MADAME PRESIDENTESS

A Novel

NICOLE EVELINA

Lawson Gartner Publishing
PO Box 2021
Maryland Heights, MO, 63043
www.lawsongartnerpublishing.com

Printed in the United States of America
First Printing, 2016

ISBNs
978-0-9967632-0-2 (print) | 978-0-9967631-9-6 (e-book)
Library of Congress Control Number: 2015959293

Publisher's Cataloging-In-Publication Data (Prepared by The Donohue Group, Inc.)

Names: Evelina, Nicole.
Title: Madame Presidentess : a novel / Nicole Evelina.
Description: Maryland Heights, MO : Lawson Gartner Publishing, [2016] |
    Includes bibliographical references.
Identifiers: ISBN 9780996763202 (print) | ISBN 9780996763196 (ebook) |
    ISBN 9780996763219 (audiobook)
Subjects: LCSH: Woodhull, Victoria C. (Victoria Claflin), 1838-1927—Fiction. | Women
    presidential candidates—United States—History—20th century—Fiction. | Suffragists—
    United States—History—20th century—Fiction. | Spiritualists—United States—
    History—20th century—Fiction. | LCGFT: Historical fiction. | Biographical fiction.
Classification: LCC PS3605.V424 M34 2016 (print) | LCC PS3605.V424 (ebook) |
    DDC 813/.6—dc23

Editor: Cassie Cox, Joy Editing
Cover Design: Jenny Quinlan, Historical Editorial
Layout: The Editorial Department

1. Fiction 2. Historical Fiction 3. Women 4. Politics

To all Incarnate Word Academy girls—past, present, and future.
Victoria was a woman before her
time and would have fit right in with us.

Speak your truth, dare to be the first, and
never doubt your strength or abilities.
Praised be the Incarnate Word. Forever. Amen!

"The truth is I am too many years ahead of this age... and the unenlightened mind of the average man."

—Victoria C. Woodhull

"For Victoria, the fight for women's equality was not simply a matter of gaining access to the ballot box—it was a matter of winning the much more basic right of self-ownership."

—Mary Gabriel, *Notorious Victoria*, p. 3

PART ONE

The Little Queen

CHAPTER ONE

By the time I was three, I had learned to fear the dark—that was when Pa came home smelling of sharp, unpleasant odors and vented his day's worth of rage on us. By five, I'd accepted that no amount of pleading or tears would stay an angry hand. At seven, the creak of my father's footfall on the rotting boards of our ramshackle house still made me shake.

But that wasn't what roused me from sleep on a blustery spring night. Somewhere in my dreams, I thought I heard my name being called. I woke, not fully aware of where I was but knowing something was not right. The air, while tinged with the ashy scent of a banked coal fire and the sourness of unwashed hair and sweaty bodies, held another heavier odor. Wood smoke. Acrid traces tingled in my nose, tickling my throat.

The house was on fire. I leaped from bed and slid, in my stocking feet, on the wooden floor as I hurriedly woke my siblings.

"Wake up, all of you. Wake up!" My cries were enough to rouse my elder brother and sister, but the younger ones slept on. I picked up Tennie and handed her to Polly. "Maldron, take Utica and get outside, all of you. I'll find Ma."

I rushed into my parents' tiny bedroom, expecting to find her asleep, but the room was empty, bedcovers askew.

"Oh, Ma, this is not the time for one of your nocturnal vigils," I said to myself as I slipped into my shoes and threw a ratty cloak over my shoulders.

I barely heard the rattle of the loose porch stairs as I bounded down them toward the orchard behind our house. There, amid blooming apple trees nearly bent double by the howling wind, was my mother, arms raised in prayer, face turned toward heaven, swaying to and fro like a charmed snake, and muttering her prayers to God.

As I drew closer, I could make out her ecstatic chanting. "Glory, glory, Jesus, Jesus. Save us from our sins. Save this bedeviled town. Glory, glory, Jesus, Jesus."

The last time I interrupted her prayer, Ma had beat me so badly my eyes were blackened for a week. But surely she would understand when our home was in danger, wouldn't she? Hesitantly, I approached her, as fearful as though I sought to tame a wolf. Her eyes were open, but they were glassy, seeing things visible only to her blessed inner eye.

As gently as I could, I laid a hand on her arm. She didn't respond or look my way but continued to chant and sway.

I shook her slightly. "Ma, it's Victoria. I need you to come back to me. Please, Ma, it's important."

A second shake got through to her. She lowered her head, eyes turning hard as flint, and smacked me across the cheek. "Haven't I told you not ta bother me when I'm talkin' to the spirits? Now you gone an' scared 'em off." She shook her head, her expression making her disappointment clear.

"Ma, I had to. The house is on fire!" I turned, pointing back at the little one-story wooden shack, expecting to see orange flames shooting from the windows or the whole thing smothered in a veil of black smoke.

But there was nothing. The house sat as still as any other night, taking the licks the wind dealt it with the stoicism of a bare-knuckle boxer.

I couldn't understand. I knew I'd smelled smoke. I looked at my mother, eyes imploring her to believe I was telling the truth.

She huffed. "Fire, eh?" She pinched my ear so quickly I didn't have a chance to defend myself. "I'll teach you not to tell lies."

She dragged me back toward the house, pausing only when Maldron came running toward us.

"Fire brigade is comin' this way." He pointed down Main Street, where in the distance, the team of horses was crossing the town's only intersection, wagon rumbling like thunder. "Tennie says it's not the house but the mill that's afire."

At the mention of my clairvoyant younger sister, Ma's face crumpled. "Tennie's never wrong in her seeings. Oh, Lord in Heaven, that mill was gonna be our nest egg! Now what will we do?" She wailed loudly.

I supported her right shoulder while Maldron took her other, and the rest of the family joined us in solemn procession to a bridge that overlooked the mill, which was not far from the house. Maldron and Polly ran to take their places in the bucket brigade that was fighting a losing battle as the wind carried the flames up to the roof and into the wheel itself. If the inferno wasn't contained soon, it would consume the very bridge on which we stood.

"What a time for your pa to be gone. This never would 'ave happened if he were here."

I didn't see what he could have done to prevent or stop the situation, but his help wouldn't have been unappreciated. "They need more hands. Ma, please let me go help. I'm fourteen, hardly a child to be trod underfoot."

But she would hear nothing of it. Shaking her head, she draped her cape around the three of us, a mama duck protecting her brood. "I gave the Lord three of my girls already. He won't be gettin' you too."

Smoke and flames reached toward the heavens as we stood silently, watching as the townspeople tried in vain to save what little livelihood we had left. Years earlier, we had lost our land and all our money. Now this. It seemed as though our trials would never end.

Mama swayed again, humming between her prayers. "Oh merciful Father, send relief, or we shall perish."

Helpless to do anything else, we joined in. But our prayers were in vain. Despite the heavy rain the wind blew in, by dawn, the whole town knew we had suffered a total loss.

Not wishing to be the subject of talk behind her back, Ma insisted we accompany her to the general store—the town's central gossip hub—while she replenished some of the supplies the fire had consumed. Even early on a Thursday morning, the store was full of women and children eager to see what goods had come in on the latest wagon from Mount Vernon. All eyes turned to us as soon as we entered.

Louisa Oldacre, a tall, thin blond woman always clad in the latest fashion and a descendant of one of the town's founding families, was at my mother's side before the proprietor, Mr. Yoakam, could even wish us good morning. "Oh my dear, you must be so exhausted. What a terrible night for your family." She clucked her tongue and plucked a basket from a shelf. "Here, let me help you."

As she led my mother away, I wandered over to the dry goods area, intending to admire the colorful ribbons and buttons we could never afford. The eyes of my friends and their mothers were weights on my back as I walked. As I stood in front of the rows of silken spools, imagining how I could dress up my old bonnets if Ma would spare but a coin, snippets of conversation reached me, each one worse than the other.

"…couldn't afford the mortgage…"

"…family of lying thieves…"

"Wouldn't surprise me if it was all a sham," Mrs. Goodman said in hushed tones to Mrs. Scott as they passed behind me. "Did you know Buck just took out insurance on the mill? I don't know about you, but that seems a mite suspicious to me."

"Especially since he's conveniently missing," Mrs. Scott replied. "Postmaster or no, I never trusted that man."

I turned on my heel so I was facing them, cheeks burning. "That's my pa you're talkin' about."

"When he treats this town and its residents with respect, I will start respecting him," Mrs. Goodman said primly before grabbing my elbow and marching me up to the counter, where my mother stood haggling with Mr. Yoakam. "Anne, you need to teach your daughter how to speak to her elders. She sassed us just now."

"Apologize, Victoria."

"But Ma, they said Pa—"

"Do as you're told." She slapped me upside the head.

"I'm sorry," I mumbled, staring at my feet.

Once the women were gone, I set my attention on my mother's conversation with Mr. Yoakam.

"If you have any more of Buck's elixir, I can give you your order in trade," Mr. Yoakam said. "Otherwise, I can only allow you to take what you have the coin for."

"But we lost Buck's latest batch of tonic in the fire. He stored his surplus in there."

"Which is probably why the fire spread so fast. I'm sorry, Anne. We've been over this before. I can't offer you any more credit until you pay your outstanding bill. There's nothing more I can do."

My mother looked near to tears. Reluctantly, she began separating the staples like flour and butter from the more luxurious goods such as tea and meat.

Louisa Oldacre, apparently having witnessed the exchange, swept over to my mother's side. "Now, Mrs. Claflin, what are you doing? Stop that right now. Mr. Yoakam, put that on my credit."

"Oh no, I could never—" my mother protested.

"Nonsense. It's the least I can do given your recent misfortune."

My mother was not one to accept charity without a fuss, but this woman's unexpected largess had left her speechless. She pressed a hand to her mouth, but I didn't miss that her lower lip trembled. "Thank you," she finally managed.

I signaled to Maldron and Polly, who were outside watching the young ones, to come inside and help carry the wares. When we were all loaded up like pack mules, we started back across the street to our house. But Tennie and I lagged behind as she dragged her feet and wearily begged me to carry her even though my arms were full of sacks of dried beans. I set them on the sidewalk outside the store and hoisted her into my arms. Behind me, Mrs. Scott and Louisa resumed their gossip.

"That was mighty kind of you, Miss Oldacre. You turn coat on your opinion of the Claflins?"

"No, sugar. But I do have a plan. Come on inside, and I'll tell you all about it."

SUNDAY MORNING WAS ALWAYS my favorite time of the week. It was special because every one of us children had to wash, put on our best clothes, and comb our hair before presenting ourselves to the Lord at church. But better than that, Ma and Pa were on their best behavior; it was the one morning of the week we were certain not to receive the switch or get a tongue lashing for some real or imagined infraction. Ma hummed as she prepared the picnic we would eat after services, and even Pa was known to occasionally grace us with a smile as he cleaned the dirt from under his fingernails.

With Pa away, visiting my eldest sister in Mt. Gilead, Maldron and Polly headed our straggling parade to the church. Ma brought up the rear, ensuring Utica kept up amid her spinning, skipping, and chasing butterflies and Tennie didn't stop to pick up any way-ward turtles or toads. The reverend still looked at Tennie askance from her last gift.

When the tall white steeple towered over us and the church doors were in sight, Maldron halted. The rest of us gathered around him, straining to see why he didn't head straight inside to secure our usual seats midway up the aisle to the left of the altar.

Barring entrance to the church was a tall bay mare hitched to a wagon loaded with supplies. Bolts of muslin lay next to sacks of wheat and corn, soft packing for the stacks of crockery, tin dishes, and two oil lamps cradled on top. A barrel of salt fish was tied to one corner, and the butt of a rifle stuck out from between piles of clothing for men and women.

"Who's leaving town?" Ma asked when she finally caught up to the rest of us.

It was early in the season to be traveling yet; next month was when most wagon trains set off, but it wasn't inconceivable some family had decided to get an early start.

The assembled crowd shifted restlessly, as if no one dared speak.

"I'm afraid you are." Mayor Tom Trumbull stepped forward, holding his hat in his hands. "It pains me to say this, but the town of Homer, Ohio, no longer welcomes you and your family, Mrs. Claflin. We must ask you to leave."

"What?" my mother cried. "Why? Have we not been good citizens these last twenty years? Why do you abandon us now?"

"Do not play for sympathy, Mrs. Claflin. Your husband is a well-known crook and a swindler. All assembled here know the truth—that he was run out of town by these very same men for defrauding them of their fortunes. Now, with the unfortunate disaster at the mill, I'm afraid we can tolerate no more."

I looked up at Ma. "Don't they know Pa is just visiting Maggie? He'll be back any day now." I said this last to the mayor in case he hadn't heard.

He regarded me stonily and crossed his arms. "Is that what you told your children? It's a sin before God to tell lies—even if it is to protect the innocent."

My heart thudded. Could the mayor possibly be telling the truth? Had Pa really been chased out of town like an outlaw by men with pitchforks who'd threatened his life? I'd seen it done before. But those men robbed banks. My father sold medicines and traded horses. No, it didn't add up.

Louisa Oldacre swept to the fore, her bright smile a jarring contrast to the grim scene playing out around us. "Please don't think us too unkind. Our church did hold a fundraiser to purchase your provisions for the journey. Added to those I secured for you late last week, you should have plenty to take with you to meet up with your husband."

Polly sneered at Louisa. "You think this makes you a good Christian, don't ya? Never mind all the ill you've spoke of us. A little charity washes away your sins? Well, that's horseshit."

I expected Ma to reprimand Polly for her coarse language, but her attention was elsewhere.

Ma raised her hands to the sky and recited, "'Blessed are those who are persecuted in tha' name of the Lord for theirs is the kingdom of heaven.' That's what we are. One of my neglectful children left a lamp burning in the mill. The howlin' wind overturned it and set the whole thing blazin'. We was helpless to stop it, 'specially without Buck, yet you stand here afore God and everybody callin' us thieves." She put an arm around Maldron. "We got our pride, you ken. We don't want to live nowheres that don't want us. Come on, children."

She motioned for us to climb into the wagon. Obediently we did so, though I grasped at my friends' hands, hugging them to me, tears pouring down my face. This was my home, the town where I'd been born, and while I was not popular, I had a few close acquaintances, and I was loathe to let them go.

But Mama's pride would brook no resistance. Without another word, she urged the horse forward, and the wagon moved. Slowly, we rumbled away from the church, away from the only home I had ever known. Once we had stopped back by the house and packed our few belongings into the cart, we said farewell to the town of Homer forever.

As we crossed the county line, Ma called out the words of the Gospel, "'If any place will not welcome you, leave that place and shake the dust off your feet as a testimony against them.' So the Lord has commanded, and so do I," she said with a smirk.

"How can you be joyful at a time like this?" Polly asked.

"Because"—she smiled a gap-toothed grin—"I know somethin' they don't."

CHAPTER TWO

MT. GILEAD, OHIO

The following day, when we arrived at the cramped farmhouse my sister Maggie shared with her husband Enos and their three children, Pa was waiting for us at the head of the drive.

"Looks like the spirits were modest in their predictions. Where'd you get all this?" he asked as he helped Ma down from the buckboard seat.

Ma grinned. "Town's more gullible than heaven knows."

"And the insurance company?"

Ma shrugged. "They ain't said nothin' yet. But all that's left is ash and blackened timbers, so they'll never know."

"Know what?" Maggie asked, her forehead wrinkling.

"Let's just say that the fire had some help," Pa said with a smug smile.

I hopped down from the wagon, aghast. "So the ladies were right? You did set the fire?"

"Don't be so high and mighty, Little Queen. The Lord helps those who help themselves. Besides, the spirits told your Ma it would all work out, and it has and then some." He guided us into the house. "Hurry to put those things away. I have something to show you."

Pa sat in a chair by the fire, feet propped on a stool, directing the rest of us as we unloaded the wagon. Then we piled back in and Pa took us into town.

We pulled up in front of a three-story brick building on Main Street. On the lowest level, the plate-glass windows reflected our image in the late afternoon sun, showing me that Polly was holding a sleeping Utica and Molly was braiding Tennie's curly locks. The second- and third-floor windows were much smaller and curtained by thin fabric, indicating those rooms were meant for private use.

"What is this place, Pa?" I asked, fascinated. I'd never seen a building so big or so fancy. Even the bank in Homer was only two stories.

"It's our new place of business." He beamed with pride. "You two"—he pulled Tennie and me into the circle of his attention—"are going to be bigger than the Fox sisters. I've already started running ads in the paper."

Tennie and I looked at one another, mirrors of each other's excitement and fear. The Fox sisters were notorious throughout the country for their communications with the spirit world. They regularly held séances and charged up to five dollars a sitting to speak with customers' departed loved ones. Tennie and I had the gift of speaking with the spirits, which we'd inherited from Ma, but we'd never done it on a commercial basis. We didn't have much experience seeking out the spirits; usually they came to us—and privately at that.

I wasn't sure how Tennie felt, but the idea of being a medium for strangers made my gut tighten. What if I couldn't reach the person they were looking for? Worse yet, what if I was wrong? I voiced these fears to Pa while he unlocked the front door and led us inside.

"Don't worry your pretty little head about that, Vickie. Your ol' pa has his ways. I'll tell you all about it later. But first, the grand tour." He made a flourishing gesture around the large room with livid blue walls the color of a fresh bruise. "This is where I'll sell my elixirs and tonics. Everyone must pass through here before they can see our girls—a chance to prime them for a sale—then back out again before they go. Annie, I'll need you to start on a new batch of elixir first thing since we had to sacrifice our stock in the fire."

Ma nodded solemnly. She enjoyed making Pa's tonics even though they weren't really the magic cures he claimed. I'd helped her enough times to know they were mostly alcohol and vegetable oil, often with a dash of laudanum thrown in for good measure. But they made his clients happy, and some even claimed they worked, so I didn't question their methods.

Pa led us up a narrow, steep flight of stairs. At the top, the floor branched off, leading to one room on either side. I stepped into the one on the left, facing the street. Sunlight streamed through rectangular windows onto bright golden wallpaper covered in black filigree. Books on magic, the occult, and the philosophy of life and death lined a tall bookshelf in one corner while settees and chairs covered in flaking gold paint and worn burgundy velvet waited to be inhabited by customers. Dominating the center of the room was a round table on which a ball of glass sat, flanked by candles. Around the table sat four stiff-backed chairs, and from the walls above, daguerreotypes of two men and two women stared down solemnly, as if reminding all present that spirits ruled this place.

"You certainly have created an atmosphere," Polly observed.

Tennie crossed from this room to the other then back again. "They look almost the same, only the other room has red walls."

Pa nodded. "That will be your room, Tennie. Victoria, you'll practice in this one."

Ma scowled at Pa. "Where'd you get the money to outfit this place? Thought we'd have ta wait 'til the insurance money came though. Did you win a bet?"

Pa reached into his coat pocket and produced a wad of colorful bank notes. "Being postmaster had its perks." He wiggled his fingers in the air. "Sometimes when people were expecting money, I had to tell them it was lost in the mail."

Shock jolted through me. I knew my father was different from other men, but I'd never suspected he was the thief many people accused him of being. It hurt my heart and soul that he could so openly flout the law when he took a rope or switch to us without a thought when he suspected us of lying. A protest bubbled up within me, words begging to be let forth, but I clamped my jaw shut, knowing from long experience that anything I said would result in a bloodied lip or worse.

"Once this place is up and running, I plan to buy the floor above." He pointed up. "We'll live there so we can be open longer and don't have to take up space with Maggie and her kin." He rubbed his palms together. "Yes, you girls are going to make us rich."

To that end, Tennie and I spent the next week taking lessons from Pa and memorizing his "blue book," a small notebook in which he kept notes on everyone in town. He'd been busy since coming to Mt. Gilead. His notes included tavern gossip—juicy secrets and scandalous accusations—and extensive cemetery records highlighting the recently departed, connecting families, and noting birth and death dates as though he'd traipsed through the entire graveyard like a storybook sleuth.

"Be a good listener," Pa exhorted. "Don't be afeared of silence. People will tell you what you need to know if you keep your trap shut."

We had certainly learned to keep silent around him.

"But what if the spirits aren't talking and neither are the customers?" Tennie asked. She had always been bright and enthusiastic to please.

Pa thought on that a moment, rubbing his beard. "Well, there are things you can do to get a response from them whether they want to give it or not. If you're trying to get a name, ask them to write six names on a piece of paper, one of which is the dead person's, and watch them close. Nine times of ten, they will hesitate on the right name. Or if you need to prove your abilities to someone who is doubtful, ask them to think of a letter, then have them recite the alphabet. They will give some kind of reaction when they reach their chosen letter."

I regarded him dubiously. It couldn't be that easy.

"Ah, the Little Queen doesn't believe her old pa. Practice it on your brothers and sisters. You'll see. It works."

Tennie believed in him. Her wide eyes shone with worshipful awe. "How do you know all this?"

"Reading people is a valuable skill no matter what your occupation. The more you pay attention, the more they reveal. And when you have the information, you have the power. You hold the purse strings. Remember that."

AT FIRST, WORKING AT Pa's shop was fun, an adventure. I liked making my own money—all of it went to Pa, but I was still contributing to the family—and it was much better than going to school or taking in laundry and sewing as Ma and I had done in Homer. I enjoyed being able to help people find peace or get the answers to questions that had long disturbed them.

When a client came in, we drew the curtains to darken the room. Then my father introduced the client, supplying me with as much information as he could.

A plump woman in a pale pink gown stood between my father and a man with the deeply lined face of someone who had spent many hours in the sun and wind.

"May I present to you Mr. and Mrs. Henry Wilkins," Pa said. "Mrs. Wilkins here lives about an hour south, but she was born here."

That was my cue to riffle through my pages of mental notes so I was as prepared as I could be. Wilkins, Wilkins. Ah yes. Family had been in the area since the 1820s, one of the first to take up residence. Most recent death was a daughter, a young girl, who had succumbed to consumption two years prior.

"My boy has been ill for some time now. The doctor doesn't know what ails him. I wondered if the spirits might be able to tell us what medicine cannot." She leaned in so close I could smell the mint that didn't quite mask her breath. "If you could tell me if he will live, there's an extra two dollars in it for you."

That was an unusual request—most people wanted to question their departed loved ones—but the unusual was common in this line of work. Once the couple was seated, we joined hands and sang a hymn. Before I even had a chance to address the spirits, a girl was there with us, her rich brown hair tumbling over her shoulders, wafting in the ghost breeze that stirred her dress.

"A girl is here with us," I said, keeping my inner sight on her while watching Mrs. Wilkins closely. "She says her name is Edith."

Mrs. Wilkins choked back a sob. "That's my girl."

I asked her about her brother. She shook her head slowly. I was about to relay the sorrowful news when Edith looked over her shoulder, held up a finger for me to wait, and disappeared. A few moments later, she reappeared with a younger boy by her side.

"Tell Mama I love her and not to cry over me," he said.

Swallowing, I repeated the boy's message. "John is here with us. He died moments ago. Edith was with him. In fact, she left us to be there when he passed from this life. He says he loves you and not to weep over him. He is at peace."

Mrs. Wilkins muffled her sobs with a handkerchief.

It was Mr. Wilkins who found the fortitude to speak, though sorrow made his eyes shine unearthly bright. "Truly, you have a gift. We did not tell you our son's name, nor could you have known how near to death he was. I only regret we were not with him at the time of his passing."

I laid a hand on his. "He was not alone. His sister was there. Take comfort in that. Being here with me is as near to being with him as you could possibly have been."

Most of the time the spirits complied with my patrons' requests, and even when they didn't, I was normally able to figure out what answer my clients wanted with the help of Pa's methods. Well, all except for once.

Pa introduced me to a finely dressed gentleman. "Vickie, this is Mr. Davis. He is a legislator in Columbus."

The state capital. Occasionally travelers passed through our town, but he was the first man of import to visit us. All the memorization I had done wouldn't help me with an outsider. I would have to hope he would give some sign of the proper way to proceed.

After shaking his hand and ensuring he was comfortable, I asked, "With whom do you wish to speak, Mr. Davis?"

He cocked an eyebrow. "I was rather expecting you to tell me."

Inwardly, I sighed. So we would play that game. Sometimes clients thought they were clever if they didn't supply me with any information at all. All it really meant was that it would take longer for me to find their answers and it was more likely they would walk away disappointed. This man could not. I had to tell him something accurate. I nervously glanced at Pa, who motioned for me to get on with my answer.

I closed my eyes, calling on Demosthenes, the ancient Greek orator who was my spirit guide, to help me wade through the press of spirits attracted to the beacon of my soul. Usually I had a name or a description, some marker to separate the one I sought from all the others. But tonight, thanks to this man's pride, I was blind.

"I am having trouble forming a connection with any specific spirit, Mr. Davis. Perhaps if you wrote out a list of names, that would help me. Only one has to be someone you know. You may falsify the others."

He did not make a move toward the pen and paper on the table or even uncross his arms. "I am a worldly man, Miss Claflin. I know all the tricks your kind use. You will not defraud me this night."

I shook my head, unable to bear his insistence that I was lying to him when I had no material with which to fashion a lie. "How can I do such a thing? You have told me nothing, sir. I can only assume you seek a loved one, or barring that, you wish to debunk my gifts and unmask me as a charlatan, which I am not. Please, either help me or leave. Your passivity does neither of us any good."

Mr. Davis began to rise, muttering to Pa that he had taught his daughters no respect, when the spirit of a woman, her hair and russet dress sopping wet, slammed into me with the force of a carriage at top speed. But it was not me she sought to reach; it was my client.

"Paul, Paul dearest!" she cried.

"Mr. Davis?" I tried to get his attention, but he was intent on berating me to my father. "Mr. Davis," I repeated more loudly. No response. Finally, I mimicked the woman's frantic tone. "Paul!"

He stopped and turned toward me slowly, fear in his wide eyes.

"A woman is trying to speak with you. She has a desperate message—"

"What woman?" His voice was strained.

"I—I don't know." I paused, listening. "She says her name is Mary Margaret. She's about your height, long curly red hair, brown eyes. She tells me she was a passenger aboard a boat that capsized in New York Harbor during a storm this very night. She wishes nothing more than to be with you, but—"

"Where was the ship's port of origin?"

The odd question perplexed me. I expected him to ask if she was injured. "What?"

He slammed his palms onto the table. "I said, where was it from?"

I looked at the woman. "Ireland—Galway, I think. She was nearly home from visiting family when the boat encountered trouble. She—she drowned, as did her sister."

Mr. Davis bowed his head for a moment. When he raised it, fire glinted in his eyes. "You lie!"

I stood, shaking my head. "I tell the truth. She wishes you to know one more thing. She was pregnant."

He shook his head. "No. You are making this up to get back at me for not giving you any crumbs of information. You are not only a fraud but a cruel little girl." He turned to my father and poked him squarely in the chest. "And you, her own father, the king of lies. I demand my payment back—now."

For a moment, as my father towered over Mr. Davis with one arm raised, I thought Pa might start a brawl.

Instead, my father gestured the client to the door. "As you wish, sir."

When he opened the door, a raised voice reached me from across the hall in Tennie's parlor. "You witch! You charlatan! You whore! How dare you tell me my wife is dead? You know nothing."

A man so resembling Mr. Davis that they had to be brothers flung open the door and stormed out. The two men swore oaths and vowed to see their wives safe in New York as they stomped down the stairs, Pa following in their wake. Tennie and I could only stare at one another across the empty hall.

"I didn't know you had a client," Tennie said.

"Nor I you." I filled her in on what had taken place during my session, which was much the same as hers.

Neither man—and they *were* brothers—would supply the slightest bit of information, but we both were visited by their wives. The younger hadn't reacted any better than my client.

"Pa will be mad."

Tennie nodded silently. "That's two dollars he's out."

"And more, two important men hate us."

"We will talk about this later," was all Pa said to us when he returned to the second floor.

To his credit, he didn't take his anger out on us during business hours, not even after he dropped Tennie and me off at home and went back out into the rain to meet friends at the tavern.

But I had hardly fallen asleep that night when I was shaken violently awake.

"Come here, you ungrateful wretches," Pa growled, hoisting Tennie and me out of bed.

The stench of hot, bitter ale assaulted me as he yanked me to my feet. When my father glowered down at me, I expected to see the glassy, unfocused gaze of a drunk. Instead, his eyes were clear. He knew exactly what he was doing and didn't care. My legs trembled, and I fought the sudden urge to urinate.

"Embarrass me in front of two bigwigs, will ya? I'll learn ya ta speak out to our payin' cusm" —he hiccoughed— "cussomers. What'd I do ta deserve daughters like you?" My teeth rattled as he shook me, heedless of my fear, as though I was one of his horses to be broken under his will. "Answer me."

I had learned long ago not to respond when he was on one of these tirades, but Tennie, only ten years old, hadn't become wise to that yet.

"Pa, we didn't lie—"

The crack of his hand against Tennie's mouth was like thunder in the silent house. Tennie clutched her bleeding mouth with only the slightest mewl of pain. Behind us, the rustle of straw and Utica's slight whimper said the other siblings were awake and trying desperately not to attract attention.

"You could've lied to 'em," Buck yelled. "Or if you had to tell the truth, give it to 'em another way. How hard is it to say, 'Mr. Davis, you mi' wanna telegram New York. The spirits are sayin' there's been an accident with a boat from Ireland'? They prolly told everyone what cheats we are. Wouldn't be surprised if we have ta close up shop within the week. All because you two have no tact."

I cowered between the bed and the wall, trying to protect Tennie with my body. We both knew what was coming. Once he raised his arm, one blow was much like the last. I couldn't even tell what he used this time. A piece of firewood? A cold iron? He was nothing if not creative. I concentrated on the cold, half-rotten floorboards as I held my arms over my head, trying to shield myself from the worst of the blows.

My head was still ringing when I woke in the morning, still crouched over Tennie in a pool of my own blood and piss. Or maybe it was hers. It hardly mattered. We were alive, and thank the Lord it was Sunday so we didn't have to go to work. My arm throbbed, but I thought little of it. This was not the first time it had been broken, nor was it likely to be the last. Maldron set my arm and wrapped it in a sling, and Polly helped make us presentable for church.

As we were leaving, Mr. Whiteside, who ran the telegraph office, flagged us down. "This message just came for you, Mr. Claflin."

I stood on tiptoe, despite the pain that shot up my legs, so I could see the note.

MR. CLAFLIN. DEEPEST APOLOGIES TO YOU AND
GIRLS. HAVE CONFIRMED WIVES' DEATHS. WILL
REIMBURSE YOU TENFOLD. LOOK FOR CHECK IN
MAIL. MR. EUGENE AND MR. WILLFORD DAVIS.

"Well, I'll be damned. You were right," was all he said.

CHAPTER THREE

Word of our heroics with the Davis brothers spread quickly, bringing in more clients than we could possibly see in a day. Around the same time, Pa collected the insurance money from the mill, and we moved into the floor above the shop and parlors. The change of accommodation was welcome, as it gave us more space and meant we were living in more luxury than we'd ever seen, even if to most townspeople it was a commonplace establishment.

But it also meant that we no longer had to spend nearly an hour in a wagon traveling to and from the shop, so Pa considered those working hours we owed him. Every morning when the church bell tolled eight o'clock, he unlocked the front door. With summer's daylight in full effect, he didn't pull down the door shade until nine most evenings.

After a month of this schedule, I began to feel like a prisoner in my parlor, hardly leaving it other than to use the outhouse. In and out the clients trooped, each with their own sad tale of loss and woe or concern they could confide to no one but the "girl healers," as we had come to be known.

When Pa decided our business as clairvoyants wasn't bringing in enough clients, he began spreading the idea that we could heal with our touch. It was true to an extent. Tennie, Polly, and I had each learned from our mother about the magnetic energy that flowed through the body and the power of the faithful to manipulate it to heal. Ma was a devotee of Franz Mesmer, who taught a method of healing that involved the laying on of hands and the use of magnets. Ma had been inducted into the art at a revival meeting in her youth, but she believed her own magnetism was stronger than most and needed no aid, so she taught us to heal using only our hands.

Many of the women seeking our help suffered from ailments brought on by a lifetime of hard labor, such as Mrs. Angelson's choleric knees and chilblains or Mrs. Jaeger's gnarled, arthritic joints and overtaxed back. But others, like Joy, the constable's wife, suffered from "bouts of clumsiness" I understood far too well. They masked a deeper hurt than bruised skin and broken bones, one brought on by the vile concoction of male temper and drink but which could not be spoken of with candor even in the hushed whispers of the parlor.

What no one, save Tennie, understood was that working in such intense conditions for eleven hours a day was extremely taxing. Each time I opened myself to the spirit world, a bit of my energy was used to intensify the glow of my soul, like trimming the wick of an oil lamp to make it burn brighter, so the spirits could see a friendly face was walking in their realm. When I worked to soothe injuries, I called upon my own magnetism to heal the ills of my patients. I tried my best to shield myself from the tales of abuse and oppression that were confided in me, but having my own experience with such things, I found it difficult not to sympathize and take on a little of their pain.

Though we were given a few short minutes to recover between clients, soon it was not enough. I was empty by the end of the day, wrung dry like laundry on the line, with nothing left to give. My mind quivered like raw liver, overwhelmed with pity and concern for the women with whom I so closely identified. I fell asleep even before I had fully climbed into bed, though Tennie gently guided me to the pillow and tucked me in.

Soon I learned I was taking on some of the ills of my patients, developing rheumatism that made the motions of healing painful, even as the women reported better health. Breaking out into a cold sweat while channeling a spirit or shivering so violently between clients that I could barely sip my tea was not uncommon for me. But I worked through it all, knowing a request for respite would only earn my father's fury and my mother's scorn.

One morning in late June, I found I could not rise from bed. My body was leaden, my limbs weak. When I moved but an inch, hot pain shot through me, tracing through the veins beneath my skin. I tried to speak but could only manage a garbled utterance that even Ma, who frequently spoke in tongues, could not decipher. When I made the mistake of closing my eyes, they would not open again.

I lay in a state of semi-consciousness while my family bickered around me. My hearing remained attuned to the mortal world, so I heard my father's oath when Ma told him I would not be working that day.

"You'd best work twice as hard to make up for your good-for-nothing sister, you hear me?" he spat at Tennie.

I could imagine her shaking in response, so I tried again to rise—but to no avail.

"You must preserve your body and spirit if you are to rise to the heights God has prepared for you." The voice was male, but it was not my father's.

My inner eye opened, and I beheld my spirit guide, a man of middle years with tightly curled brown hair, wearing the white toga of an ancient Greek. He had been with me for nearly seven years now.

I found all my senses returned to me in this spirit world, which made an odd sort of sense as I spent nearly as much of my time in it as I did in the realm of mortals. "Demosthenes, what ails me? Am I dying?" I certainly felt as though I was.

Demosthenes smiled. "No. You have many things to accomplish yet. You will rise to great distinction, emerge from the poverty you have known, and live in a grand house. You will amass great wealth in a city crowded with ships and become a great leader of your people."

As he spoke, I saw it, this fabled future of mine. There I was, grown and beautiful, standing in the drive of a spectacular brick mansion overlooking a bay teeming with merchant and passenger ships, their tall sails billowing in the breeze. Gone was the adolescent awkwardness I saw in the mirror each morning, smoothed into the sleek lines of adulthood. I was outfitted in a sumptuous gown of navy silk with black lace trim, my brown curls piled artfully beneath a matching feathered cap. At my side was the most handsome man I'd ever seen. He was tall, a good half foot taller than me, with smiling eyes of deepest brown. He held himself erect like one of noble bearing, and most importantly, he was holding my arm the way gentlemen often did with women they fancied. That meant this stunning creature was mine.

"Victoria."

I heard my name not from his lips or those of my spirit guide but as though from a great distance. I looked around to find its source, only to find I was alone and the gray of the spirit realm was brightening as if with its own personal dawn. My name sounded again, and my eyelids fluttered open. At first I was blinded by bright sunlight, then a figure blocked its source. As my eyes focused, I found myself staring into the face from my vision. An involuntary sigh slipped from my lips as I tried to understand if I still dreamed or was awake.

"Victoria, this is Dr. Canning Woodhull. He's here ta fix ya right," my mother said from somewhere out of my line of vision.

He could have been the president or Jesus himself for all I cared. I had eyes only for him, the man of my vision, the one who stood by my side in that wonderful future that was so unlike my present.

"Can you feel this?" he asked.

A sharp pain pricked my wrist. "Ow!"

The doctor's face lit up in a charming grin. "Good. That's the first reaction we've gotten from you in three days. And you can speak too. I predict you'll be well soon enough. Still, I would like to visit you daily until I am confident you are on the mend. Would that be agreeable to you?"

It was more than agreeable; it was ideal. I nodded.

He gave my mother some parting instructions before leaving with a promise to see me every afternoon at four.

When he had gone, Ma sat on the edge of my bed just as she had done when I was small. After feeding me a spoonful of bitter liquid—doctor's orders—she stroked my forehead. "You gave me quite a fright, my girl. I was afeared you were dead."

"I think I may have been." My voice was rusty from disuse. I cleared my throat. "Oh, Ma, you would not believe what the spirits have told me. This"—I raised a hand to indicate our living conditions—"is not our fate. So much more awaits us. And the good doctor is part of it. I have seen it." My cheeks were burning, but whether with fever or girlish excitement, I could not say.

"Is he now?" Her gaze was appraising, as though she was simultaneously weighing my worth and deciding whether I could snag such a man. "He *is* a bachelor and a good age—twenty-six." She spoke more to herself than to me. "Good breeding. He could practice medicine anywhere, yet he chose this town. Mayhap it *was* fate." Her eyes sparkled. "Well, we'll see. It's not enough that you fancy him. He has ta take a shine ta you too."

True to his word, Dr. Woodhull visited me daily, checking my temperature and pulse. When he placed his strange, pipe-like wooden stethoscope on my chest to listen to my heart, I was certain he could hear it flutter at his nearness.

As my strength increased, he insisted on accompanying me in a turn about the small back garden to get me on my feet again. During those brief walks, he would grasp me firmly under my left arm. Ma supported my right until I was strong enough to walk with only him—but still under her watchful gaze. At first he and I spoke of nothing at all—mostly goings-on around town, the idle gossip of strangers seeking to gauge one another. But as the days passed, our conversation turned more intimate, and he charmed me with tales of his adventures in the big city while I told him of my work with the spirits.

One day he surprised me by pausing before we turned back toward my mother to bring our time together to an end.

Dr. Woodhull turned to face me, one hand resting lightly on my waist as though we were about to dance. "You are nearly recovered, Victoria, but I find I do not wish to end our acquaintance. If your parents are agreeable, I'd like the pleasure of your company at the Fourth of July picnic. Will you accompany me?"

Every ounce of my willpower was required to avoid nodding enthusiastically like a fool. "Why yes, thank you for the invitation. I would be honored."

❦

PA WAS LESS ENTHUSIASTIC about letting me go with Dr. Woodhull than Ma had been—truth be told, she was over the moon about the match—but he agreed to let me, provided we stayed within the watchful gaze of Maggie and Enos.

We must have made quite a picture strolling down Main Street in our summer finery, he in his smart white suit, I in my white dress and new shoes, hollyhocks twined in my hair like a fairy princess. I *felt* like a princess, more alive than I had in weeks, with that strong, handsome man at my side. As we walked past the bank and the barber, the general store and the boardinghouse, all decorated with red, white, and blue bunting, I felt the open stares from Mrs. Goodwin and her pudgy spinster sisters and heard the calls of "You've got a prize one there, Doctor!" from the men gathered around a barrel of beer in the town square.

But they had it backward; it was I who had indeed snagged a prize—the man my spirit guide had shown me, the one who would rescue me from my life of drudgery, lies, and scheming. Between the compassionate way he'd treated me during my illness and the gentle way Dr. Woodhull held my arm, I knew he was not a man of violence like my father. With him, I would be safe. The spirits had all but said so.

We watched the volunteer militia march, re-enacting the time when our country had won its independence from England, with great solemnity. Behind them marched men in bandages, leaning heavily on crutches, representing those who were wounded or had died in battle. Following were the families descended from those who had fought in the war, holding flags and mementos from lost loved ones, and transporting elderly uniformed veterans of the Revolutionary War in carts, followed by the survivors of countless conflicts since. Bringing up the rear, the mayor stood in a black wagon pulled by a team of white horses, reading the Declaration of Independence at the top of his lungs.

It was the first time I'd ever given thought to what it meant to be a citizen of the United States, to live in a country of unprecedented freedom. Tears of pride sprang to my eyes unbidden. Suddenly, I was moved by the sacrifices made by these men for people like me, generations of Americans they would never know but for whom they had given everything so that we might live in peace. We were truly blessed to call this country home.

"What a sight." I sighed. "It pulls at the heartstrings, does it not, Dr. Woodhull?"

He smiled. "Please, call me Canning. I believe we know one another well enough to call each other by our Christian names." He squeezed my hand. "It does indeed put the day into perspective. But enough solemnity. Let us join the party, my little chick."

My heart soared. He felt it too, the connection between us. Were his words not proof?

In the park, the townspeople milled with great joy, calling to one another over the patriotic tunes played by a brass band in the grandstand, laughing, dancing, and enjoying the high summer sunshine. I noted the envious stares of the town darlings, the McKenzie sisters, as we passed. Chuckling inwardly, I gloried in the irony that I, whom they'd once called the "spawn of a two-bit con man and a madwoman," was the one to land the man every woman desired. All of their money couldn't help them one bit when a man valued other qualities more.

Maggie and Enos waved to us from a blanket under the shade of a great maple. Their children ran in circles, chasing one another and playing games only their fertile imaginations could understand. After filling our plates beyond capacity with slices of ham, turkey, all manner of casseroles, and several types of desserts, we sat next to them. Maggie handed me a cup of cider while Enos and Canning passed a flask of whiskey between them.

"So, Dr. Woodhull, you know all about us from treating our dear Vickie," Enos said. "But we know so little about you. Where are you from?"

Canning removed his hat and wiped sweat from his brow with a handkerchief. "I was born in Brooklyn, New York. My father is a judge and my mother, a woman of fine standing from just outside Rochester."

"Sounds like New York is in your blood. What brings you out our way?"

"Fate," I answered for him, patting his arm affectionately. "Why, if you hadn't come, surely I'd be dead."

"Victoria!" Maggie scolded. "Don't be morbid. Eat your food and let the men speak."

I dutifully spooned a bit of casserole into my mouth, then I stuck my tongue out at my older sister.

She cringed, but Canning laughed. "I love your spirit." After a brief pause, he returned to Enos's line of questioning. "Yes. New York is where my family calls home. In fact, my uncle is the mayor of New York—"

"Truly?" Maggie fawned as though he'd just admitted to being European royalty.

Canning chuckled, obviously amused. "Indeed. I could have set up practice anywhere in the area, but my heart has never been in the big city. I love small towns such as this. They have a personality, a feeling of intimacy you can't get in a big city. Here, you all know one another—"

As if on cue, Mr. Reddings, the head of the town council, called to Maggie and Enos in greeting, which they returned with a wave.

"You see, that's just it. You care about one another. I wanted to start a practice somewhere I could get to know people and their children and hopefully treat their children's children. To me, that's the place to settle and start a family, preferably a large one."

Canning regarded me with warmth as he said that, and my heart flipped. Was that his way of saying he hoped I would be the mother of his children? My face flushed at the thought. I could see it already.

Enos and Canning spent the better part of the afternoon talking about all things Mt. Gilead, from its history to the farming conditions over the last several years. Finally, Canning inquired about the medical needs of the local orphanage. The two of them left us to speak with the ladies' group who oversaw the needs of parentless local children, leaving Maggie and me alone to gossip about my handsome suitor.

By nightfall, my head was swimming from the cider, and my stomach was giddy with butterflies. I rested my head on Canning's shoulder as he led me back down the lane toward home. I wondered if he would kiss me before we parted. Part of me hoped the answer was yes, but a larger part was terrified at the prospect. It would be my first kiss.

When we stood on the sidewalk in front of the steps leading up to my home, Canning turned to me. My hands immediately grew slick with sweat. This was it, the moment when I would know for certain whether he cared for me as I did him or whether it was all a figment of my girlish imagination.

Canning's eyes were soft as he took me in, holding my hands. "Victoria, this is the greatest evening I can recall in ages. I know it is sudden, but I want you for a wife—provided you agree, of course."

Shock rendered me mute. Here I was wondering about a silly little kiss when he had marriage on his mind. Marriage! A surefire way to get out from under my father's thumb and start a life with a man who had a real profession, a steady income, and who loved me for who I was, not what I could do for him. It was all too much. I swayed, feeling as though I might faint with joy.

Canning's arms came around me in a tender embrace. "Say yes, my little puss, before I have to revive you with smelling salts."

I grinned up at him, content to have him support me fully. "Yes!"

His lips met mine in a soft kiss. When he finally pulled away, he added, "I have already secured the blessing of your parents, so worry not on that score. They were thrilled at the match. We will be wed as soon as arrangements can be made."

After one more kiss and a promise to call on me the following day, he left, and I floated up the stairs and into the room I shared with Tennie. Who would have thought that falling ill would lead to this? That my recovery was really a courtship in disguise? Certainly not traditional circumstances, but nothing in my life or in my family was ever conventional. I lay in bed, staring at the ceiling and trying to imagine my wedding day. This was the chance I had dreamed of during those long hours of channeling and healing, the chance to begin my own life with a loving man at my side. I knew the spirits had called me to more than life in Mt. Gilead, Ohio. Now I had the opportunity to find out what more they had in store.

CHAPTER FOUR

My dreams of wedded bliss were shattered after only three days of marriage. I woke on the fourth day not to the pleasant warmth of my husband sleeping next to me but to an empty bed and a cold, abandoned room.

Lighting the fire and chewing my lower lip, I tried to shake off sleep and recall the events of the previous night. We'd had dinner downstairs in the boardinghouse where we let our room, then we'd retired to bed. We made love and slept, same as the last two nights. But where was Canning? Perhaps he'd gone out to seek a more permanent place for us to live or to follow up on a business lead. That would only have been sensible. As much as I wanted it to, our honeymoon couldn't last forever.

But as day faded to night and my husband failed to return, worry ate at my heart in earnest. What if something had happened to him? He could have fallen ill or been set upon by robbers. Any number of atrocities could have befallen him.

Pulling my fur-lined cloak over my shoulders, I headed out, intent on finding my husband. As I passed through the lower rooms, the proprietor, Mrs. Abrams, inquired about my destination.

"My husband has not yet returned. He didn't tell you where he was headed this morning, did he?"

Mrs. Abrams pursed her lips. "No, but you'd best start at the tavern two blocks over. In my experience, nearly all missing husbands can be found at the bottom of a mug of ale." She tsked disapprovingly.

I had a hard time believing Canning to be of that sort, but it was a place to start. If nothing else, it was a gathering place for people who may have seen him and could give me further direction.

At the threshold of the tavern, I paused. No woman with any self-respect would enter such a place unescorted, especially after dark. I would be taken for a whore. But I had to risk it. Pushing open the door, I ignored the sudden silence and the stares of the patrons. I marched straight up to the bar and asked its tender if he'd seen my husband.

"Ma'am, with all due respect, if I could recall every wayward man who passed through these doors, I'd have a far better lot in life than tending this shithole." He gave me a piercing look that said he'd be no help. "Now, either order something or leave."

I huffed, affronted by his brusqueness. Turning to leave, I briefly entertained the notion of yelling my inquiry to the entire room, but that would only have brought undue attention my way. As I stomped to the door with no clear plan of what I was going to do next, a hand seized my wrist, stopping me.

I was about to retort that I was not for sale and the man should keep his hands to himself when I realized the person who had stopped me was not a man but a woman.

"You lookin' for a doctor, right? Dark hair, about this tall?" She held up a hand above our heads.

"Yes, my husband, Canning Woodhull. Have you seen him?"

She snorted. "Yeah, I seen him. But I daresay the ladies down at Miss Evelyn's are seeing a lot more of him." Seeing my confusion, she added, "It's a brothel. He left with one of my sisters."

Surely she must have been mistaken. My dear, sweet Canning would never have been caught with the likes of a prostitute, especially not now. He had a young, nubile wife who was discovering she liked her marital duties very much. He had no need for such a place.

"I'm sorry. You must be thinking of someone else—"

The short brunette shook her head. "No, I remember him. Unusual name for one. And handsome." She fanned herself with her hand. "He was bragging on being newly married to a young wife. I assume that is you."

"I suppose, yes, it could have been him, but why—"

"Not our job to ask why, missy, just to do as the dollars please." She hooked her arm in mine. "Come on. I'll take you there. If nothin' else, you'll be relieved that I was wrong."

She didn't give me a chance to respond but pulled me out into the night and through a series of winding alleyways I never could have navigated on my own. All of my fears about large cities came back to me, but she didn't seem to share them, taking sharp turns and negotiating narrow passages as though she had been born to them. Now that I thought about it, she may have been.

We reached a dark lane halfway across the city, where trash and muck overpowered even the wood and coal smoke pouring from chimneys up and down the street. One house was ablaze with light, music and laughter spilling out into the otherwise quiet darkness. My companion walked right in, not pausing to knock or ring a bell.

"Hey there, Miss Lana," called a lithe blonde, her face painted with layers of rouge and eye coloring. "Brought us a new recruit? She's a pretty one—in a mannish sort of way."

Lana shook her head. "No. This one is looking for her husband."

The blonde's face lit up. "Oh, can I come? It's so much fun when the wife gets involved." She giggled. "He's not the graying senator, is he?"

"Nope. A young, good-looking doctor. Probably came in with my sister."

"Oh yes, Jeannie's upstairs. They have quite a party going on."

Without so much as a glance in my direction, Lana led us up the stairs. She opened the door on a scene that I couldn't have conjured in my worst nightmares. Canning lay on the bed, shirtless, drinking from a bottle of wine, surrounded by four women in varying stages of undress. One had her mouth pressed to the open slit in his pants while two kissed and fondled one another under his rapt gaze. The fourth writhed on her knees as he stroked between her legs.

I swallowed hard, fighting the urge to vomit. This was a scene of wantonness I could not have imagined taking place even in the bowels of hell, but yet there it was, with my husband, my vowed love, at its very center. Stamping down all feelings but outrage, I focused on channeling my anger to help me through this horrid situation. The other emotions could wait.

"Canning Woodhull!" I yelled, and his eyes snapped to me. They were dull and unfocused, so I knew he was drunk. Good, that would make him all the easier to drag back home. I pushed through the naked women, shoving them aside so I could take the bottle out of Canning's hand; I certainly was not going to touch his other one. "Three days married and you already defile our vows. Did I displease you so greatly?"

I pulled Canning to his feet. He blinked, grinned at me, and put an arm around my shoulders.

"'Ave you met my new friends?" he slurred. "Oh, I'm 'fraid I can't remember their names." He giggled.

I rolled my eyes. No sense in berating him when he wouldn't even remember it. I had to get him home so he could sleep it off.

Ignoring my husband, I turned to Lana. "Is there a carriage we could take back home? I'm afraid I can't find my way, and he will be no help."

"You can get anything here for the right price," she said, bored now that the drama had fizzled out.

I threw a wad of bills and a few coins at her. "Surely this should cover it and any expenses he incurred." On impulse, as we passed through the entry hall, I grabbed a vase, tossed the flowers aside, and dumped the water on Canning's head. "Time to sober up, Doc."

I'd spent too many nights pulling my father out of his cups to put up with the same from my husband. Besides a grunt of indignation, Canning gave no reaction. It was only once we were inside the cab and Canning's eyes cleared and hardened that I realized what a mistake it was to have shocked him from his stupor. For several long moments, he stared at me quietly, rage and humiliation stoking a fire behind his eyes. The anticipation was more unnerving than if he had yelled. Finally, he fisted a hand in my hair and yanked me toward him so that his lips were next to my ear.

"You had no right, Victoria, no right to interrupt my business." His voice was a throaty growl, low and sinister and cold as ice. "I may be your husband, but what I do is my own affair. You have humiliated and disrespected me, and for that, you must be punished. I will not have my wife going about seeking to bend me to her will." Before I realized what was happening, he was rooting beneath my skirts.

I batted his hand away. "Canning, what do you—"

His fist silenced me, making my ears ring and birthing stars in my field of vision.

He pinned me to the carriage seat. "You will be silent and submit to me as a woman should. The least you can do for the trouble you have caused is finish what the whores started."

It was then I noticed the bulge in his pants and realized he intended to take me then and there. I pushed against him, seeking to at least delay the inevitable until we were in a more private setting. "Don't you think we should wait until we get back to the house?"

He growled. "I said shut your mouth."

He smothered any additional objections with his lips. He was a far cry from the gentle lover I had known before. These kisses were demanding, feral, raping my mouth with tongue and teeth. His hands dug bruises into my breasts. When I tried again to push him away, he pinioned my arms behind me, making me cry out in pain as they twisted at unnatural angles. Finally, he plunged inside me, thrust his hips half a dozen times, grunted, and collapsed on top of me.

By the time the carriage pulled up in front of the boardinghouse, Canning had set his clothing to rights, finger-combed his hair, and straightened my skirts. The driver and those we passed on the way to our rooms would never know anything had been amiss. But I knew. In the course of a single day, my whole world had changed. The tears would come later, in the dark hours when I could think and begin to feel the ramifications of all that had occurred this night.

But for now, as I washed and took my place in bed beside my unfaithful husband, one thought chased itself around my mind—my husband was no better than my father. I had escaped the fisherman's hook only to be impaled by his trident.

❧

WHILE SOME WOMEN IN my situation would have wept and carried on in hysterics, I had never taken to emotional overreaction. I tried to see my situation reasonably, soberly, as the weeks passed. From the stories I'd heard in the parlor in Mt. Gilead, I knew that as bleak as my situation seemed, others had it far worse. Yes, my husband was a drunkard, but I couldn't keep every bottle from his hand any more than I could control where or with whom he spent his nights.

Like my mother before me, all I could do was pray. And pray I did. While Canning was out building his medical practice, I spent my days on my knees, begging God to bring back the charming man who had courted me, to cast out the abusive devil who possessed him since that night at Miss Evelyn's. When I wasn't praying, I was holding séances, speaking with my dead baby sisters and my childhood caretaker, Rachel, desperate for any bit of advice they could impart.

When I returned to Mt. Gilead for a short visit with my family, I was loathe to tell Ma I had fallen into the same trap as her, but I could find no real way to hide it. She didn't laugh or yell as I'd expected. Rather, in a rare moment of compassion, she twined her fingers in mine and brought them to her lips.

"You're his wife now, an' no matter what he does, you belong ta him. But as the Good Book says, 'This too shall pass.' I didn't name you for a queen for you ta live like this. I may not know what, but you were meant for more."

Her words lightened my spirit, and I returned home hopeful, with a heart full of joy. I had discovered something else while I was away—I was pregnant. Surely a babe would calm my husband's temper—or at least buy me time. Canning might have been a lot of things, but there was no way he'd hit me and endanger our child.

Our room was empty, though a mess, when I returned. Canning's clothing was scattered all over the floor as though while I was away, he hadn't bothered to do more than simply drop it wherever he liked. The laundress would be by later to pick up our washing, so I grabbed a basket and filled it, first with my travel-stained clothes then with Canning's discards. I shook my head as I walked the room, picking up trousers and shirts, ties and underclothes, some of which were clearly female and most decidedly not mine. I forced myself to take deep breaths and ignore the implications, though I couldn't resist tossing her clothes into the fire rather than the basket.

Picking up a jacket, I paused. Something was sticking out of an inner breast pocket. Curious, I removed it—paper of some sort—and dropped the jacket in the basket of dirty clothes. I approached the window and turned the page over in the light. It was an envelope addressed to my husband with a letter inside. It was written on fine cream stationery in a looping, feminine hand. I knew I would have nothing but grief for reading it, but I couldn't stop myself.

Dr. Canning Woodhull,

Though you have treated me worse than a gutter whore, as a Christian woman, I feel I owe you the respect of informing you that your son was born this day in Terre Haute, Indiana. He is healthy and well but will not bear your name. He will never know his father, of that I will make certain. Any man who can send his pregnant lover to a backward country town on the day of his wedding to another woman does not deserve to be called a father.

I would offer my felicitations on your nuptials, but all my heart can muster is pity for the poor girl foolish enough to have been charmed by your lies. Tell me, did you marry that child because she too was en famille? *You never could control your lust, and I doubt God has wrought a miracle and made you faithful in the last several weeks.*

I wish you to know also that I have uncovered all of your lies. I have had plenty of time during my confinement to investigate your claims of connections and success. That successful medical practice of yours has no basis in fact. The closest you came to a medical education is having an uncle who is a trained doctor. Did you tell that wife of yours the same cockamamie story about your family? You are no son of a judge—a son of a bitch, certainly—but your father was only a small-town justice of the peace. Hardly the same thing. And this uncle of yours? The mayor of New York is indeed a Caleb Woodhull, but I took the liberty of writing to him, and do you know what he said? Not only does he not have a relation by your name, he has never met you. How odd.

What would your little wife think if she truly knew the man she married? And what would happen to your practice if you patients knew you were no better than a slightly educated charlatan? I will tell everyone the truth. In fact, I have taken measures to be sure the press in half a dozen major cities have copies of my proof. Do not ever approach me or my son. And be certain of one thing – I will ruin you.

Your wife has my everlasting sympathy and daily prayers. But you, my former love, can rot in hell.

The letter wasn't signed. But it didn't need to be. This woman had revealed enough of herself to ruin the last ounce of hope in my heart. The letter fluttered to the floor as I slid down beside it, clinging to the basket of soiled clothing. Her accusations swirled in my head. Canning had had a lover the whole time he was courting me. He'd sent her away so he could marry me even though she was pregnant. He had a son he would never know. He wasn't the educated, well-connected man I thought I'd married but a fraud frighteningly similar to my father, whose shadow I'd thought I had escaped.

I buried my head in my hands and wept. There was nothing else I could do. Would that I had known this before I'd wed him—or at least before I had became pregnant—then I could have at least considered filing for divorce. But now, what choice did I have? I could not support myself, much less a child as well, on my own. If I left, I'd have to go back to Ma and Pa in shame and endure their wrath—no doubt they would find a way to make this my fault. I couldn't let my child be raised the same way I had been. At least with Canning, I'd have some say in how he or she grew up; back in Mt. Gilead, Ma and Pa would wield the power. No, I'd made my bed, as they say, and lain down with a dog, so now I had to endure the flea bites even if the dog wasn't the breed I'd expected.

A heavy knock on the door stirred me from my thoughts and had me leaping to my feet.

"Constable, Mrs. Woodhull. Open up, if ye please."

I flung open the door to find two uniformed policemen supporting an incoherent Canning under each arm.

"This man your husband?" one asked.

"Yes, sir."

"We found him wandering the streets, barely able to walk. Couldn't tell us his name or where he was from. We've had him in a cell for the last ten hours or so. Lucky for us one of Miss Kitty's girls recognized him. Said he'd been kicked out of her place the night before."

They gave Canning a shove toward me. He stumbled then leaned on me limply as if we were engaged in some macabre dance.

"He's your problem now. Do us a favor and keep tighter control over him, or we'll have to press charges, you hear?"

They spoke as though I had *any* control over him. "Yes, sirs. Thank you for returning him to me safely."

Canning muttered and giggled to himself while I undressed him. He stank of alcohol, sweat, vomit, and the strong perfume of the whorehouse, so I bathed him like a babe, hoping the cold water would sober him into some condition resembling sense, while he faded in and out of consciousness.

Placing the chamber pot next to the bed in case his stomach roiled, I tucked him into bed. His eyes opened briefly, lighting on the letter that still lay discarded on the floor.

"You know, then?" he slurred. Without waiting for me to respond, he went on. "Talked to some o' the boys at tha press club. They know too. It's going to come out. We have to leave town."

Though I didn't disagree with him, now was not the time to try to reason with him. I stroked his forehead. "Sleep now, Canning. We can discuss this in the morning."

Inwardly, I raged. Damn him, damn the bottle, and damn the laws that kept me tied to this man. I could have proved adultery easily enough, but even a divorce would have done me no good. There had to be a way around the rules of society that bound innocent women to good-for-nothing men—me, all the women I had known in Mt. Gilead, and the thousands in the city around me. Somehow, someday, I would find a way. But that was another day's quest. Now I had to make sure my husband didn't drink himself to death and that we escaped before the press could prove Canning was worthless.

CHAPTER FIVE

Canning's mistress was so thorough in her revenge that we lasted in Chicago only eight months—long enough for our son, Byron, to be born—before reporters came nosing around again. So we hopped a ship from New York to San Francisco, a burgeoning town still bustling from the Gold Rush, where patients were plentiful and news traveled slowly—or so we hoped.

We settled in on one of the many long, narrow streets where brick houses stood shoulder to shoulder on both sides of the lane like spectators at a parade, watching impassively as men and women, horses, carriages, and even wagon trains turned the dusty road to mush and mire. While it was more advanced than I had anticipated—some parts of the city had gas lights—San Francisco lacked the positive energy of Chicago, the bustle of activity leading to commerce and growth. Its endless activity was focused on survival and greed, for he who found fortune best keep it to himself lest it be stolen or surpassed by another.

It was certainly not the kind of town in which I wished to raise my child, but it was better to be here and anonymous than dogged by reporters in Chicago. I was fortunate that Byron was a placid child. He rarely cried, but then again, he rarely showed interest in anything. During the day while Canning was out, I held Byron, sang to him, played with him, did anything I could to elicit those sweet baby coos every mother longs to hear. But no matter what I did, he regarded me with disinterest. It was as though he were in the grip of a relentless lethargy that kept him from fully connecting with the world around him.

Finally, I could take no more and asked Canning to check him for signs of blindness and deafness.

"I don't know why you're so worried," he said, waving a finger in front of Byron's face and watching his eyes track its movement.

"He's your son. Don't you worry that he doesn't smile, doesn't cry, doesn't reach out to grasp your hand—all the things most babies do? I'm scared for him, Canning. I know there's something wrong with him. I can tell."

Canning stood behind Byron's cradle and clapped sharply. Byron startled then settled back into his malaise as though nothing had occurred.

"Hmmm... he's not deaf or blind, but that should have frightened him enough to make him cry or at least seek out the source of the sound. We will have to watch him."

"That's it? That's all you can say?" I asked as he resumed drinking his whiskey.

"My dear, it's all I would say to any parent. Babies develop as they will. Give him a few months, and he'll be fine, you'll see." He put his feet up on a stool by the fire and savored his drink, leaving me to tend to the family ledger.

That was the third bottle of whiskey Canning had opened this week. He didn't drink the cheap swill they served at the local saloon either. It was some special brand imported from back east that cost nearly as much as he made in a week.

After tallying the numbers three times, I was forced to tell him, "We don't have enough money to pay the butcher."

Canning didn't even open his eyes. "He'll extend us credit."

"This *is* the credit."

"So ask him for more."

"And if he doesn't offer any? What then? I think I may have to look for work."

That got Canning's attention. He snickered. "Doing what? Selling fortunes? I'm not your father. I won't collect clients for you." He laughed harder. "I know! You could always be a cigar girl."

I couldn't believe my husband would speak of me becoming a prostitute—even in jest. I swiped his bottle of whiskey. "And you could be drinking rotgut down at the tavern rather than paying your whole weekly wage for a case of this."

He jerked the bottle out of my hand and brought the back of his other hand down across my cheek. "At least I contribute to this family. What a man does in his private time is his business. Or would you rather I go back to staying at the brothel?" His eyes glinted with malevolent challenge, daring me to say yes.

I would not win this battle of words with him, that much was clear. But I could still win the war. Tomorrow, I would prevail upon one of our neighbors to watch Byron while Canning was at his clinic, and I would find work.

FIVE DAYS OF TRUDGING up and down the steep lanes of San Francisco and answering ads for domestic help had netted me nothing. One thing I hadn't accounted for in my fevered quest to do right by my family was that so many others were trying to do the same for theirs. Time and time again, doors closed to me. I was too old, too educated, not skilled enough, or the clients wanted live-in help. But worst of all, I had a family. Nearly twenty times I had lost promising domestic work to Chinese immigrants who could accept lower wages or, in some cases, work for room and board alone—compromises I could not make because I wasn't supporting only myself.

I paused before a fine townhouse in a fashionable area of town. It was made of gray stone and had its own gaslight illuminating the doorway in the waning evening light. From the stoop, I could see down into the harbor, where hundreds of ships rocked. I had a sudden memory of my spirit guide telling me I would find great success in a town with many ships. Maybe this was it. Maybe it was a sign. It had to be. This was my last stop before I had to hurry back home so Canning wouldn't know I was gone.

Buoyed by that hope, I pulled the tassel that rang the bell. A scurry of footsteps, the yapping of at least two small dogs, and a woman's shushing voice followed. The door opened, and I beheld not the butler I expected but the lady of the house, a small dog with dandelion fur tucked under each arm.

"May I help you?" she inquired with a placid smile.

I cleared my throat. "Yes, ma'am. I am here to inquire about your need for domestic help. You are Miss Cogswell, I presume?"

Her lovely face fell. "I am. But I'm afraid you are too late. I just hired a girl for that position." She gestured behind her, where a Chinese girl no older than ten stood at attention, waiting for her mistress's command.

My heart sank. Perhaps I would have to become a cigar girl after all. I blinked back tears and fought to keep my voice steady. No sense in losing my dignity in front of such a fine lady. "Oh. I'm sorry to have bothered you."

I started to turn away when Miss Cogswell stopped me. "Wait. There is one thing I believe you may be able to help me with. Can you sew?"

"Yes. I have many years of experience working with my mother. I can tailor, darn, and embroider."

Miss Cogswell clapped. "Wonderful. Li, bring that pile of clothing I showed you earlier." While Li scurried off, Miss Cogswell leaned toward me confidentially. "She's bright and strong but has never held a needle in her life. Poor dear. I'm an actress, you see, and I am responsible for taking care of my own costumes. But I don't have much time for that, what with learning my lines, performing, and entertaining patrons after the shows. You may just be the angel I've been praying for."

Li returned bearing a basket of assorted garments, everything from ripped hose and sagging underthings to crinoline skirts with dropped hems and dresses with torn seams.

Miss Cogswell explained what needed to be done to each piece. "Bring this back on Sunday, and I'll inspect your work. If I like what I see, you'll have a job. Plus, I'll tell everyone else in the neighborhood and in the theatre what great work you do. You'll have no shortage of clients. That's a promise."

❧

ANNA WAS GOOD TO her word. A week later, I had more offers of work mending garments than I had hours to complete them. She advised me as to which would be the most profitable and who was trying to sneak in some labor on the cheap, and we became fast friends.

Within three months, I was spending my days at the theatre, mending garments almost exclusively for the company. On weekends, I tended to the needs of the rest of my clients while Canning drank away most of our profits.

Byron was the hit of backstage. Chorus girls fussed and cooed over him while the stagehands shook their heads in awe that he never cried or fussed amid the noise and confusion. One day, while I was letting out one of Anna's dresses so that she could fit into it despite her recent weight gain, one of the newer actresses, a beautiful brunette named Josie Mansfield, took a seat next to me.

After watching Byron for a long while, she shook her head. "I don't know how to tell you this, Mrs. Woodhull, so I'm going to say it straight. I hope you won't be offended." Her eyes were pleading. "I believe your son may be an idiot."

I dropped my needle and bowed my head. Someone had finally voiced my greatest fear. That my child was born deformed in the mind was something I'd fretted over from his first days of life. A mother—even a first-time mother—knows when something is wrong with her child, and I knew. He wasn't lusty enough; it was as though he didn't realize he'd been born and was still blissfully ignorant in the dark world of the womb. Tears leaked from beneath my pressed lashes despite my efforts to hide them, and I let out a small involuntary sob.

"Oh, Mrs. Woodhull, I didn't mean to make you cry," Josie said, remorse in her voice. She placed a gentle hand on mine.

"No, it's quite all right," I said, clearing my constricted throat. "I'm glad someone finally acknowledged he is different."

She gave me a wan half smile. "My little cousin is the same, you see. I remember what he was like growing up, what it was like for my aunt. I'm happy to help in any way I can. I might be able to help you calm him. He'll get more fretful as he grows."

I reached into the basket of material scraps at my feet and found one to use to wipe my eyes. "Thank you. Having someone to speak to about this lifts a great burden from my heart." I picked up my needle again. "My husband is a doctor, but even he won't admit that Byron isn't developing normally."

"Oh, of course not," Josie said as though it was the most obvious fact. "If he did, he'd have to admit he sired a malformed child. No man with any amount of pride would do so."

I put the sewing aside, picked up my son, and looked into his deep brown eyes so like his father's. "Why do you think this happened? Did I not love him enough while I was pregnant?" *Could it be because he was conceived in violence in the back of that carriage?* "I certainly love him now. I could never give him to one of those institutions for children of his ilk. He is my son." I gave Josie a pleading look. "What did I do wrong?"

She shook her head, toying with one of Byron's tiny hands. "I wish I knew. My aunt blamed her husband's propensity to drink for her son's condition. He beat her all through her confinement."

I nodded, my eyes growing glassy as I remembered my own similar experiences with Canning. What a fool I'd been to think being with child would be a shield of protection. If anything, it had made him worse. He'd been fine until my growing belly interfered with our martial relations. Then he went to the brothel instead. When they finally kicked him out, he'd come home and take out his frustrations on me. It was one of his blows that had started my labor.

I set Byron back into his little box as the rage inside me grew lest I accidently squeeze him too hard. "Damn Canning, and damn his drinking. Damn his wicked fists and my weakness as a woman.

If I were a man, I'd beat him back. I'd hit him so hard he'd never wake up."

Josie hugged me close. "I know, sweetie. I know. And when you do fight back, it only angers them more. Every time I tried to fight against my stepfather, to stop his depravity, it only enraged him more. Nearly killed me one time."

I nodded, still holding her tight. Here was a woman who truly understood what it meant to be helpless and abused. "Me too. Early in my pregnancy, I decided to give Canning back every bit of pain he inflicted on me, so I closed my eyes and pretended I was one of those muscled dairywomen who carry heavy pails. I kicked, punched, bit him, pulled his hair, poked at his eyes, anything I could to show him I wasn't going to settle for the same treatment I'd gotten from my Pa."

I was shaking now. I could feel it, could see my upset reflected in the trembling of her lace collar. "But the harder I hit him, the more aggressive he became. I think he would have killed me had I not finally shoved him in such a way he tripped over his discarded shoes and hit his head on the wardrobe. A neighbor found us the next morning. Doctor said we were both an inch from dying. How I didn't lose my babe, I will never know. The angels must have been watching over him."

Josie pulled away, searching my face. Her own eyes were pink and puffy, rimmed in black by makeup that had yielded to her tears. "The angels *were* watching over you both. This is the plight of women. The law allows it, the preachers allow it, but I don't think God does. All we can do is endure and pray that one day they will see justice before God's throne."

"Does that have to be the only answer? Surely we can change the laws, talk sense into our preachers?"

"There are those who are trying. Women who call themselves suffragists are right now fighting the very laws we rail against. But they are women of breeding and education with the bank accounts to make people at least pretend to listen to what they have to say. You and me? We're lucky people hear the words we say onstage, and those are written for us. Can you imagine the reaction if we spoke our own minds?"

I gave a small, derisive puff of laughter because it was the response Josie expected. But she had triggered an idea in my mind. We couldn't speak our minds, yet people listened when the spirits spoke through me. If only they would tell Canning to cease his abuse or, I laughed inwardly at the thought, give a message for our lawmakers. Perhaps then they would listen. Perhaps someday...

My train of thought was interrupted as the dressing room door shot open and Anna bustled in, script in hand. "Josie, the director wants to see you. Victoria, will you be a dear and run lines with me one more time? I can't seem to get this scene right."

Yes, there was something there, the seed of an idea that needed to germinate before it would come to fruition. But when it did, it would change everything.

CHAPTER SIX

"Christ in Heaven! This is the last week of the show. Where are we going to find someone willing to learn this bit part for a pittance?" The director's near-hysteria carried through the dressing room door and over the laughter of actors, clanging of gears, and whining of pulleys as the set men prepared for the evening show.

Anna looked over her shoulder as I sewed her into her costume. "You and I have been running lines from this show for months now. Surely you know the part of the country cousin?"

"I think I know all the parts," I said around a mouthful of pins. I spit them out and set them on the table in front of Anna. "But that doesn't mean they will give it to me."

The idea was tempting. The more I'd watched the actors over the last two years, the more I'd come to realize that what they did wasn't all that different from what Tennie and I had done in Pa's shop. In fact, acting was easier. They only had to say the lines prepared for them; they didn't have to worry about real spirits changing the script.

And the money… as the director said, it wasn't much, but it would be a nice supplement.

"Yes, they will." Anna shrugged away from me. "Just you watch."

That was how I found myself onstage for the first time that night, wearing a costume rather than mending one and saying a few simple lines in front of the gaslights. I wasn't onstage for long, but when I was, the feeling was like nothing I'd ever experienced, not even when I was in touch with the spirit world. I felt as though the power of all those eyes on me transformed me into the best version of myself. Or maybe because I got to be someone else, I felt free enough to be who I really was and more. After all, for those brief minutes, I wasn't Victoria Woodhull, seamstress and wife to an alcoholic bastard of a husband. I was the country cousin of the great actress Anna Cogswell.

By the time *New York by Gaslight* closed that Sunday, San Francisco had begun to take note of the newest actress on its stage. There was even a small blurb in the paper that mentioned me by name in the closing night review.

"Look, Canning, isn't it exciting?" I said to him the next day while we ate breakfast. "Anna says the director was so impressed by my talent he's thinking of casting me in his next show. Can you believe it?"

Canning looked up from the review I'd shoved beneath his nose. "Another bit part or a real role?" He sniggered. "The more time you spend onstage, the more time those Johnnies are going to expect from you after the curtain falls, and I won't have any wife of mine playing the demimonde."

I waved away his concerns. "This is a real part. It pays fifty-two dollars a week. That's nearly three times as much as I make as a seamstress."

That caught Canning's attention. "I'll give you my blessing, but know I will be there almost every night and I will be watching what you do after the show. If you so much as look at one of those backdoor bastards, I'll pull you from the show by the roots of your bleached wig, you hear?"

❀

CANNING MUST BE AROUND *here somewhere. Please let him show up soon.* I never thought I'd actually want to see my husband backstage— most nights he flitted around like an annoying mosquito—but tonight I could have used his temper to rid me of this particularly persistent admirer.

"Come on now, darlin', I'm only asking you to dinner." Anton Joss's cigar-stained breath ruffled my hair as he trailed a finger up my arm from wrist to shoulder then back down again. "What happens after that is up to you."

He had me pinned against one of the stage walls, one arm on either side of my neck so I could barely move, much less escape. "Mr. Joss, your offer is very kind, but as I've told you before, I am married to a very jealous man who would not take kindly to my being out at all hours with you when I should be at home in his bed."

I glanced away from his thick mustache, my gaze darting around the wing. When I caught her eye, Josie sent me a concerned look. But there was nothing she could do, nothing anyone could do. Mr. Joss was one of the show's backers, and if I wanted to keep my part in *The Corsican Brothers*, I had to keep him happy—even if that meant spreading my legs for him. I'd managed to fend off his advances thus far, but it appeared his patience was at an end. *Where is my husband?*

I swallowed hard, seeing I would have to consent. Perhaps I could slip out after the show without him noticing? But then I'd just have to face him the next day. There were only two ways this could end: I could say yes and submit to whatever depravity he required, or I could refuse and watch my job disappear.

"Your offer is very kind, but I simply do not feel right accepting it as a married woman."

Mr. Joss stepped toward me, closing the inch of space between us. "If that's the way you wish to play it—"

"The lady said no." Canning's voice from somewhere behind my admirer was a blessed relief. Before I could even let out my breath, Canning had pulled him away from me and landed a punch square on Mr. Joss's nose. "You can play with the other actresses all you wish, but my wife is off-limits. And if you don't heed me, I will personally see that you don't have the equipment"—he shot a purposeful look at the man's crotch—"to ever make a play for another woman again."

Mr. Joss recovered quickly, straightening his rumpled suit. "Remember that I hold your wife's employment in my hands. One word from me and she will never find another job in these theatres again as an actress or seamstress."

Canning answered by throwing a rude gesture over his shoulder as he hustled me toward my dressing area. "I think it's time you find another line of work."

"Doing what, Canning? This is all I *can* do. I know I'm meant for something higher, but what? And how? Will you lay off your drink and your laudanum long enough for us to find out?"

Canning blanched at my mention of his newest habit.

"Don't act like you think I don't know that gin and whiskey alone don't satisfy you anymore. Am I to become a cigar girl, as you once joked, to support your new habit?"

Canning smacked me hard, but I hardly noticed. After five years of marriage, I barely registered his blows anymore. If I didn't react, he was less likely to do it again. I'd figured out long ago it was the rise, the reaction, he enjoyed. If I robbed him of that, he lost interest.

I was saved from any further conversation by the shrill call of "Places!" as the director made his last-minute pass through our dressing area, ensuring everyone was prepared for the opening scene.

Without another word, Canning left to take his seat. I paced through the first several scenes, waiting for my cue. Maybe it was my encounter with Mr. Joss or the words Canning and I had exchanged or perhaps that the moon was full, but I was restless, unable to still my body or mind. Something was tugging at my edges like a communication from the spirits I could not quite hear.

Thankfully, all that melted away when I took the stage. Under the lights, amid the swell of music from the orchestra that accompanied our ballroom scene, I was able to think clearly again. My lines spilled forth without conscious effort as I charmed the audience and my castmates with graceful aplomb.

The conversation onstage centered on an exchange about the separation of the two titular brothers, but I couldn't pay attention. My restlessness returned with a force I could barely contain. The gaslights faded, and I saw Tennie in my mind's eye. She was dressed in a striped calico dress, holding her arms out to me.

"Victoria, come home," she said with no small amount of urgency.

Something was wrong. I had no idea what, but whatever was going on, my sister was in dire enough straits to send her spirit directly to me to beg for help. Without a thought for the play taking place around me, I dashed off into the wings and didn't bother to remove my pink silk dress or slippers. I gathered up my few valuables from my dressing area and ran headlong into the foggy drizzle.

Canning met me around the front of the theatre. "Vickie, are you unwell? What is going on?"

I shook my head, trying to catch my breath while simultaneously urging him back toward our home. "We have to go."

"What? Why?"

"I've had a vision of my sister. All I know is we are needed. We must be on the morning steamer to New York."

CHAPTER SEVEN

Tennie rushed into my arms at the train station. "You came! Oh, thank God you came."

I held my sister close, only mildly surprised to see she was wearing the same dress as in my vision. "What is it, Tennie? What's happened? Is it Ma?"

She kissed my cheek. "No, nothing like that. Ma and Pa are both fine. Everyone is. I"—her cheeks colored, and she looked away— "I couldn't stand another day alone in this place. You have no idea, Vickie. It's even worse than it was before." She looped her arm in mine, finally nodding at Canning. "Come home. You'll see."

"Home" was a large house on the outskirts of Columbus where Tennie saw clients, Buck sold his snake oil, and Utica and Maggie, now divorced with four children to feed, entertained gentleman clients. Tennie occasionally saw clients in that way as well.

Once Canning and I moved in, Pa put me back to work in the parlor, but he didn't pressure me to entertain men, the one thing for which I'd give him credit. Maybe he was respectful of my marriage or scared of Canning—I didn't really care because it kept me from the worst of my father's schemes.

After several years of this life, working thirteen-hour days, I understood Tennie's desperation, for this was no way of living. But we were all well and truly trapped unless we could find a way out. Byron was growing and, as Josie had promised, becoming more erratic and sometimes even violent, especially around strangers and loud noises, both of which our house had in excess nearly all day and all night. He needed dedicated care, but none of us had time to sit with him; it fell to whoever wasn't busy at the time to be sure he ate and was tended to. I was ashamed to admit that some days, we forgot he existed and he spent the better part of the day sitting in a corner, rocking back and forth, grunting to himself.

When I voiced my concerns to Canning, he dismissed them almost before I had finished speaking. "Why should we move? We have income and a house. What more could you wish for?"

Of course he didn't understand—no, he *wouldn't* understand. He and my father were bosom friends, sharing clients by day as both "doctored" in their own humbugging way and sharing a taste for alcohol by night. For them, it was a dream life with a solid income and little responsibility.

Against all logic, I found myself praying to God for another child, one who was whole and smart and beautiful. In my darkest hours, I knew my need for what it was—a desperate desire for the love I didn't get from my husband or my family. Tennie was the only one who truly cared about me, but even that wasn't enough to fill the void that ate away at my heart with every beat. I needed someone who would be devoted to me, wholly dependent on me.

But I rarely admitted that…even to myself. I told myself that if I had another child, Canning and I could get away from all of this. The last thing my father would want was a screaming babe interrupting his trade, so we would be forced to leave, breaking the bond that made Canning immobile, forcing us into another phase of life.

Finally, the Lord heard my prayers. Late in the summer of 1860, I found myself with child once again. But rather than being upset by the news, my parents welcomed the impending birth of their next grandchild with unusual solicitude. It seemed that part of my plan had failed. But then fate intervened again.

One afternoon in early 1861, snow fell in large flakes outside our building amid a bitter cold snap, keeping away our clients and forcing my nieces and nephews into a single room to entertain themselves when all they really wanted was to play outside in the snow—a desire they voiced loudly any time one of the adults came near. After several skirmishes that ended in scratches and tears, Utica was elected to stay with them and ensure they didn't kill one another.

When I brought in trays of soup and bread for their midday meal, I found the kids so engrossed in their games they didn't look up when I opened the door. At least I thought they were playing until I paused on the threshold to listen. Then I realized I had walked in on a very different scene.

The kids were gathered in a semicircle near the rear of the room, their backs toward me, taunting something. I assumed they'd cornered a rat or one of the neighborhood tomcats who'd tried to escape the cold. But before I could move to break up their circle, I realized it wasn't an animal they were after but my son. I could just barely make him out between their tiny bodies, cowering against the wall, arms clutched over his head protectively.

"Monster!" one of the boys yelled. "You ain't even a person."

"My mama says you the devil's spawn," Polly's daughter Rosa said.

"Yeah, you more like a dog," an older boy said, removing the rope that held up his pants. "An' you know dogs need whippin' to keep 'em in line."

He raised his arm to strike. I flung aside the tray of food and was in motion in the same moment, determined to protect my son. But Byron sprang up with shocking ferocity and tackled the boy, snarling like a crazed beast, his hands clamped around his attacker's throat. The kids shrieked that Byron was going to kill Jessup, drawing Utica out of her morphine-induced haze and bringing the other adults scrambling into the room.

Before I could pry Byron's surprisingly strong grip from Jessup's throat, the accusations began. I finally got Byron to let the gasping boy go, and I held my son to my breast, where he shook with a rage I'd thought impossible for one so young. Ignoring the ravings around us, I whispered soft words to him, stroking his hair, telling him all was well, until he calmed enough for me to look up. When I did, it was into a circle of grim, silent faces.

My father broke through the ring, pushing siblings, nieces, and nephews away so that he towered over me and my now-quiet son. Byron clung to my protruding belly as though seeking comfort from his unborn brother or sister, refusing to look at his grandfather. I didn't blame him. The hatred on my father's face was such as I hadn't seen since I was a child myself.

Emboldened by the years that had passed since then, I dared speak first. "Whatever you may do, do not punish my son for the taunts of his kin."

"He tried to kill my boy," Maggie screeched from somewhere behind Pa's broad shoulders.

Pa ignored us both. "Vickie, I cannot have this happen again. Imagine if we'd had clients here. What if your son attacked one of them? He needs to be locked up like the wretch he is. And if you won't do it, I will. Otherwise, get out."

I couldn't believe my own ears. "You would abandon your own kin, your pregnant daughter and her family, based on one tussle? I've seen Utica and Polly come to blows over who took the last sugar cube, and you would toss us out over this?"

Pa turned his back on us. "Be gone by morning and do not come back. You aren't welcome here."

❀

WE HAD NOTHING. NOWHERE to go. For the first time in my wretched life, I was homeless.

After begging one night's stay with friends in Columbus, Canning decided we should visit his father and uncle in New York. "They'll take us in," he said with great assurance.

I sold my few remaining pieces of jewelry from our time of prosperity in San Francisco to book passage to New York. Though I'd known for years that Canning's connections were not what he made them out to be, I was not prepared for the coldness with which we were received. His uncle, the "mayor," was traveling and so could not receive us, and his father flatly refused to let us in. I wondered what had really taken place all those years ago when Canning left New York for Ohio. It had to have been something big for his father to still be holding a grudge. One thing was for certain—Canning's tale of admiring small-town life and wanting to settle down in one had been just as much of a lie as his made-up familial connections.

Seeing I was soon to give birth, Canning's step-mother took pity on us and paid a month's rent at a local boardinghouse so I wouldn't have to birth my child on the street. Our lack of funds also meant

Canning lost his ready access to alcohol and laudanum, which meant he was frequently sick as his body went through withdrawal. He was in no condition to see patients, so we lived on the charity of neighbors.

Finally, my time came. In between contractions, I prayed Canning really did have some medical education because this time, I would have to rely upon him to help me deliver my child, a frightening prospect given his hands shook constantly and he was covered in more sweat than I was. As pain ripped through me, I prayed to Demosthenes, Jesus, and every spirit I could think of to be with me and my new child, to deliver us safely.

Canning told me we had a healthy baby girl, whom I named Zula Maude, before I succumbed to exhaustion and fell into a deep sleep. I awoke a few hours later to a pool of warm liquid on my left shoulder just beneath where my sleeping daughter lay. *Damn it, Canning, couldn't you have at least swaddled her correctly?* But when I looked at my hand, it wasn't covered in urine; it was red with blood.

I sat straight up in bed, looking around for my husband to ask for his help, but the small room was silent. I was alone. I held my baby girl carefully and checked for the source of the bleeding. A large crimson stain covered the front of her tiny gown right where the stump of the umbilical cord protruded from her stomach. As I removed the soaked cloth, she emitted a weak cry, bathing my hands in fresh blood. He was a doctor. How could he have not tied the umbilical cord off properly? Panic built in my throat as I searched for something to use to re-clamp it so my child wouldn't bleed to death. Finding nothing at hand, I tried to stand, but my legs gave way and my head swam with dizziness. When my ears stopping ringing and my eyesight cleared, I tore the edge of the bed sheet and used it as a makeshift tie.

I breathed deeply, knowing the worst of the danger was over, but my daughter still needed help. She had lost a lot of blood, and I had no idea how to know if she would live or die. I laid Zula on the bed and tried to stand again. This time I made it a few steps before collapsing into a rickety old chair, which splintered beneath the weight of my sudden fall. Now I too was bleeding, and I had not the strength to rise again.

Desperate, I called out for help, but no one responded. I heard a scuttling on the other side of the wall, so I knew our neighbors, the Collinses, were home; I just had to get their attention. I pulled a piece of the broken chair out from beneath me and banged on the wall with it. For what felt like hours, I knocked on the wall, scratching the wallpaper and gouging out pieces of plaster, until my front doorknob rattled.

"Mrs. Woodhull, are you all right? What is going on in there?" Mrs. Collins called.

"I need help," I cried, my voice hoarse and throat dry. "Get a doctor."

The handle rattled again, and a loud bang startled me as she threw herself against the locked door, trying to get it open. "Don't you worry, dear. I'll get someone right away."

By the time Mr. and Mrs. Collins finally got in through a grate in the basement, I managed to pull myself to my feet and collapse back into bed, cradling my baby girl. The doctor was there soon after, assuring me Zula would be fine and treating the wounds I had sustained in my fall. He tried to give me a dose of laudanum syrup to help me rest, but my stomach rebelled at the sugary sweet scent I'd come to associate with my husband's breath. Failing that, he gave me something else, something bitter. Before I lost consciousness, Mrs. Collins promised to stay by my side and care for Zula.

It was dusk two days later when I woke. Byron had crawled to my side from wherever he had hidden during the chaos of the birth and its aftermath, and he was sleeping peacefully snuggled up against me. Mrs. Collins was there, as promised, with a heavyset young woman with kind eyes and long brown hair piled on top of her head in a manner that reminded me of a Viking maiden. Mrs. Collins introduced her as her daughter, Celeste, who was nursing her own babe and was happy to lend her other breast to Zula.

"Your daughter is just fine," she assured me, holding my baby girl out so I could hold her and see for myself.

"And my husband?" I asked, looking around for some sign of Canning.

Mrs. Collins shook her head. "He's asleep in our parlor. Or should I say passed out. My husband was home when Canning entered our house thinking it was his own. It took him an hour to convince your husband he had the wrong address, but by then, it was clear Canning wasn't going to make the short trip over here. He's letting him sleep it off."

I hid my face beneath the covers, mortified. As if it wasn't bad enough the bastard had left us for dead, now he had humiliated us in front of the few people we trusted. I breathed deeply, willing myself to face them and pulled down the sheet. "I am so sorry for all the trouble we have put you and your family through, Mrs. Collins." I smiled at Celeste. "And so grateful for the care you have given. I'm afraid I cannot pay you for your kindness."

Mrs. Collins waved off my words. "Nonsense. We were doing what needs be done." She took my hand. "Tell me—and speak plainly now. Do you really wish to be married to that man?"

Her blunt question shocked me. Did I wish to be married to a man who couldn't be bothered to deliver his own child safely? One who would rather be supported than support his family as his honor and wedding vows compelled him? One who was so lost to alcohol and drugs that he didn't even recognize his own home? No. I'd tolerated his antics for the better part of a decade, and for what? What did I have to show for it? No money, no viable connection to my family, and a temporary home that was only paid up for a few more days. So what if the law said we were bound? It also said we could be unbound. I could prove adultery twenty times over and more. That was what I would do.

I gazed at the sleeping baby in my arms and stroked Byron's temple. I had been raised by a good-for-nothing father, and all I had gotten was a good-for-nothing husband. For once, I was grateful Byron likely had no memory of Canning's abuse. As for Zula, I would rather raise her by myself than have her know pain from her father's hand.

It wouldn't be easy, but I could open my own shop. I'd had enough experience working for my father to know I could use my gifts of clairvoyance and healing to attract clientele on my own. Why should I not keep the money I earned?

"No," I answered after a lengthy pause. "I do not wish to be married to him any longer. And why should I?"

She nodded. "I thought so. We'll take care of you until you're well. Then tell us where you want to go, and we'll see you get there safely. No woman should have to live as you do."

CHAPTER EIGHT

I never told Canning I was leaving. I gathered up the children, said farewell to our neighbors, and took off for the small towns of the Midwest, moving often so he was unlikely to find us. Even though I stayed well north of the Missouri Compromise Line that divided slave-holding states from free, the war years were tough on my children and me. Despite our humble conditions and the need to travel from town to town, following regiments and supply trains to fill our purses and our bellies, Zula prospered and was growing into a bright young girl whom all of my customers loved. Year after year, Byron remained the same, a perpetual child in the body of a growing young man. But I was able to keep him near me and manage his fits, so we never had another episode like the one in Ohio.

I crossed paths with my family on occasion, coming the closest to them in Chicago, where I worked only blocks from the latest incarnation of Pa's business, a clinic he ran while styling himself with the audacious title King of Cancer. His advert in the paper claimed boldly that between his magical salve and Tennie's laying on of hands, they could cure all manner of cancers—and fast.

A few my clients were also patients at the clinic, not making the connection between us because I chose to continue using Canning's last name even though we were separated. A few claimed to be helped by Ma and Pa's concoction, but most wrote them off for the charlatans they were, having only burn scars to show for their faith in his mixture of what one woman deduced was nothing more than lye and mustard seed.

"Be glad you've never taken up with the likes of them," she said to me one day. "I hear now they's on the run from the law." She nodded sagely. "The papers say one woman died from that rot, and Miss Tennie's been charged with manslaughter. Poor girl. Everyone knows it's that Pa of hers who should have charges laid at his feet."

I prayed for Tennie nightly, asking the spirits to tell me if anything happened to her as I planned to rescue her as soon as my situation allowed. Beyond that, I put my parents and my past behind me as no good came from dwelling on such things when I had a new life ahead of me.

After years of wandering around the Midwest, the spirits directed me to St. Louis, where they promised good things awaited. I set up a small office downtown at Sixth and Washington under the name Madame Holland. Not knowing the climate of this city, I put it about that I specialized in healing women's ailments as the majority of the clients I had seen over the years were women. I'd come to realize that no matter the city, religious affiliation, political leanings, or economic status, their stories were the same—tales of physical or emotional abuse, of sexual exploitation, abandonment, and pain. Granted there had to be some women who were happy in their marriages or with their families, but they weren't the sort to seek out a healer; they had nothing to be healed. My heart went out to my clients, and I prayed again, as I had in San Francisco, that Demosthenes was right and someday I would be able to help them. For now, I healed as my gifts allowed and comforted them as I could.

But it wasn't long before word of my clairvoyance spread and I had war widows and soldiers at my door seeking to speak to lost husbands, sons, brothers, fathers, and brothers-in-arms. So when a tall stranger in uniform strode into my chamber, I expected he would be like all the others. What I did not expect was a rush of information from the spirit world. Before I had a chance to greet the man or even focus on his face, I fell into a trance.

"This is him. This is the one," the spirits whispered. "It's all been leading to him."

I had no idea what they were talking about. I shook my head, trying to clear it, but the spirits buzzed around my mind like excited cherubs in a Renaissance painting.

The dark man sat across from me, silently appraising my battle with the spirit world.

Still half in trance, I took his hands. "I see our futures linked. Our destinies are bound together." In my mind's eye, I saw our souls wedded as it were, blessed by the Principalities, Powers, Thrones, Dominions, and other angels. "We are betrothed by the powers of the air."

His chuckle brought me back to myself. "My, that is quite impressive. It is certainly one way to make an impression. Tell me, do you greet all your clients thus?"

I was grateful for the low lighting so he could not see me blush. Now that I was back in my right mind, I saw how ludicrous I must have sounded. I had practically declared my undying love on first sight. I wouldn't blame him if he left, much less made a few sarcastic comments.

"Forgive me, sir. The spirits are not usually that... passionate in their responses. There must be something about you that they like."

He shot me a sly grin. "They? Or you?" He cocked an eyebrow.

Me? I hadn't even had a chance to get a good look at him yet. He was tall, that I remembered from my first glance, but now I really looked at him, at his dark brown hair, matching beard and mustache, luxurious side whiskers, his finely tailored suit and gold pocket watch. He was certainly not a poor man, and his eyes captivated me. They were rich and dark, the color of Dutch cocoa, with seemingly endless depths. I could see the spirits in them.

I sat back in wonder. "You are a believer, a Spiritualist."

He nodded. "I am. What else can you tell me?"

I gave a small laugh. With the spirits hovering around me, I could have told him his date of birth, the names of his family for five generations, and where he'd served in the war. But that would have likely only scared him off, and I wanted to keep this man around. He was attractive, yes, but there was more to him than that. He had a depth of soul and intelligence I'd rarely encountered. This was a man who had much to teach me.

Wanting to get it over with, I mentioned the one thing I did not like that the spirits were telling me. "You are here on behalf of your wife, who suffers from female troubles. You heard about me and wanted to see if I was genuine before bringing her here."

He frowned, clearly disappointed I'd chosen not to continue our repartee. "Indeed. But given you have only recited to me what it is you claim to do, how can I know you to be genuine?"

I shrugged. "I could use my healing ability to relieve you of the pain you still suffer from removing bullets from your own body during the war. Would you like me to start with your right shoulder, your right arm, or your left hand? I do not think your wife would like me working on so intimate an area as your left thigh, though that is what pains you most." It was my turn to arch an eyebrow at him.

A smile lit his features. "You are not only genuine but clever as well. I like you, Madame Holland."

"And I you, Mr....?"

"Surely you need no introduction, but I shall supply one anyway." He stood and held out his hand. "Col. James Harvey Blood, commander of the Sixth Missouri Regiment and City Auditor of St. Louis. It is a pleasure to meet you."

Rising, I accepted his hand. "Please call me by my given name, Victoria Woodhull. Madame Holland is only a name I use in business."

Colonel Blood nodded. "How kind of you, Victoria." He dug in his pocket and produced a card. "I am president of the St. Louis Society of Spiritualists. We would love to have you attend a meeting and share your experiences. We meet on the first Thursday of every month. Our next gathering is this week, in fact."

I gave him a dazzling smile. "I wouldn't miss it."

❧

COLONEL BLOOD BECAME MY most regular client, dropping by every Tuesday and Thursday afternoon and staying well into the evening. After so many years of keeping my thoughts to myself, it was refreshing to have a man to speak with who believed in the spirits as I did, who had served in the war and understood privation, who could sympathize with my plight.

From this shared experience grew a bond that was not meant to remain platonic. He had a wife, and technically I had a husband, never having gotten around to filing for divorce. But James explained that in Spiritualism, the legal bonds of a piece of paper, the blessings of a church—they were both meaningless. For those of us who lived our lives in communication with the spirits, the bond of the soul was what mattered.

But unlike Canning, he didn't pressure me to become his lover; rather, he let our attraction build slowly over nights of conversation and healing. As I found out the night I renewed my offer to treat his old war wounds, with James, the laying on of hands was not just an outlay of magnetism. It was an intoxicating exchange of energy unlike anything I'd ever felt.

Still, we had physical urges as well. James showed up at my office one balmy spring night, intentions writ in his eyes. He paused in the doorway, his eyes drinking me in. Then he was in motion, removing his hat even as the door swung shut behind him. He flung his coat carelessly into a corner and stepped out of his boots before reaching me. I fumbled with the buttons on his vest as he tugged at his tie before giving up on his clothes and hastily removing layer after layer of mine. He squeezed my derriere as his mouth found mine, and I moaned, tugging at his clothes, desperate to get him out of them.

He stepped away long enough to remove his shirt, leaving only his breeches in place. I let him guide me to the couch, where his weight came down on me, a delicious heat igniting where our skin touched. He licked and sucked my nipples while his hand explored the forbidden place between my legs. I moved against him and moaned, nipping at his skin as I kissed him from his collarbone to his temple and back again. Then I wrapped one leg around him as the heat within me grew, finally exploding in a shower of stars behind my clenched eyelids.

Temporarily sated, I rolled him over so I was on top of him, then I teased him by running my hands slowly down his naked torso, grinding my hips against him as I went. Torturously slowly, I unbuttoned his breeches and peeled them down his legs, taking my time as I ran my hands up the hard muscle of his calves to his thighs, where my lips took over. I licked the delicate skin of his inner thigh before finally taking him into my mouth.

I brought him to the brink several times before positioning my hips over his and guiding him inside me. I bent forward, and our lips met again as I moved up and down, drawing him in deep only to rise once again and prolong the pleasure. Not willing to let me have all the fun, he rolled us onto our sides so he could thrust as I rotated my hips, our bodies never losing connection. As his rhythm increased in speed and roughness, I held on to him with my legs, letting him ride me over the edge and digging my nails into his back as I shuddered in ecstasy.

"James," I cried out.

Not long after, he groaned my name, and our motions slowly ceased. We stayed intertwined as our heartbeats slowly returned to normal, and we separated only when I rolled onto my back, guiding his head to my breast.

"I didn't know such a thing was possible," I said, pushing sweaty strands of hair off my forehead.

"It is—but only between two healers, two Spiritualists of pure faith." He leaned up and gently kissed my nose. "Only between two bonded souls."

"And so we are."

❁

WHEN JAMES CAME TO visit me the following week, he wasn't alone. For one horrifying moment, I thought he'd finally brought his wife with him. My stomach kissed my toes—after what had taken place between us, the last thing I wanted was to now meet his wife—but then she drew closer, and I realized this woman was far too old to be his wife. I breathed an audible sigh of relief.

James said nothing but gave me a curious look before introducing his friend. "Victoria, I hope you do not mind my taking the liberty of bringing a guest, but I believe the two of you will have much in common." He addressed the older woman. "Mrs. Virginia Minor, this is Mrs. Victoria Woodhull. Mrs. Minor leads a group of local suffragists. Mrs. Woodhull has expressed an interest in helping women gain more rights but does not know where to start."

She approached me with an almost regal bearing, regarding me as though she knew in the very fiber of her being that she had been ordained to impart her wisdom to me. The woman's high eyebrows gave her an air of perpetual surprise but also lent her a disarming quality of openness and curiosity, which I found appealing.

I rose and took both of Mrs. Minor's hands in mine. "I am so pleased to meet you."

"Likewise, my dear. It's always such a joy to meet young women interested in our cause."

We sat, and I poured the tea I had prepared for my visit with James, adding an extra cup for Mrs. Minor.

"I am sorry to say that it is still a benefit for a woman to have a male backer even in this female fight. I have my husband's support, and I must say, you've done well in choosing James to be your guide as you enter our cause." She looked at him with great admiration. "He has a history in the movement already, so associating with him can only elevate your own name. Tell me, how would you like to help?"

"I-I really do not know. All I know is I can't stand the thought of my daughter being raised to fear her father or her husband's wrath or going through life beholden to laws she cannot have a say in creating or voting for or against."

Virginia nodded, a tiny smile playing about her lips. "Motherhood is one of the strongest motivators of our cause. The desire to protect our offspring, to provide for them a better life than the one we have experienced, is innate. You will do well with that as your motivation." She took a sip of her tea before continuing. "I will not lie to you and say we have an easy road ahead of us. We were close, so close, to getting the vote before this cursed war derailed everything. You and I would be casting our votes this year if the South hadn't foolishly seceded. Mark my words, peace will come soon, but we'll have a whole new fight on our hands with the emancipated slaves seeking their own suffrage."

"Perhaps that is to our advantage," I said, thinking of what it was like when both of my children ganged up on me to get their way. "Wouldn't we be much like many children clamoring for the attention of our mother? Maybe if we speak as one, the government will be so tired of listening to us cry, they will give in."

Virginia smiled ruefully. "If only it were so easy. I do not believe the emancipation leaders will want to work with us anymore after the war. Suffrage is a complex subject that touches on more than the right to vote. At its core, it's about the value of a life, the affirmation of dignity and personhood. Many men, even Negro men who are just beginning to taste freedom, will argue they have more of a right to vote than do we, the inferior sex."

"So what can we do?"

"The best thing we as women can do is band together. As soon as this war is over, I plan to organize our local women's suffrage advocates into a formal group. We must show our government we know our rights and are willing to demonstrate them with or without their permission. Only by demanding our rights of suffrage at polling places and using courtrooms to challenge state laws that bar us from voting will we see change."

"But that could be years off," James noted. "Surely there is action to be taken now."

Virginia nodded. "For now, I advise you to do what you can in your life. Come to our meetings, tend to the women in your life, and tell everyone you know about our cause. It doesn't seem like much, but once this war is over, we'll be able to organize again. And then the country will see what we women can really do."

ON APRIL 15, THE nation woke to the news that President Lincoln had been assassinated the previous night. I could scarcely believe it. Shocked, I sought the company of others, wishing to join with them and grieve together as citizens of a broken nation. After feeding Byron and Zula and leaving them in the care of a matronly neighbor who preferred to process the horrible news in private, I followed a steady stream of pedestrians headed to a local memorial for the president at the riverfront.

Walking through the streets was a strange experience more akin to traveling in the spirit realm than in the real world. Black bunting hung from every available surface, from balconies and porch finials to lamp-posts and telegraph wires. The usual hum of voices was nonexistent as people walked in silence, heads bowed and shoulders stooped. Horse-drawn carriages still clacked and clopped across the cobblestones, but their bells had been removed. Even the church bells were silent. Public clocks had been stopped at the time the president expired, allowing the hours to pass unmarked.

Many people I knew—clients, friends, and neighbors—were

among the mourners heading toward the river. Even so, I was relieved when I crossed paths with James where Broadway turned toward the landing docks. He didn't speak, only took my hand and squeezed it as we followed the funeral procession for our dead president.

Once at the designated spot, the mock funeral continued with soldiers guarding an empty coffin surrounded by American flags and larger-than-life images of the president, which were shrouded in black crepe. Around us, women dressed in widow's weeds cried and wailed, mourning openly in a style reminiscent of the Old Testament tradition of rending garments. From two makeshift stages, men gave eulogies through megaphones, messages the crowd hastened to relay to those in the back, bending the meaning to suit their wills as information passed from ear to ear.

Occasionally, snippets from the speakers reached us, phrases of praise and grief, calling the slain president a second Jesus who was martyred on Good Friday in accordance with God's will, another quoting the president's recent injunction against malice and urging peace in this time of grief.

"The world doesn't make sense anymore, does it?" James said, tears in his eyes.

"No. Nothing does. If a man so pure and good can be gunned down during a night at the theatre, what chance do any of us have?"

I cast a wary eye across the street, where a very different group of people were gathered. Rather than mourning, they were celebrating. We had been a city divided, dancing on a knife's edge, ever since the war had pitted brother against brother in this town that couldn't decide whether it was for the North or the South. Now we were stepping ever closer to the point when blood would be spilled.

I do not wish to stay here anymore. Even as I thought the words, James voiced them.

I looked at him in surprise. "I was just thinking the same thing."

"I don't mean here at this memorial. There is nothing left for me in this city. My wife and children will be fine, maybe even better off without me. You are all that matters. We can go on the road together, make some money. Once we have enough, I'll send some back here to pay my debts and secure the family that no longer feels like mine. But I can't stay here."

"Surely you can't abandon them to take up with me. You will only be exchanging one family for another, and I fear that with Byron you will be taking on additional responsibility."

James took my hand in his. "Don't you see, Victoria? The day we met, everything changed. The vows, the bonds that formerly held me were cut off. As you said, we were 'betrothed by the powers of the air.' But my soul was not only joined to yours; I also accepted your family, formed a bond with them."

"Don't be ridiculous. You did not even know my real name, let alone that I was a mother."

"Ah, my mind did not, but my soul vowed then and there to accept all that was yours."

Could it really be as simple as he made it out to be? Men left their wives all the time to seek their fortunes in the wilds of the west. But that was different. There was an implicit promise they would either return or send for their families. No matter how James chose to see it, this was abandonment, plain and simple. How could I, a woman who had experienced much the same in my own first marriage— though Canning left me for the brothel rather than another family— be party to such a situation?

I shook my head. "James, as much as I want to share your enthusiasm, I cannot condone this."

James shook his head. "It is not as though I am leaving my family penniless. My wife lived comfortably before she married me, and she will go on as such. She and my children will want for nothing. Do not fear I am wronging one of your sex, for in fact I am doing her a favor. Our marriage has not been the same since I returned from the war. She learned to live without me then; she can do so again now. I am not abandoning her. I am setting her free to find true happiness with someone who will be good for her spirit, just as I have found you. That is, after all, what Free Love is, is it not?"

He made a convincing argument. In the face of it, it was pointless for me to continue to protest. He had his mind made up, and there was no swaying him. Finally, I said. "You are right. I must learn to shake off the teachings of my youth and embrace this new philosophy. "I will leave with you, but there is one thing we must do first. I wish to get Tennie back."

❧

TWO DAYS LATER, OUR brightly colored wagon with a ball-fringed top pulled up in front of Buck's latest makeshift office, a plain two-story building near the train station in Cincinnati. The only thing differentiating it from the rest of the buildings on the block was the sign outside proclaiming it to be the home of "Tennessee Claflin, healer and wonder worker." We certainly had the right place.

My stomach flipped with each step up the cracked stairs leading to the front door. The last time I had seen my family, Pa made it clear I was not welcome in their presence, and now I was here to take my sister, their golden goose, away from them. One thing was certain—this would not end well.

"I'll get Tennie. You distract my family," I whispered to James.

He nodded and pushed open the door without bothering to

knock, as though he was any other customer. From the porch, I heard Pa greet him and James inquire about their services. They conversed for a few moments, Pa giving James a spiel that hadn't changed in the last fifteen years, extolling the virtues of Tennie's miraculous gifts. Eventually their voices faded; Buck had probably ushered James into a back room to do business.

When it seemed the front room was silent, I cracked open the front door, peering in. No one was within the reception area, so I slipped inside. Trying to avoid any creaking floor boards, I scurried to the stairs, certain Tennie was holed up somewhere in the upper rooms as had been the case in so many similar buildings over the years. I prayed I would get to her before Buck brought James to her.

Pausing to listen outside each closed door in the narrow hall of the second floor, I eventually heard soft weeping. Years of hearing my sisters cry after beatings or beratings had attuned my ears to each of their particular moans and sniffles. This was definitely Tennie.

I turned the doorknob slowly and gently pushed into the room. She was sitting on the bed, back toward me, head in her hands.

"Dear God," she prayed, voice muted by her palms, "tell me, have I got to live like this always?"

I stepped up behind her. "No, you don't. You don't have to live like this another minute."

Tennie jumped up, barely suppressing a scream by clamping a fist to her mouth. "Vickie! What are you doing here?"

"Taking you away from this place." I seized her wrist. "Hurry. We haven't got much time. Pack your things and come with me."

Tennie bent and pulled a carpet bag from beneath her narrow bed. "I am ready." She held it up with a watery smile.

"How did you know…?"

"The spirits told me you were coming. I just didn't know when.

Wanted to be prepared." She interlaced her fingers with mine. "Let's go."

We bounded down the stairs, less concerned with making noise now that escape was in sight. But we drew up short at the bottom of the stairs. Pa, Ma, Polly, and James were gathered in a tight circle around the wooden desk set just inside the front door. They all looked up when Tennie and I entered.

"I should have known," Buck snarled. "There was something not right about him from the start." He hooked a thumb at my lover. "Who are you really?"

I was at James's side in three long strides. "He is my husband." Pa didn't need to know we weren't legally wed yet.

Pa noticed Tennie standing a few feet behind me, and his eyes bore into her bag. "And where do you think you're going?"

"With Vickie and James. I have to be rid of your dead weight, or I shall die." She held her head high, but her voice quavered, betraying her ongoing fear of Pa's wrath.

He took a menacing step toward her. "You will do no such thing. Remember what happened last time you threatened to leave me?"

Tennie rubbed her neck, calling attention to fading bruises I hadn't noticed until now. She regarded me hesitantly, as though her resolve was wavering.

James stepped between us and Buck, keeping one eye on him while watching us as well. "Tennie, you never have to work for them again. I swear to you I will do all in power to protect and keep you. Go to the carriage. If he makes a move to follow either of you, I will lay him out."

Tennie and I slipped behind James and out the front door. He followed, never taking his eyes from my parents.

"Tennie, baby girl, how can you do this to poor old Ma?" our mother wailed. "I cannot live without you. You'll see—you'll be the death of me."

Tennie burst into tears at Ma's dramatics. "Let's go, please, or I shall be rent asunder with grief," she said to James.

"Vickie, you cussed devil," Pa called, shaking a fist at us as James helped us into the surrey. "This is all your fault. You will regret this, you ungrateful lot. Don't forget, Tennie, the law is still looking for you. We will show you up. We will put you in the papers. We will ruin you."

PART TWO

Future Presidentess

CHAPTER NINE

I had been mad to come to New York City. That's what people would say if they knew I'd left my life, husband, and children behind to follow the instructions of a spirit guide who'd been dead for two thousand years. Traveling across a couple of states wasn't even a question; Demosthenes had told me to go to 17 Great Jones Street, where I would find lodging prepared for me, so that was what I did.

It had been that simple back in the Ozarks. But now, standing in the flickering glow of a gaslight on the doorstep of the brownstone Demosthenes had indicated, the first twinges of doubt nipped at my gut.

"Did Demosthenes give you any indication what we're supposed to do now?" Tennie asked.

"No."

With that single word, my old fears were released from their cage. What if we ended up in the slums or on the streets? I couldn't live like that again. Besides, Demosthenes had prophesied greatness. *From that place, you will fulfill the destiny written in the stars from the moment of your birth. One day you shall speak before the highest men in the nation. Your namesake is a queen, and one day you shall rule this land.*

It sounded outlandish—even to me. I, a mere woman with no political connections or even the right to vote, as president? Preposterous. Yet something inside me yearned to make his words come true even though I had no idea how. If I had power, who knew what positive changes I could bring about for the country and its women? Still, the Executive Office was a huge leap from Great Jones Street. I took a deep breath and squared my shoulders. There was no room in my plans for doubt. I had to have faith. Demosthenes hadn't let me down yet.

"I suppose we'll set up shop like we always do," Tennie suggested. "We can put a card in the papers advertising our healing and clairvoyant services and make the rounds in the neighborhood. It won't take long to figure out who is amenable to our line of work and who is not."

Besides, my husband would be joining us in a few weeks. We only had to get along until then.

Tennie grimaced and took my hand. "Ready? Remember, we're in this together."

I nodded, letting out a deep breath, and struck the iron knocker on its plate three times before stepping back. The sound echoed then all was still, save the evensong of the crickets somewhere in the darkness around us. A moment later, the door was flung open, and a smiling woman with a pile of red hair pinned atop her head greeted us as though she was expecting us though we had made no reservations or inquiries.

"You've come about the rooms, I suspect," the woman said in a thick Irish accent. "Come in, come in." She ushered us into the hall. "I'm Katherine, owner of this building. You wait here while I see about the beds. The maid was supposed to dress them this morning, but one can never be too careful." With that, she bounded up the stairs without even asking our names.

My breath hitched as I crossed the threshold, cloth bags swaying in my trembling grasp. Tomorrow, bruises would mar the skin where they'd knocked into my thighs. A small "oh" of wonder escaped my lips, and I placed a steadying hand over my pounding heart. Had I only a few moments before imagined cracked plaster walls and roach-infested corridors? Nothing could have been further from the pristine foyer I faced, with its fine green-and-gold wallpaper that was smooth as silk under my curious fingertips and its polished black-and-white tiled floor. No, this brownstone was nothing like the cramped apartments I had known.

"Victoria, come here. You must see this." Tennie's voice was a ripple in the calm quiet.

"What's got you so bothered?" I crossed the room with small, cautious steps. *Please, Lord, do not let my dirty old shoes mar this lovely floor.*

Tennie pointed at a black leather book resting on a marble table beneath a large vase of fragrant gladiolas. I let out a small gasp. Written on the cover in gold lettering was the title *The Orations of Demosthenes.* The book was a collection of speeches given by my spirit guide when he lived, a sure sign that our journey was not in vain.

I shivered. No matter how many times my visions proved true, I would never get used to the eerie feeling that accompanied their confirmation. Looking up to heaven, I mouthed, "Thank you."

Now I had to figure out what would propel me from this brownstone to the glory Demosthenes had promised. But such plans would have to wait until morning. After Katherine showed us to our rooms, I dropped my bags and collapsed on the bed, lost in the bliss of dreamless sleep until the rumble of carriage wheels and the cries of people on the street below woke me well past dawn.

Over coffee and toast, Katherine helped us get our bearings. Great Jones Street was the dividing line between two very different neighborhoods. Northwest, toward Broadway, were the upscale bordellos, saloons, and dance halls frequented by the rich. In the opposite direction was the working class neighborhood of Bowery, with its shady street gamblers, pickpockets, pimps, and prostitutes.

Demosthenes certainly picked an appropriate location. The house sits in limbo, as do I. On one side, the poverty and lawlessness of my past; on the other, the wealth and prestige of my dreams.

After breakfast, Tennie headed up to Broadway while I left the upper-middle-class brownstone behind for the Bowery neighborhood. I stopped in a few shops, explaining my business and leaving my card when I was met with interest. Only once was I chased out by a broom-wielding elderly woman who called me a witch.

As I traveled farther south, the sidewalks slowly emptied, and the condition of the brownstones became markedly less well-maintained. Crumbling staircase finials and cracked steps became the norm along with peeling shutters, some hanging haphazardly from rusted hinges. Here and there, ill-kept women stood on stoops, gossiping and casting appraising looks at any potential clients who might pass. This was the area I'd been searching for. Tennie and I had plied our trade in neighborhoods such as these throughout the Midwest for years.

Three houses down, a jaunty piano tune, along with the sweet scents of perfume and floral potpourri, drifted out an open front door. A disheveled man stumbled out.

"I don't care how much coin you have," an angry female voice shouted after him. "If I see the likes of you around here again, you'll be in for worse than a black eye."

I climbed the stairs and knocked on the doorframe. A young woman with blond hair beckoned me in.

"You lookin' for work?" The woman eyed me up and down, taking in my light blue gown with its high neck buttoned to my chin, cinched waist, and bell sleeves hanging below my wrists. "Cuz you sure ain't gonna get any dressed like that. You may as well be a nun." She cackled at her own joke.

I shook my head. "I'm afraid you misunderstand my purpose. I am a healer inquiring about the needs of your establishment. Is the lady of the house available?"

The girl snorted. "She's here, but she ain't no lady. Madame, a woman to see you," she yelled before disappearing into an interior room.

The music trailed off. The piano player stuck his head into the foyer, tousled brown hair flopping over his forehead and into his eyes. "You'll have to excuse Clarissa. She's not at her finest first thing in the morning. Please, come in and have a seat."

I smiled at the young man with the kindly, open face and gold-wire spectacles. "Thanks, Professor."

He was momentarily taken aback. "Not your first time in a bordello, I see. I'm impressed. Not many people know that title goes along with the job."

"And I doubt most know or care that you have employment other than playing for their entertainment." I studied him, taking the measure of his tan suit pants, striped suspenders, and white shirtwaist. "I'm guessing you're an accountant."

"Journalist, actually."

I raised my eyebrows, interest piqued. Befriending the press never hurt—that had been one of Pa's how-to-bamboozle-the-world life lessons. I turned on the charm, eyeing him through my lashes. "How impressive. For whom do you write?"

"The *New York Herald*. I'm Johnny Green. I'm still a junior copywriter, so I have to earn some extra coin however I can."

"And your employer doesn't object to your choice of venue?"

He scratched the back of his neck. "Naw, they let me do as I please. Besides, you wouldn't believe the tips you pick up working in a place like this." Johnny cocked his head as though listening, his ears attuned a sound I could not hear. "Ah, here she comes now. I'll leave you two in peace." He tipped his hat to me and quietly slipped out.

I gasped when a gray-haired, plump woman entered, leaning on a cane. We had shared a carriage the night before, but I had not been expecting to find her here. "Madame de Ford."

A spark of recognition lit Madame de Ford's eyes. "My oh my, what a joy to see you again. Less than twenty-four hours. That is fate. Mrs. Woodhull, was it?"

"Yes, ma'am. I must say I'm surprised. I didn't think…"

"That I was a madam?" Madame de Ford supplied, stroking the length of pearls wound round her throat. "Not many people do, my dear, and I strive to keep it that way. Why, if I had known you were a working girl, I'd have offered you a position last night. You and your sister would fetch a pretty penny."

"Oh no, Madame. I'm not in that line of work." I handed her a card.

Madame de Ford squinted at it. "A healer and medium, eh? Aren't you the talented one. What kind of healing do you do?" She gestured to the couch, indicating we should be seated.

"My sister and I are both magnetic healers, but we also specialize in herbal remedies. I can offer your girls methods to prevent pregnancy, but I don't traffic in abortifacients. We also have a sweet water that is excellent for cleansing as well as a clove oil that prevents pain and helps make a woman's desire apparent to her partner."

Madame de Ford considered me. "And what can this 'magnetic healing' of yours do for my girls?"

"It's good for anything that ails you. All I do is touch you and let the invisible healing energy flow through my hands and into you, sort of like how words flow through telegraph wires. It helps heal all manner of pain. I'm happy to demonstrate it for you if you'd like."

Madame de Ford raised a finger. "I have just the girl in need of your help." She called to someone named Minnie.

A small mulatto girl with long dark hair plodded in, eyes downcast. I suppressed a shudder. Minnie couldn't have been older than thirteen. Her face was bruised and swollen, and she stood with one arm hugging herself as though to ease the pain in her ribs. What I hated most about my job was knowing the girl had likely done nothing to provoke the wrath that had rendered her nearly unable to stand. At least I could help speed her recovery.

While I worked on her injuries, Minnie slowly relaxed, eventually telling me of the experience that had led to her injuries.

"A couple of times a year, the rich men hold grand parties where the rules of society are suspended," she explained. "On those nights, us girls are their property to be passed around. You would not believe the things they do. They treat us worse than worms, and we can't report it; they very men we would tell are the ones who hurt us." Minnie shrugged, grimacing, indicating the movement caused her pain.

"Why does Madame de Ford allow you to attend such parties? She seems to me to be a kind woman who would not wish you harm."

"She has to. She's indebted to those who protect us—the police, the politicians, other men. I don't know who all."

I shook my head, inwardly railing at the injustice of such traditions. While I understood that men needed a place to satisfy their needs, that did not mean mistreating women—or girls, in Minnie's case—was justifiable. But as she said, what could one do when the very men who were supposed to protect them were the perpetrators? And how was this any different from wives being abused by husbands? No matter where I looked, women were getting a raw deal.

I was just finishing up Minnie's treatment when a knock sounded at the door. A woman bearing a tray of tea and sandwiches entered soon after. Minnie waved her away. "Take that to Alice, please. She needs it more than I do."

The woman was momentarily taken aback, but then she silently nodded and backed out of the room.

"Minnie, you need to eat. You have to keep your strength up in order to heal," I chided.

She ducked her head. "I know, but your magic has made me so relaxed all I want to do is nap." She yawned. "Besides, I know Alice hasn't been making enough money to cover her keep lately so she goes without food."

I watched the battered girl carefully getting to her feet in front of me. This was a special soul, to be so young and endure what she has with such strength then to still be able to put the needs of others before her own.

Then suddenly, Minnie turned, throwing her arms around me with abandon I had only ever seen from Byron. "Thank you, Victoria. Please, come back often. No one had treated me with such care since my mother left me." A tear rolled down her tanned cheek.

For a moment, I could not speak, stunned by her gratitude. Here was a girl desperately in want of a mother figure, and she felt she had found what she needed in me. "I promise," I croaked, throat thick with suppressed emotion. It was a vow I would do my utmost to fulfill.

When Tennie and I compared notes from our day that evening, we sat by the fire in the parlor, sipping glasses of applejack provided by

Katherine to celebrate the end of a successful first day. We had secured several clients, all brothel owners. But the healing session with Minnie wasn't far from my mind. My own experiences with a good beating mixed with my memories of Minnie's bruised and broken body.

"I can't abide to watch those women suffer. I have to do something for them, for Minnie if no one else," I added.

"You only like her because she reminds you of us," Tennie observed.

"Yes, true, but that's not all of it," I said, watching the amber liquid curl around itself as I stirred it with my pinkie finger. "It's more than the kinship I feel with that girl. How many women have we seen over the years who were suffering from maltreatment at the hands of the same fathers, brothers, and husbands who then blame them for bringing on such abuse?"

Even now, when I thought of that time, my throat constricted and I struggled to breathe. I closed my eyes and willed myself to be calm. That was the past. Buck would never raise a hand to Tennie or me now, not with James to protect us.

I swallowed hard. No woman should be made to feel that way—ever. I hadn't had a savior, but maybe I could be one for other women in my situation. If Demosthenes was right and I was meant to be a queen, then they were half of my subjects. I would do all I could to protect them—starting now. I had to convince Tennie to join in my cause.

"I understand what you're saying about unfair treatment," Tennie said. Her cheeks were rosy from the drink. "While I was visiting, Miss Wood had a row with the local minister. He refused to bury one of her former girls who died from consumption in an asylum up north. Said she was too vile for a Christian burial, yet he was one of Miss Wood's best clients."

"Someone has to do something. Stand up, fight back. Why not us?"

"But we're only... us."

"So? Do you think President Lincoln imagined he could end slavery when he was living in that log cabin in Illinois?"

Tennie scoffed. "We can't even vote, and you're comparing us to a former president? You sound like one of those suffragists James speaks so highly of."

"Maybe I am." I stared off into the distance, my vision blurring. "I don't know very much about them, but perhaps I should listen a little more closely to my husband in the future." I rubbed my weary eyes. "Mark my words, we may not be influential yet, but we will be someday. Demosthenes didn't bring us all this way to work in brothels. "

Tennie's eyes lit up, and she dashed out of the room, stocking feet thumping on the stairs. I shook my head. What was my unpredictable sister up to now?

In a flash, Tennie returned, waving a small, green leather-bound notebook. "We may not be important yet, but we know a few people who are."

"What is that?"

"You told me to keep a list of wealthy people we meet or hear about. This is it." She opened the book, and I snatched it.

A list of more than a dozen names written in pencil ran the length of the page: John Jacob Astor, Horace Greeley, Benjamin Butler, Boss Tweed, Cornelius Vanderbilt, Henry Beecher. I recognized some of these names. They frequently appeared in the business papers.

"Tennie, are *all* these men clients of the houses?"

Tennie shook her head, sending her auburn curls swinging. "A few are, but the rest either are friends of people we've met or simply names I jotted down from conversation. No lead is too small, right? We need to start building up our wealthy clientele anyway. The brothels are solid income, but they'll never elevate us to the heights to which your spirits aspire." She gave me a friendly poke in the ribs. "What do you say we start tomorrow by tracking down their secretaries, agents, mistresses, or whoever has their ear?"

❧

WEEKS STRETCHED INTO A month, and still James hadn't arrived from St. Louis with my precious babies. He sent a telegram explaining it was taking longer than expected to transition his legal and accounting business to his brother, so I went about my business, praying every night for their safe journey.

One morning in early September, my prayers were answered. Less than a minute after Katherine announced their arrival, seven-year-old Zula Maude burst into my room, all bright smiles and bobbing brown curls.

"Momma!" she cried, throwing her arms around me. "I've missed you so."

I smiled and pulled my daughter close, running a hand over the girl's hair, a few shades lighter than my own and just as unruly. "I've missed you too, my girl. Have you been good for James?"

Zula nodded. "He promised that after we unpack our things, we could see the city." Her dark eyes were huge with excitement.

I was going to say we'd see about that, but I didn't get a chance to reply before James and Byron appeared in the door.

"Hello," James called. "We were waylaid by your lovely landlady, but I see our young filly found her way."

I rose to hug Byron, who had grown into a handsome young man with his father's dark eyes and hair. He smiled broadly, grunted his greeting in his special language few others could understand, and planted a wet kiss on my cheek. Then I embraced my husband, rising to tiptoe to kiss his cheek.

"I am so glad you are all here. It is wonderful having our family back together again." I turned to my children. "Would you like to see your room? You'll be staying across the hall with Aunt Tennie."

Getting them settled in was simple, but convincing them to nap before their next adventure was another story. Zula whined in a high pitched singsong that she wasn't tired. When James agreed they needed to rest before venturing out in the city, Byron threw one of his fits, groaning, grunting and waving his arms about wildly.

"Hush, son," I cooed, rocking him in my arms as if he was a babe, not a young man of fourteen. I made soothing sounds and stroked his hair until he finally calmed enough for sleep to overtake him.

"I'm sorry for overexciting him," James whispered as we quietly sneaked out of the room and shut the door. "He wants to see the animals in the Central Park menagerie."

"Do not apologize." I wrapped my arms around him. "It doesn't take much to upset the boy. In that respect, he takes after Canning. I wish his father had some of Byron's kind, gentle nature." Shaking off thoughts of the past, I turned my attention to my husband. "What about you? Would you like to rest before we set out again? You look as drawn as death."

His dark eyes were bloodshot, his thick brown hair disheveled from travel, and his side whiskers were too long, as though he hadn't groomed them since leaving St. Louis. But he sighed and sank onto the bed as I kneaded his shoulders. "I would. But there is one thing you should know first. When we were traveling in from the station, our carriage stopped to take on additional passengers. You will not believe who one of them was."

"Who?"

"Buck."

My hands ceased their motion. I searched James's face for signs of jest, but his eyes held no mirth and his lips were pressed into a straight line. "My father is here?"

"So it appears. The rest of the Claflin clan too. Utica and Maggie were with him. He wouldn't acknowledge me. Still sore about us rescuing Tennie from their household and their schemes, I reckon. The carriage dropped him off in a rundown part of lower Manhattan the driver called Five Points."

"I know of the area," I said, but I wasn't listening. I was fighting a wave of panic that started in my gut and was crawling up my throat, threatening to bring my breakfast in tow.

How had he found us? And why were they here? With my family, everything was done by design for their own profit. But what did they stand to gain from me? I wasn't destitute, but I was by no means rich.

"Victoria? You look ill. Have I erred in telling you?"

I smiled benignly at him. "Not at all, dear." I kissed him softly. "I appreciate the warning." I helped him remove his clothing until all that remained were his underclothes and socks. Then I tucked him into bed. I kissed his forehead before placing my hat on my head and taking up my pocketbook. "Rest well. I have an appointment but will be back by noon to show you the city."

Once in the hall, I leaned heavily on the door, my mind spinning. No good could come from the Claflins taking up residence in New York. Wherever they went, trouble—usually in the form of lawsuits for fraud and the ire of swindled customers—was sure to follow. It was one of the many reasons I had left them behind. Or so I'd thought.

I slowly descended the stairs, biting the inside of my lip as I tried to decide what to do. As I neared the bottom, my heart skipped a beat.

What if they were here to get Tennie back? She was an adult now, but they could easily have dragged her back into the fold by blackmail—they had plenty of secrets to use—or by force, if necessary.

What was worse, my poor sister was all alone in the city right at that very moment, completely unaware of the familial threat lurking around any corner. I had no idea where Tennie had gone, but thanks to James, I knew where to find my family.

I hurried out the door, already scanning the street for a taxi whose driver could be convinced to take me into the slums. It would take only a quarter of an hour to reach my parents; hopefully I would not be too late.

The stench of rotting garbage, slaughtered carcasses, and excrement invaded the carriage long before the dilapidated buildings of Five Points came into view. I clutched a handkerchief to my nose and swallowed the bile rising in my throat. We slowed near the center of town, hampered by the sheer mass of people in the streets yelling, cursing, and calling to one another in a variety of languages. Chickens and goats wove in and out of the throng, adding their own cries to the cacophony.

The driver pulled to a stop beyond the neighborhood water pump. "This looks to be as far as I can go. You'll have to go the rest of the way on foot."

"This is fine," I said, passing a few coins to him after he helped me out of the carriage.

I lifted my skirts enough to rescue them from the filth underfoot and began the slow ascent up the hill to a storefront with glass windows bearing the name Claflin Cancer Clinic and Cure-All.

I shook my head. My father was back to his old tricks. Had he learned nothing from his brushes with the law, including more than a dozen charges in three states? In the window, lined up like soldiers for inspection, were rows of dark green bottles bearing Tennie's likeness, now ten years outdated, along with the name "Miss Tennessee's Magnito Life Elixir for Beautifying the Complexion and Cleansing the Blood." For the patients' sakes, I hoped the contents weren't a decade old too.

Inside, Pa was sitting behind a desk, his feet propped up, a lit cigar hanging from his mouth. I took a deep breath. No time like the present. I pushed open the door to the dimly lit shop.

"You're still selling that snake oil?" I said by way of greeting.

"The prodigal daughter returns." Buck looked up from the newspaper on his lap, not showing an ounce of surprise. "There will always be a need for healing, Victoria."

I scoffed. "You mean humbuggery. I know what's in that medicine of yours, Pa."

Buck rose, appraising me. "Didn't take you long to find me."

"Dirt has a way of coming back—even when you're sure you've scrubbed your hands free."

Buck threw down the paper and grabbed my arm. His face was a hairsbreadth from mine, his breath hot and ashen on my cheek. "Ungrateful wretch, that's what you are. How's about I teach you some respect?"

I shrank back, a reaction based on years of fear. Experience warned me not to push him too far, especially when his voice took on that black tone. I was saved from responding by the creak of the door as a customer entered. Buck's dark expression changed to one of pleasantry in the space of a breath.

"What can I do ya for, sir?" he called to the small, stooped man while throwing me a look that said we were not finished.

While Buck swindled the unsuspecting resident out of his hard-earned money, I browsed, opening jars and inspecting their contents.

I sniffed at one that contained a greasy yellow paste and immediately recoiled at the pungent, metallic scent. That was the stuff Buck had once claimed could cure cancer, the same "cure" that ended up getting Tennie charged with manslaughter in Illinois since she had been the one who applied it to the unfortunate patient. I set the jar back on the shelf and perched on the side of the desk until my father's transaction was complete.

As the man left, letting in a fresh gush of rotten air, my eyes watered. "How do you stand it down here?"

"I like to think of it as the city's perfume." Buck sat back down, carrying on as though we'd never been interrupted. "Speaking of smells, I hear tell you been sniffin' 'round the wallets of this town." He leaned back, a smug smile spreading across his face at my surprise.

"Have you been watching me?"

"Nah, nothin' so time-consuming as that. But the city has ears, girl. You best remember that."

"Why are you here, Pa?" I asked, desperate to change the subject. "And why drag the whole family with you? James told me he saw Utica and Maggie. I know Ma's here too. You couldn't have all this supply without her."

"Time for a change of scenery is all. Thought it was time to catch up with my two best girls. You two have been quite busy from what I hear, cozying up to them bankers on Wall Street."

"You've been quite busy yourself." I gestured to the shop around us.

"I hear there's one prize bird you can't seem to snag though," Buck went on as though I hadn't spoken. "A commodore, no less. But I may be able to help you out there…if you will trust your dear old dad."

I snorted. "What reason have you ever given me to trust you? We all still have scars from your hand."

Buck contorted his face into something resembling contrition. "I want the chance to make it up to you, to show you I'm a changed man."

I stood, crossing my arms. "Let's hear it."

"Your Mr. Vanderbilt may be closely guarded, but he's got his weaknesses, same as any man." Buck began to pace, slowly warming to his audience of one. "Nothin' the man likes more than horses. And I know a thing or two about them creatures."

"Pa, you stole horses and sold them for profit. You didn't breed them."

He waved away my interruption. "Six of one, half a dozen of the other. I happen to know a few people at the track he favors. Them jockeys is always looking for a leg up on the competition"—he guffawed at his own joke—"so they buy my elixir. Anyway, no one will question my coming or going. If I can get you an audience with Vanderbilt, can we say all's forgiven?"

I narrowed my eyes at my father. He never did anything for free. "What's in it for you?"

"Peace of mind knowing that I can die in my girls' good graces. I'm not getting any younger, you know."

"You're losing your touch, old man. Try again."

Buck hooked his thumbs around his suspenders and rocked back on his heels. "I do want to make things right between us, darlin'. Is that better?" When I continued to be unmoved, he changed tack, leaning forward onto the balls of his feet. "Look, he's ripe for the taking, and you want in with his crowd, so why shouldn't I do this for you?"

"Why *should* you—that's the real question."

Buck threw up his hands. "Ask around. Everyone knows Vanderbilt believes in the spirits and willingly supports any medium or fortuneteller who crosses his path. Why shouldn't he benefit from you? At least you're not a crook."

"If he's such an easy mark, why aren't you moving in on him?"

"Well, for one, I no longer have my best medium." He glared at me, obviously still sore over the loss of Tennie. "And two, I have enough of an in to arrange a meeting but nothing to hold his attention. If there's one thing the commodore likes more than horses, it's young women. Let your sister entertain him while you talk to his dead mother or son or Ben Franklin if he wants."

I watched him closely, analyzing his every change of expression, every flush and paling of his skin. A suspicion had been niggling at the back of my mind, and I was waiting to see if he'd admit it. When he fell silent, I pounced. "You want a cut of whatever Tennie and I make from him, don't you?"

Buck scooted back his chair, trying and failing to look offended. "Of course not. Why would you think such a thing?"

I advanced until I was leaning over him, in the position of power for the first time in my life. "You do! God, Pa, we left for a reason. We will never work for you again. You can take Ma and the whole stinkin' family back to Chicago or Cincinnati or wherever it was you came from. We will not have you humbug us in our new life." I stomped toward the door, fuming.

"Vickie," Buck called after me, "please wait. I don't want anything from you. Let me do this for you to prove I mean it."

I slowly turned around to face my father. He was begging me with his eyes to give him one more chance. I took a deep breath, weighing my options. "If I let you do this, I owe you nothing. Tennie owes you nothing. You will never again interfere in our lives or disturb our peace. Is that clear?"

"Yes. Yes, of course." Buck put out his hand. "I'll shake on it like any business deal."

"I know the nature of your business," I muttered, but I took my father's hand anyway, praying I hadn't made a deal with the Devil.

CHAPTER TEN

Tennie and I scampered up the front steps of 17 Great Jones Street, arms interlocked at the elbows, giggling, hands full of parcels from a morning of shopping. Our levity faded, however, when we nearly tumbled into Katherine on the porch, barring our entrance.

"Katherine, what's this?" Tennie asked sweetly. "We're paid up for the next two months, and I don't believe we've broken any rules."

"No, no. 'Tis nothing of the sort. I thought you'd like to know," she dropped her voice to a conspiratorial whisper, "that there's a gentleman to see you in the foyer." She tilted her head in the general direction of the front door. "Claims to be your father. I can have him removed if you like."

Tennie stiffened and pulled away from me, edging backward toward the steps, but I clamped down on her arm, preventing her escape.

"No need for that, Katherine, thank you. We'll see him." I tugged at Tennie's arm, ignoring her acerbic glare. "Come on. You can't avoid him forever."

As soon as we stepped over the threshold, Buck greeted us with a blinding grin and open arms. "Girls, so good to see you. Hope you don't mind me tracking you down like this, but I couldn't wait to share my news."

I couldn't make myself move toward my father, much less embrace him. I eyed him, my wariness increasing at the sight of his formal attire. He was wearing his best suit, so something had to be afoot.

"You're leaving town?" I said with a measure of hope.

Tennie stood stony-faced, arms crossed.

"Confound it! No." He scowled at us. "Remember that favor I said I'd do for you?"

I set down my packages, using them as a makeshift fort between my father and petrified sister. I tapped my chin and pretended to think. "I don't recall asking you for a favor, but I do remember a business agreement."

Buck gave a small nod. "One and the same. I'm here to tell you you're expected at the Vanderbilt residence at one this very afternoon. The commodore would like to speak with you both."

I turned to Tennie, greeted by a mirror of my own shock. Tennie's mouth was slightly agape and her blue eyes wide.

"You're not cutting a shine on us, are you, Pa?" I asked, finding my voice first.

Buck shook his head and rocked back on his heels, stuffing his hands into his pockets. "Not at all. I'm as serious as a gravedigger." When we didn't respond, he stepped aside, giving us a clear path up the stairs. "Well, what are you waiting for? Go on. Get up there and make yourselves pretty. You want to impress the old coot, don't ya?"

Tennie needed no more encouragement. She scooped up her packages and scurried up the stairs as if her shadow was on fire.

I picked up my bundle and stood before my father. "You came through." It was a statement, but there was a hint of question in my voice.

Buck held up a hand. "Don't thank me yet. I got you in. It's up to you two to make the sale."

Within the hour, we were dressed and taking a short carriage ride to Washington Park. Cornelius Vanderbilt's home was in keeping with his imposing reputation. Though made of the same brownstone as many others in the city, its four floors and grand staircase with wrought-iron railings made it more akin to a palace than to the place Tennie and I called home.

Buck ushered us up the stairs with a slight pressure on our shoulder blades. I tensed at his touch and sensed Tennie stiffen next to me, but neither of us said a word. After rapping the door knocker several times, Buck stepped back, waiting. A tall, thin man with graying black hair opened the door and greeted us.

Before I had a chance to speak, Buck slid in front of us, blocking us from the butler's view. "Please tell Mr. Vanderbilt that Mr. Claflin and his daughters are here for their appointment."

The butler eyed us dubiously but did as requested.

A few moments later, the servant returned and stood to the side of the doorway. He motioned Tennie and me inside but put out a hand to stop Pa before he could step foot in the foyer. "Mr. Vanderbilt thanks you for accompanying your daughters and will consider that a formal introduction, but he wishes to speak to them alone. Good day." He closed the door before Pa could offer a rebuttal.

Having shed my unwanted chaperone, I relaxed, trying not to stare in obvious wonderment at the white marble floors, gilded walls, carved wainscoting, and frescoed ceilings of the foyer. I glanced away so as not to soil them with my lower-class gaze.

"A lot of the places over on Broadway try to look like this, but this isn't some cheap imitation. This is the real thing," Tennie whispered to me. "Look at that fireplace. You could fit half a dozen women in there."

"Maybe that's what Mr. Vanderbilt does with his mistresses when he's done with them," I joked, a smile lighting my voice. "Let's hope he likes us, or we may be forced to find out." At Tennie's outward distress, I hastened to add, "He's a man like any other client. Remember that."

"A filthy rich one," Tennie mumbled.

The butler led us through a set of tall French doors leaded with blue glass and through an airy sitting room painted in pastel blue and peach. After a few more turns, we arrived at a dark corner office. The dim illumination from a few oil lamps and the meager afternoon light that survived the sheer curtains gave the area a sense of foreboding, as if we were trespassing on sacred ground or delving into secrets meant for others' eyes and ears.

The hair on the backs of my arms and neck stood on end. "There are spirits here. I can feel them."

"But can you hear them?" asked a booming voice from somewhere behind us.

I pivoted on the ball of my foot. A tall, sinewy man in a black suit with white cravat stood in the doorway, posture ramrod-straight despite the white hair and balding head that dated him as old enough for a well-earned stoop. He peered at me with intelligent blue eyes that sought answers but not only from me.

I closed my eyes and tried to focus on the swirling gray figures all around us. At first, they had no form, but as I concentrated, a young boy in a suit, maybe fourteen years of age, took shape. "I see a young boy. He has your nose, your bearing."

Please tell me your name that I may let him know you are here. I opened my eyes, still seeing him in my mind's eye.

"He says he's named after a president and wants me to guess which one." I scrunched up my forehead, unsure of the meaning of the riddle.

The commodore clapped in glee. "That's my boy all right. It was one of his favorite games to play with strangers. His name was George Washington Vanderbilt. Please, please, sit down." He motioned toward two leather chairs on the fore side of a heavy wooden desk that, like so much other furniture in this house, was inlaid with gold. He took a seat on the opposite side. "Please forgive my rudeness in not asking your father to join us. I wished to meet with you alone for it is you with whom I would be working, am I correct?"

Tennie leaned forward. "Yes, Mr. Vanderbilt. I'm Tennessee Claflin, a medium like my sister." Her voice came out in a rush, like a girl forcing herself to speak to her first crush. She extended her hand.

He grasped it gently, taking in her reddish-brown curls, bright blue eyes, full lips, and cleft chin with obvious pleasure. "And you must be Victoria." He extended me the same warm greeting.

"I am, sir. So nice to meet you."

"I don't quickly trust those claiming to have your gifts, but I have to say I'm impressed with what I've seen so far." He removed a small container of chewing tobacco from one of the drawers and placed a wad between his lip and gum. "Now, your father tells me you can predict the stock market." His eyes shifted between the two of us expectantly.

Does he? It would have been nice to know that before we came in. The bastard hadn't breathed a word to me about this. Reformed, ha! Traitor more like. I'd have words with my father later. But true or not,

Mr. Vanderbilt needed an answer. What had I read in the paper that morning? Surely there had to be something that would save us. Mr. Vanderbilt had made his fortune in railroads and water shipping, so it was likely he'd want to know about one of those. But which one? And what if I was wrong? I shot Tennie a pleading look.

"You're an expert in that already," Tennie said, coming to my rescue. "I'm sure you have plenty of advisors. Plus, you probably have a natural instinct for that sort of thing." She batted her eyelashes and leaned onto the desk, giving him a clear view of her ample cleavage. "We're also healers—if you're interested in those services."

"Are you now?" He spit tobacco juice into a spittoon hidden behind the grand desk. "I want to hear about that, but first"—he turned back to me—"I want to hear more about the market. Give me a prediction about Canada Southern Railway. If you're correct, you're hired."

I swallowed hard, praying he couldn't see the sweat beading on my brow. The spirits had spoken to me of many topics over the years, but I'd never asked them for financial advice. If they remained quiet, I had an equal chance of being right or wrong. I closed my eyes again, trying to remember something, anything, I'd read about the railroad.

I started as Demosthenes appeared. "Tell him this, 'No man can tell what the future may bring forth, and small opportunities are often the beginning of great enterprises.'"

Of all the times for him to be unclear. Trembling inside, I faced the commodore with a steady gaze and repeated Demosthenes's answer.

He was stock-still for a moment, pondering my words, then a grin split his features. "By golly, you do have a talent, young lady. There's no way you could have known that earlier today I was approached to buy stocks of Canada Southern, to get in at the ground floor as they say. It's a small sum, but your spirits seem to think it won't remain that way for long."

"This is absurd!" a male voice shouted behind us.

Tennie and I whipped around. A tall, middle-aged man with brown hair and a carefully waxed handlebar mustache stalked into the room. Within three long strides, he was at the commodore's side.

"You can't actually believe them, Father. Tell me you don't believe them," he demanded.

"As a matter of fact, I do." Mr. Vanderbilt laced his fingers together and rested them on his protruding stomach, a gesture that implied the matter was closed. He nodded toward the fuming gentleman. "My son, William." Next, he inclined his head in our direction, introducing us.

William bowed politely and murmured a rote "How do you do?" before returning his attention to his father. "That last thing *she* told you"—he pointed at me—"is a well-known quote from a famous Greek orator. Anyone could have said the same."

"Indeed, it is a quote from Demosthenes," I acknowledged. "He is my spirit guide and has been for some thirty years. He brought me from abject poverty to sitting in your salon, so you cannot say his advice is unsound."

"I can say anything I please," the younger man bellowed. "It is not him I question. I care not for a man who has been dead for centuries but for the two swindlers sitting across from me. I suppose they've told you they can contact Mother?"

"No. Only your brother George. But she knew about his clever name game," the elder Mr. Vanderbilt said, mouth turned down in a frown.

"Names she could easily have read in the papers." William pressed a fist to his mouth as if to stop an expletive. "That's how these people operate, Father. I've told you this before. They are thinking only of how to part you from your hard-earned money."

"Money you believe would be better off in your hands, I suppose," I interrupted, rising. I stepped toward William. "Tell me, how would it profit your father for you to gamble it away?"

I was taking a risk with that guess, but if there was one thing I knew about rich young men, it was that two influences easily parted them from their cash: women and sporting bets. This one was too uptight, too refined, to be tied by his prick to a woman, so gambling had to be his vice.

I tapped my cheek theatrically. "It's the ponies, isn't it? Gave up on the dog races—too small-time—and moved on to something more lucrative."

William's eyes bulged, but his father laughed, clapping once with a loud smack. "She's got you there, son. To a tee."

William stared between his father and me before finally finding his voice. "How dare you accuse me of such a thing, you who admittedly grew up in the gutter." He turned to his father, his voice rising in pitch. "I will not see you humbugged by a pair of harlots. Harold!"

The butler appeared.

"Remove these women at once."

Mr. Vanderbilt held up a hand to stop Harold. "William, please. You're making a damned spectacle of yourself. *You* should be the one to be removed." He flicked his long fingers at his son in a gesture of dismissal. "Harold, while you're here, please tell Cook there will be two more dining with us this evening. I do hope you ladies don't have other plans."

"Why, no, of course not," I said.

"Bully for you!" Vanderbilt came around the desk, offering his arm to Tennie. "I do hope you will tell me more about this healing gift of yours over cocktails."

Aperitifs in the Vanderbilt house were more than fancy drinks consumed at table. Mr. Vanderbilt had a passion for whist, which we played for more than an hour while Tennie and our soon-to-be employer indulged in imported cigars and outrageously expensive liquor. I nearly spilled my rum punch when William, who had been pressed to be my partner because we needed a fourth, laid down a winning hand and Tennie let out a curse so foul it wasn't spoken in most bordellos. I cringed, barely able to look at Mr. Vanderbilt. Beside me, William stiffened.

"Praise God!" Mr. Vanderbilt hooted around a hardy laugh that reddened his cheeks and shook the table. "After seventy-three years, he finally sends me a cherry, not one of these prim, powdered persimmons. Tennie, you are my kind of woman." He squeezed her rump, eliciting a delighted giggle from Tennie.

"Father, I do not think such behavior is appropriate from either of you," William chided.

"Settle down. We're just having fun."

The butler announced dinner then, and Mr. Vanderbilt led Tennie into the dining room. William took my hand, but instead of following his father, he pulled me aside into an alcove.

"Why, Mr. Vanderbilt, if you wanted to get me alone, all you had to do was ask," I teased, giving him a flirtatious smile and batting my eyelashes while praying that wasn't what he was really about.

William made a show of holding me at arm's length. "I am not after that, you cussed devil. I wish to make a deal with you."

"Pray tell."

"I have made it no secret that I do not want you in my father's life. As you do not seem keen to heed my wishes, I will sweeten the deal. My offer is this—one year in Europe for you and your sister, first-class, fully paid. In exchange, you will never bother my family again."

I nearly rolled my eyes. What a sneak! So the esteemed heir to the

Vanderbilt fortune thought he could buy me off. Well, he'd have to try much harder to oust either one of us from the house now that we finally had our hands on a well-paying client.

"No, I do not think we will accept. We may never be able to convince you of it, but we're not after your father's money. There are far easier ways to a man's fortune than through his employ." I stepped around him in the direction his father had gone. "I do so look forward to the day you realize we were in earnest from the start," I called over my shoulder before entering the dining room unescorted.

William did not meet my gaze and spoke very little throughout the lengthy meal, during which Mr. Vanderbilt and Tennie flirted like a courting couple, and was quick to make his excuses once the candles burned low. The very room seemed to breathe a sigh of relief when he departed, taking his ire with him.

We repaired to a small sitting room, where Mr. Vanderbilt addressed me, rubbing his hands together as though hatching some grand scheme. "Well now, if you're amenable, I would be obliged if you would show me more of your skills with the spirits by speaking with my mother." He nodded at a painting above the fire.

I followed his gaze, and a plump woman with dark eyes stared back at me. The painting had to be old, or at least the woman favored outmoded fashion because she wore the dress of a much earlier time, her hair and face nearly obscured by a bonnet that hugged her forehead and squeezed her cheeks like a nun's wimple. A heavy shawl with one broad stripe across the center was pulled close around her shoulders. A Bible lay in her lap.

"Of course," I said as Tennie and I took seats opposite Mr. Vanderbilt. "What is your mother's name?"

"Phebe Hand der Bilt."

"Hand der Bilt?" Tennie questioned, brow scrunched in confusion.

"That was how our last name was pronounced in the old country. My mother liked it better than the Americanized Vanderbilt, which I prefer."

I nodded. "The spirits are attracted to music. Is there a favorite song that might lure her to us? You do not have to sing; humming will suffice."

Mr. Vanderbilt hummed a tune that took me back to the unpredictable, outdoor revival meetings of my youth, my mother shaking in ecstatic prayer, babbling nonsense she swore was the language of the angels.

Pushing aside those memories, I clasped his gnarled, wrinkled hands and closed my eyes. Within a few heartbeats, Demosthenes was beside me, and I relaxed, now fully able to concentrate, knowing he would protect and guide me as I sifted through the unfamiliar spirits who reached out to anyone open to their touch.

I concentrated on contacting the woman in the portrait. I wandered through a sea of gray formless beings. Then Demosthenes signaled for me to stop. He bowed before the plump, stern woman and introduced me as the one who would mediate communication with her son Cornelius. The woman acknowledged his words with a slight nod.

"She is with us," I said.

"Ask her to tell me something you couldn't possibly know."

I listened, a small smile tugging at my lips. Mrs. Hand der Bilt was handing out a tongue lashing, half in English, half in Dutch.

"She is a little cross to be tested," I said. "She wishes me to say that your family's loyalties were split during the Revolutionary War."

"That is correct. We had one dissenter who joined the king's army." He was quiet a moment then cried out, "Oh, she *is* here. I can smell her scent." He inhaled deeply. "Strong soap and lavender. Takes me back to my boyhood."

"She is not keen on being asked questions but wishes to advise you to be wary of your children for they are plotting to force you to take a new wife."

"Not surprising." Mr. Vanderbilt bit back his annoyance. "But she needn't worry. I have no plans to do any such thing."

In my mind, Phebe carried on.

"She also says to be careful whom you back in public lest a kitten turn out to be a lioness." *Once a mother, always a mother. She is still trying to protect her son. How sweet.*

But then Phebe clarified that she was referring to me.

"Your mother does not like me and wishes you would 'stop taking in strays.' Those were her exact words."

Mr. Vanderbilt chuckled. "She said that to me so often as a child." The audible groan of his chair suggested he had shifted position, and the nearness of his voice indicated he was leaning toward me. "Why does she not trust you?" His voice was grave.

I shook my head slowly, trying to get the departed Mrs. Hand der Bilt to stop yelling long enough that I could ask her son's question. "She says I will one day shame you and you will regret the day we met."

I brought a hand to my head, which was beginning to pound. Between the long day, emotional whirlwind, and this shocking revelation, my powers were flagging. I gestured to Tennie, who placed her hands on mine in a gesture of support. I would have to draw strength from my sister to continue.

As if sensing the situation, Mr. Vanderbilt said, "Perhaps that is enough for one sitting. I do not wish to overtax you so late in the day."

I thanked the spirit of Mrs. Hand der Bilt and bid her farewell. Slowly, I made my way back through the spirit realm into the present. I opened my eyes and blinked rapidly, eyes tearing up from the sudden brightness of the fire. My mind was full of cotton, opaque as though I had just woken from a dream.

Mr. Vanderbilt said nothing, only pressed the thumbs of his interlaced fingers to his lips for a moment as though deep in thought. Eyes unfocused, he reached into his breast pocket and produced a can of chew and a small piece of white paper. He studied the paper for a moment before handing it to Tennie. "I nearly forgot I was going to give this to you."

I peered over Tennie's shoulder as she turned it sideways then around completely, trying to make meaning of the series of dots and dashes separated by spaces.

"What is it?" Tennie asked.

"Today's closing stock prices for Canada Southern." His words were a bit garbled by the wad of tobacco in his cheek. "Mrs. Woodhull's prediction was spot on."

"You learned all of that from this?" I asked when Tennie handed it to me. "Can you teach me to read it?" I scooted to the edge of my chair, holding the paper between us.

"Me too," Tennie chimed in.

The commodore chuckled. "Not all in one day, but yes, I can teach you the symbols. They aren't too hard. We'll make that a part of each visit. Once you've consulted the spirits or done your healing, I'll teach you a bit of Morse code—that's what it's called."

"Will you also teach me how to know if a stock tip is good?" I asked.

Vanderbilt's bushy eyebrows shot up. "You want to learn about the stock market?" He guffawed. "But you're a woman."

I stood. "Indeed I am. But if I am going to be giving you tips, shouldn't I at least know if they are worth relaying? No one ever said the spirit world doesn't deceive. Look at what happened to poor Adam and Eve."

"You have a point."

"If I'm told something that seems wrong, it is best if I can question the spirit then and there. That way we may unmask it for what it truly is. Unless you wish to follow the advice of the spirits blindly, something I doubt you tolerate with any of your other advisors."

Mr. Vanderbilt rose, looking down on me sternly. I cringed, bowing my head. He was going to reprimand me for failing to hold my tongue as a respectful woman should.

Instead, he wagged a finger at me. "There are two things I admire: horses and pluck. And you, my lady, have pluck. Keep giving me arguments like that, and I'll start thinking you missed your calling in a court of law." He offered a hand to each of us and threaded his arms in ours as he walked us toward the hallway. "There are books in my office that may serve as a good starting place. You're hired, by the way."

❧

I paid my first visit to the Broadway brothels several weeks later, standing in for Tennie, who had her first date on the town with Mr. Vanderbilt. She was well on her way to securing her desired position as his mistress.

Freshly painted with neatly trimmed fauna adding a splash of color on either side of the stone staircase, the exterior of Miss Wood's establishment was like any other house on the block off Broadway. A porter dressed in the height of finery greeted me with a small bow and, after I relayed my business with Miss Wood, escorted me inside.

Far above, on the soaring ceiling, dozens of cherubs frolicked. Some carried bunches of roses. Others prepared to take aim at unsuspecting patrons with their arrows *de l'amour*. Chandeliers of beaded crystal hung in stately rows, each set with fresh, fragrant beeswax candles. The walls were white but patterned with gilded carvings of flower garlands, lions' heads, and naked couples in sex acts that defied the flexibility of the human body.

Before I could take it all in, Miss Wood greeted me with a light kiss on each cheek. "Thank you so much for coming, dear. Tennie told me you were every bit as talented as she." The madam's voice was sultry and deep, and the way she rolled certain letters gave her a catlike purr. She gave me an appraising once-over. "And you're just as beautiful. A little thin maybe. The men here like their girls with some meat."

"Then it's a good thing I'm not here for the men."

Miss Wood laughed. "Speaking of men, I understand your sister has caught herself a rich fish." The woman raised a reddish-gold eyebrow.

Word traveled fast. But why did Miss Wood care what Tennie did? She was fishing for something. Best not to give away too many details. "She and Commodore Vanderbilt are quite companionable, yes."

Miss Wood tapped my arm gently, her black lace shawl slipping off one shoulder of her low-cut crimson dress. "Honey, please, you can be honest with me. If I'm going to lose my best healer to a man, I should at least get to know if she's a lightskirt."

"You know my sister. She's a flirt, but this one seems different."

"Those are the truly dangerous ones," Miss Wood huffed, leading me down a hallway tiled in light blue and white toward a large room decorated to resemble a French salon.

Around the room, women in sumptuous gowns with feathers and jewels in their upswept curls talked in small groups or entertained well-dressed men in three-piece suits who gazed at heavy gold pocket watches with as much adoration as they did at their partners. A pale brunette looked up from her perch across the back of a rose-patterned divan as Miss Wood approached. Her pose, so elegant yet careless, was that of a leopard sunning herself. There was something familiar about her, but I couldn't place what it was.

"Mrs. Woodhull, I'd like to introduce you to our most popular girl, Miss Josie Mansfield." Miss Wood wedged herself between Josie and her client, effectively separating the two.

"Victoria? Victoria Woodhull?" Josie leapt to her feet and let out a squeal quite incongruous with the refined atmosphere. "What are you doing in this part of the country?"

"I could ask the same of you. The last time I saw you, you were on a stage in San Francisco."

"As were you," Josie said as we embraced.

"It appears you have already met." Miss Wood glanced at Josie then at me, a slight depression marring her brow. "Josie was Tennie's scheduled client today, so I will leave the two of you." She turned to the man, whose red face and clenched fists betrayed his opinion of the interruption. "Come now, Mr. Fisk. Let's see if we can't find something to soothe you. I have a fine imported brandy I've been saving for a gentleman such as yourself." She led away the mustachioed client.

"Come, come." Josie giggled, dragging me by the hand into yet another hallway. "We must catch up."

Once inside her spacious bedroom suite, Josie plopped onto the bed, and I sank next to her into the down-filled mattress, running a hand over the heavy material of the duvet. It was finer than anything I'd ever seen.

"You sleep here?" I asked.

Josie gave a snorting laugh and rolled onto her side to look at me. "Among other things. It's meant to look like Marie Antoinette's rooms in Versailles." She shook her head, regarding me as though peering at a long-deceased relative. "I cannot believe you're here. When you ran offstage that night in the middle of the performance, I thought for sure you'd gone mad. Then when no one heard from you, we feared the worst."

"It was nothing like that." I propped my head up on my arm. "I had a vision of my sister Tennie calling me home, so I went."

"Tennie is your sister? I had no idea."

"One of several but the only one I like."

"Miss Wood called you 'missus.' Does that mean you're still married to that drunk bastard Canning?"

"Oh Lord, no." I put a hand to my chest. "I use the name because it suits me. I didn't want to be associated with my family so I couldn't use my maiden name, and now that I am re-married, I believe using Woodhull shows I am my own woman, not beholden to my husband."

I filled Josie in on the last decade of my life, including returning to my family, meeting James in St. Louis, our torrid affair and my subsequent divorce from Canning, all the way through coming to New York and becoming employed by Cornelius Vanderbilt.

Josie put a hand to her head as if to ward off dizziness. "My, you have had an exciting few years."

I went to her side, concerned. "Are you unwell? What is it Tennie is treating you for?"

Josie attempted to wave me way. "Nothing of great concern. I have these headaches that sometimes give me the vapors."

Slipping around behind her, I placed my hands on either side of her head, close but not quite touching her, and directed my magnetism into her as we talked.

"What's your story? It can't be any less dramatic than mine."

"You'd be surprised." She picked at the lace edging of a pillowcase. "After divorcing the actor who brought me to New York, I was broke. I tried to turn back to the stage but without much success."

"Oh, Josie, I'm so sorry." I placed my hand over Josie's. "I know how happy you were in the theatre."

She shrugged. "This is its own form of acting, plus it pays better. Jim, Mr. Fisk—that's the man who was with me earlier—has been around ever since. I'm sorry about him, by the way. He *is* a good fellow, not that you would know it from his reaction just now."

"So Mr. Fisk doesn't mind what you do?"

Seating herself at the dressing table, Josie frowned at her reflection. "He must not since he keeps coming back. At first I held him off. The longer he couldn't have me, the more enamored he became, especially when he had to watch me bring other men back to my room." She picked up a silver brush and ran it through her hair. "Now he's so smitten he's pledging to buy me a house of my very own with his next big stock windfall. He tells me about his plans all the time."

Johnny's comment about being able to get tips easily in a brothel danced through my mind. If it worked in journalism, why not in stocks? This might be the break I needed. "He's in the stock market?"

Josie ginned at me. "He's one of the big bugs, right up there with your Mr. Vanderbilt. Those two don't like each other much, not after Jim nearly bankrupted Mr. Vanderbilt over that Eire stock. It was a right awful thing to do, but that's Jim for you. He's all greed, especially in the bedroom."

I knelt beside her now so I could look her in the eyes. "What would you say to a little deal that would benefit both of us?"

Josie stopped brushing. "What are you proposing?"

"Thanks to my no-good father, Mr. Vanderbilt thinks I can predict the stock market with my clairvoyance. I can't bear to tell him the truth—that the spirit world tells me many things but the direction of the market isn't one of them. How would you like to be my 'spirit'? I'll pay you, of course."

Josie stared at her reflection, considering the offer. "It wouldn't be too hard to get information out of him. It's one of the things Miss Wood trains us to do. She wants to know exactly what business her clients are up to so she can use it to her advantage. Can't say I blame her."

"So you'll do it?"

Josie nodded, turning away from the mirror to face me. "Here's your first tip: tell Mr. Vanderbilt that Central Pacific Railroad is going to go up." She linked her arm in mine. "If you thought the two of us knocked 'em dead onstage in San Francisco, just wait. New York isn't going to know what hit it."

❧

THE NEXT MORNING, I worried a path from one end of the small office I shared with Tennie to the other. This tip had the potential to make us very rich women if Mr. Vanderbilt kept to his promise to split the proceeds with us as remuneration for our advice.

The ticker spit out its first report right after trading opened at ten o'clock. Central Pacific Railroad was valued at $134 a share. Mr. Vanderbilt sent word to his associates that they should increase his number of shares. Then we waited.

Throughout the morning, Tennie and I studied Mr. Vanderbilt's texts on finance while he handled his other business. At noon, I looked up from the newspaper I'd been reading, trying to learn all I could about stocks. It was slow going. Men like Mr. Vanderbilt studied for years, decades even, to become experts. Why did I think I, with my meager three years of schooling, could do any better? *Maybe I should give up this charade and admit that my father was mistaken and this whole thing was based on a lie. Or maybe I should wait and see how this first test goes.* There would be time for the truth later.

In the early afternoon, Tennie sat on Mr. Vanderbilt's lap and read the paper to him as he dozed. How could he remain so infernally calm? I was ready to crawl out of my own skin. Finally, the clock on his desk chimed, signaling the market's closing time.

I hurried over to the ticker machine and held up the long ribbon of paper, searching for Central Pacific Railroad. "I don't believe it. The stock closed at $165. That's a gain of more than thirty dollars a share."

Tennie tugged gently on Mr. Vanderbilt's side-whiskers to wake him. "Wake up, old boy. It's closing time."

Mr. Vanderbilt snorted awake. "Wha? What's that?"

"I said you should say thanks to Victoria. You are now a much richer man than when you fell asleep."

Mr. Vanderbilt looked at me, puzzled, as he slowly shook off sleep. I tore off the ticker tape and brought it to him.

"By the horn spoons!" A smile spread across his face. "Do you know what this means?"

"That you've made nearly two hundred fifty thousand dollars," I answered.

Mr. Vanderbilt nudged Tennie, and she rose so he could do the same. "That *you* made me nearly two hundred fifty thousand dollars," he corrected, indicating me. "Or should I say the spirits did?" He limped over to his desk, shaking one leg as though it was still asleep, and opened the top drawer. He removed his check ledger. "I don't forget my promises either."

I grasped Tennie's hand and held it tight while Mr. Vanderbilt scribbled an entry then handed us a slip of paper.

"I promised to pay you half if your tips were correct." He raised his head when neither of us made a move to take the proffered paper. "When the banks open tomorrow, you will find the money in your account. This is surety of my payment." He waved the paper.

Tennie took it, looking from it to me in silent wonder.

"So it is true?" I asked. "We are rich?"

Mr. Vanderbilt smiled before patting me affectionately on the back and kissing Tennie on the lips. "Indeed. That is the beauty of the stock market. But keep in mind that as quickly as it can give you wings, it can tear them away if you aren't careful."

I stood still for a long while, contemplating my sudden good fortune. I would have to pay a fourth of what we'd earned to Josie, but that still left us with a sudden influx of wealth, which meant I could do more for the women I cared so much about.

"I hope this doesn't mean you're leaving me." Mr. Vanderbilt's voice broke into my thoughts.

"Oh no, quite the opposite. We've only just begun."

Word of the commodore's coup had already spread by the time we left for the evening. As we were getting into a carriage, Johnny Green, the piano player-cum-journalist, jogged to the front doors of the mansion.

"Commodore, Commodore. One question, if I may," the reporter called, trying to get Mr. Vanderbilt's attention before the door shut between them. "All of Wall Street is buzzing over your incredible windfall today. What advice do you have for our readers who wish to emulate your success?"

As the carriage began to pull away, Mr. Vanderbilt's gleeful laugh followed. "Do as I do. Consult the spirits."

I smiled to myself. The spirits. If he only knew. But at least now I had the money to make good on the plans Tennie and I had hatched back in August. With our newfound wealth, we would be accepted by the suffragists, who were key to any reform involving women. The next step was joining their ranks.

CHAPTER ELEVEN

The distinctive buildings of the nation's capital rose up around me in the winter cold, but I couldn't get my mind to accept that I was there, much less that in only a few minutes, I would be hearing the pioneers of the women's movement speak at the National Female Suffrage Convention.

"James, this is the best Christmas present you could have given me." I snuggled against him as we walked, grateful for his generosity and encouragement in getting involved with the movement.

"I know how much it means to you," he said with a warm smile. "I only hope I can be of help in establishing you among their ranks."

He had been a supporter of the movement from its pre-Civil War roots, so his name held sway here. My hopes were high that by the end of the weekend, my name would be known too.

Carroll Hall was crammed with people, all talking animatedly while they found their seats. Onstage, plump and cheerful Elizabeth

Cady Stanton, dour Susan B. Anthony, and skeletal Lucretia Mott were oblivious to the commotion, awaiting their turns to speak.

They look like the Fates.

As soon as the thought crossed my mind, a glimmer of light caught my eye, a gossamer thread lying in their laps. Mrs. Stanton's fidgeting fingers appeared to be weaving it; Mrs. Mott, brushing away lint from her skirt, could have been taking its measure; and Miss Anthony's crossed fingers closely resembled the shears that cut the thread of life.

Certainty settled into my core as though I had swallowed a cannonball. These women would have a profound effect on my life; today was only the beginning.

Elizabeth Cady Stanton was the first to speak. "At this very moment, Congress is debating the Fifteenth Amendment. If it is passed, it would give black men the right to vote. But I ask you, how are we, as women, any less important? How are we to be left out of such legislation? Shall American statesmen make their wives and mothers the political inferiors of unlettered and unwashed ditch-diggers fresh from the slave plantations of the South?" She went on to refer to black men and immigrants as "Sambo and Hans and Yung Tung," railing that women might be subjugated to men of inferior intelligence simply because of their sex.

While some members of the audience gasped at her use of such language and others muttered in agreement, Frederick Douglass, the famous former-slave-turned-orator, came forward to challenge her.

"The right of women to vote is as sacred, in my judgment, as that of man, and I am quite willing to hold up both hands in favor of this right. But I am now devoting myself to a cause not more sacred but certainly more urgent because it is one of life and death to the long-enslaved people of this country, and this is Negro suffrage. As you very well know, woman has a thousand ways to attach herself to the governing power of the land and already exerts an honorable influence on the course of legislation. She is the victim of abuses, to be sure, but it cannot be pretended, I think, that her cause is as urgent as ours."

"I don't know about that," Tennie whispered to me over the remainder of Mr. Douglass's remarks. "He goes too far. I am a bit insulted that he would insinuate that simply because I can marry or sleep with a man, I have more access to power."

"But don't you? We both know what men are willing to do for sex." I eyed the tall black man with wild hair as he spoke. "I think he's saying that the Negros must have the right to vote as a matter of survival now that they are free. They need to be able to influence their government as they shape their lives."

"But what of our lives? That's what Mrs. Stanton was saying. Are ours any less precious?"

"No, and Mr. Douglass would be the first to say so. He doesn't deny our right. He's simply asking us to wait our turn."

"Why should we?" Tennie huffed.

The debates continued for the next two hours, both onstage and between Tennie and me, until the crowd finally adjourned for cock-tails at one of the nearby hotels.

The first person we encountered was Lucretia Mott. James made the introductions.

"My, yes," Mrs. Mott said. "I always enjoy meeting new members. You girls are so young you could be my granddaughters. What did you think of the speeches?"

While Tennie answered Mrs. Mott, James excused us and escorted me to the side of the event's host, Representative Benjamin Butler, the most powerful man in the House of Representatives.

He had been speaking with a finely dressed woman but turned his back to her as we approached. "Colonel, delighted to see you again," Mr. Butler said, pumping my husband's hand and giving me a polite bow. "Are you enjoying the convention?"

"Most definitely, though I am afraid my wife and her sister are much at odds over the Stanton-Douglass debate."

"Aren't we all," the representative said. "I thought I knew where I stood before coming here today, but I've found they both made some excellent points that make it hard to choose a side."

"But choose we must," interjected the woman to whom Mr. Butler had been speaking. Her deep voice and large bones would have looked more at home on a farmstead than in fashionable society, where dainty features and a sickly pallor were deemed desirable.

"Forgive me." Congressman Butler gestured to her. "This is Lydia James, wife of one of Washington's most prominent lawyers. She was telling me why she favors Mrs. Stanton's arguments."

Mrs. James preened. "I said to Mr. Butler that as members of the newly formed National Woman Suffrage Association, we have a duty to keep out the unlettered, ignorant women who are unfit to appear before an audience such as ours. If the press, not to mention the government, is to take us seriously, we must show them we are worthy of their attention."

"Is that so?" I asked, inching closer to the woman. "And what of women who start out poor and unlettered, as you say, but rise to be in your midst? What do you say of them?"

James squeezed my elbow in warning, but I shook him off.

Lydia peered down her nose at me and gave a sharp, hooting laugh as though I had told an amusing joke. "Oh, my dear, I don't think we are in danger of encountering many of those. Though the war made some women more independent than they'd been previously, we are, for the most part, well-contented within our social ranks."

"*You* may be," I muttered into my drink.

James shot me a warning look, angling his body away from me and toward the politician. "So, Congressman, I hear rumors that you wish to introduce a bill into the House calling for the vote for women."

Mr. Butler beamed. "You have good sources. I do have plans."

As Mr. Butler outlined his ideas, I listened, enthralled by the magnetism of this small, rather ugly man. He had an overly large head and sunken eyes surrounded by puffy, wrinkled flesh. One of his eyelids drooped, and his bristly mustache hid thin lips. But something about him, about his passion and vitality, made it impossible for me to take my eyes off of him.

"Do you believe such a bill has a fighting chance?" I asked.

Mr. Butler grimaced. "I honestly don't know. We have some strong support but equally powerful resistance, namely John Bingham in the House and the Beecher family in the public. Perhaps if we can sway one, we will be victorious. Either way, I'm determined to keep trying until we succeed."

"As well you should." A tall, black-haired man in a tailored suit joined them, clapping Mr. Butler affably on the shoulder. He extended a hand to my husband and me. "I'm a reporter for the *New York World*. I'd tell you my name, but my column is anonymous." After we introduced ourselves, he addressed me. "I believe you are a new face in Washington, Mrs. Woodhull. What is your opinion of the convention and its leaders' views?"

I swallowed, not enjoying the attention, especially since my words might end up in print. Icy sweat broke out on my neck and back, and I was suddenly burning up and unsure how to answer. This was my chance to making a lasting first impression. "I am new to the movement, so I don't know its intricacies as well as many of the women here, but I agree with them to a point. While I believe in woman most completely, I also believe in man most thoroughly."

"What do you mean by that?"

"Well, I believe Mr. Douglass is right that the black man winning the vote will help build momentum for women. But I also agree with Mrs. Stanton that we cannot allow ourselves to get swept under the rug while the issue is decided." I cleared my throat. "Where I disagree with her is on the topic of worthiness. I'm a healer and have heard stories from all walks of life, and each person—man and woman, rich and poor—is worthy of the right to vote. It seems to me the only question is when it will become a universal right."

"And do you see yourself playing a role in bringing that to pass?" the reporter asked.

"Absolutely." The word was out of my mouth before I had even thought it, but I knew deep within my bones it was true. I had found my calling.

I told James as much that night as we lay in bed.

"I will support you if you wish to pursue this," he promised. "You have something few of the other women in the movement can claim."

"A handsome husband who actually wants his wife to speak her mind?"

His chest shook as he laughed. "Not what I was thinking but yes." His tone quickly sobered. "You speak from experience. You've seen both the highs and lows of life and can offer a validity none of the blue-blooded biddies at this convention could ever affect. They will always be window dressing to the movement. You, on the other hand, could prove to be very powerful."

With James's support and my newfound conviction, I approached the second day of the conference not as the wide-eyed innocent of yesterday but as a potential future leader. The urge to speak out, to give voice to all of those whom society silenced hummed in my veins. The only remaining question was how.

Among the morning's speakers was my old friend from St. Louis, Virginia Minor. After she was introduced, Mrs. Minor wasted no time in getting to the point of her speech. "You may know that my husband and I are vocal proponents of the idea that the Constitution already gives us the right to vote. But we are willing to put before you an additional piece of supporting evidence, found in the Fourteenth Amendment, that I believe gives all *women* the right to vote.

"As persons born in the United States, women are citizens. Nowhere in the text does it specify 'males' or 'men,' only 'persons,' which is a term without gender and therefore should include both men and women. The Constitution gives all *citizens* the right to vote. Therefore, as citizens, we already have the right to vote. The next line of the amendment elaborates, noting that no state is allowed to legally deprive citizens of their rights or deny them equal protection."

I followed Mrs. Minor's words closely, taking in each argument and dissecting it carefully. I was not trained to debate the finer points of law, but I could find no flaw in the woman's logic. In fact, the longer I listened, the more I found myself agreeing. Around us, women whispered to each other, nudging husbands and companions in agreement with Mrs. Minor's peaceful call to arms.

"Therefore, if the right is already ours, all we need do is take it back. Yes," her voice rang out like the peal of an Easter church bell, "I mean we must take action. Perhaps you have heard of the Spiritualist town of Vineland, New Jersey? There, late last year, nearly two hundred women cast their votes. They pledge to do so annually until they are acknowledged. This is what I call on you to do.

"What I am asking of you is revolutionary, this I know. It goes against all we are raised to believe and how society demands we behave, but I urge you to open your minds to the idea. As a group, we have the power to change state laws, something which Miss Anthony, Mrs. Stanton, and other leaders of this group will be working to put into action. But each of us bears personal responsibility as well. So on your next election day, I ask that you hand over your ballot, not meekly but with pride, and demand to be counted among the citizens of this fine country. Only in that way can we hope to affect change in time to cast our votes for the next president in 1872."

The crowd roared with applause, and I leapt to my feet, clapping as loud as my hands would let me. This woman was onto something.

"We should do this," I mouthed to Tennie, who nodded enthusiastically. I would have to discuss the possibilities taking shape in my mind with James.

"They've got motivation now," said a man in the row behind me. "Too bad they don't have the money to see it through."

His offhand comment snagged my attention. The party needed money, and I needed a way into its upper echelons. If Josie's stock tips had taught me anything, it was that there was money to be made in the stock market—lots of it. Perhaps that could be my entry into suffrage society. I mulled over the thought as other people spoke. By the time Elizabeth Cady Stanton delivered the closing address, I was determined to work with Tennie to see how our budding business relationship with Mr. Vanderbilt might help advance our work for women.

When Mrs. Stanton said, "The need of this hour is a new evangel of womanhood to exalt purity, virtue, morality, true religion, to lift man up into the high realms of thought and action," a chill raced down my spine. Those words were meant for me.

My sight blurred, and I blinked as a vision took over my consciousness. I stood in the center of a spotlighted stage, speaking to throngs larger even than the crowd gathered for this convention, as Demosthenes had promised.

A flash, then I sat on a platform next to the three Fates who ran the organization. I was the golden child sent to breathe new life into a movement desperately in need of new energy.

The next thing I knew, Miss Anthony was announcing me as president of the National Women's Rights Convention.

Another shift and the vision began to fade, but not before a newspaper headline blared the fulfillment of the highest of Demosthenes' prophecies: "Victoria Woodhull Makes History as First Woman President."

Yes! I will bring this movement to the masses. I will show them that a woman like them, raised in the dirt, who works for a living, can be an agent of change. Then they shall see one Victoria sitting on the throne of England while her namesake guards the interests of women in the United States. Less than four years from now, I shall be president.

CHAPTER TWELVE

"Victoria, you must see this," James called the morning after we arrived back in New York.

I was still in bed, snuggled beneath the blankets, watching the leaden clouds disgorge a light but steady dusting of snow. I sat up as he entered carrying several newspapers under his arm.

"What? What is it?" I asked as he leaned down to kiss me.

"See for yourself." He set the papers in my lap.

I wiggled into a sitting position and opened the *New York World* to a lengthy article about the convention in Washington. I read aloud the part James pointed to, my incredulity increasing with every word. "'Mrs. Woodhull takes the most lively interest in all the genuine reforms of the day and entertains her own distinctive views. Upon the woman question, I deem her particularly sound. She has just been attending the National Female Suffrage Convention but only partially agrees with the doings of that body.'" I stared at my husband, mouth agape. "James, how is this possible?"

"Do you remember the man we spoke to while having cocktails the first evening? It sounds like he was none other than the 'Alpha' who writes this column. But there's more. Read on."

I did as he commanded, skimming over flowery phrases that would make me into the next Florence Nightingale rather than a woman sympathetic to the plight of prostitutes. "'I can fully agree with the writer in the Washington paper that this woman is to rise to a very conspicuous position, destined to act a part in the coming conflicts and reforms in the country.'"

James gingerly removed a copy of the Washington *Evening Star* from the pile. "This is the one Alpha referenced." James read in a dramatic voice suffused with pride. "'Victoria C. Woodhull is the Coming Woman, make no mistake of that. She represents the next generation of reformers, full of vitality and passion. Mrs. W. possesses a commanding intellect, refinement, and remarkable executive ability, and will undoubtedly play a conspicuous part in such changes, should they come.'"

"'The Coming Woman,'" I repeated in awe. "But I didn't even talk to an *Evening Star* reporter. How could he think so highly of me if he doesn't even know me?"

James sat next to me on the bed. "Any of the men we spoke with could have been reporters. Plus, who knows who was listening?"

"In Washington, you said you'd support me as a member of the association. Do you still feel the same way?"

"More than ever." Without breaking eye contact, he picked up the rest of the papers. "I thought these might be a good place to start. They are back copies of the weekly paper Elizabeth Cady Stanton and Susan B. Anthony run. It's called the *Revolution*. They only began printing it last year, so it shouldn't take you too long to catch up." He kissed the top of my head. "While you do that, I'll see about arranging meetings with some of the people I know who are allies in the movement."

I threw my arms around his neck. "Thank you. You can't possibly know what this means to me."

He kissed me softly. "I can, and I do. I meant it when I vowed to be with you in fortune and famine when I took you as my wife. You were always destined for greater things." He swatted me as near to my backside as he could reach. "Now get up. We have a world to change."

"And I know just how to start," I said, waving the *Star* and *World*. "Can you get additional copies of these? I think our friends who ran the convention may like to see them, along with a kind note thanking them for putting on such an enlightening event."

James smiled. "They are already downstairs. I bought out every newsstand within four blocks. I thought you may want to send some to your family to show them what you've made from the nothing they gave you."

In between absorbing every word of the *Revolution*, I hounded Mr. Vanderbilt, greedily lapping up every scrap of financial information he tossed my way. In the evenings, I talked about the money to be made in the stock market so much that even Katherine became intrigued.

Slowly, Mr. Vanderbilt's tutelage expanded beyond Morse code and the basics of investments until Tennie and I were more than secretaries to him. If we'd been men, we would have been called apprentices, perhaps even be groomed to follow in the commodore's footsteps. But such a thing was unheard of for women. Yet we were at his side each day, reading the ticker tape, passing him tips from "the spirits," and learning to make our own educated predictions about the market. Occasionally he would even give us a small sum of money to invest as a test of our skill.

Many times, while my head was bent over dry tomes on finance, I chewed on Elizabeth Cady Stanton's words from an 1868 issue of the *Revolution*: "Let women of wealth and brains step out of the circles of fashion and folly and fit themselves for the trades, arts, and professions and become employers instead of subordinates, thus making labor honorable for all and elevating our sex by opening new adventures for aspiration and ambition."

The longing to take action overwhelmed me. We were getting an excellent education from Mr. Vanderbilt, but what good would it do if we couldn't put it to use? I couldn't spend the rest of my life as a middleman between Mr. Fisk and Mr. Vanderbilt. I was already itching for more. Was it possible? Would Mr. Vanderbilt hire Tennie and me on as stockbrokers if I asked? While women couldn't hold a seat on the stock exchange, there were plenty of ways to do business without being present in the building itself. If he said yes, we would have to give up our work as medical healers. I would continue seeing Minnie, though; she had become like a second daughter to me. There would always be more healers to tend the ills of Broadway and Bowery; women willing to take on Wall Street were a far rarer commodity.

One bright morning, I screwed up my courage to ask— with Tennie by my side.

"Mr. Vanderbilt, you have been so generous and so kind to us already. I hesitate to ask for more"—I cleared my throat, which was suddenly like a cat's tongue—"but I was wondering if you would be willing to allow us to try the skills you've taught us in the actual market, to work as your brokers, at least temporarily."

Mr. Vanderbilt was silent for a moment as though he hadn't heard me. Then he burst out laughing, holding his belly as if I'd told him the most amusing joke. "Oh, Victoria, you are a stitch." He wiped his eyes then frowned at our somber expressions. "You are serious?"

"Yes, sir," Tennie mumbled.

"You wish to run my investments? You, who six months ago didn't know a bull from a bear, want me to entrust my wealth to you? I'd sooner set a blind newborn pup to guard a viper pit."

"But, Commodore"—Tennie leaned on his desk, bringing herself closer to his level—"we already provide you with your most lucrative tips and have learned the workings of your mind. Where would you be if your mother hadn't agreed to the bargain you struck with her on your sixteenth birthday? That was the beginning of your career with the ferry boats, wasn't it?"

"I never should have told you that story," Mr. Vanderbilt griped.

Tennie gave him a hard look, one that said she meant business. "We are proposing a similar bargain with you. Give us six months to prove ourselves. If you aren't satisfied, you can throw us out if you wish."

Mr. Vanderbilt sat back in his chair, making a production of lighting a cigar as he pondered our offer. "Finishing plowing a rocky field by my birthday in exchange for the money to buy a periauger is quite a different story than what you're proposing. What am I to tell my other advisors? They will laugh me into the harbor when they find out I've employed two addle-brained women to replace them."

"We don't intend to replace them. You can still consult them. It is smart of you to retain their services as a barometer of our wisdom. Plus, you would be showing the world you're still a maverick even at an age when some would write you off into dotage." I flinched inwardly. Hopefully my veiled insult touched his pride rather than gave him umbrage.

Mr. Vanderbilt puffed on his cigar, sending a cloud of black smoke into the air, where it formed a veil between us. "So you wish to test your mettle against the big boys, eh? I must admit you've done remarkably well these past months, passed nearly every test I devised for you, and have made me even richer than I was before." He trailed off into pensive silence. "Why not? Simply because other men don't employ women doesn't mean I can't. The idea that something can't be done has never stopped me before." Mr. Vanderbilt stood suddenly, offering us his hand. "I'll do it. But remember, I am your client now, so you cannot ask me for advice. You will sink or swim on your own merits. Do you understand?"

"Yes, sir," Tennie and I chorused.

Inside, I was beaming. We were going to prove Mrs. Stanton was right and show that women could enrich the workplace. That we stood to make a profit at the same time made the situation all the better.

Vanderbilt shook his head in wonderment at us, his protégées. "You've always had spirit. It's one of the many things I like about you."

Tennie and I eyed one another. We had done it. Now it was time to focus, to prove we could be the best stockbrokers Wall Street had ever seen. It would take up most of our waking hours, but the work would be worth it. We would prove that women could do all the same things as men—and then some.

CHAPTER THIRTEEN

When we arrived at Mr. Vanderbilt's mansion for work, an unfamiliar face greeted us. Instead of Harold, a tall, imposing woman with her dark hair pulled back into a tight bun surveyed us with assessing black eyes.

"You must be the assistants." She stepped back so we could enter.

We had barely crossed the threshold when William was upon us. "May I present Mrs. Frank Armstrong Crawford Vanderbilt, my father's new wife?" The last part was punctuated with a smug, pointed look in Tennie's direction.

Frank? What an odd name for a woman. Wait, did he say wife?

"Wife?" Tennie echoed my thoughts, hand going to her mouth. Her shock had slipped out with the word.

The new Mrs. Vanderbilt gave us a thin smile. "Yes, we were married some weeks ago, but I was only now able to transfer my residence to this place."

I opened my mouth to congratulate the woman on her good fortune, but William stepped between us. "So you see, there will no longer be need for your services here. Mrs. Vanderbilt can attend to her husband."

I straightened, purposefully drawing my head up a little higher. "Indeed?" I turned to Mrs. Vanderbilt. "You are a stockbroker then?" I asked politely, already knowing the answer.

"Oh, no. I have no such skills."

I shot William a triumphant grin. "Then until she can make your father hundreds of thousands of dollars a day, I'd say he does have need of our services."

"You have also lost him a hundred thousand in one day," William said.

My eye twitched at the reminder. "How much have you made him lately?" I countered, touching a finger to my chin. "Oh, that's right—you only make money for yourself and then gamble it away." I brushed past him without another word, calling, "Dear Commodore, where are you? The spirits have a message for you."

Once we were safely ensconced in our office with the door firmly closed, Tennie let out a stifled wail. "Married?" she asked in a harsh whisper. "How can he possibly be married?"

I shrugged. "I don't know, but he clearly is." Thinking of William's reaction, I added, "My guess is his children made him a match that he would have been unwise to refuse."

"He was always concerned about their interference in his life. Remember what his mother said at his first séance? You saw the way William tried to push us out. We may have won for the moment, but what does this mean for us in the long run?" She worried her lower lip between her teeth.

"Calm down, Tennie. We've spent the last year building up Mr. Vanderbilt's trust. He's not going to toss us out simply because a new woman has taken his name. No one else can boast my connections—to the spirits or otherwise—and I doubt his need or desire for you will be any different. Did you see that woman? She's as warm and inviting as a block of ice."

Despite herself, Tennie laughed. "You have a point. And even if she is doing her duty in the bedroom, the old goat has enough fire in his blood for two women."

"See? We're going to be fine."

A brief, sharp knock on the door signaled Mr. Vanderbilt's arrival.

"You are going to be more than fine," he greeted us. "You're going to be great if I have anything to say about it." He kissed Tennie on the cheek warmly as though nothing had changed. "Your spirits certainly are in good form," he said to me. "A contact of mine confirmed your last prediction. That bastard Fisk is using his connections to the presidency to monkey with the price of gold."

"This isn't going to end well, is it?" Tennie fidgeted with her tie. "We're lucky to know what's coming, but what of all the investors who don't?"

"You are so kind to be concerned, my little sparrow," Vanderbilt said, regarding her fondly. "That is the risk we all take when we enter this field."

We spent the morning refining our gold strategy for the next day's trading. I was preparing instructions for the men at the Stock Exchange when a rapping on my office window broke my concentration. When would those damn birds realize they couldn't fly through glass? I squeezed my eyes, refocusing on the words before me, but I barely had a chance to register them before the sound came again four times in rapid succession. That was no bird.

I looked up and gasped at the woman who stood on the porch outside. Josie's brown hair was hastily pinned into a lopsided twist, her outfit was a simple house dress—rather than the elaborate walking or visiting gowns she usually wore in public—and she was clutching her shawl around her shoulders as if the very act sustained her life. She kept glancing around as though afraid to be spotted.

Something had happened to my friend, something bad.

I set down my pen and went out to the patio. "What is going on? You look a fright."

"I came here straight away. Is there somewhere we can be sure to not be overheard?"

I glanced around. The elder Mr. Vanderbilt was out in the stables, and William and Frank were lurking about the house. The woods.

Once we were far enough into the trees that Josie was certain we were not followed, she spoke at such a rapid pace I had to strain to keep up. "I needed to make sure you heard this before the markets close. Jim and his crony, Mr. Gould, just left my house. They don't know I overheard, but they were discussing what to do when the market opens tomorrow. They finally landed on a plan to drive up the cost of gold to one hundred fifty dollars then sell their shares before the bottom falls out."

I pressed my lips together. That would be worse than Tennie had feared. "I can see why you didn't want to tell me this in writing, but you took a terrible risk in coming here. What if Jim learns you told me?"

Josie shook her head. "I don't think he will. He hasn't sunk so low as to have me followed. I certainly didn't want you to come to me though. *That* he would be sure to hear about. Go"—she swatted at my arm—"tell that financier of yours that you've had a vision. I will disappear a different way than I came."

I took my time walking back to the house. This tip was more than the casual advanced information of my previous intelligence. This could affect the whole country. I yanked a stem of late-blooming honeysuckle off a bush, shredding its petals as I walked. If Josie was right, tomorrow night at closing, Mr. Vanderbilt could be the richest man in the country. At half the profits, Tennie and I stood to gain much as well.

As I neared the house, my pace slowed even more. I paused at the forest's edge, leaning against the trunk of a stout oak and gazing at the house where Tennie and Mr. Vanderbilt went about their business, oblivious to this newest threat. I trusted Josie but not the men. What if Mr. Fisk somehow knew Josie was my source and had deliberately given her false information? Then Tennie and I, and possibly even Mr. Vanderbilt, would be living in the gutters along with all of the other innocent victims of tomorrow's scheme—not to mention what Mr. Fisk would do to all of us for double-crossing him.

I sighed. What would be would be. No sense in delaying the inevitable. I started back toward the house again.

Mr. Vanderbilt looked up from bouncing Tennie on his knee when I entered. His laughter quickly died. "You look like you've seen a ghost, my dear."

I flashed him a halfhearted smile. "I have, in a manner of speaking. I've had a vision of a great golden bubble." I let my eyes take on a distant quality as I imagined it. "In its center was the number 151. It expanded at a rapid rate, then suddenly it burst." I focused on Mr. Vanderbilt once again. "I believe this means you should sell your stock in gold when it reaches exactly one hundred fifty dollars."

Mr. Vanderbilt considered my words but not for long. "You are the expert in the realm of the spirit, my dear. If that is what you advise, that is what shall be done."

❧

THE NEXT DAY DAWNED clear and beautiful, one of those perfect autumn days where the sunlight and breeze danced as they caressed the skin and the sky appeared endless. Sitting outside the stock exchange in my carriage, the future was full of infinite possibility for me as well.

Gold had opened at one hundred fifty dollars when trading began, but I wasn't ready to make my move, and neither was Mr. Vanderbilt. To sell all our shares too soon would send a signal something was going on, attracting attention neither of us wanted, so we sold most off quietly in small increments, reserving some for later when we would make a grand gesture that others could follow. The price would likely rise before coming back down again—that was when we would sell.

As a woman, I wasn't allowed in the exchange, but I had plenty of men to work for me. Not even an hour into trading, they were coming to me with outlandish stories of the chaos taking place inside.

"You should see it, Mrs. Woodhull. It's a madhouse in there," Dirk O'Malley reported in his thick Irish brogue. "Men are sweating like they're facing the headsman while they're telegraphing their clients. That poor fountain in the middle of the room is getting the worst of it; I saw half a dozen brokers splashing their faces with the water in the pool, and two even dunked their heads in the streams coming from the golden dolphins' mouths." He laughed. "Ain't never seen anything like it."

As the morning progressed, a crowd formed in the street nearby. Without being asked, my driver took on the role of my personal guard when I needed to leave the carriage, but for the most part, the crowd was peaceful, merely curious. As prices continued to rise, more and more businessmen joined them, loudly shouting orders over one another at their brokers, openly fretting and more than once coming to blows over disagreements of strategy.

I was paying for my lunch at a nearby restaurant when a commotion drew my attention to the street. Straight as a set of stick pins, a unit of Seventh Regiment National Guard soldiers approached the crowd. Their weapons and grayish-blue uniforms left no doubt of their orders to keep the peace. I eyed them cautiously as I made my way back to my carriage.

I took a deep breath as I settled in for the afternoon's trading. While I was away, another carriage containing at least three passengers had pulled up on the opposite side of the street. The silhouettes of two men in bowler hats were visible beyond the frame of a busty brunette. That had to be Josie with Fisk and Gould, the orchestrators of this scheme. Nothing else made any sense. Feeling suddenly sick, I sank back into my seat and hoped they would have no reason to look in my direction. I didn't want to have to explain my presence.

From outside the carriage, a soldier said, "I'm sorry, sir, but I can't allow you to approach."

For a moment, I feared it was Fisk or Gould come to inquire about my business here, but when the man protested, I relaxed. It was Dirk.

"It's all right. He's one of mine," I called.

Dirk appeared at my window, diving in without preamble. "Tensions are running high inside. Gold has shot past 150 to 164."

That was even higher than Josie had said. Mr. Fisk and Mr. Gould were losing control of the market. "Sell what we have left. Get us out before the whole thing comes crashing down. Make sure Mr. Vanderbilt's assets are protected before those in my name."

"Yes, ma'am." With a tip of his cap, he was off.

It wasn't long before unrest once again surfaced in the waiting crowd, and with it came an increase in grumbling. Without warning, brokers burst out of the exchange like water from a dam, frantically consulting their clients in the crowd.

"What is it?" I asked as Dirk approached once more.

He blew out a deep breath. "We got out just in time, right at one hundred fifty. As soon as word came from Treasury Secretary Boutwell that the government is going to sell gold tomorrow in order to prevent a national collapse of the markets—which they should have done days ago—the price started falling. If I thought it was crazy before, I was wrong. People are actually crawling over one another to sell off their stock. This is going to be a disaster."

He was right. It wasn't long before prices plummeted to $132 a share. Brokers wandered aimlessly in the streets, shirtwaists untucked, suits rumpled, wearing forlorn expressions.

"We're ruined," one cried.

"Ruined!" echoed another.

Others simply sobbed.

I stepped out of my carriage and placed a gentle arm on a passing broker's shoulder. "Please, I cannot undo what has happened today, but let me help." I pressed a handful of coins into his palm.

Slowly, as though waking from a dream, the man looked at his hand then at me. Instead of thanking me, he spit in my face, throwing the coins back at me. I recoiled, using my handkerchief to wipe away his saliva. I picked up the discarded money, straightened my dress, and tried again.

The next man shrugged me away.

The following growled that he "was no rich woman's charity case" and shoved me aside.

Finally, I met a pair of red-rimmed brown eyes.

"Sir," I said, approaching him slowly like an unfamiliar animal, "may I offer you a bit of assistance? It's not much, but it should buy your family a meal and board tonight." I held out my open palm so the coins were clearly visible.

The man stopped before me, studying my palm. Then a grin lit his face, chased by twin tears from each of his eyes. "God bless you, ma'am. I was praying for a miracle, and here you are." He held up a brown glass bottle. "I was of a mind to drink myself into the arms of death this night, but you've saved me." He embraced me. "Thank you."

By closing, newsboys were shouting from the street corners about extra editions with headlines declaring "Black Friday." They carried tawdry stories about brokers hanging themselves or leaping from tall buildings—twenty men dead in all. Some gloried in the public drunkenness of businessmen who had lost everything and the wailing of newly made widows. Other articles speculated on the effect the crash would have on businesses and what the government could do to reverse the disaster that had left many with nothing.

I had read the papers, but the misfortune of others was far from my mind as I stood in the parlor of the Vanderbilt mansion, surrounded by my family and his. Champagne was flowing; music filled the air, and laughter bubbled along with light from every window. My burning cheeks reflected my joy, warm from not only the wine but also the heady realization I was now a truly wealthy woman even after I paid Josie handsomely for her help. My personal speculating had netted me a small amount; my main income was related to Mr. Vanderbilt's success.

He raised a glass to his guests. "I would like to make a toast to Victoria Woodhull, the woman of the hour. Without her guidance, I would be crying in the streets tonight rather than celebrating a great financial coup. You may have guessed I came out on top today, but I want you to know just how well this bold operator guided me. I made more than 1.3 million dollars today, half of which is hers according to our agreement."

I ducked my head, embarrassed by such a public declaration of my newfound wealth.

"I'm sure you will agree with me"—Vanderbilt pinioned William with a sharp glare—"that Victoria and Tennie have more than proven their worth as brokers in their own right. Agreeing to take them on as my protégées was one of the smartest decisions I've ever made."

"Hear, hear," James said.

The company followed suit, lifting their glasses and sipping their drinks.

"What are you going to do with all your money?" Mrs. Vanderbilt asked. "If you are interested in charitable donations, I may be able to make some recommendations."

"Certainly you deserve a rest after such an accomplishment," William put in. "My offer of a European vacation still stands."

"Thank you, but we will be staying nearby for the time being." I blew out a breath and glanced at my sister, who nodded slightly. "Up until half an hour ago, I would have told you I had no idea what I should do with my unexpected good fortune. But the spirits are guiding me once again. They say that instead of going to secure staterooms for Europe"—my gaze flickered briefly to William before alighting on his father—"we are to go down to Wall Street." I forced the rest of the words past my lips. "To secure a banking office."

Mrs. Vanderbilt's hand fluttered to her lace collar. "Why, whatever for?"

I hesitated but continued when a hand softly squeezed my elbow. James. He both knew about and approved of my plans. "To open our own brokerage firm."

CHAPTER FOURTEEN

Beginning a business on Wall Street wasn't nearly as easy as I had imagined. I couldn't simply hang a sign on the door and wait for customers to arrive, not if I wished to be successful. Mr. Vanderbilt helped by establishing a line of credit in my and Tennie's names with his friend, the banker Henry Clews, and introducing us to his many connections. Luckily, all it took to get them to extend their allegiance was Mr. Vanderbilt's blessing and a witty remark from me or a beguiling glance from Tennie.

One of those leads secured our office space. As the former home of Williams & Grey, the building had been hastily abandoned by its occupants: a forger, bank robber, swindler, and murderer. In their haste to flee, they took only what they could carry, so as a result, the heavy walnut desks trimmed in gold, oak chairs upholstered in green silk, and rich carpets were included.

"It is perfect," I declared before James and I ever set foot inside.

Down the street to the right, the massive Greek columns of

the New York Stock Exchange cast wide shadows across the street, obscuring men and horses in pockets of darkness though it was barely past noon on a sunny winter day. Four doors to the left of the office, a brightly painted sign marked the office of Jim Fisk. Hold your enemies in nearest regard had been another of my father's lessons, one I could practice well from this location, especially after what Mr. Fisk had pulled in September. Above the street, telegraph wires crisscrossed in a spider's web, connecting the many businesses in the financial district to one another and to our clients, assuring the most up-to-date information. One glance inside at the fine furnishings and we made a deal.

Tennie's budding relationship with Johnny Green—whom she had begun dating once Mr. Vanderbilt got married, though she hadn't stopped being his lover—proved an unexpected benefit. Thanks to his coverage of the financial crisis, he had been promoted at the *Herald*, relinquished the title of professor at Madame de Ford's, and taken the lead on preparing the public for our eventual leap into the public sphere as stockbrokers.

"Here is something for the consideration of Susan B. Anthony and her sister apostles in women's rights," he wrote in the *Herald*. "With what complacency must she and they regard the success which has so far attended their efforts. If finesse is woman's gift, why not finance also? We all know the skill with which she administers the domestic exchequer. And as to Wall Street, she would be quite in her element."

Articles like this helped draw crowds to our doorstep for the grand opening of our firm on February 5. As our carriage rocked over stones and ruts, I drew in long, slow breaths, closing my eyes against the bouncing that was doing nothing to quell my queasiness. The whole situation was like a dream that could shatter into wakefulness at any moment. Who would have thought two poor, nearly unlettered sisters from Homer, Ohio, were about to become the first females in the country to run a business buying and selling stocks—and at a company that bore our names, no less?

As if sensing my distress, Tennie squeezed my hand. "The hard part is already done. All we need to do today is greet our clients and conduct our business as best we can. I'm sure we will have detractors, but they will be no different than those who mocked our spiritual skills. And like them, we will show these ninnies how wrong they are."

I smiled and was still smiling when the carriage pulled up to our office. But my amusement faded quickly when faced with crowds lined up for blocks in either direction.

"There must be a thousand people out there," Tennie said.

My stomach flipped on its side. I leaned around Tennie, gawking. "They can't all be here for us."

Tennie grinned as she stepped out of the carriage with me close behind. "I believe they are. Put on your theatrical face, Vickie. We're about to make our debut on the Wall Street stage."

Women whispered behind their hands to one another, and men openly ogled us, taking in our matching outfits, chosen precisely for our entrance into the male world of finance. We'd traded in jewelry and makeup for silk bow ties and white rose buds. Eschewing corsets and bustles, we wore blue jackets embroidered with rich velvet which were broad at the shoulders but tapered to contoured curves at the waist over matching skirts that brushed the tops of our shoes—a carefully planned statement designed to draw attention and remind onlookers that while we were too modest to show our ankles like common whores, we also were no ordinary women.

Two uniformed police officers escorted us from the carriage up the front walk, pushing back anyone who dared get too close to the

Bewitching Brokers, as we were already coming to be known. Reporters, protesting men, and curious onlookers shouted at us, but I couldn't make out anything specific in the general clamor.

Sighing in relief, I crossed the threshold of Woodhull, Claflin, and Company for the very first time as its proprietress. I embraced James, who stood in the doorway to his office. He would help manage the business and serve as my secretary—as well as be the firm's silent partner.

"I am so proud of you," he whispered into my hair. "No matter what happens today, remember that."

I cupped his cheeks and kissed him. "I will."

Behind me, a man loudly cleared his throat. I turned. There stood my father, almost unrecognizable with his well-groomed hair and beard, dressed in a fine brown suit with polished shoes.

"I always knew you two had heads for business." He held his arms open wide as though to embrace us. "That's why I employed you from such a young age—but I never imagined anything like this." He discreetly wiped a tear from his one good eye.

I must have inherited my acting talent from my father. It is thirty years too late for him to suddenly become the devoted patriarch. I still didn't want to let him anywhere near our business, but Tennie's argument that we owed him at least a token position for the role he'd played in our introduction to Mr. Vanderbilt won out. Ignoring his show of emotion, I ushered Pa behind the ornate desk we had reserved for him.

"Remember, if anyone asks, you taught us law and what you knew of finance before falling on hard times and becoming impoverished," I stressed, making sure he would play his part in the tale we were paying him handsomely to uphold.

"It's not far from the truth."

"Anyone can hang up a shingle and call themselves a lawyer, Pa. It's the training that establishes a professional, and that is what you lack."

"Ignore her." Tennie sent me an admonishing glance. "She's just nervous."

While Tennie made sure everything was in place in our shared office, I checked on the back room, which was hidden from casual view by a walnut partition decorated with glass. This room, accessible by its own entrance from the outside—but only from within through the office Tennie and I shared—was set aside specifically for our female clients, who for various reasons may not have wished to be seen conducting their transactions. On a small side table, chocolate-covered strawberries rested on a block of ice, and a bottle of champagne chilled in a nearby bucket. Only the best would be served to the women to whom we owed our first livelihood in New York.

Once I was seated behind my desk, I took in the room one final time, trying to see it as our clients would. The office was elegant, with oil paintings on the walls, marble statues in the corners, and ample upholstered sofas and chairs for clients. In truth, it was more like a parlor than an office, but we wanted people to be comfortable, not intimidated, as was the case in some other offices. On the wall behind me, directly in the sight line of each client as they sat facing me, was a small frame containing Tennie's handiwork, the words "Simply to the cross I cling" in careful cross-stitch, while next to it was a photo of Cornelius Vanderbilt. It never hurt to remind people of the two men in which we female brokers placed our trust.

A nearby clock struck ten.

Taking one more deep breath, I switched on the ticker-tape machine at my right. "It's time."

"Open the doors," Tennie called to the doorkeeper we had hired to help control the crowds until they dwindled to our normal clientele.

Our first visitor of the day—a tall, bearded man in an old-fashioned long coat—introduced himself as Mr. Edward H. Van Schalck. After taking a seat in a chair positioned squarely between us, he declared, "I would like to place an order of stock. I'm told that is what you do here?"

Tennie ignored the slight condescension in his voice and answered politely, "Of course, Mr. Van Schalck." She removed a solid gold pen from behind her ear—a gift we each had received from Mr. Vanderbilt—and prepared to write. "We expect to be overwhelmed by the crowds today, so if you would please let us know in what companies you are interested and how much you'd like to purchase, we'll gladly make the purchase as soon as we are able."

After we took down his order, the gentleman bowed and left the room, pausing to speak with James and Buck. Callers continued this way for about an hour before Mr. Van Schalck returned, this time freshly shaven, his cheeks still rosy from the barber's blade. Accompanying him was a motley group of companions, all of whom he introduced quite cordially before taking up his previous post in the chair facing us.

The shortest of the bunch, who resembled a pig ready for the spit, exclaimed, "By God, I thought you were joking. There *are* two women doing business on Wall Street."

As I stared in mute astonishment at his audacity, he raked first Tennie, then me, with beady eyes.

"You cannot succeed," he declared. "It is against the laws of God and nature."

At this, Mr. Van Schalck leapt to his feet, outraged. "Hugh Hastings, you lout! You of all people should know that women make the best lobbyists in the home, so I see no reason why they should not be successful bankers as well."

The two men argued for a few moments before Mr. Van Schalck finally convinced the group to leave.

Not long after, the tinkle of a soft bell signaled the arrival of our first female customer through the back entrance. I slipped behind the partition, curious as to whom it would be. Madame de Ford and Josie awaited me, dressed in their best promenading gowns and feathered hats.

Madame de Ford embraced me warmly. "My dear, my dear, what a showing you have made for yourself. Your name is on everyone's lips from Madison Avenue to Five Points."

"I'm so happy you came. Please sit. Enjoy some strawberries." I struggled with a champagne cork that refused to give before it finally came out with a loud pop.

"What finery," Madame de Ford observed, looking around as I brought out two crystal glasses and filled them. "I knew there was something special about you from the moment we met, but I could never have imagined all this."

"We've worked hard, but we could never have gotten here alone. We've had so much support along the way." I winked at Josie. "Not the least of which came from the two of you."

"Oh yes, and we don't intend to stop now." Madame de Ford sipped her drink and coughed on the bubbles before continuing. "We would like to invest as well."

"There is great interest in your firm at Miss Wood's, especially since we now have a private meeting place," Josie added. "We'll stop in whenever we can." She gave me a meaningful look, one that hinted the pipeline of stock tips and business leads was just heating up.

My gold pen hovered over my notebook, waiting. "How would you like to begin your venture into the stock market?"

The two women turned to each other with uncertain expressions.

"We only relay what we hear," Josie said, breaking the uncomfortable silence. "We need you to work your magic. What do you advise?"

I gave them a primer on how the stock market worked along with a few suggestions for safe starter investments. When I sat back down at my desk, the small clock on a side table was chiming half past noon.

"Oh my, was I back there so long? I'm sorry to have left you all alone. What did I miss?"

Tennie shrugged. "Not much. A few of our competitors dropped by out of curiosity, but they were polite at least. More well wishes and stock orders from businessmen. Mr. Charlick had some fascinating advice on Long Island Stock. Remind me to tell you about it later. Oh, and our favorite men were back—twice."

I groaned. "What did they want now? And how are they getting through the crowd so easily?"

"I have no idea." Tennie sighed and shook her head. "Perhaps they know one of the police officers? I can't fathom what they are playing at. The first time they simply listened to the conversation in the room then left. The second time they wanted to know how Central was doing, so I consulted the tape and told them. That was it. The funny thing is each time they come in, they've changed something about their clothes or appearance. It's like they believe we won't recognize them."

"I can't decide if they are smitten with one or both of us or are simply crazy."

"Neither can I. I thought about having them barred from entry, but how would that look if, on our first day, we denied legitimate customers access to our office? The press would eat that up."

I rubbed my temples and closed my eyes, relishing the brief moment of calm. I opened them again when the doorman cleared his throat, trailed by a man of six feet with voluminous gray hair and a full beard.

"Mr. Walt Whitman to see you," the doorman said with a bow.

When the poet's gray eyes met mine, the blood drained from my face, and I grasped the desk as a wave of dizzy unreality overtook me. Here, standing before me, was a great man of letters, one of my personal favorites. I stood on shaky fawn's legs, maintaining my hold on the desk so I could remain upright and he wouldn't see my hands shaking.

"Mrs. Woodhull, Miss Claflin." Mr. Whitman greeted each of us with a slight bow. He removed his hat, tracing the brim with his fingers as he spoke. "It is a pleasure to meet the women who are shaking up Wall Street."

Tennie recovered her composure first, quickly rounding her desk and guiding him to a chair. "Please have a seat, Mr. Whitman."

I winced as Tennie poked me in the ribs before sitting on the couch opposite.

"My sister and I are both great fans of your writing, especially *Leaves of Grass*. Isn't that right, Victoria?"

"Oh yes. We used to read it to one another every night when we were growing up. It was one of the few books our mother owned."

Mr. Whitman smiled at me kindly. "What was your favorite poem?"

"There are so many to choose from—" Tennie began.

"'I Hear America Singing,' without a doubt," I cut her off. "I love how you show us the dignity of the working man through your words." I dropped my gaze to my sweaty palms in my lap, too embarrassed to make eye contact with my idol while talking about my past. "We were raised poor, you see. So your words made us feel valued." When I raised my eyes, I found his were twinkling with joy, encouraging me to continue. "Your sense of individual worth always resonated so strongly with me. I too believe each person is a beautiful combination of body and soul, both of which are worthy of praise and respect. But listen to me rambling. You came here to visit us, not to listen to me wax philosophical about your poetry." My cheeks grew warm with embarrassment.

"No trouble at all. It gives me great joy to hear how others have been affected by my work. To be praised is an honor, sure, but to know one's words have changed lives is the true reward of art." After a moment of silence, Mr. Whitman continued. "I read with great interest your impetus for becoming stockbrokers. With that act, you succeeded where so many preachers have failed. You embody what you teach to others. You"—he made a gesture that encompassed Tennie as well—"are representative women. Whether you realize it or not, you are showing women everywhere what they are capable of." He reached into his coat pocket and produced a folded piece of paper. "I wrote a short poem for you to commemorate this occasion. Would you like to hear it?"

"Of course," I breathed, unable to believe my ears and still blushing furiously under his praise.

Mr. Whitman cleared his throat. "'I came here to see two great children of nature / in this swarming vortex of life. / You have given an object lesson to the whole world. / You are a prophecy of the future.'"

My eyes filled with tears, and I wiped at them. I wouldn't cry in front of such an elegant man, but I could not help myself. He truly understood me and all that I was aiming for.

"Thank you, thank you so much," was all I could say through my tears. Though it was not proper, I rose and embraced him. It was the only way I could express what his kindness meant to me.

He clasped my hands. "You are an example to us all. I look forward to watching your star rise." Then he held up the page covered in his elegant scrawl. "Would you like to keep this as a memento of the day you turned the financial world on its ear?" His bushy eyebrows lifted with mirth.

I laughed, tears drying to streaks. "Yes, please. Will you do me a favor and autograph it?" I plucked the gold pen from behind my ear and reached for a vial of ink.

Mr. Whitman and Tennie chatted as he signed the page, and I slowly regained my composure. Far too soon, the bell at the back door chimed, and Tennie excused herself to see to the new client. Mr. Whitman and I exchanged a few more words as I escorted him to the front door.

"I was serious about wishing you well," Mr. Whitman said. "I will scan the headlines with great eagerness to find your name, as I'm sure I will."

When we reached the front door, we paused.

"I would like to call on you whenever I visit New York." He nodded to James, who was standing in the doorway of his office. "That is, of course, if your husband has no objections."

James shook the older man's hand heartily. "It would be an honor to have you in our home. Thank you so much for your visit today."

Once the farewells had been said, I floated back to my desk, where I safely tucked away the poem. I would put it in my clippings book alongside copies of the newspaper articles mentioning Tennie and me.

But first, I had work to attend to. The day had generated a mountain of paperwork, more than the three of us could hope to finish before dinner, but we made a go of it between the trickle of remaining visitors. When the shade was pulled on the front door at four o'clock, we were still filling out forms and creating files for new clients. My head popped up as the doorman's voice reached us from the porch.

"I'm sorry, gentlemen, but it is after business hours. If you have any orders to give to Mrs. Woodhull or Miss Claflin, they will gladly be received after nine o'clock on Monday morning. Good eve to you."

Tennie snickered. "Our two admirers must have come back."

I nodded. "That reminds me, we should tip our doorman extra for his fine work today. If those two don't soon weary of our office, I'm hiring him as security."

"COLONEL BLOOD! COLONEL BLOOD! Come quickly!"

I woke in the dead of night the following week to Katherine's harried shouts amid an insistent banging on our door.

While I rubbed my heavy eyes, James slipped into his robe and let in the woman. "Katherine?"

She gulped in air. "There are men downstairs. Say your firm's been burglared."

By the time James, Tennie, and I dressed and arrived on Wall Street, the constable was there, along with a handful of policemen, which was surprising given the police normally didn't rouse themselves from bed for such a minor offense. Our association with Mr. Vanderbilt must have increased the urgency. All were examining the damage to the shattered front window and splintered doorframe, shaking their heads and muttering.

"What happened?" I asked.

"Looks like vandalism," the constable said. "One of the night watch noticed smoke coming from inside and broke the door in to try to put it out."

"Smoke?" Tennie cried. "Is everything ruined?"

"No, no, it was a small fire, not well set. Our man doused it. But there was other damage inside." He gestured into the dark office with a lantern. "Have a look."

I took the light and nudged past the men at the door to survey what remained of my once-pristine office. A brick lay on the floor inside the front window, shards of glass glinting around it like stars. Our precious busts were no more than piles of marble and dust in the corners, while the sofas and chairs bled stuffing from deep gashes in the upholstery. The ticker machine was smashed to bits, gears, metal, and screws trailing out of the broken glass dome like entrails from a gutted pig.

When I reached our desks, I froze. Tennie's was charred and dripping, a craggy patch of black on the surface indicating where the fire had been set and later extinguished. A glint of light drew my eye to my desk, and my breath caught. Bathed in a circle of moonlight in the center was a butcher's knife, forcefully impaled in the wood. Breathing in the lingering traces of burned paper, I moved slowly toward the weapon as if it might spring to life and stab me of its own accord. I hovered over it, taking in the six words written in bold black strokes on a note pinioned to the wood: *The hearth is a woman's place.*

I removed the note with trembling fingers, ripping the paper rather than touch the knife. Heavy footfalls echoed behind me.

"I suppose you've seen this?" I asked the constable.

"We have."

I retraced my steps, joining James and Tennie in the front office. "Someone certainly took umbrage to our opening day." I held up the note so Tennie and James could read it.

"It was that unnerving Mr. Edward Van Schalck. I just know it. He and his friends were in and out of here all day, acting like loons," Tennie told the officer. "What other explanation is there?"

"It could have been anyone," James said gently. "There were plenty of protesters outside too."

"We'll look into Mr. Van Schalck," the officer assured Tennie.

"May I keep this?" I asked, holding up the note. My fingers itched to crumple it up or rip it to pieces, but that was what the perpetrators expected of me. I had another use in mind.

"Yes." The officer's voice was wary.

"This is a reminder of what we face and what we will overcome," I said, answering his unspoken question of why I would want to keep such a thing. "Tennie, send this to Johnny and see that the papers cover it well. Our clients need to know we've had a jolt but we will not let this defeat us. Frighten us momentarily, yes, but we will not let one tantrum by a jealous man—or group of men—change our business." I signaled to one of the night watchmen. "Go to Mr. Vanderbilt's home at dawn and tell him what took place here. Tell him also that we plan to be open for business as usual."

Back on Great Jones Street, sleep was fickle, teasing me into heavy-lidded exhaustion, but my memories of the damage and imagined fears never allowed the full release of slumber. Before I knew it, we were at the brokerage once more.

The damage was much less threatening by the light of day. By noon, Mr. Vanderbilt already had our furniture replaced and had arranged for one of his men to sleep in the office at night in case there was any more trouble. The only signs of last night's break-in were the boarded-up front window, which was being repaired at that very moment, and the gash in the desk I refused to trade in for a new one. I wanted to see it every day, to remember we had persevered.

Business was brisk, especially with word having spread about the break-in. While Katherine watched Zula and Byron, Tennie and I answered questions about what had happened and assured clients of our well-being and intent to continue on as though nothing had taken place. In some ways, the vandals had done us a favor, bringing in more traffic than we would have attracted on our own.

We remained after closing time, finally having the time to review the coverage of our momentous debut.

"Look at these headlines," Tennie crowed. "They are calling us the 'Queens of Finance' and the 'Sensation of New York.'"

"Did you see this one?" James called out from the front office. "'The extraordinary coolness and self-possession and evident knowledge of the intricacies of the difficult role they have undertaken is far more remarkable than their personal beauty and graces of manner, and these are considerable.'"

"I can't believe how many reporters are shocked that we have wits in our heads." I searched for a particular paper and, after finding it, snapped it open. "This one, for example, seems surprised that we can speak of financial matters intelligently and spends more space describing our clothes and figures than our business." I reached for another. "The highest compliment this one could muster was that we are 'straightforward, well-bred American women who were perfectly capable of taking care of themselves in the dangerous byways of Wall Street.' They make it sound as though we enter a war every time we open the front door."

James was standing in the doorway, leaning against the frame. He frowned. "In a way, you do. You are still the enemy. Your very presence threatens all men and the territory they've carved out for themselves. Look at what happened last night. Doesn't that scare you?"

I gave a small, bitter laugh. "Of course it does. But if I gave in to everything that scared me, I would have died the first time my father hit me or when I had my children or when we moved here or any of a thousand times in between. I have faith in the spirits and barrel through adversity. It's the only way I know how to survive."

"We will defeat the naysayers with our mighty golden pens," Tennie declared, wielding her pen like a sword.

I mirrored her gesture with my own. "Or die trying."

CHAPTER FIFTEEN

MARCH 1870

Slowly, life on Wall Street developed its own rhythm. Every morning, Tennie and I rode to the brokerage in a carriage with white horses and red velvet seats just like the male brokers. We opened the office doors at nine, completed what work we could, and began seeing clients when trading began at ten.

"Thank you, Mr. Alley," I said as I walked one of our most prominent clients to the front door. "We appreciate your business as always. I will make your purchase as soon as I am back at my desk."

"It is always a pleasure seeing you, Mrs. Woodhull," the older man said. "If you don't mind, I'll have a chat with your husband while I wait for my friend to finish his business." He gestured over my shoulder.

I turned. Mr. Abram Baylis was deep in conversation with my father. Pa was not allowed to give the clients financial advice, so what could the two have been talking about so earnestly? I edged closer.

"Blasted knee pains me in chilly weather," Mr. Baylis was saying.

"It's an old war wound. Makes a right mess of my hunting plans when I cannot mount a horse."

"Never you worry, sir. I know just the thing to help you." Buck slid open the bottom drawer of his desk.

I inched forward, craning my neck to see over Mr. Baylis's shoulder. Half a dozen dark glass bottles gleamed in the light. I scowled. They were the same as the ones I'd seen in my father's shop a year and a half before. I *would not* have him peddling that slop from my office.

"All you need to do is take a swing of this before eating, and you'll find you're back to your old self," Buck said, lifting out a bottle.

I intercepted it before Mr. Baylis could take it and turned to him with a tight smile. "Forgive me, but my father sometimes fancies himself a doctor. A nip of whiskey or brandy will likely have the same effect—they are the main ingredients." I steered my flabbergasted client to the door, taking Mr. Alley's arm as I passed him. "Thank you both for your patronage. I or my sister will be in touch when we have news of your stock."

Once the door shut, I let the smile fall from my face. "You two-bit scoundrel! How dare you try to sell your swill right under my nose? Do you have any idea how hard Tennie and I worked to get here? One whiff of impropriety and we'll all be ruined."

"Now, Vickie, I—" Pa stood, hands in front of his chest in a defensive position. His voice was calm, but his expression was black.

"No, save your excuses. I never should have let Tennie convince me to let you work here."

"Is that any way to treat your ol' pa? I should take you over my knee right here. Don't think yourself too grown or too important."

Tennie and James came out of their respective offices, drawn by the commotion.

"What's going on here?" James asked. "Did I hear you threaten my wife with violence? Because if so, you will have to contend with me." He slid between Pa and me.

Pa sat back down. "I only meant she should show some respect."

"For what?" I cried. "For you taking advantage of our generosity?"

"Now, Vickie," Tennie said, coming up behind me and placing calming hands on my shoulders, "Pa was just trying to earn some extra cash."

"We pay him plenty and not so he can humbug our customers. I want no more of this."

"What else do you want me to do? You won't let me do any lawyering or talk about money. Should I count the grains in the wood of my desk?"

"He has a point," Tennie said. "We need to find him something meaningful to do."

I threw up my hands. I was trying to get my father out of the firm altogether, but Tennie kept getting in the way. I looked around for something that would take up his time but not give him the opportunity to cause mischief.

The door opened, and a man laden with two large canvas bags entered. "Postal delivery. Where would you like these?" The letter carrier gestured with his head to the bags. Each one likely carried more mail than he saw in a typical day, but everyone wanted to contact the Lady Brokers.

"Right here," Tennie said, pointing at Buck's desk. "You can sort mail, right, Pa?"

Buck stood so he could see over the mail bags. "I used to be postmaster. I most certainly can." He threw me a triumphant look.

I pointed at my father. "No more snake oil. If I catch you selling even the smallest jar of cream or giving any medical advice, you are out. Do you hear me?"

Buck nodded.

James grabbed him by the collar. "And if you ever threaten my wife again, you'll be looking at the inside of a coffin."

※

EVERY EVENING AFTER THE firm closed, Tennie and I dined out with James. So when he was called out of town to help his brother, I thought nothing of suggesting Tennie and I take our evening meal at Delmonico's, a favorite haunt of local brokers.

We were seated with the utmost decorum, as befitted a place of its renown and class. A waiter filled our water glasses, took our drink orders, and retreated, giving us time to choose our meals.

"Tomato soup to begin?" Tennie suggested. "Cornelius raves about it. Says it is the best in town, and he rarely compliments anything."

"Yes, that sounds lovely. With pheasant and then custard pie for dessert."

Feeling a presence at my side, I looked up, expecting to see the waiter ready to take our order. But to my surprise, Lorenzo Delmonico himself stood next to me.

"My dear Mrs. Woodhull and Miss Claflin, so wonderful to see you again," he greeted us with a warm smile. "My sincere congratulations on the success of your business."

"Thank you, Mr. Delmonico." Tennie smiled sweetly.

His face turned grave. "I'm afraid an error has been made in seating you. We assumed a gentleman was joining you."

I shook my head. Why should that have mattered? "No, it is only us."

Mr. Delmonico gestured for us to rise. "No matter. Pretend to be talking to me, and I'll walk out the door with you. Then people will think you only came to speak to me. That will make the situation appear proper."

"Make what look proper?" I asked.

"I can't let you eat here without a man. It would start an awful precedent."

"Don't let us embarrass you," Tennie said with a small snort of disbelief before throwing down her napkin and marching outside.

"You do understand, don't you, Mrs. Woodhull?" Mr. Delmonico clasped his hands together in a pleading gesture, as if willing me to agree with him.

"No, not at all. I understand that you are a traditional establishment, but to deny two paying customers who have done nothing to earn your ire except dare to be female is in the height of bad taste."

Tennie returned, dragging behind her our reluctant coachman, out of place amid the dark suits in his scarlet coat and leather boots. She shoved him into the seat next to her. "We are buying you dinner tonight." She stared at Mr. Delmonico with a defiant sparkle in her eye, daring him to escort us out now.

He stepped back, clearly fuming but not willing to make a scene. I motioned to the waiter. "We shall have tomato soup for three."

❧

THE FLUSTERED COACHMAN REMAINED silent throughout the meal even when I smoothed out a copy of the sporting paper *Days Doings* and pointed at a cartoon of Tennie and myself, asking him, "Which one of us do you think they've captured best today?"

Tennie nudged him in the side. "Come on, Joe. You must have an opinion." She cocked her head and studied the drawing. "They have shortened the length of my skirt yet again. Look at all that exposed ankle."

"I look like a shrew." I laughed. In truth, the cartoons were humiliating, but laughing at them was the easiest way I had found to cope. I'd rather have done that than cry as the illustrators had intended. "But this one is better than most lately."

We put away the papers when the waiter arrived with our dessert. The coachman begged off, expressing his gratitude, and quickly slipped outside.

"I suppose I embarrassed the poor fellow. It never occurred to me that it would be difficult for him to eat in public with us." Tennie shrugged. "Ah, well, we were allowed to stay, weren't we?"

I glanced around, relieved no one had yet noticed our table was once again females only. "They may never allow us in again, but yes, you made your point."

Before I had a chance to crack the surface of my custard, a portly, balding man with gold spectacles perched on his nose approached our table.

"Mrs. Woodhull, Miss Claflin, good evening."

"Good evening, Mr. Greeley," I greeted the newspaper editor, eyeing an older man standing several steps behind him. "To what do we owe the pleasure?"

"Ah." He gestured to the stranger. "I was having dinner with a former colleague of mine, and he asked for an introduction. This is Mr. Stephen Pearl Andrews, author, reformer, and utopian leader. Mr. Andrews, Mrs. Victoria Woodhull and Miss Tennessee Claflin, distinguished lady brokers."

I presented my hand to the imposing older man, studying him closely as he took it. He may have been handsome once. Behind his bushy hermit's beard, his skin was clear though wrinkled with age, and his eyes—oh, they were captivating—were a deep, serious brown that hinted at the secrets of the universe. When he smiled, they lit with an inner fire that may have been the force of creation itself.

"You forgot to add that Mrs. Woodhull is an up-and-comer in the women's movement. I read all about you in the *Revolution*. Tell me"— he released my hand—"how did Miss Anthony treat you during your interview? She can be such a shrew, but her article gave the impression she liked you well enough."

"Would you like to join us?" Tennie asked, gesturing to the two empty chairs at our table. "We'd love your company."

I bit back a smile as the men seated themselves. Tennie was an incorrigible flirt. "To answer your question, Mr. Andrews—"

"Please, call me Stephen. We are among friends here, are we not?"

"Stephen," I amended. "I found her to be pleasant enough, though a little cold and severe in appearance. I am ever grateful for the kind words she wrote about us. They will do much to secure our place in the movement."

"Indeed." Stephen signaled the waiter to bring him a brandy. "What was it she said?" He glanced upward, feigning thought. "Ah yes. 'These two ladies, for they are ladies, are determined to use their brains, energy, and their knowledge of business to earn them a livelihood. This woman firm in Wall Street marks a new era.'"

Tennie gave a little giggle. "My, you have a remarkable memory, Stephen."

"I make it a point to commit to memory that which is important. So tell me, Mrs. Woodhull, what are your plans to advance the women's movement?"

"Well, Miss Anthony did ask us to officially join the movement.

I told her we needed to get our firm established first, but once we do, she will see what we will do for the rights of our sex."

"What do you mean by that?" Mr. Greeley asked. His eyes were narrowed, lip slightly upturned, and his nose wrinkled as though he smelled something offensive.

Was he put off by the idea or merely curious? Either way, I'd best choose my words carefully. "Well, we need the vote of course. It's our constitutional right. But it doesn't end there. I've worked with women on many levels of society and have clearly seen that we need rights within marriage as well. Otherwise a wife is no better off than a common prostitute, for both trade their bodies for some assurance of material comfort."

Mr. Greeley's mouth dropped open, and he struggled to form a response but was interrupted by Stephen, who clapped and hooted loudly.

"Yes. This is exactly the kind of thinking we need. I've been saying for years that individual rights are key to our country's future. Taking the idea deeper to the level of the individual woman is pure genius. Victoria—may I call you Victoria?"

I nodded.

"I am so glad old Horace here introduced us. I think we shall be great friends. May I call upon you sometime? I have many things of immense importance which I want to communicate, and I believe you are exactly the person to help me do so."

Stephen made good on his word by calling upon us the very next night and nearly every day for the following month until he was a regular fixture in our rooms at Great Jones Street. When I wasn't working in the brokerage, I spent my free hours with him and James, discussing matters of women's rights, social theory, and reform. Those conversations were among my happiest moments, for

I was finally among people to whom I could speak freely without fear of reprisal and who, in turn, could expose me to a wider world that would enrich my mind and strengthen my resolve to run for the presidency. I scarcely dared to admit it even to myself, but I had begun to believe that Demosthenes was right; I might yet live up to my queenly name.

Stephen's presence meant I also had the opportunity to get to know his wife, Ester. The tall, olive-skinned woman had the wild curly locks of a gypsy and expressive black eyes. She was also a Spiritualist and magnetic healer with impressive skills in trance communication. I took an immediate liking to Ester when we clasped hands upon meeting and the woman's light and buoyant energy filled me.

Given our shared ability to speak to the spirits, it was only natural to invite Ester to our weekly séances, which were conducted in Katherine's darkened parlor, where the windows let in wide silver swaths from the moon.

I took a seat at a small rectangular table, James on my right. Next to him was Tennie, then Stephen. Ester, who insisted on serving as medium, was seated across from me, the chair to her left vacant, reserved for any spirit who might make contact. The table was bare save for a single sheet of paper upon which the twenty-six letters of the alphabet were written.

"My methods for communing with the spirits are different from those used by our fair hostess," Ester said. "I follow the traditions laid out by the Fox sisters, the first Spiritualists. Do not be alarmed. Everything I do is perfectly harmless." Ester looked at each person in turn. "If we are all ready, please join hands."

I took Ester and James's hands, laying them palm up on the tabletop.

"Spirits, we call upon you in humility. If anyone here this night would like to speak with us, please make your presence known," Ester said, her voice carrying throughout the room.

It was more difficult than I expected to be an observer when I was used to being in control. Even though I wasn't the channel, I could not turn off my otherworldly senses. Spirits were all around us; I felt maybe a dozen or more. Most were simply curious, but there was one strong tug directed toward Ester. This spirit wished to speak. No sooner had I thought it than I felt a shift in the air pressure at my side like the charging of the atmosphere before a thunderstorm; the chair across from me was no longer empty.

A single loud knock split the quiet.

James and Tennie jumped.

"Ah, yes. Someone is indeed willing." Ester smiled. "Spirit, we welcome you. Is there someone here for whom you have a message?"

Another knock.

"Is it for one of the men?"

Two knocks.

"No. For Tennie?"

Two more knocks.

"For Victoria?"

A single knock.

I looked at James, puzzled. What spirit would choose to speak to me through another medium? Why not come to me directly? As if understanding my thoughts, he shrugged and gave my hand a reassuring squeeze.

"What is your name?"

Ester barely finished asking the question before the paper skittered across the table toward the empty chair. The medium reached forward, her fingers touching letters at an astonishing speed.

Stephen called out the letters in turn. "R-A-C-H-E-L."

"Welcome, Rachel. Victoria, does that name have meaning for you?" Ester asked.

I blinked a moment, still in shock. "Yes. She, Rachel Scribner, was my childhood neighbor. She took care of me when my parents did not. I"—I choked back the memory of a narrow bed in a hot, suffocating room—"I was there when she died." But why approach me now, after all these years? And why could I not see her?

Another rap. An affirmation?

"What is your message for Victoria, Rachel?"

Ester's hand flew across the page, spelling out words, pausing, then spelling out more.

"She's going too fast," Stephen cried. "I can't keep up."

"Neither can I," the medium said.

Suddenly, Ester's hand fell to her side, limp. Her eyelids fluttered then closed. Her head tipped forward.

"She's going into a trance," Stephen put out a hand to stop Tennie, who had started to rise. "I've seen it before. It will be all right. Rachel must have more to convey than she can do in letters."

Ester raised her head and opened her eyes.

I gasped. Gone were the laugh lines around Ester's mouth. Gone too were the furrows in her brow. This was the face of a much younger woman. And her eyes, oh, how they sparkled with joy I had not seen since I was five years old. Ester's body may have been in front of me, but Rachel was looking out of her eyes.

"Victoria, how you have grown." Even Ester's voice was different—higher, softer, suffused with pride. "I have been watching you, have missed nothing."

Tears streamed down my face. How much I wanted to go to her, to kneel at Ester's knee as I had with Rachel when I was young, to feel her loving caress again. I fought back the urge. To break the circle would mean releasing Rachel's spirit before we heard the reason for her visitation.

"I come here tonight with a warning," Rachel/Ester stated. "Beware the Judas kiss. One of your own blood will betray you."

Others may have been frightened at such a pronouncement, but I nearly laughed. I didn't need the spirit world to tell me the Claflins were trouble. That was a lesson hard learned long ago. Still, Rachel had her reasons for crossing to this side, so I should learn all I could.

"What will this person do? For what should I be watchful?" I asked.

"Guard your secrets well lest they return to haunt you."

The others fidgeted in their seats, but I could not look away.

Rachel watched me with maternal compassion. "I am proud of you, daughter. Be strong on your journey, resolute as the pioneers who settled this land. Your name will not be forgotten."

I closed my eyes and smiled. When I opened them again, Rachel was gone and Ester was beginning to stir.

All night, I relived my time with Rachel, turning the prophecy over and over in my mind and repeating every word the spirit had said to me. By morning, the dire prediction was still in the corner of my mind, but it was my caretaker's charge to be resolute that I felt most keenly.

Emboldened by the support from the spirit world, I made a decision I'd been toying with for months. Today I would change a woman's life. It may have only been one, but I had to start somewhere. I paid Madame de Ford a visit.

"My dear, I wasn't expecting to see you here. What may I do for you?" she asked as we sat in her office, sipping tea.

I shifted in my seat. What I had to propose was not easy, and I was unsure of Madame de Ford's reaction. "How much does Minnie still owe you on her contract?" I tried to sound casual, as though this was only of passing interest.

Madame de Ford's bushy gray eyebrows rose. She set down her teacup in its saucer and pushed it away. She placed both arms on the surface of her desk, dark eyes boring into me. "That is between her and me. What business is it of yours?"

I bristled at Madame de Ford's coldness. So be it. If she was going to be frank, I would too. "I would like to buy her out of her contract. With my financial business, I am able to spend less and less time at home, and my son needs someone to care for him while my daughter is in school. Our landlady watches him now as a favor to me, but that cannot continue indefinitely."

Madame de Ford considered my words. "Why Minnie?"

I shrugged. "I've always had a fondness for the girl, and she has a sweet temperament that I think would suit Byron's needs well."

"Does she know of your son's condition? What if she refuses?"

"Then you've lost nothing and we can pretend this conversation never took place."

"How much are you offering?"

"What is left on her contract plus half to make up for your temporary loss of a worker."

Madame de Ford clenched and unclenched her jaw as she thought this over. Finally, she called one of her girls to fetch Minnie. The girl arrived quickly, shoulders bent and eyes downcast as though she expected a punishment.

"Oh, don't look so dour, girl. I'm not about to send you to the gallows."

Minnie dared look up then, meeting Madame de Ford's eyes.

"Mrs. Woodhull has something she would like to ask you."

I turned to Minnie. "How would you like to work for me?"

Minnie wrinkled her brow. "Doing what, ma'am? Are you opening your own house?"

Of course the girl would think that. This was the only work she had ever known.

I shook my head. "I need someone to care for my son. He is a few years older than you but has the mind of a young child and he cannot speak, though he has ways of communicating you will learn in time. But he is the sweetest child you will ever meet."

"So I would be a caretaker to him?"

"And a companion, yes. You will be paid well for your services."

Minnie looked to Madame de Ford. "What about my contract?"

"Mrs. Woodhull is taking care of that. You will leave here in no debt to me."

Minnie turned back to me, her eyes shining. "You would do this for me? With no conditions?"

"None," I promised. "You would be free to quit if you find the work is not suitable for you."

Minnie nodded, suppressing a smile. "Yes, I will work for you."

I breathed a sigh of relief, and Madame de Ford did the same, only hers was of resignation.

"Go pack your things, Minnie, while Mrs. Woodhull and I finish our business here," she said.

That night, when Minnie was tucked safely into bed with Tennie, and Zula and Byron were asleep in their room, I turned to my husband, who lay awake beside me. I wanted to talk about Minnie, to make sure he was comfortable having yet another person in our rapidly expanding household. Plus, I wanted to broach a few delicate subjects with him.

"That was a fine thing you did for Minnie today," James said as though reading my thoughts. "But we cannot expect her to sleep in the same bed with Tennie forever. We should probably look into finding a house of our own, especially if our family continues to grow. We have Minnie now, and Stephen is here more often than not. We can't impose on Katherine's hospitality much longer no matter how much we pay her."

"You make a good point. Plus, my father has been hinting that my family needs a better place to live." My entire family—mother, father, brothers, sisters, and their spouses and children—were all crammed into two rooms, sleeping atop one another like flowers crushed in a child's poesy. "He is right. With all of our good fortune, the least we can do is buy them a house or find one of our own that is large enough for them to live in as well."

James grumbled, "I don't like the idea of your family living with us. Your mother already thinks I steal from you. Now with Ester's prophesy, it seems like too much risk."

I turned my head so I could face him. "You think I don't see that? They will be in our home all the time anyway. They are like ants. Once one gets in, you can be sure the rest of the colony will follow. The only way we could escape them completely is to move out of the city, and that didn't work out too well when we came here. Plus, if they live with us, we will be paying for only one home."

"But it is not as though we are short on money."

I sat up. "No, but I've been thinking of other possible uses for our funds. All this talk with you and Stephen has made me want to take action. Hiring Minnie was a small first step, a way I could affect change here, in our lives. Now I want to expand, to work on behalf of all women. I want to prevent as many as possible from feeling the shame and sting of abuse."

James levered himself into a sitting position as well. "What are you thinking?"

"It will be years before I can work my way up in the suffrage movement, and even then, I doubt Miss Anthony or Mrs. Stanton will concede their leadership positions before death claims them. While I still wish to work with them, I've thought of a way of going around them as well. If women want true rights, women need to be in power, yes?"

James nodded slowly, as if wary of agreeing too openly until he heard me out.

"Well, I've already broken one barrier to women by opening our firm and showing we can be successful in business. Why not in politics as well? We've made plenty of connections."

"You are saying you wish to run for office?" James's voice was skeptical.

"Yes." I bit my lip and took in a deep breath. I let it out with a puff before continuing. "But not just any office. The one that can truly affect change." I clasped his hands. "Do you remember the night Demosthenes instructed us to come to New York? He said I was named for a queen and that I would become queen of this land. James, it's time. I want to run for president."

CHAPTER SIXTEEN

APRIL 1870

Scarcely a fortnight passed between James's first spluttering of "You want to *what?*" and my formal announcement of my candidacy for president. Each time I explained my reasons, along with my qualifications, it came down to the same set of basic points. Tired of repeating myself, I set them down in the first of a number of columns contracted in the *New York Herald*—thanks to Tennie's relationship with Johnny.

"You couldn't ask for better timing," Stephen assured me when I voiced uncertainty about announcing my candidacy two and a half years before the election. "The suffrage movement is badly divided right now. Lucy Stone, Henry Ward Beecher, and their ilk want to step back and take the fight state by state, while Miss Anthony and her group are forging ahead with their national strategy. They need someone who is neutral to step in and lead them on a path that can bring both sides back together. Whoever can do that will have the attention of the whole country. And if you don't do it soon, Anna Dickinson will beat you to it. She's already got Theodore Tilton's support to be the leader of a unified party."

In my mind, I sneered Anna Dickinson's name. The woman already had everything I'd ever wanted. She was a famous lecturer on women's issues and could command sold-out audiences from the East Coast to the wilds of the West. I'd be damned before I'd let that blue-blooded pompkin beat me to the head of the women's movement. What reason could Anna have to want to lead us? She certainly didn't understand how the law oppressed women. She wasn't even married. How could she understand? But I knew all too well. Women deserved to have a leader who was not only passionate and well-informed, for any fool could become so, but one who had experienced the pain and degradation we were fighting against.

"You're right. Whether or not men wish to admit it, women's suffrage will be the issue of the next election. The Republicans have yet to put forth a rallying topic since their abolition victory, and the Democrats seem not to care about anything. If we can force the issue, we can capture the voters."

Stephen nodded. "It will be all the stronger because you are a woman. I'm pleased at how fast you are learning the political landscape."

Over the next few days, I expanded upon what I wished to say. Then James and Stephen gave it a finishing finesse, molding my ideas into the type of language the public was used to seeing from political candidates and adding the basis of what would become my platform—formalities far beyond my knowledge, at least at that point.

When I opened the paper on Saturday, April 4, before office hours began at the firm, my heart swelled with pride. There was my soul's desire in black and white under the headline, "The Coming Woman:

Victoria C. Woodhull to Race for the White House – What She Will and What She Won't Do."

"As I happen to be the most prominent representative of the only unrepresented class in the republic, and perhaps the most practical exponent of the principles of equality, I request the favor of being permitted to address the public through the Herald. While others of my sex devoted themselves to a crusade against the laws that shackle the women of the country, I asserted my individual independence; while others prayed for the good time coming, I worked for it; while others argued the equality of woman with man, I proved it by successfully engaging in business; while others sought to show that there was no valid reason why women should be treated, socially and politically, as being inferior to man, I boldly entered the arena of politics and business and exercised the rights I already possessed. I therefore claim the right to speak for the unenfranchised women of the country, and believing as I do that the prejudices which still exist in the popular mind against women in public life will soon disappear, I now announce myself as a candidate for the presidency.

"I am well aware that in assuming this position, I shall evoke more ridicule than enthusiasm at the outset. But this is an epoch of sudden changes and startling surprises. What may appear absurd today will assume a serious aspect tomorrow. I am content to wait until my claim for recognition as a candidate shall receive the calm consideration of the press and the public. The blacks were cattle in 1860; a Negro now sits in Jeff Davis's seat in the United States Senate. The sentiment of the country was,

even in 1863, against Negro suffrage; now the Negro's right to vote is acknowledged by the Constitution of the United States. Let those, therefore, who ridiculed the Negro's claim to exercise the right to 'life, liberty, and the pursuit of happiness,' and who lived to see him vote and hold high public office, ridicule the aspirations of the women of the country for complete political equality as much as they please. They cannot roll back the rising tide of reform. The world moves.

"All that has been said and written hitherto in support of equality for women has had its proper effect on the public mind, just as the anti-slavery speeches before secession were effective; but a candidate and a policy are required to prove it. My candidature for the presidency will, I confidently expect, develop the fact that the principles of equal rights for all have taken deep root. The advocates of political equality for women have, besides a respectable known strength, a great undercurrent of unexpressed power, which is only awaiting a fit opportunity to express itself.

"The simple issue of whether woman should not only have this complete political equality with the Negro is the only one to be tried, and none more important is likely to arise before the presidential election. These important changes can only be expected to follow a complete departure from the beaten tracks of political parties and their machinery; and this, I believe, my canvass of 1872 will affect. I have deliberately and of my own accord placed myself before the people as a candidate for the Presidency of the United States, and having the means, courage, energy and strength necessary for the race, intend to contest it to the close."

It was done. It was there for the whole country to read. A woman was running for president. And not any woman—one who had a history of breaking down barriers in the very halls men held sacred and would like to cement them out of.

Some men would snicker and dismiss me as yet another crazy suffragist, while others may see me as an object of curiosity to be watched simply for my oddity. Then some would hate me for this simple act, for daring to do what many would never consider—and several of those may well have been my clients.

My stomach clenched as I considered the implications on my fledgling business. I had been so caught up in the glory of declaring myself a candidate I hadn't stopped to think I may hurt Tennie, not to mention our main source of income. What if dissenters broke into the firm again or worse?

My burst of anxiety was temporarily assuaged when I read the highly favorable editorial the *Herald* had printed along with my letter, supporting the Sixteenth Amendment and encouraging women to vote for me. That was a major coup; to have the backing of a major paper upon declaring my candidacy went a long way in establishing myself as a legitimate candidate.

I likely would be receiving visitors and well-wishers all day, in addition to the usual clients, so if I was going to reply, I had to do it now. I picked up a pen and tried to order my thoughts of gratitude to the paper and its editor. Normally I would have had James rewrite it in his more elegant hand, but I wished them to know this one was genuine. When finished, I signed it as I would all other documents from this moment forward: Victoria C. Woodhull, Future Presidentess.

Three days later, we embraced another much needed change as James, Zula, Byron, Tennie, Minnie, and I bid Great Jones Street farewell and moved a few blocks north to a mansion in the fashionable, moneyed Murray Hill neighborhood.

I chose the four-story brownstone at 15 East Thirty-Eighth Street between Madison and Fifth because it was the tallest on the block, as befit the home of a queen. Set apart from its neighbors by a generous plot of land, the house was surrounded by oak, maple, and pine trees so tall and thick they likely had memories pre-dating the Revolutionary War. Sprawling before them was an oval garden dotted with carefully maintained flowers in their first budding of the spring: cheerful yellow and white jonquils; clusters of purple, white, and gold crocus; and spikes of fragrant hyacinth.

We emerged from the carriage at the foot of two staircases that fanned out from a granite foundation to lead upward toward the massive black walnut door. Scrolling wrought-iron banisters led the eye upward toward two ten-foot parlor windows with black walnut sashes. Above them were twin balconies jutting out from the stone façade, supported by Corinthian columns.

Standing on the staircases in formal lines, six on each side, was the household staff Mr. Vanderbilt had helped us secure: a tall, thin man with regal bearing; an equally tall younger woman who had the serious posture and tightly wound bun of a schoolmarm; a plump woman with wild blond curls tucked beneath a chef's cap; two young girls who clustered around her like assistants; half a dozen maids and footmen; and a man I guessed was a gardener.

"Welcome to your new home, Colonel Blood, Mrs. Woodhull," the tall man greeted us like a steward of old. "I am Mr. Cross, your butler." He gestured to the woman next to him. "This is Helena Beauchamp, your housekeeper."

Tennie poked me in the side. "Who would have thought these two country bumpkins would have a dozen servants by age thirty? Momma's gonna faint when she sees this."

After introducing the rest of the staff, Mr. Cross led us inside. Though I had been on a brief tour of the house before James signed our lease, this was the first time I was truly at leisure to marvel in the luxury that was now mine, decorated according to my exacting instructions. The entryway of polished marble with its white, green, carmine blue, and gold frescoed ceiling depicting satyrs, cupids, seraphs, and the old Greek gods feasting in their heaven along with gilded mirrors and gold-and-crystal chandeliers combined what I liked most about Mr. Vanderbilt's classic style with the French extravagance of Miss Woods's parlor. Light filtered down through a pale stained-glass dome in the center, casting rainbows willy-nilly on the walls and floor.

The parlor was one of the largest rooms, its patterned violet-and-cream curtains giving way to deep blue silk-covered couches and chairs. Niches in each corner boasted marble statues of great thinkers of the past—Aristotle, Plato, and Shakespeare among them—for this was where I would receive guests, and I wished it to convey both my feminine sense of style and the masculine gravitas of my mind. The place of honor above the fireplace was reserved for a bust of Demosthenes, to whom I'd dedicated the house in gratitude for his unfailing guidance.

Before us rose a wide, gently curving staircase with a delicate iron-and-wood banister that led up two flights. At the top of the first flight, where the stairway split into two along a hallway lined with white doors, was a single room with glass French doors, its far wall a semi-circle of glass looking out upon the lush back lawn. Seating was arranged to complement the view yet not obstruct the eye from the potted ferns, palms, and vines growing along the walls. Mixed in were clusters of orchids and other exotic flowers along with gilded cages containing small songbirds, whose sweet chirps could not fail to brighten any mood.

The Claflins, who were due to arrive later that day, would move into that floor while Tennie, James, the children, Minnie, and I occupied the uppermost floor. Stepping into the hall on the third floor, I relaxed my shoulders and took my first truly deep breath of the day. It was silent, for the noises the maids and footmen made conveying our trunks and setting everything in order did not penetrate this far. With any luck, the chaos that followed in my family's wake would be shut out as well. I needed a place of sanctuary.

Tennie dropped out of the party as we reached her bedroom, allowing me to catch only a glimpse of the dark purple velvet and lilac-patterned silk she had special ordered from France to decorate her room before she shut the door. Minnie ushered the children into the suite she would share with them. Finally, James and I were left alone in the doorway of our own spacious room.

"It's a far cry from the room we first shared in St. Louis," James observed.

"There was barely room for a bed and washbasin, let alone a chest for our clothes."

Now we had room enough for a large four-poster bed with gold-fringed, sage-green silk curtains and canopy plus a separate sitting area with gilt chairs and a small table, several free-standing wardrobes for each of us, a vanity for my toilet, and a white marble fireplace.

James swept me into his arms. "I may not have been able to carry you over the main threshold, but the least I can do is escort you properly to our marriage bed."

I clasped my arms around his neck. "What do you plan to do once you get me there?" I asked, my voice already husky with desire.

"I'm sure I can think of something." He kissed me softly before kicking the door closed.

❦

A CRISP KNOCK, FOLLOWED by Mr. Cross's announcement, "Mrs. Woodhull, you have a visitor," drew me from my rooms later that day.

As I hurried down the stairs, I prepared myself to face the Claflin brood come home to roost. Instead, a pale, gaunt Canning Woodhull, shaking from the tips of his oily brown locks to the soles of his well-worn boots, stood just inside the main doorway. He spoke my name with the trembling of someone fresh in from subzero cold, not a warm spring day.

I rushed toward him and helped Mr. Cross remove his coat. "Canning, what on earth are you doing here? You are clearly unwell."

"I knew I'd find you," he said as his body involuntarily jerked. "I needed you. I'm sick. No one knows how to care for me like you do." He snickered, leaning against me heavily.

"You're also drunk." I recoiled from the whiskey on his breath.

"Among other things," he muttered, giggling at some private joke.

That explained the tremors. He was going through morphine withdrawal. The last time I had seen him like this was just before Zula was born, when our poverty had kept him from affording his illicit pleasures. He had been sick for weeks, ultimately turning back to the drug when I left him.

James and Tennie entered the room, probably drawn by Canning's slurred speech.

"Will you two please help me get him upstairs?" I asked.

"You will do no such thing," James said in an uncharacteristically stern tone.

"James, he needs our help."

"I'll be damned before I let that lout stay in our rooms. It's bad enough he made it inside the house at all."

Canning was starting to collapse, his knees slowly giving out. He babbled quietly to himself, seemingly oblivious to the argument going on around him.

"It's not like I asked him here," I said with a grunt as I struggled to rebalance his weight and keep him upright.

"He is not welcome under my roof."

"It's *our* roof," I reminded him. "He can't be left alone now. He could die."

"Let him."

Tennie, who was examining Canning's greening countenance, moved to help me. "We'll never get him upstairs anyway. Let's take him to the empty servants' room off the kitchen. Mr. Cross, fetch a bucket. He's going to vomit soon."

"How would you know?" James asked in a biting tone, reluctantly following up and dragging the case Canning had brought in with him.

"When my family gets here, he won't be the only alcoholic or morphine addict in this house. My mother and at least one of my sisters share his vices. I have plenty of experience." She gave him a sour smile.

James's expression turned contrite. "Oh. I apologize, Tennie."

"No need." Tennie hoisted Canning's legs onto the narrow bed while I wrestled with his upper half.

He had passed out, which made him more pliable but also more unwieldy. With a grunt, I rolled him onto his side so that he wouldn't choke on his vomit when it came.

"There isn't room in here for all of us," I said, taking the bucket from Mr. Cross and wetting a cloth from the basin one of the maids brought in. "James, my family will be here soon. See that they are arranged and that no one breathes a word that Canning is here. I'm going to stay here with him until I'm sure the worst has passed. Then we can talk about this."

James scowled. "I suppose we can't just toss him into the gutter."

Tennie took James by the arm and led him out before closing the door to the small room. Canning flailed in his sleep. I continued stroking his brow. How many times had I done the very same thing as his wife? Too many to count. No, he didn't deserve my compassion, but my heart ached for him all the same. He was the first man I'd ever loved. He'd rescued me from my father's abuses and a life of humbuggery. Granted, our marriage wasn't much better—what was the old proverb? Out of the frying pan and into the fire—but he was still the father of my children, so for that reason alone, I could not abandon him to life on the streets.

Canning moaned, and his eyes flew open. Knowing what was coming, I braced him with one arm around his shoulders while placing the bucket under his head with the other. Once his retching ceased, Canning lay back on the pillow, pale and sweating. As I cleaned his beard with the wet cloth, he seized my wrist.

"Victoria." My name was both a question and a statement on his cracked lips. "Thank you. You are all I have." His eyelids fluttered shut, and he passed out again.

I made sure he was securely on his side and took the bucket to the kitchen to have it cleaned. On my way back to check on Canning, my mother's grating voice carried to me.

"She was better off with him than a thief like you. At least with him, we saw her whenever we wanted."

So my family was here and they knew about Canning already. And my mother was wasting no time lighting into James for abuses that had occurred only in her gin-soaked mind.

James was likely fighting the urge to throttle her, something he had threatened to do once before but refrained because she was his mother-in-law. "Annie, I am no thief. No matter what you may believe. As for seeing your daughter, you are living in the same house with her now, so you may see her as much as you like."

His words were delivered through gritted teeth, a sure sign his patience was wearing thin. I had planned to sit with Canning again, but it sounded as though my husband had more need of me. After placing a fresh bucket within easy reach and making sure Canning was still breathing, I entered the parlor only to find James sitting alone, a glass of rum in his hand. He wasn't drinking it so much as staring through it at the flickering candles as though divining the future.

"Strange how one day can turn your life upside down, is it not?" he asked without looking up.

I sat next him and laid my head on his shoulder, kicking off my slippers and pulling my feet beneath me. "Life certainly is full of surprises."

We were both silent for a while, lost in our thoughts.

"It is very quiet. Where is my family?" Looking up at him, I added wryly, "You didn't make good on your threats to kill them, did you?"

"Tennie's out back burying the bodies," he answered without missing a beat. "She took them out to dinner. We decided that would be best for all concerned."

I sighed. "Good."

"You want him to stay, don't you?"

I stared at him. James had always been good at reading my thoughts, but this was eerie. "Has some of my clairvoyance worn off on you?" I joked, trying to change the subject.

"Victoria." James's tone was chiding, as though reprimanding a child.

"Yes, I do. What life is there for him out there if he came all this way to seek help? I cannot in good conscience hand him his hat as soon as he is well enough to stand and send him off, hoping for the best."

James shook his head. "Someday one of your strays is going to turn on you, and you'll find yourself without a hand. First, you allow your horrid father to work in the firm despite all he's done to you and Tennie. Then you invite the whole family to live with you, and now you've taken in your drunkard ex-husband. Mercy is a noble virtue, but it can also be the sign of a fool."

"James Blood, how dare you call me a fool?" I shoved him so hard he nearly fell off the settee. "You are the one who left a promising career and a stable family to live the life of a gypsy with me. If anything, we are equal in our foolishness."

"I regret nothing." He set down his glass on a nearby table.

"Nor do I. I know this must be strange for you, having Canning here. But I swear to you he no longer means anything to me. You have nothing to fear. He is here simply because he needs help and I am the best person to provide it because I know his patterns."

"I'm not going to talk you out of this, am I?"

"Have you ever?" I smiled. "I'll talk to Canning tomorrow. If he's agreeable, and I think he will be—out of desperation if nothing else—we'll tell the rest of the family of our arrangement. Let's see how he does. If he commits even a small transgression, you have my permission to terminate his residency."

James slumped, defeated. "So we have another *flâneur* in the household, eh?"

"No. He won't be useless. I was planning to ask him to help Minnie take care of Byron and Zula. Byron has always had a deep affection for his father, so perhaps having him here will help ease the transition into his unfamiliar surroundings. Besides," I added petulantly, "my father works at the firm, so it's not like none of them are employed."

"If by 'works' you mean gives me endless unsolicited advice and makes a general nuisance of himself." James shifted his weight so that he was facing me more fully. "Victoria, this is an awful lot of trust to place in your family. Do you truly believe they will not try to use your generosity against you? You are in the public eye now, like it or not, and that makes you vulnerable. Have you forgotten Ester's prophecy? Why aid its fruition?"

It was a valid question. Blackmail was one of my mother's favorite pastimes, one my brothers and sisters occasionally indulged in as well. I was giving them the fodder they needed to ruin me if they ever decided to turn against me, but if we were all to live under one roof, I could see no way around it.

"I will make them swear an oath of silence." I said it as though it was the solution to all my concerns, but little pinpricks of fear deep in my gut told me one of them would someday break the oath. But for now, it was a chance I had to take.

CHAPTER SEVENTEEN

MAY 1870

"Stephen, I don't know about this." I paced as I read the paper in my hand. "This goes far beyond what we discussed. All I want to do with these columns is explain to people where I stand on the matters they care about, not give them a lesson on utopia and universal government." I gestured to the papers. "No one will be able to understand all this, let alone believe I wrote it."

I stopped pacing only when Stephen placed his hands on my shoulders, forcing me to sit in the chair opposite him. "First of all, you did write it—the basis anyway."

"But that was simply a follow-up to my ideas on government and about women's rights being equal to men's. That is what I know. Not this." I sighed. "Anna Dickinson might have written this but not me. I've got tactics in my mind—plans for how to make the world better. This is philosophy—your specialty, not mine."

Stephen placed a comforting hand on mine. "Victoria, you are a much more intelligent woman than you give yourself credit for being. None of these people have heard you speak. You may not be an eloquent writer, but when you speak with passion, it's as though music flows from your lips." He shook the pages at me. "Are these not the very things we've burned up the late-night hours discussing? Do you not see yourself, your husband, and me reflected here? We are a team of thinkers, stronger for our unity of purpose. As for what people will and will not understand, how can we know unless we test their mettle? This is our job—to show them what can be. The rest will follow."

"Maybe you're right," I conceded. The wall clock chimed six, and I hurried to the door. "I cannot spend any more time arguing about this today. Tennie arranged for our first 'at home' to take place tonight. She's invited an interesting mix of politicians, Spiritualists, and suffragists." I turned back after opening the door. "Stephen, are you even listening to me?"

He raised his gaze from the sheaf of papers he was already editing, striking through a phrase with a thick line of ink. "Hmmm? Oh yes. Your 'at homes.' They are an evolution of the parties you held at the hotel while you were living on Great Jones Street, yes?"

"Yes, but on a more intimate basis. They are meant to allow people to get to know the woman behind the public façade. After all, there is no more personal place than one's home. Will you be joining us?"

He waved his pen at me without looking up. "Perhaps. I have some work to do on this first."

"By all means, don't let me be an impediment to your genius," I muttered as I stomped off down the hall.

The kitchen staff was ready, so now all I had to do was decide what to wear. Would it be better to appear professional in a navy or black dress? Or shed my dour broker image in favor of a yellow or lime dress that better matched my zest for life?

I was still weighing my options when the sound of laughter reached me from the dining hall. *Loafing again. If I catch those maids one more time…* I swung open the doors.

My mother and Utica stared at me from their seats at the head of the dining table, porcelain tea cups frozen halfway to their lips.

"Join us for tea, won't you, dear?" My mother grinned, revealing missing teeth.

"Ma, what are you doing in here? Don't you know I have a gathering starting in a few hours?" I approached them, clearing pieces of the tea service as I went.

Utica held out her cup to me. "Have a sip, why don't you? It will do wonders for your nerves."

Humoring her, I took the cup with my free hand and brought it to my lips. The liquid was spicy and sharp, burning my throat. I spit it out, spraying the tablecloth. "This is not tea," I croaked between coughs.

My mother and sister cackled.

"It's bum's tea," Utica sang. "Would be gin, but you didn't have any."

I cleared my throat, eyes watering from the cheap rum, and fought to keep my already fragile temper in check. I needed this room ready to receive guests, and here they were drinking and playing dress-up. Come to think of it, they didn't have such fine clothes. I examined them closer, plucking at Utica's peach gown. "Is that my dress?"

"Maybe," my sister replied.

In a flash, Utica and my mother were on their feet, scampering out of the room like little girls well aware of their transgressions.

I called for Helena to clean up the mess and set the room to rights before I chased after my family. "As God as my witness, if I catch the two of you…" I yelled as I bounded up the stairs.

"Did I hear Ma?" Tennie met me on the landing to the second floor.

I nodded, pausing to catch my breath as Tennie ran toward the row of doors, pounding on one.

"Ma! Where is my pearl necklace? I know you took it from my case." Tennie jiggled the door handle. "It's locked."

"She was wearing it a few minutes ago," I volunteered, removing the room key from a set I wore at my waist for such situations—which were not as uncommon as I would have preferred.

"And what about my sapphire comb?" Tennie shouted through the door as she fumbled with the lock. "I was going to wear that tonight. Utica, if I find out you've been pawning my jewelry again, I will toss you both out on your ungrateful ears."

"The same goes if you interrupt us tonight," I put in for good measure.

Less than two hours later, the drawing room was filled with glittering women and smartly dressed men, the floor-to-ceiling gilt mirrors reflecting their images and creating the illusion of a crowd twice its size. Above the soft strains of a string quartet, their voices rose in merry chatter on topics both serious and trivial.

As I told my guests at the start of the evening, these soirées were more than parties; they were the beginning of a revolution that would end only when women were fully acknowledged as equal to men, both at the ballot box and in the bedroom. Therefore, they should feel free to give voice to radical ideas and speak of reform.

Whereas I had previously been contented to be in the company of journalists and wealthy businessmen, these folk were most assuredly a step up on the society ladder from my first attempts to ingratiate myself into New York's inner sanctum. In one corner, President Grant's father was surrounded by a knot of men seeking his son's ear, including James and several politicians I knew from various suffrage meetings. Not far away, Stephen debated Elizabeth Stuart Phillips, the famous Spiritualist author, likely on some point of utopia, which he was still trying to achieve despite multiple past failures.

At my side, Laura de Force Gordon, a lawyer who had also come into the women's rights movement through Spiritualism, was chattering about the need for reform out West. "I tell you, ever since the Wyoming territory gave women the vote in December, the rest of us have been chomping at the bit. Then Utah goes and does the same in February, and we're all fit to be tied. If it's good enough for women in two territories, why not all of us? Just because California is an incorporated state doesn't make us inferior to them. If anything, you'd think it would be the other way around."

I opened my mouth to commiserate.

"Listen to me," Laura barreled on like a steam engine on a downhill grade. "I can't even practice law in my own state. And do you know why? Because I'm a woman obviously. But do you know what the state bar told me? They were afraid the rustling of our skirts would distract men in the courtroom. Can you believe that?"

Again, I made to respond but was interrupted, this time by Horace Greeley. He kissed my proffered hand in warm greeting and introduced the short man at his side as Representative Benjamin Butler. As soon as Mr. Greeley said his name, I recognized him from the convention in January.

He took Laura's hand first. "I know exactly who this is. The Suffragist of the West, that's what they call you, isn't it?"

"They say it as though I am the only one," she said with a self-effacing eye roll.

"But you are the leading one; that is what's important." He turned to me. "And here we have the Coming Woman. I remember you from the convention."

"And I you." I gestured, and a waiter appeared with a silver tray covered by a matching dome. "I heard you might be in attendance tonight, so I took the liberty of having some of your favorite foods set aside especially for you." I lifted the dome to reveal a pyramid of doughnuts surrounding a cut-crystal glass of whiskey.

Congressman Butler let out a roaring laugh that carried above the din of conversation. "Ah, my reputation precedes me, I see." He plucked the top doughnut from the pile and offered the tray to Laura.

"Don't mind if I do." She snatched the glass from the center and took a long swig. "Oh, that tastes like home. You New Yorkers and your fancy drinks—you've forgotten the simple joys of a good whiskey."

I pinched my eyes shut in horror. I whispered to the waiter, "Please see that a new drink is brought to Representative Butler as quickly as possible."

The congressman slapped his leg, laughing so hard he had to wipe tears from his eyes. "Oh Horace, I owe you for tonight. You have placed me in the company of the two most fascinating women in the country," he said to the man next to him.

"Thank you, sir. You are too kind."

"Come now, you know I am right. Don't be modest."

The waiter reappeared with the congressman's drink and whispered to me that dinner was ready to be served. Gliding over to the orchestra, I motioned for them to end after their current song. When the music stopped, the dining room doors were flung open and the commencement of the meal announced.

As hostess, I was to escort President Grant's father, the highest-ranking man, in to dinner, so we would enter the room last.

When Congressman Butler neared with Laura on his arm—a pairing I suspected would suit them both well personally and professionally—he lingered at my elbow. "Would it confuse your dinner arrangements if I begged to be seated at your left so that I might enjoy the company of you both this evening?"

I smiled, suddenly grateful I had asked James and Stephen to consult on the place settings, a duty normally reserved for the hostess. "As the Fates would have it, that is already your place this evening. See for yourself." I gestured through the open doors toward the table.

Representative Butler beamed. "What a thoughtful hostess you are. I should much like to speak to you both about Mrs. Virginia Minor's ideas and how we may use them to force Congress to act on the issue of women's suffrage. Oh, this will be a lively supper indeed."

❧

AFTER THE LAST GUEST departed, I slipped quietly up to the roof, wishing to be alone after the hubbub of the day. Breathing in the chilly night air, I sat on the cold slate roof, my skirts bundled beneath me. I closed my eyes, but instead of the peaceful oblivion I sought, my mind gave me flashes of the day's events: a forged check at the brokerage I had missed but Tennie spotted, my argument with Stephen, my mother and Utica in their purloined dresses, Laura's shocking breach of manners with Congressman Butler's drink, the president's father spilling his soup at dinner—all events out of my control. But wasn't everything lately?

I pulled up my knees in front of me and rested my chin against them, watching the tall ships bob in the harbor to the north. Tears pricked at the corners of my eyes, but I refused to let them fall. I was simply out of sorts after a long day; it would pass. But what if it didn't? In announcing my intent to run for president, I had set myself up as a representative woman. If I was to be a model for all others, I had to get my life in order.

Prayer had always helped me, and I turned to it now, ashamed at how I had allowed the spiritual part of my life to lapse since coming to New York. Now that I no longer gave daily sessions to clients—only occasional séances for Mr. Vanderbilt—I found I had little time for my own conversations with the other side. That would stop now. Maybe they had some advice which could help me plot the overwhelming journey I was attempting to take.

I closed my eyes, listening to the sounds of the city beyond. The trees rustled, and in their breeze, the spirits danced. I was aware of them only marginally at first, as if they were hesitant to approach me. Then as they drew near, I recognized four of my most beloved spirits—my sisters Delia and Odessa, who had died as young children; Rachel Scribner, a frequent visitor since Ester's séance; and of course Demosthenes.

"I'm sorry for abandoning all of you. Thank you for not doing the same to me," I said.

I poured out my heart to them, voicing all the fears I had been afraid to admit even to myself—that tomorrow my first editorial as a presidential candidate would appear in the paper, and I wasn't happy with it, no matter how many times Stephen said it would be fine; that the nation would consider me a laughingstock for trying to affect change; that Mr. Vanderbilt would one day learn the true source of my stock tips; that for all my current success, I would end up viewed as a fraud like my father.

The answers that came echoed what my heart was telling me if I stripped away all my fears and the lies I told myself. No one was above reproach, least of all my father and Mr. Vanderbilt. The commodore had employed his fair share of devious tactics to get to his station in life, so he had no right to judge me for anything. If I didn't like what was being written in my name, I should take control and write it myself, once again employing Mr. Vanderbilt to aid me.

When I opened my eyes, the world was blurry and I was cold. I fondled the coarse threads of a blanket wrapped around my shoulders that hadn't been there before. Confused, I looked around only to find James sitting at my side.

"Welcome back." He smiled, used to my spirit communications from our early days of marriage.

I blinked several times in rapid succession. "How long have you been here?"

"Long enough to hear you argue with the spirits. At least you don't reserve that only for me."

I shoved him playfully. "You should know better by now. What part did you hear?"

"That you want to start a newspaper." James looked confused.

I grinned. "I do. Follow my lead when the papers come out tomorrow."

I was up at dawn, eager to see our first column in print. When I passed the parlor, I found James, Stephen, and Tennie already there. Tennie handed me the paper.

I quickly read the familiar lines and the commentary below. "They hate it," I declared, collapsing onto the settee and crumpling the *Herald* in my lap.

"Oh, stop being so dramatic," Tennie chided.

"How can you say that? See here"—Stephen pointed at a column of type—"the editor writes that he is 'dazzled by the profundity' of your writing."

"*Your writing*, you mean. It also means they had no idea what it said."

"It's only the first column. We have them under contract for several more. They'll come to understand. You'll see." Stephen flashed his most charming smile.

Which I ignored. "How am I to get the American voters to take me seriously as a candidate when they don't know what I stand for? I'm treated as a novelty by the press, who may spare me a word here or there—usually pejoratively unless I'm paying them to write words of praise. I'm treated as a pet by those in power, who pat my head and tell me what a good girl I am for standing up for my beliefs when all they want me to do is roll over and play dead."

"Victoria, please, calm down."

"No, Stephen. I've had enough of your silver tongue. I don't need pretty words and lies. What I need is a way to break free, to take action." The words of the spirits returned to me, humming through my head like the current through telegraph wires. *You must help yourself.* I stood, once again examining the paper. "What makes this so special? It's simply ink printed on paper. What makes people listen to what they say is the authority which the readers place in the name, right?"

"And trust," James added.

"True. But that comes over time, and it doesn't always matter. Look at the *Sun.* Everyone knows it's full of tall tales and gossip, but people read it anyway."

"Where are you going with this?" Stephen asked.

I tossed the paper at him. "What is to stop us from starting our own paper? That way I could express my opinions more strongly and frequently than all the begging, charming, and bribery in the world could allow at the established rags. Why should I"—I waved my arms wildly as if to include them all—"why should we, wait upon the whims of others to make known our thoughts when we have it within our power to do so ourselves? It's not as if it's unheard of—even in our own circles. After all, Mrs. Stanton has her *Revolution,* and the Bostonians have the *Women's Journal.* As a dear friend once said, 'I have many things of immense importance which I want to communicate.'" I winked at Stephen.

"I've always wanted my own newspaper," he replied, mulling over the idea.

"Well, we have names that everyone knows now," Tennie offered. "And it's not like we couldn't afford it."

"I don't know about that," James said. "Running a newspaper is quite costly."

"Who says *we* have to pay for it?" I grinned at Tennie. "Your dear Mr. Vanderbilt loves new and daring enterprises. Perhaps you could find a way to *convince* him to back yet another scheme from his famous Lady Brokers. Especially if we promise to put in a good word for him and his businesses from time to time."

"He'll do it. I just know it."

James's expression was still pensive. "I'm not against the idea—I rather like it, in fact—but I want to make sure we've thought this through. Even if you get the funding, what do any of us know about journalism?"

Stephen raised a finger. "That's where I come in, my friend. In the old days, I worked for the *Tribune*. I know all the ins and outs of the business. I could easily teach you. It's not as difficult as one might think."

"I'm sure Johnny would be willing to help out, too," Tennie added.

I squeezed Tennie tight. "Call Johnny and everyone else we know in the press for an impromptu luncheon. Tell them we have something that will interest and astound the political world. Tease them that I'm willing to spend a fortune to get my message out about equality and governmental policy. Better yet, tell them that we're promoting a revolution."

❧

A MONTH LATER, I was holding the inaugural issue of *Woodhull & Claflin's Weekly*. Launching it on a Saturday morning when the warring Boston and New York suffragists were fighting with one another across town had been a collective decision. This way they couldn't fail to notice my name and note I was a serious new player on the women's suffrage scene, one they would do well to watch.

The strategy paid off—with many of my now-rival papers praising my efforts.

At the *Herald*, Johnny wrote, *"While the two hostile divisions of women's righters are passing their time in refusing to coalesce with each other and in flooding the country with resolutions and chatter, there are at least two advocates of the woman movement that endeavor to show by example and precept that their sex, with ordinary fair play and industry, can take care of itself. The example of Woodhull and Claflin is a highly commendable one, as they do more and talk less than any two divisions of the female agitators put together."*

CHAPTER EIGHTEEN

Throughout the summer and autumn, Representative Butler and I became close friends, uniting under our shared passion for women's rights. He praised my work with the *Weekly* and offered to help me refine my argument, borrowed from Virginia Minor, that women already had the right to vote thanks to the Constitution so I could get my message to as many people as possible through my paper.

At the same time, we were coming to realize that in Washington, D.C., the Sixteenth Amendment—which would have given women the right to vote—would go no farther than the Judiciary Committee.

"It's the classic way to kill a bill no one wants to deal with," Congressman Butler explained. "But it's a moot point because our argument overrides the need for it. That's what Washington needs to hear."

The answer, according to Mr. Butler, was for Tennie and me to spend some time in the nation's capital. He would do his part to persuade Congress to grant permission for me to speak about women's suffrage if Tennie and I agreed to bear the risk of being the first women to make such a brazen request.

When we arrived at the Willard Hotel, a massive five-story structure within walking distance of the Executive Mansion, I immediately spotted Susan B. Anthony and Elizabeth Cady Stanton sitting in the lobby with a group of suffragists. Though I nodded to them and said hello, neither woman acknowledged me. But why would they? I might have earned praise for my financial efforts in New York, but Washington was a different story. Here, I wasn't yet one of them, only a usurper who was lucky to get my name in the press after the last convention.

"Why do you think they are here?" Tennie asked, an edge of concern to her voice.

"Probably to try to push the Sixteenth Amendment through. Little do they know their labors are in vain or what we have in store." I smiled wickedly, imagining their reactions if Representative Butler was able get permission for me to speak. That would shock them to the roots of their carefully coiffed hair.

As we waited for our luggage to be unloaded, I peered through the haze of cigar smoke at the spacious hotel interior, with its soaring columns and hanging lamps dangling over the heads of its patrons, who were clustered in highly polished wood-and-leather chairs. Most of the patrons were men—politicians and wealthy business owners or heirs, judging from the fine cloth and tailoring of their suits—but besides the suffragists, there were few women. According to what Mr. Butler had told me, the wives, daughters, and mistresses of these men were cloistered on the hotel's second floor, where they wouldn't interfere with business. I smiled again. I did so enjoy interfering.

After settling in, we met Representative Butler in one of the public rooms.

"I trust your journey was uneventful?" the congressman asked.

"And I trust you have the committee in suspense waiting to hear what I have to say?" I joked.

"Patience, my dear. You've just arrived. Plus, we still have to finalize your petition." He gestured for us to sit.

I declined, preferring to stand after so many hours on the train.

"That's actually why I'm here. I have good news and bad news," he offered.

"Tell us the good news first," Tennie insisted.

He removed a long, cylindrical tube from his coat pocket and unrolled a large piece of paper. "This is the most recent draft of the petition. I think it's nearly complete. But there are still a few points of convention I'm unsure about." He looked up at us. "That leads me to the bad news. I'm needed back home in Massachusetts for a few weeks."

"But that means you'll be gone into December," I said. "I thought we wanted to get this before Congress before they adjourn for their holiday recess."

Representative Butler held up his hands in a defensive posture. "I do, and that hasn't changed. The other part of the good news is I found a lawyer willing to convert your petition into the legal language these types of documents need. His name is J.D. Reymart. He's from New York but is spending the rest of the congressional session at this very hotel. He comes highly recommended."

"I don't care if he's a saint. He won't compare to you." I may have been laying on the flattery a little thick, but I wanted him here with me, not halfway across the country. I needed him to finish my mission. "When will I meet this prodigy of all things legal?"

"Right now, if you like."

My breath caught. I spun, cursing inwardly that he had heard my mocking. My heart skipped a beat when I took in the man who now stood face to face with me. He was not at all old and balding like the congressman as I'd expected. This man was young, perhaps even a year or two younger than my thirty-two, and taller than me by a few inches. Dressed in a light brown coat with long tails, a matching vest, and high-necked shirtwaist, he was what many men, including James, would have called a dandy. But the only word that came to my mind was stunning. Clean-shaven, with high cheekbones and amber eyes, he was temptation incarnate. Suddenly, I was very grateful my husband was back in New York.

"Mrs. Woodhull is our esteemed memorialist, and this is her sister, Miss Tennessee Claflin," Mr. Butler said in introduction.

Mr. Reymart bowed to us. "Charmed," he said in a husky voice, taking my outstretched hand.

The frisson of excitement that passed between us was so strong that I nearly yanked away my hand in surprise. That was a sign our souls were linked—or so my Spiritualist beliefs said. Just as I could manipulate the magnetic energy within someone to heal them, so too would my own body recognize someone with a kindred energy, just as it had with James. This man was likely a healer too whether he knew it or not.

"Forgive me, but we've had a long day of travel," I said by way of explanation for my bizarre behavior. "I'm afraid I'm a little out of sorts this evening."

"Have you eaten? I know Mr. Butler has to be on his way, but I would be happy to accompany you to dinner," Mr. Reymart offered. "I find food helps settle me."

I hesitated.

"I'll join you even if she won't." Tennie looped an arm in his.

Mr. Reymart ignored her, waiting for my answer.

"Yes, of course. Thank you," I finally managed.

"Well then, Victoria, I leave you in Mr. Reymart's capable hands. Tennie, I forgot to tell you, I've told several of my colleagues about your firm. You'll find a list with appointment times at the main desk. I thought you may wish to call on them while your sister works on her petition. We wouldn't want those pretty little hands of yours to be idle, would we?"

❦

As I suspected, Mr. Judah DeWitt Reymart had little need of my help in drafting my petition, or memorial, as it was properly called by those in the legislature. Still, he sent word to my room after breakfast, and I attended on him in a small study on the first floor reserved under Congressman Butler's name.

While he hunched over a cherry wood desk, I reclined in a stuffed velvet chair near the fire where I had a direct line of sight to him. He had removed his coat, revealing a brocade vest of burgundy and goldenrod, and rolled up his white shirt sleeves, exposing tanned, muscular forearms. I could better appreciate his trim physique without the bulky outer layer.

Lost in imagining the muscles rippling beneath his clothing, I was startled when he called my name and crooked a finger to call me to his side. My face burned. Hopefully he would think my blush was from being too near the heat—if he noticed at all.

I leaned over him from behind, inhaling his clean scent punctuated by the grassy, vanilla hints of the coumarin in his aftershave. The slightly sweet aroma of tobacco clung to him, but he did not stink of cigar smoke as most men, including the congressman and James, often did.

"I need a point of clarification here, if you please." He pointed a long, thin finger at a line in the document he was working on. "I'm beginning with your paper on Constitutional Equality and then will draft your memorial. In speaking of the sovereignty of the citizens of the United States, you refer to the governing power as a monarch. Do you not think some might misconstrue that you refer to a king rather than a president or that you intend to set yourself up as a queen?"

He had a valid point.

"I meant not that our country was a monarchy but that it is the system through which most of the world receives its power. Here"— my hand brushed his as I indicated another line of text above, and I quickly withdrew it. Had he felt the same blossoming heat where our skin touched?—"perhaps we need clarity in this line that citizens of a republic confer sovereignty rather than receive it from their ruler. That is what makes them free, male and female alike."

Mr. Reymart considered for a moment then nodded. "That would be helpful." He turned his head to look up at me and smiled. "Thank you."

I nodded, unable to speak.

He rummaged through the pile of documents on his desk and finally held out to me two large sheets of paper. "I had my assistant make a copy of each document for you. It would be helpful if you would read through them again and mark any points where you purposefully used certain language so I can be sure to carry your original intent over to the final documents. Also, if there is anything you wish to change, you may note that too."

I took the documents and turned back to my place by the fire, but Mr. Reymart stopped me with a light touch on the sleeve.

"Please, sit with me." He slid over his chair and positioned another next to him at the desk. "This way, we might observe one another's work and ask questions with minimal interruption."

We passed the better part of three days this way, side by side, so near but not touching except in occasional brushes of fingers or bumps of shoulders and elbows, all too fleeting contact. I was near to bursting when I returned to my room each night to face Tennie's scrutiny.

"Tennie, he is brilliant," I found myself saying one night. "His arguments have added so much to both documents. Not only that, he truly supports and understands our cause. He told me today he admires my dedication and courage. Can you believe that? A man outside of our inner circle who actually supports us? I can't wait for you to see the final products. I don't know how Mr. Butler and I would have got on without him."

Tennie wagged a finger at me. "Don't try to couch this in your working relationship with Mr. Butler. This is about you and Mr. Reymart. You sound like a young girl in the first throes of love. You are a married woman, or have you forgotten that?"

"And you are having an affair with a married man," I reminded her.

Tennie waved her hand, dismissing my comment. "That's different. His wife doesn't love him. James loves you."

"Yes, but we have a different sort of a marriage."

When he'd left his wife, James and I agreed that marriage should not be bound by a legal agreement issued by the state but by the bonds of love that united two people, which were fluid and could change. "Love those who you will when you will," had been our motto since meeting. Free Love had been his excuse for bedding me before he was divorced from his first wife, and I was relatively certain he'd been with a few women since then. Surely he would understand any indiscretion that might arise.

"Does love stop him from late-night games of chess with other women? You can't tell me all those suffragists have only board games on their mind when they linger after meetings. Surely you've noticed when he fails to return from one of his outings with Stephen, showing up just in time for breakfast. It is my turn now. "

Our fourth morning in Washington was spent attending to separate duties. Tennie was off to her prearranged appointments, Mr. Reymart to a series of meetings, and I to drafting articles for the *Weekly*. It was in James and Stephen's hands while I was away, but that didn't stop me from telegraphing stories and tips to them from the hotel. I was the editor, after all. Plus, I couldn't give Stephen free rein over my paper. Not after he had openly attacked one of the country's most beloved preachers, Henry Ward Beecher, and accused him of a litany of charges ranging from falsehoods to lewd conduct unbecoming of a Christian minister. Stephen had no proof; the whole sordid mess had stemmed from an unnamed personal grudge.

After demanding space to apologize on behalf of the paper, I let them know my memorial would be coming the next day, for Mr. Reymart assured me we would finish our work tonight.

"Please hold the entire editorial section of the November 19th issue for it," I wrote. "The memorial is to run in its entirety along with a shortened, simplified version of my Constitutional Equality paper coming tomorrow as well, which will serve as a layman's explanation, under the headline 'Startling Annunciation… 16th Amendment a Dead Letter.'" As an afterthought, I added, "You may as well lay out the text of the Constitution on nearby pages so that readers can use it to judge the merits of my argument."

Stephen would have said I was being too proscriptive, but it was my paper and this was the most important issue I'd ever printed, perhaps even more so than the debut issue. It had to be perfect even if I was several states away.

I said as much to Mr. Reymart over dinner, and he agreed.

"Your name is on the masthead. That means you get to dictate the content, not him. The others, no matter your relationship to them outside the paper, are your employees and must do as you say. Remember that. Besides," he added, toying with his fork, "any man who dares stand against you is a fool."

I was still smiling from the compliment when he opened the door to our study, guiding me inside with a light touch on the small of my back that sent a shiver of pleasure up my spine. It was probably an unconscious gesture, but it was also incredibly intimate, a small sign of ownership and comfort, a confirmation that he returned my feelings.

Full dark had turned the windows into mirrors in the candlelight. For a moment, we were reflected as a couple, I in my cranberry-and-cream dress, my short hair pinned in tight curls atop my head, he in his blue cutaway coat, white silk cravat, and tan breeches. Then he turned to shut the door, and the illusion was shattered.

Once again, we took up our places behind the desk, his coat thrown over the back of his chair, my seat closely at his side.

He slid a sheet of paper toward me. "This is the final translation of your memorial. Please read through it and let me know if it expresses your intentions accurately."

I examined the page, my heart fluttering when I saw the words I'd so long dreamed in my mind finally on paper in the parlance of government. It was quite difficult to understand with so much archaic language and large words, but I comprehended enough to know it said what I intended it to.

"I've never seen the word 'whereas' used so many times in one place."

He smiled apologetically. "It seems to be a favored word in the legal community. But otherwise, it looks correct?"

"Yes. You did a wonderful job. Thank you."

"Splendid. I'll have my assistant send a copy to Representative

Butler first thing in the morning and have a copy delivered to your rooms as well. Now, I took the liberty of making some final suggestions to your paper. For example"—he pointed with his nobleman's fingers—"might I suggest that here you strengthen your argument with the idea of *ita lex scripta est*?"

"You may if you explain what that means," I teased.

Mr. Reymart gave a small, embarrassed smile. "I apologize. It's Latin, a legal term that translates to 'so the law is written.' It means the law must be obeyed notwithstanding the apparent rigor of its application. So we must obey the law without inquiring into its reasons. That means if the Constitution says all citizens are entitled to the right to vote, we must take it at face value without arguing over who is and is not a citizen."

"I like the way you think."

"Good. I think that concludes my work on the memorial. Now you have to get the committee to agree to hear your petition. Mr. Butler will be of more value with that than I." He bent forward to cross off a list of changes, and a curl of light brown hair fell over his forehead, auburn highlights sparking in the flickering candlelight.

I reached up to brush it out of his eyes but barely stopped myself before he turned his head. I was caught with my hand in midair, reaching toward him.

We locked eyes, and for several heartbeats, the only sounds in the room were the crackling of the fire and our soft breathing. Mr. Reymart took my hand, intertwining our fingers in his lap. With his other hand, he ran his fingernails along my left cheek then dragged his fingertips across my right jaw before cupping my chin. The expression in his eyes was questioning, seeking permission I gave him with a slight smile.

Our lips met softly, tentatively at first, as we explored our new nearness and became acquainted with one another. My hands delved into his thick hair as our kisses grew more intense, lips parting and tongues exploring. His arms came around my waist, and after a brief moment of weightlessness, I found myself sitting on his lap, his hands roaming across my back. I pressed against him as his soft lips slid over mine. I gently sucked his tongue, tightening my grip as he pulled back slightly in surprise.

"Victoria," he moaned.

Our foreheads were still touching, our lips only a hairsbreadth apart as we panted.

"We shouldn't… you're…"

"Yes, we should." I tangled my fingers in his hair and yanked back his head before covering his mouth with mine. I slowly slid my body up and down over his, inwardly cursing the skirts that prevented me from straddling his legs.

He turned his head to the side. "Then we should at least find a better location."

I let my lips caress his jaw and nibbled his ear as he seemed to consider a plan.

"It would never do for us to be seen entering my room together or me to be entering yours. Your husband could sue me."

I purred a laugh into his ear. "Always a lawyer." Lips still on his earlobe, I reached behind him, blindly searching in his coat pockets until my fingers grasped cold metal. I held up his room key, its numbered tassel dancing a jig. "Meet me upstairs in ten minutes. Send whatever you need to your assistant. Pretend it's an ordinary night, and everyone else will believe so too."

We said our good nights with the door open. While Mr. Reymart finished up with the papers, I went to my room as I would have any other night, relieved to find it still dark. Tennie must have been out with one of the politicians on Mr. Butler's list. Good. I didn't want to face my sister in light of what I was about to do.

After washing my face and making sure enough time had passed, I sneaked up one floor to Mr. Reymart's room and let myself in, lighting candles as I went. Hastily, I removed my hair pins and clothes, piled them out of the way on the floor, then slipped under the bed sheets. When the door handle turned a few minutes later, I slid out, standing next to the bed in all my natural glory.

"You are beautiful," he said, taking my measure from head to toe while the door swung shut.

His mouth was on mine before I could move, capturing me, possessing me. I willingly submitted to his touch, reveling in the feelings he provoked, intense and thrilling. I wanted to drink in every moment then make him feel as alive as he made me feel. Fingers caressed, tongues tasted, and soon we were joined in frenzied passion.

Once we were spent, I laid my head on his chest, unable to believe I'd given in so easily.

"What will you tell your husband?" Judah mumbled, already half asleep.

"He needs to know nothing."

A few moments passed in silence, then he chuckled. "I bet you'd have no trouble getting an audience with the Judiciary Committee if they could all see you like I did tonight."

I grabbed a small pillow and whacked him in the face with it. "That would be a sight, wouldn't it? The Lady Godiva of the women's movement. Exactly how I wish to be remembered."

He kissed my chest. "I guarantee you'll be remembered for much more than your sexual prowess."

CHAPTER NINETEEN

JANUARY 1871

Though I wished him to linger, I was relieved that Mr. Reymart had to return to New York. That way, no awkwardness or stolen glances could feed the Washington rumor mill. Not that it needed more fodder. Other rumors were quickly surfacing in the gossip-laden streets, as I found out at lunch the day I was set to testify before Congress. The people at a nearby table began talking loudly about me.

"I can tell you one thing for certain," said a woman with an affected high-class accent. "Some of the women in the movement, particularly Mrs. Isabella Beecher Hooker, look down on this Mrs. Woodhull for her impolite opinions and lack of breeding. She said to me once, 'Who is this woman but the daughter of a crook? What have I to fear from the spawn of sin?'"

"That sounds more like Catharine Beecher than Isabella. Are you certain of the source?" asked a man at the same table. "Either way, it would ill become these women, especially a Beecher, to talk of antecedents or cast any smirch upon Mrs. Woodhull, for I am reliably assured that Henry Ward Beecher preaches to at least twenty of his mistresses every Sunday."

A tittering followed at their table and ours.

"Victoria, what have you done to earn the ire of Mrs. Isabella Beecher?" asked the wife of a New York congressman.

"Nothing personally," I answered, buttering a roll. "But one of my colleagues at the paper published a story accusing her brother of many of the same things that gentleman's words confirmed. Catharine is so conservative; she probably thinks my running for president is a sign of the Second Coming."

The table burst into laughter.

"Well, you have nothing to worry about from that old biddy," said Eustace, the wife of a senator. "Remember, everything about tomorrow has been carefully chosen to throw more fuel on the fire between our warring suffragists. While they quarrel with each other, you'll quietly sneak in and get the victory and the credit."

"Speaking of victory," said Caroline Willard, the wife of the hotel's owner, "how did you finally get Benjamin Butler to give you access to the committee? It seems like they kept saying no, then all of a sudden it was yes." She leaned toward me conspiratorially. "Is there any truth to the rumors?"

"What rumors?"

Mrs. Willard glanced over her shoulder then lowered her voice. "They say he offered to help you in exchange, and I quote, 'for the opportunity to feast his eyes on your naked person.'"

I coughed, choking on my bread. One of the other women patted my back while another thrust a glass of water toward me.

Mrs. Willard kept on talking, oblivious to my misery. "I heard that when he was asked about this gossip, all Mr. Butler would say was 'Half-truths kill.' Now, I don't know about you, but I think he fanned the flames with that statement and made it sound like much more happened."

I stopped coughing and wiped my tearing eyes with a napkin. "Mrs. Willard, did you ever consider he could have meant the true half was that he helped me?"

Mrs. Willard had the grace to look chagrined as she inspected the tablecloth. "No, I hadn't thought of it that way."

I crossed my arms. "Well, you need to start because there's no truth to it."

Although the rumors were alarmingly close to the truth, I'd never admit that to anyone. All they had gotten wrong was the name. While Mr. Reymart hadn't had anything to do with the committee's change of heart, Congressman Butler may have. What exactly had Mr. Reymart shared with him? For a lonely old man whose wife was dying of cancer in Switzerland, details of a torrid night may have been enough to get him to exert extra effort.

But what did it matter? Both houses of Congress had reviewed my women's voting plan, and in a few hours, I was speaking before the Judiciary Committee, the very body that held a woman's right to vote within their grasp. How I got there was irrelevant.

The short carriage ride from the Willard Hotel to the US Capitol that afternoon was a bitterly cold one, with an icy wind tossing gusts of prickling sleet against the glass carriage windows. I huddled against Tennie, trying to shield myself from the draft, while Representative Butler sat stonily. The only sign of his annoyance was the incessant rolling of his unlit cigar from one side of his mouth to the other.

Upon arriving, we found the room in which the hearing was supposed to take place closed due to a malfunctioning heating stove which was spewing smoke throughout the House building. The acrid stench was noticeable even in the temporary chamber, which was quite cold because the windows had to be left open to air out the smoke.

As Tennie and I filed in behind Representative Butler, dozens of reporters, suffragists, and curious onlookers turned toward us. I tensed, shoulder blades drawing together as their scrutiny bore into me from the tip of my alpine hat to the soles of my leather boots. I wished I was wearing a shawl like Tennie so I could pull it more closely around me. But as it was, I had to face them without more than my black dress and navy jacket as armor.

I fought back a wave of disappointment at how empty the room was. Out of more than thirty committee members, only seven had bothered to show up so far. They were gathered around a large mahogany table in the center of the room. William Loughridge of Iowa was leaning on his hand, his keen good-natured eyes alive with expectation because he was fully committed to the women's movement. He winked at me when our eyes met. Mr. John Bingham sat opposite him, his dour expression showing he was not pleased to be hearing my petition. Mr. Burton Cook of Illinois and Mr. Charles Eldridge of Wisconsin were the only other representatives in their places, heads bent together in confidential conversation. The others milled through the crowd, shaking hands and laughing heartily at jokes only they could hear.

I took my place at one end of the table, Tennie at my side. I removed my hat and peered around, seeking a friendly face in the crowd. Directly behind me were the suffragists, the nearest being Mrs. Hooker with her soft curls held down by a hat with curling blue feathers. Snuggled in next to her was Mrs. Anthony, clad in her traditional black, spectacles already in place on her nose. Behind them were the trio of Paulina Wright Davis, an ancient suffragist with a cloud of snowy curls; the Reverend Olympia Brown, pastor of a Universalist church in Bridgeport, Connecticut; and Mrs. Josephine S. Griffing, an abolitionist and women's rights advocate. Leaning against the bookshelves at the back wall of the room were the press, the only two familiar faces being those of the handsome Theodore Tilton and Tennie's boyfriend, Johnny.

The Capitol clock struck the one o'clock hour, reverberating down my spine. It was time. I blew out a deep breath. All I had to do was read from the paper.

Representative John Bingham, House Judiciary Committee Chairman, opened the proceedings. "Mrs. Woodhull, I have read the petition you bring before us. As the one who sponsored the Fourteenth Amendment, I am here to tell you, madame, you are not a citizen."

Rage flooded me, and I clamped my hands into fists at my side, reminding myself this man commanded my respect even if his words indicated otherwise. Still, I couldn't remain silent. "Then what am I?"

"You are a woman. You may now speak."

"I knew that before I came to Washington," I said under my breath, standing.

Almost immediately, the blood drained from my face and my head began to swim. I grasped the edge of the table for support, and Tennie took my left elbow. Dragging in a few deep breaths, I reminded myself I had been onstage in front of people before. This was no different. Didn't Demosthenes say I would one day speak in public? This was my moment.

I took one more deep breath and read from the paper grasped in my shaking hands. "To the Honorable Senate and House of Representatives of the United States—" My voice, so strong and determined in my mind, came out as a quiet whisper. I had to take long pauses between words to catch my breath, which was coming shallow and rapid. "In Congress assembled, respectfully showeth."

I paused, reciting a brief prayer to my guiding spirits to help me through this ordeal. As if in answer, a warm ray of light pierced my soul, bringing with it a determination and strength I could only have heretofore dreamed. My cheeks flushed, and I read again, this time in a voice that matched the one in my mind, growing in authority with every word. "That she was born in the state of Ohio, and is above the age of twenty-one years; that she has resided in the state of New York during the past three years; that she is still a resident thereof, and that she is a citizen of the United States, as declared by the Fourteenth Article of Amendments to the Constitution of the United States.

"That since the adoption of the Fifteenth Article of Amendments to the Constitution, neither the state of New York nor any other state, nor any territory, has passed any law to abridge the right of any citizen of the United States to vote, as established by said article, neither on account of sex or otherwise.

"That, nevertheless, the right to vote is denied to women citizens of the United States by the operation of Election Laws in the several states and territories, which laws were enacted prior to the adoption of the said Fifteenth Article, and which are inconsistent with the Constitution as amended, and, therefore, are void and of no effect; but which being still enforced by the said states and territories, render the Constitution inoperative as regards the right of women citizens to vote.

"And whereas, Article Six, Section Two, declares 'That this Constitution, and the laws of the United States which shall be made in pursuance thereof, and all treaties made or which shall be made under the authority of the United States, shall be the supreme law of the land; and all judges in every state shall be bound thereby, anything in the Constitution and Laws of any state to the contrary notwithstanding.'

"And whereas, no distinction between citizens is made in the Constitution of the United States on account of sex, but the Fourteenth Article of Amendments to it provides that 'no state shall make or enforce any law which shall abridge the privileges and immunities of citizens of the United States,' 'nor deny to any person within its jurisdiction the equal protection of the laws.'

"And whereas, the continuance of the enforcement of said local election laws, denying and abridging the Right of Citizens to Vote on account of sex, is a grievance to your memorialist and to various other persons, citizens of the United States, being women—

"Therefore your memorialist would most respectfully petition your Honorable Bodies to make such laws as in the wisdom of Congress shall be necessary and proper for carrying into execution the right vested by the Constitution in the citizens of the United States to vote, without regard to sex.

"And your memorialist will ever pray. Victoria C. Woodhull."

When I finished speaking, I smiled at the committee and bowed graciously before sitting down abruptly, dizzy and limp as an unstarched cloth. Several people patted me on the back and whispered their congratulations, but I barely noticed.

"You did wonderfully." Tennie gave my hand a gentle squeeze.

"Thank you, Mrs. Woodhull," Representative Bingham said. "The committee will take time to consider what you have said and render a decision." Though his words were neutral, his expression remained steadfastly unimpressed.

Behind me, a man rose to make the next speech, and we stood to leave. I shuffled along, disappointed in my failure to move Representative Bingham. Hopefully the others had a more positive reaction.

As we passed the bank of reporters, I got my answer.

One senator was telling a man from the *Evening Star*, "Though

Congressman Eldridge thought it appropriate to giggle as though the whole thing was a good joke, I believe Mrs. Woodhull appeared in as good a style as any congressman could have done."

Closer to the door, Miss Anthony had cornered Johnny and was positively beaming. "You see, good *can* come out of Washington. The national capital shall yet be the glory of her sex and the rest of man and womankind."

Out in the hall, I was scarcely able to take a breath before Mrs. Stanton embraced me. "You made us so proud." She beamed.

"Indeed," Miss Anthony agreed. "You must read your memorial at our suffrage convention. Our delegates would be most interested to hear your argument."

By the time the convention was over three days later, I was not only initiated into the fold, I was welcomed into its upper echelons. I spent most of the time listening to the movement's greatest thinkers and strongest advocates call for equality in justice, as well as having those same women, especially Miss Anthony, flatter me within an inch of my life.

On the final night, I was named to the National Committee of Women. That meant remaining in Washington through the spring and working to garner support for the right to vote. Finally, the chance to make a difference on a large scale was within my grasp.

When the group asked for my financial support, I gave generously, elated to be able to do what I had felt called to at my first convention. Ten thousand dollars was not excessive, at least not to me, but it did raise a few eyebrows. While some whispered behind my back that I simply wanted to show up everyone yet again, I was quick to tell those who cared to listen of my long desire to make a difference in the movement.

There was no time for petty jealousy. We had to use every

moment, every advantage we had, to show Congress women were behind us on the issue. If we were successful, we might be able to force a declaratory act even if the decision of the House Judiciary Committee came in against us. Mr. Butler was directing the printing presses of Capitol Hill until they smoked and threatened to over-heat, cranking out thousands of electrotype copies of my memorial, as well as five thousand petition letters asking for women's signatures for the right to vote.

I was already preparing the next issue of the *Weekly*. The next four issues would be dedicated to the women's movement, spreading the word about suffrage as far and wide as possible and encouraging women to write to their representatives by the end of the month, when a decision was expected.

❧

A YOUNG MAN IN a crisp blue military uniform greeted me when I emerged from the dining room of the hotel the following morning. "Mrs. Woodhull, President Grant requests the honor of your presence."

I staggered back a step, hand to my heart. "What? Me? You must be mistaken."

"No, ma'am. Please come with me."

A short walk down Fourteenth Street and a warren of Executive Mansion corridors later, I was standing before the massive oak doors to the president's office.

My escort knocked, announced me, and stepped back. At the president's command—a simple "enter"—the doors where flung open and I was admitted. Before I even crossed the threshold, a cloud of sweet, cloying fumes from a black cigar greeted me, momentarily rob-bing me of breath.

I coughed once and blinked rapidly, straining to see through the haze. The walls were painted in turquoise, gray, and green, the pale carpet stained by tobacco juice and ash. A meeting desk and chairs took up a good portion of the room, and two chairs sat ready to receive guests before the fireplace. The presidential seal watched over us like a guardian angel perched in the center of the ceiling.

President Grant was sitting slouched over his desk, his back to three large south-facing windows, the smoldering cigar between the fingers of his right hand and a document of some sort in his left. He snubbed out the cigar and stood to greet me. "Mrs. Woodhull, it is an honor. You have done the women of your country a great service these last many days."

His firm grip enfolded my hand with power and warmth.

"The honor is all mine, Mr. President."

He pointed at his presidential seat. "You may well occupy this chair one day. You certainly have the courage and the drive. Although I must say, I wish you'd wait until I wasn't running." He chuckled. "Please, sit."

I took a seat facing him, entranced by his bright blue eyes.

"Not only am I pleased that a woman finally broke the invisible boundary before Congress, I'm thrilled it was a fellow Ohioan." He grinned at me.

I nodded, smiling delightedly—though I could hardly believe our meeting was taking place. People would talk about this moment for days to come, the first meeting of the current president and future presidentess.

My time was limited, so I wasted no time in turning the conversation to suffrage. "I'm happy to hear I have your support, Mr. President. If you don't mind my asking, what is your personal opinion on the topic of women's suffrage?"

"It is a just cause and deserves to succeed," the president admitted. "Do you know what I think would fix everything? I would give each married woman two votes, one to please her husband and one for herself. Then wives would be represented at the polls without there being any divided families on the subject of politics."

"If you believe in it so strongly, then why have you not moved to make it law?" The question was out before I had a chance to think it through. Had I just made an enemy of the most powerful man in the world? I squirmed in my seat, awaiting his reaction.

The president was silent, but his expression was not one of anger, rather of contemplation. Finally, he sighed. "I wish it was that simple. People believe the president is all-powerful, a being like unto God. But it's not like that. I can veto or sign laws, but I can't simply make a law because I desire to. I have to go through Congress and all of the other checks and balances that make this wonderful nation of ours a democracy rather than a monarchy." He leaned forward.

I unconsciously did the same, drawn in by the intimacy of his tone.

"Think of it this way. As a citizen, you can violate the law. You may be punished for it, but you can do it. The President of the United States cannot violate the law. That's what I would be doing if I acted alone."

"But surely you can make your position clear." I bit my lip to stop myself from challenging him further.

"I can, and I have. And I will. I promise you I will be more forthright about it. But there is only so much one man, no matter how powerful, can do... but I tell you one thing, Mrs. Woodhull, I will be the loudest person cheering when your petition is taken up by the House then passes into law. I'll even invite your family to be present when I sign it. How does that sound?"

My eyes widened. "Do you believe it will go that far?"

"I do. You've masterfully explained to Congress why they are bound by their own Constitution to enforce this right. How can it not?"

I grinned.

"Oh, be sure to look for a letter from the First Lady. My wife was an early adopter of your cause—from the moment you stormed Wall Street, she was in your corner—and keeps telling me how much she wishes she could have been here to meet you today. Unfortunately, a letter will have to suffice."

"I am honored. Please extend my gratitude to her."

A knock sounded at the door. After receiving permission, a page stuck his head into the office. "Mr. President, a reminder you have a meeting in ten minutes."

"Yes, George, thank you." He stood and held out his hand again. "I'm sorry our visit must be so short, Mrs. Woodhull. But as they say, duty calls." He kissed my hand and escorted me to the door.

"Thank you again, Mr. President. It has been a pleasure and an honor to meet you."

"I would ask you to vote for me in the next election—because you'll be able to, I'm sure—but something tells me another name will be on your ballot."

"I'm afraid so, sir."

"No matter. It's an honor to be in such respectable company."

I had to stop myself from dancing as the guards escorted me out and back to my hotel. The president backed female suffrage and believed my petition would force Congress to recognize that right. Not only that, the First Lady supported me as well. With the two most powerful people in the country behind me, it was a sure bet that the name Victoria Woodhull and the ratification of woman's right to vote would be forever linked.

❧

BY THE END OF January, my nerves were tingling with excitement. The long nights, hoarse throats, and hours of cajoling and convincing that the other suffrage leaders and I had endured in our quest to drum up support for my memorial and women's right to vote had paid off. Not only was the president in favor of my petition, we were able to present Congress with eighty thousand signatures of women from as far away as California who demanded the vote through a declaratory act.

But no victory, even one as assured as this, was without a speck of tarnish. The opposition had been hard at work as well, and one thousand women had signed a petition asking Congress not to give women the right to vote. Led by Isabella's conservative older sister, Catharine Beecher, they believed women should be at home, cooking and taking care of their children, and that only men should engage in business, especially politics. As Catharine wrote, "The Holy Scripture indicates for women a sphere higher than and apart from that of public life because as women they find a full measure of duties, care, and responsibilities and are unwilling to bear additional burdens unsuited to their physical organization."

This troubling mindset could well be the excuse Congress would latch onto in order to dismiss my petition despite the strong support behind it. It weighed heavily on my mind as I stood on the steps of the Capitol Building on January 30, waiting to hear the committee's decision. With me in the lightly falling snow were Susan and Isabella, along with Tennie and nearly three hundred other supporters

I had come to know over the last three months. Above me on the landing, Representative John Bingham stood stone-faced, waiting for some unknown signal. Next to him was my friend and mentor, Benjamin Butler.

Representative Bingham spotted me in the crowd, and a slow smirk spread over his features. He looked me square in the eye as he raised his voice to be heard by everyone in the crowd. "Ladies and gentlemen, it is my honor to present to you the findings of the House Judiciary Committee on the matter of the memorial of Victoria C. Woodhull, which seeks to give women the right to vote on the grounds that it is already granted by the United States Constitution under the rights given to citizens of this country. After careful study and consideration of the matter, it is our finding that a citizen of the United States means nothing more or less than a member of the nation. Therefore, while we affirm this point, we reject the notion that the Constitution entitles women to the right to vote. As this is not a matter of federal law, those who oppose our findings should take their complaints to their individual states, who have the authority to extend the rights to women if they so choose. Furthermore, we have passed a resolution absolving Congress of any commitment to further consider the subject of women's suffrage. We consider this matter closed for the foreseeable future."

I couldn't speak, couldn't do anything but stare numbly at this man who'd pretended to take me seriously. Despite the eighty thousand women we had on our side, this had been a losing battle from the beginning. The man who had blatantly declared I was not a citizen never intended to let his committee prove him wrong.

As the crowd rumbled around me with oaths to carry on and fight injustice and Mr. Butler stepped forward to give the minority report supporting my memorial, Representative Bingham slipped down the stairs to stand next to me.

"Give up, Victoria," he whispered. "You have every right to take your memorial to the New York legislature and try to get the state to act, but remember, I hold sway there as well, and that's one place where even your darling Benjamin can't help you."

I clenched my jaw, willing my anger not to show. *Go to hell.* Oh, how I longed to say those three sharp-edged words, to spit them in his face. But no, I would not insult the person who held my only remaining hope of victory in his hands. Instead, I swallowed my pride. "I will fight with every avenue that is open to me, no matter who believes my efforts futile. Besides, I have supporters who hold more power than even you."

The congressman's laugh came out as a puff of white in the cold air. "If you're referring to the president, your faith is misplaced. You'll see."

Over the following days, the media hounded me for an interview. But I would not talk, not yet. The story would be very different once President Grant came through for me—or at least made a statement denouncing the committee's decision. Then, and only then, would I speak.

Days passed without a single word from the president. I held fast to my belief in the man who had so warmly welcomed me. But then I overheard two reporters, one from the *New York Sun* and one from the *Washington Star*, talking in the Willard lobby.

"I asked President Grant what he thought about Bingham's dismissal of Woodhull's memorial," the one from the *Star* said. "At first he wouldn't say a word. I kept on him, and finally he said, 'The matter of women's suffrage is closed.' What do you make of that?"

My muscles tensed to deflect the blow my mind was ill-prepared to receive, and I sucked in air as though I'd been stabbed. Mr. Bingham was right; everything the president had said to me had been lip service. I ground my teeth. How dare he lie to me! The president may have been the highest power in the land, but that did not give him license to deceive his constituents.

I glared at the reporters. The one from the *New York Sun*, a Mr. Charles Gibson Dana, had been hounding me for an interview for more than a week. Well, he would get his wish and then some.

I stomped over to him. "Get your pencil out, Mr. Dana. I'm ready to make my statement."

"Here? Now?"

"Yes. Take it or leave it."

Mr. Dana fumbled for his notepad. When his pencil was poised, he said, "Go ahead."

"You have asked me for my reaction to the outcome of my memorial. It is this— President Grant has got so many weak men in his Cabinet who control him that he is afraid to do what he knows to be right. Politically, the administration is throughout weak and corrupt. We would be glad to have the president's assistance because he is president; but he knows very well that we don't care for him and mean to depose him. If he had done what he knew to be right at the outset, we would have sustained him, and he would have been strong today; but his weakness and cowardice have been his ruin."

CHAPTER TWENTY

I rubbed my aching temples. All I wanted was to return home to New York and lose myself in the brokerage business while I recovered from the sting of Congress's rejection. But now that I had the National Committee's attention, they weren't going to let me go easily. They had already scheduled my first speech for that very night at Lincoln Hall.

I was no speaker. I had more than proven that in stumbling through my memorial not once but twice. However, Mr. Butler and Isabella were determined to turn me into one, as well as into a woman acceptable in high society.

Just that morning, Isabella had marched down to my room, not even greeting me before beginning my first lesson.

"This should be burned." Isabella waved a letter in my face. It was my handwriting on lined paper from the brokerage firm. "I want you to use nice notepaper hereafter—and send your correspondence in envelopes. You are no longer a banker or a businesswoman but a prospective queen, a lady in every sense of the word. These are too rough, a dreadful eyesore, and so mannish. If you are to be our accepted standard bearer, be perfect, be exquisite in neatness, elegance, and decorousness." She took one last look at the note before tossing it into the fire. "And we must work on your handwriting. You can't rely on your husband to be your secretary forever."

Now Mr. Butler was modeling for me the proper mode and manner of speaking, showing me how to imbue my voice with fire that would transfer to my listeners.

"You remind me of the Methodist preachers Ma took me to see when I was young, full of bluster and power and utterly compelling."

As I rehearsed, reciting my speech over and over, I called those same men to mind, doing my best to transmit my own personal zeal in the words I delivered.

"That was better," the congressman said when I finished. "Your delivery is gaining in force and confidence. Remember to stand up straight. It will help you breathe more fully, which will enable you to speak louder. Take your time. If you rush, your echo will fall all over itself, and your words will be tangled together for those in the back. You want every single person in the theatre to hear you as though you are having a one-on-one conversation."

I nearly hugged him. That was the personal connection I was striving for, what I so admired and envied in speakers like Anna Dickinson and Kate Field. It was what would move my listeners from passive thought into passionate action.

The clock on his desk chimed. "Ah, now I must leave you. Don't worry. You are ready. I'll be there to introduce you."

But as eight o'clock neared, it became clear he wasn't going to show up after all. I sat backstage with Isabella, trying to hold myself completely still. I would be as calm and collected as the women I admired.

As the auditorium filled, however, my resolve cracked, and I fought back a wave of panic that threatened to send me hurtling toward the alley to vomit. Someone had mentioned earlier that the hall seated more than a thousand people. Now they were setting up extra chairs and people were standing in the aisles. That meant my audience had to be closer to thirteen or fourteen hundred.

I grabbed Isabella's arm as the older woman stood. "Will you pray with me? It's the only thing that calms my nerves."

"Of course, my dear."

My trembling hands clasped in Isabella's cool, dry palms, I closed my eyes. "Heavenly Father, great spirits that guide our lives, be with us and empower us this night. Embolden our voices and give power to our words that your truth of universal equality might be heard through us. In Jesus's name we pray."

"Amen," Isabella answered. "Do you feel better now?"

I nodded. "Much."

Isabella led me out onto the stage, where Paulina Wright Davis, fellow suffragist and organizer of the first National Women's Rights Convention some twenty years before, already sat, waiting to introduce us. Paulina rose and approached the footlights, raising her hands to signal quiet from the crowd, whose anticipation to see this new renegade speaker was palpable.

"The objective of this lecture is to present to you concisely the legal and moral arguments in favor of enfranchising half of the citizens of the United States. If neither parties existing now are ready to take this issue, which is the only live one of this day, a new party will spring up that will grind these to a powder." Paulina paused before continuing in an even stronger tone. "The one demand is for equal justice, not reformed laws, not crumbs and favors, but equal justice." She gestured behind her to where I was seated. "Our first speaker tonight is the first woman to see clearly and present persistently the demand for suffrage as a right plainly guaranteed by the Constitution and its amendments. I give you Mrs. Victoria C. Woodhull."

Polite applause followed me as I walked unsteadily to center stage, taking my place before the footlights. Lightheadedness threatened to overwhelm me just as it had before delivering my memorial. *Breathe. Remember what Mr. Butler said. Breathe.*

"I come before you…" I paused, alarmed at how timid and uneven my voice sounded. "I come before you to declare that my sex are entitled to the inalienable right to life, liberty, and the pursuit of happiness." I stopped again, glancing back at Isabella for support and saying a silent prayer to my spirits.

Isabella joined me at center stage, wrapping an arm about my waist. Warmth and love radiated through her, giving me the courage to go on.

"The first two," I continued, "I cannot be deprived of except for cause and by due process of the law, but upon the last, a right is usurped to place restrictions so general as to include the whole of my sex and for which no reasons of public good can be assigned. I ask for the right to pursue happiness by having a voice in that government to which I am accountable."

A whisper of movement, and Isabella's hand fell away. I was alone in the spotlight now, but I was ready—passion for my subject replaced my fear.

"I and others of my sex find ourselves controlled by a form of government in the inauguration of which we had no voice, and in whose administration we are denied the right to participate, though we are a large part of the country."

As I spoke, I caught glimpses of the audience. Women, and a few men, sat in rapt concentration, hanging on my every word. My

old theatre training came back as I warmed to the role of outspoken advocate for women—not only women like me but women like
Minnie and the poor farm wives of the Ozarks, all those I had cared
for over the years.

"I am subject to tyranny," I declared. "I am taxed in every conceiv-
able way. For publishing, for engaging in the banking and brokerage
business—I must pay. I must pay high prices for tea, coffee, and sugar.
To all these I must submit that men's government may be maintained,
a government in the administration of which I am denied a voice, and
from its edicts there is no appeal.

"Women have no government. We mean treason," I thundered.
"We mean secession and on a thousand times grander scale than was
that of the South. We are plotting revolution; we will overslaugh this
bogus republic and plant a government of righteousness in its stead,
which shall not only profess to derive its power from the consent of
the governed but shall do so in reality."

Letting my powerful words serve as their own conclusion, I gave a
small bow to the audience, signaling the end of my speech.

Applause erupted along with joyous cheers and whistles.
Though both Isabella and Representative Butler—who arrived halfway through my speech—gave additional speeches that night, I was
the one the crowd wanted. One by one, they trickled up to me after
the event, expressing their praise and gratitude for my courage and
forthrightness.

A few days later, a letter from Elizabeth Cady Stanton echoed
their sentiments. "We have waited six thousand years, and the time
has finally come to seize the bull by the horns, as you are doing in
Washington and Wall Street."

CHAPTER TWENTY-ONE

I was finally home in New York and eager to get back to business. I had more fire in my belly than since announcing my candidacy for president. Both the press and the suffrage leaders were on my side, and I wasn't going to lie down simply because Congress had told me no. That hadn't worked for my father when I was little, and I'd be damned if it was going to work for them.

If my own enthusiasm wasn't enough to motivate me to step up my efforts to get out my message, the overflowing bags of mail waiting on my desk at the brokerage on Monday did the trick.

I picked up one envelope and removed its contents. It was a scathing rebuke from Mrs. Catharine Beecher. She accused me of not only "making a shameful mockery of womanhood" but of corrupting her younger sister, Isabella, by filling her head with "lies no God-fearing woman should entertain, much less subscribe to." If that wasn't enough, she continued, "You are a witch who has cast a spell on my poor, innocent sister. As a righteous Christian woman, it is my duty to do all within my power to drive the Devil back to hell and destroy you. You have my word I shall do just that until my dying day."

I sat back, appalled at the vitriol contained in so few lines. It was as if Catharine had been channeling a demon when she wrote it. But I was not threatened. Catherine could rail against me until she'd spilled as much ink as water in the ocean, and it wouldn't be more than hateful words. I tossed the letter onto the rubbish pile where such filth belonged.

The next letter I picked was written in a spidery, shaking hand by a woman who claimed to be ninety years old. "I was born on a little farm outside of St. Louis. And oh, have these old eyes seen some sights. I grew up during the birth of our nation, witnessed firsthand the terrors of the Civil War, wept as our president was assassinated, and watched as the Negros were set free. Each one seemed a nightmare or a miracle that wouldn't ever be topped. But here you are, Mrs. Woodhull, a beacon of light. A woman running for president—never thought I'd live to see the day—and one that ain't got no 'punction 'bout bothering those powerful men 'til they finally turn an ear your way. I been tellin' my girls and their girls after them 'bout you and that they oughta do more to get the vote. Please know y'all are in our prayers and we're fighting right alongside you in spirit. May God bless you." It was signed Ella Mae Johnson.

This was it—the proof I needed that women were responding to my call. The thousands of signatures Susan, Isabella, and Elizabeth had captured were wonderful, but most of them came from society matrons and their brethren. But these letters—postmarked from towns large and small across the country—were from ordinary people, the salt-of-the-earth types I had known all my life. As such, they meant more to me than all of the signatures in Boston, Washington,

D.C., and New York combined. These were the women who Congress needed to hear from.

Sudden inspiration overtook me like a fever. Rising, I barreled into the parlor, where James and Stephen were working on the next edition of the *Weekly*.

"Am I too late? Have you put it to bed yet?"

"No, not yet. Why?" Stephen regarded me with a mixture of curiosity and worry, half rising from his chair to meet me. He squinted as he examined my face. "Are you unwell?"

"On the contrary, I've never felt better." I grabbed a proof out of Stephen's hand. "What do we have in this issue? Can anything wait?"

Stephen crossly snatched back the paper. "I'm sure something can. What is so important?"

I was already scribbling across the back of a discarded page. "I want to run my Constitutional Equality speech again along with a brief article asking people to petition Congress. You should see these letters, see what they are already doing without any prompting from me. If we include a sample petition, I know women will take action. Do you have room for that?"

While Stephen and James conferred, arguing over what should stay and what should go, I re-read what I had written.

"Everyone should feel that he or she is a leader and should set about the good work; should draw a petition and sign it themselves and get everybody else whom it is possible to do the same, then forward it either direct to their representative in Congress or to Mrs. Josephine Griffing, Secretary of the National Suffrage Association, Washington, D.C., who will see everything of this kind attended to. It is my sincere hope a million names should show Congress our steadfastness in this matter.

"Not only must these petitions flow from the people upon Congress so as to overwhelm it, but the same power should be brought to bear upon the legislature of every state. Friends of the cause should act in concert. Their real power has never been felt. But when our individual lights shine as one, we shall become a flame to burn the blindfold off the eyes of Lady Justice, so that we, her sisters, might take our equal place alongside men."

My brief article provoked an immediate response, with misdirected petitions from across the nation pouring into the *Weekly* offices, spreading my name and exploits from coast to coast. This was aided in no small part by Susan and Elizabeth, who were both on lecture tours and freely using my name when speaking of the new spark within the movement.

The previous morning, I'd received a brief note from Susan who was taking her speech, "The New Situation," across the Midwest, Upper Plains, and East Coast. "Dear Woodhull, I have just read your speech of the sixteenth. It is ahead of anything said or written. Bless your dear soul for all you are doing to help strike the chains from woman's spirit. Go ahead! Bright, glorious, young, and strong spirit and believe in the best love and hope and faith of Susan B. Anthony."

That was the boost I'd needed for my flagging spirits. For all my newfound passion, the gossip could be fatiguing. Last week I had been out to dinner with James, Mr. Vanderbilt, Tennie, and Stephen, celebrating the success of both the *Weekly* and my burgeoning speaking career. Tennie and I had excused ourselves to the powder room only to encounter a cluster of busybodies who failed to notice our entrance.

"Have you seen Queen Victoria out there holding court?" one woman asked.

"Yes, indeed," a second answered. "She's got them all in attendance tonight: Colonel Blood, her king consort; Mr. Andrews, her minister of publicity; and her sister brought along the minister of finance, Commodore Vanderbilt."

They collapsed into giggles before Tennie cleared her throat and gave them a mocking finger wave, sending half of them skulking out like chastised dogs while the others laughed all the harder.

Such was the life of a public figure, or at least, so I told myself as I made my final preparations to leave for my first lecture tour. I would begin in Boston, where I was sure to face staunch resistance as it was the home of the conservative American Woman Suffrage Association and the Beecher family.

Simply anticipating their reaction turned my mood black. I felt like the figures on the swords suit of tarot cards some of my British Spiritualist friends used to contact the dead—bound by my position, blinded by betrayal of those who were supposed to support me, and pierced through by poisonous tongues.

The perfidy was most keen when, as with Catharine and the women in the restaurant, the disdain came from others of my sex. Why couldn't they see that I was fighting for them too? If women would lay aside their differences and unite, the government would have no choice but to listen to us. But even Jesus knew there would always be those who would oppose him, so who was I to expect otherwise?

I wasn't sure if I was leaving the backbiting behind by going on the road or riding the train into worse territory. I quickly learned life on the lecture circuit was not the glamorous affair it appeared. By the third day, I was peering through bleary eyes and dragging leaden limbs, and that was with James and Tennie handling most of the transportation, publicity, and logistical arrangements.

To the outside world, it appeared all I had to do was show up and speak, but I had to keep my campaign in mind, which made each stop doubly important. Meetings, teas, and dinners with local suffrage leaders filled my time between speeches. After all, as Election Day neared, I would need supporters willing to work for me, printing tickets, distributing them, and stumping on my behalf—best to secure them early.

Sold-out crowds greeted me on every stop on the tour, with more and more people wanting to see this "Notorious Victoria" for themselves. The female support was overwhelming; they greeted me like a queen. Women pledged to join my cause at every event, which endeared me to the local suffrage leaders all the more, as did the complimentary tickets to my events.

By the time I made it to Philadelphia, the final stop on my tour, I was grateful to be dining with a dear friend, the elderly Lucretia Mott, whom I'd met at my first suffrage convention and who had become like a grandmother to Tennie and me. Standing on the doorstep of Roadside, the Mott mansion in the town bearing Lucretia's surname, I rolled my neck, feeling my muscles slowly ease. Even if only for a night, I was home.

"My dear Victoria, you look like a hen that's barely escaped plucking." Lucretia placed a gnarled, translucent hand on my hair, drawing my head down to her shoulder in a maternal embrace.

"I feel like one," I admitted. "I have more than a few feathers out of place, I'm afraid. This tour was only three stops. I don't know how the others do it for months on end."

"You will grow accustomed to it," Lucretia assured me. "As with everything else in life, it simply takes time and practice. Why don't you follow Martha upstairs and take some time to wash and rest before dinner? My daughter, Maria, and her husband, Edward Davis, will be joining us at seven."

Later that night, over a delightful meal of soup and fish, Mr. Davis dispensed with polite conversation and asked me straight out, "What is this I hear about you planning to start your own political party?"

"You hear correctly, though I was hoping to keep my plans under my hat for a while longer." I eyed him across the table, trying to judge how much to reveal. He was a stranger to me but kin to dear Lucretia, so confiding in him was likely safe. "It is my feeling that if neither established party is willing to support a candidate, she has no choice but to form her own. It's not as though this is unknown. It seems there is yet another party at every election."

"True enough," Mr. Davis said. "What will your party stand for? Have you given any thought to your platform?"

I laughed. "I have thought of little else since I decided to run. I will save the particulars for a later speech—which you must all attend. I'll make sure you have tickets before I leave. But I will say this—lately my thoughts have turned toward matters of equality beyond simply those which affect women."

"That much is clear to anyone who reads your paper," Martha, Lucretia's sister, put in.

"Yes, that's what started my train of thought. These railroad monopolies, land-grabbing schemes, and material favoritism we write about are all signs of unequal distribution of material wealth in our country. My past has made me sympathetic to the plight of the working class, and now exposing such corruption has given me pause to think that my party should be based in humanitarian reform that bridges both suffrage and labor issues."

"Do you not fear alienating wealthy voters or those who might be instrumental in supporting your cause?" Mr. Davis asked.

I gave him an appraising look before addressing his wife. "I daresay you made a fine choice in your husband. He has quite an astute mind." I turned back to the man who had addressed me. "You speak of Mr. Vanderbilt, I presume? Yes, I suppose there is some risk, but I am a rich woman in my own right with my own source of income, so I am not beholden to anyone's favor. Let them think what they may."

"Few women would have the boldness to say such a thing," Marie remarked. "Though I know my mother would be one of the exceptions."

Lucretia nodded. "Indeed. When I see what these businessmen get away with in the name of profit, it makes my heart sick. I would gladly support a party that includes both labor and suffrage reform, as I supported the abolitionists before you."

I smiled. "Thank you. Your approval means so much to me. The Bible says the poor will always be among us, and I have no doubt that is true, as it has been for centuries, but who are we to say that as wealthy individuals, we have a right to widen the gap between rich and poor at the expense of those with nothing? Are we not called as Christians to help those in need? I tell you, the first principles of life have been utterly lost sight of, and we are floundering about in the great ocean of material infidelity. A party which would become successful and remain in power must be firm in the advocacy of all growth and reform. All sectionalism, all favoritism, all specialism must be swallowed in the greater interests of the whole."

"Now you sound like the radicals in France," Mr. Davis said with a scoff.

I shrugged. "I know nothing of them, but perhaps I do say the same things. I would imagine revolutionaries worldwide all sing the same basic song."

Lucretia's eyes jerked to me, suddenly dark and distant. Caught in their deep stare, I could not look away.

"They do," my hostess said softly, "but they often meet the same dark ends. Watch yourself that you do not share their fate."

I shivered. Was it my tired imagination reading too much into the concerns of a friend, or was that a genuine warning from the spirits?

CHAPTER TWENTY-TWO

APRIL 1871

"I am going to stop reading the news if it continues to be this grim," Tennie declared, shaking her head over the journal in her hand.

"What is going on now?" I asked, buttering a piece of toast.

"The French Communards are fighting against their government," Stephen said like a child tattling on a rival, allowing a maid to pour him another cup of tea.

"That's not what I'm talking about." Tennie shot him a dark look. "Have you seen this?" She held up the most recent edition of the American Woman Suffrage Association's *Women's Journal*. "They said that the National Woman Suffrage Association's alliance with Victoria is 'worse than if they'd allied with a bigot.'"

"They already have. You've heard Susan and Elizabeth speak about Negros and immigrants, right?" Stephen quipped.

"No one asked you," Tennie responded testily.

I took the paper from Tennie and clucked my tongue as I read. "That cow Mary Livermore has the nerve to bring up our family's dealings in Chicago. I never did trust her. And she dares to say of me 'her hands are unclean' when I wasn't even in Chicago during that whole scandal." I looked up, seeking support from my husband, but I found his expression grave. "James, what is it?"

"That's not the worst of what's being said. I've shielded you from it as long as I can, but you may as well know the whole truth. There are rumors that you're both running a blackmail scheme through the paper, and many of the companies you've exposed as frauds have threatened to shut us down. I doubt any real action will come of it, but you need to know, especially since people are dragging up your past too."

My gut twisted like twine. "Is there anything we can do to stop this?"

"You can prove them wrong or give them something else to talk about. Other than that, it's nearly impossible to fetter people's tongues when they latch onto something juicy," Stephen observed.

"Keep Ma and Pa—the whole family—away from the press," I ordered everyone in the room. "God knows what they would say. That whole blackmailing scheme makes me wonder if Ma is up to her old tricks with Polly again. Though if she needed money, all she'd have to do is ask—she knows that."

"I'll have a word with her," Tennie said.

"Thank you. Now can we please talk of something else? What were you saying about France, Stephen?"

"Oh yes, *la révolution*. It's all very thrilling. After years of oppression, during which rumor has it they ate cat and rat meat, the working people are fighting back. It's glorious—the kind of revolt we need here." Stephen's eyes shimmered with an unsettling light.

"Surely you aren't saying you support slaughter in the streets." I pointed at a headline on the back of the page Tennie held, which memorialized those who had been captured or died supporting the cause.

"No, no." James stepped in for his zealous friend. "He's merely saying the government they have installed is an example of true freedom at work. I'm surprised you haven't heard of this yet. Rumor has it that Wall Street fears a similar workers' uprising here based on meetings the International Workingman's Association is having, demanding an eight-hour work day."

"Perhaps no one feels it to be a subject to be discussed in front of two lady brokers." At my sour look, Stephen added, "I meant that they may not want to give you any ideas. The women of France are demanding many of the same things you advocate."

I sat up straighter. Maybe this was an example I could use in the formation of my own party. "Tell me more."

Stephen plucked the paper from Tennie's fingers. "Ah, well." He cleared his throat as he scanned the columns of closely set type. "It says here that the Communards guarantee the economic, social, and political equality of women with men. Women are forming groups that demand gender and wage equality and the right of divorce." He ran a finger down the page then ticked off points on his fingers. "They also demand the abolition of the distinction between married women and concubines, an end to labeling children legitimate or illegitimate, the closing of legal brothels, and an end to prostitution."

My heart soared. Halfway across the world, women were living my dream of reform. "Oh, that I were there to march with them." I saw myself wearing a red sash and carrying a pennant, demanding freedom in a language I didn't even know.

"No need to buy a ticket on a steamer ship for that." James chuckled. "There are plenty of groups you can ally yourself with right here at home. I have friends in the American Labor Reform League, some of whom you've met at your 'at homes' without knowing their affiliation."

"And I am a member of the International Workingmen's Association," Stephen said. "Our local chapter is one of the most liberal. They would think nothing of admitting a woman, especially not one who could bring their cause as much attention as you. I'll take you to the next meeting. You may even get some ideas for your platform from these hard-working men."

I looked around the table at my family and dear friends. *Thank you, Lord, for such good fortune.* What had begun as an ordinary Sunday morning was soured with rumor then redeemed by fresh new ideas that could mark a turning point in my candidacy and personal mission. God did indeed work in mysterious ways.

CHAPTER TWENTY-THREE

MAY 1871

"You're certain this is a good idea?" I asked Isabella while we waited upstairs at Murray Hill for Isabella's older sister, Catharine, to arrive.

"Oh, yes. I've finally made her see sense. I'm sure once the two of you meet, all your differences will be resolved. She merely needs to see for herself how wonderful you are."

I doubted one meeting would be enough to sway the most conservative, vicious, and outspoken Beecher sister to my radical ways, but I was willing to try. If I could at least broker a tentative peace with Catharine, it would mean I'd have a chance to ingratiate myself with the Boston arm of the suffrage movement. Making strides there—something no one, not even Susan or Elizabeth, had been able to do—would assure a vocal majority to help carry my presidential campaign. I had more reason than anyone to try to broker peace.

The bell outside the front door tolled. Catharine had arrived. I stirred from my thoughts and smoothed my dress.

Isabella squeezed my arm tightly as she made for the stairs, adding, "Remember, I didn't hold you in high esteem before I met you. You have a powerful presence. All will be well."

By the time I descended the stairs, Mr. Cross had let Catharine in. She was standing beneath the large crystal chandelier in the foyer, gaping at the frescos. I fought back a laugh, seeing the pagan gods through Catharine's more traditional eyes. Staying in was out of the question lest Catharine find further fault with the sumptuous nature of my décor or, God forbid, encounter a member of my family.

"Mrs. Beecher," I greeted my guest with a tight smile that was as fake as George Washington's wooden teeth. I held out my hands so Catharine could feel my magnetism. "How do you do?"

Still grousing over her surroundings, Catharine reluctantly took my outstretched hands as Isabella formally introduced us. Catharine nodded then looked longingly after her sister as she disappeared into the parlor so as not to disturb us.

"Would you object to a carriage ride in Central Park?" I asked. "It will give us a chance to enjoy the mild air while we talk."

Catharine regarded me coolly, dark eyes raking over me as though weighing the idea of being seen in public with me or the odds that my offer was some sort of trick. "Fine."

Half an hour later, we settled back into the crimson velvet of my brougham, or rather I did, letting the sun warm my face and the soft breeze caress my skin. Catharine sat with perfect posture, as though nothing could induce her to relax.

"I have no doubt your feelings about women's oppression are sincere," Catharine began the moment the wheels started spinning, her tone stern like that of a schoolmaster lecturing a student and allowing me no opening to get a word in edgewise. "But even you must see your methods are destroying any hope of progress. Here you are, standing up in front of not only your husband and neighbors but the entire United States Congress, daring to tell them they are wrong. You, a woman with two children you obviously neglect, preferring to place your attention on your business and political matters rather than on hearth and home where it belongs."

I opened my mouth to interject that I saw my children every morning and evening and explain how I personally ensured their welfare when they were not with Minnie.

"No woman of breeding should challenge a man," Catharine continued, oblivious to my desire to speak. "The very notion is satanic. Much less a woman like you from a family of seven-by-nine hucksters, but that's where breeding wins out. A woman with proper antecedents would use the only power that is proper for a woman—that of gentle persuasion. She would not seek out undue attention in lecture halls or on street corners as though she was his equal."

Again, I moved to interject, but a woman from a passing carriage called to us. I smiled and waved, losing my opportunity to speak.

"As for this notion of marriage reform that you so proudly tout, it is ridiculous," Catharine barreled on. "The Bible tells us that man and woman, once united under God, are not to be rent asunder. God in his infinite wisdom deigned this to be so. Who are you to purport to know better? Advocating divorce and Free Love"—she shuddered at the phrase—"is the same as asking civilized human beings to return to the lustful instinctiveness of animals. You are asking us to take all that raises us to the height of God's creation and trample it underfoot like so much refuse."

I took a deep breath, the soft perfume of the park's blooming flowers calming my temper a bit. "Catharine, I believe you misunderstand—"

"No," Catharine cut me off, surprising me with a pat on my forearm. "It is not I who misunderstand but you." She shook her head, making the decorative flowers in her cap do a merry dance that was at odds with her grave tone. "I have struggled these long months to understand what my sister sees in you and how you can hold such views. The only conclusion I can reach is that your position must come from a misunderstanding of women's role in the world—which is understandable given how you were raised—or else you are in the possession of some powerful malignant spirits." Her tone dripped pity as though she was speaking to the most unfortunate person she'd ever encountered.

"*You* are misguided," I said, willing myself to remain calm at yet another insinuation of my unworthiness because of my antecedents. "Many great people have already accepted and are living my theories of social freedom, though they are not ready to become its avowed advocates as I am."

I watched Catharine closely to see if she suspected whom my veiled reference was actually about. No recognition. I should have remained silent and pretended the conversation had never occurred, but the temptation to put this condescending witch in her place once and for all was too great.

"You speak of Free Love with derision while your own brother, Henry Ward Beecher, the most powerful preacher in America, openly practices it. I do not condemn him; I applaud him. Would that he had the courage to join me in preaching what he practices."

Catharine's eyes bulged, and her mouth gaped, making her resemble an unnatural cross between a toad and a beached fish. She clutched at the broach at her throat with one hand while pointing a bony finger at me with the other. "Evil"—she cringed into the corner of the carriage—"that is what you are. I know my brother is unhappy, but he is a true husband. I will vouch for my brother's faithfulness to his marriage vows as though he were myself." She pulled herself even farther upright and sniffed derisively.

"But you have no positive knowledge that would justify your doing so."

"No positive…" Catharine spluttered. "Mrs. Beecher is a virago, a constitutional liar, and a terrible woman altogether, so terrible my brother's friends and family seldom visit. But unfaithful—no. I will hear no more of it." She crossed her arms and turned away from me, directing her full attention to the gardens and pond we were passing.

I snickered. "If you frequent the market, the milliner, or even your own church, you will be hard-pressed not to hear that he is in concubinage with his parishioner's wife—it is common knowledge. And if you were a proper person to judge, which I grant you are not, you should see that the facts are fatal to your theories." I sat back, satisfied I'd finally landed a blow that the old woman would not forget.

Catharine raised her fist, shaking with rage. "Victoria Woodhull"—spittle flew from her mouth as if she were rabid—"I will strike you for this. I will strike you dead."

I looked down my nose at the woman who was clearly now my strongest enemy. "Strike as much and as hard as you please. Only don't do it in the dark so I cannot know who is my enemy."

"Stop!" Catharine rang the bell for the driver. As the carriage slowed, she narrowed her eyes at me with the chilling calmness of a bird of prey. "You will know exactly whom it is who strikes at you." As she slid out of the carriage, she added in a menacing tone, "I will strike at you in every way I can and will kill you if possible. That is a promise."

Light one passenger, the coachman returned me to the mansion, and I stormed up the stairs, itching to tell Isabella about how the meeting she was so sure would make us bosom friends had backfired. But the sound of raised voices inside made me pause with my hand on the doorknob.

"Useless? I built a brokerage firm on Wall Street. How can you possibly call me useless?" Tennie's voice was raised in anger and high-pitched in indignation.

A snort came in reply. "Using your thighs to dupe a gullible old man into parting with his fortune." It was our sister Utica.

"I can think of worse ways to humbug someone," added a male voice. It sounded like Canning.

Why were they ganging up on Tennie?

I quietly opened the door and peered inside. The foyer was empty. The commotion was emanating from the dining room. I peeked in, unnoticed. My mother and Utica were once again playing dress up in frocks belonging to Tennie and me. They were seated at the dining room table, which was fully set for high tea. Canning was across from them, one ankle on the other knee, dressed in a mismatched mockery of formal best, including a bowler hat even though he was indoors. The room reeked of alcohol.

"The apple don't fall far from the tree, does it?" Annie asked, elbowing Utica and giving her a toothless, leering grin.

"Ma, give me some credit," Tennie wailed, voice quavering as though she were close to tears.

"Why can't you be more like your sister? Victoria's out makin' all them speeches, and she's gonna be president. What are you doing other than playing around with all them numbers up in your office?"

It was time to intervene. I stepped inside. "She's making the money that's supporting my campaign, Ma. Not to mention putting a roof over your head, food in your belly, and"—I sniffed my mother's cup—"drink in your cups. Don't be so hard on her." Drugstore brandy, the lowest form. No wonder they were all drunk.

"So that's all I am to you?" Tennie asked me, crossing her arms defensively. "I'm your trust fund?"

"That's not what I meant, and you know it."

Annie giggled, clearly enjoying the row. "Maybe you should run for office too, Tennie. First Claflin to get voted in wins."

I stared at my relatives, who were near to falling out of their chairs with merriment. At least Canning didn't seem to find the situation funny.

"I'm happy to know my career means so much to you." I rang the bell to have the maid come take away the "tea" service. My alcoholic family clearly needed no more encouragement.

Canning stood unsteadily and made his way over to me. He kissed my hand before I could stop him. "All in jest, my love."

I jerked away my hand. "I have not been your love for more than a decade. Do not touch me."

Canning made to respond but was distracted by the arrival of the maid, who handed me a stack of envelopes—the afternoon mail—before clearing the tea service amid protests from Annie, Canning, and Utica, who held on to her cup until Tennie forcibly removed it.

I squinted at the top envelope, not recognizing its origin. "Who would be writing to us from Ohio?"

"A relative maybe or a former neighbor from when we were young?" Tennie guessed. "Or perhaps it's a contribution to your campaign."

"No, they all hated us. Held a collection to run us out of town. You were too young to remember. And I have my campaign funds sent elsewhere to keep them safe from sticky fingers." I meant my father, who was known to lift checks delivered to the brokerage firm.

Her addled mind presumably catching up to the conversation, Annie cried, "That's mine!" She lunged at me, knocking over a candlestick and sending the centerpiece crashing to the floor.

I easily maneuvered out of her reach and removed the contents from the envelope. A letter and a slip of paper fluttered to floor. I snatched them up before Ma could try.

Holding it up to the light, I read the letter aloud. "'Dear Miss Claflin. A pirate has just left this letter with me, an old woman who said she was your mother. I believe from what she said that she was crazy. She said she had been told to get three hundred dollars out of me for that letter, but as she couldn't read, I believed that she did not know what she had been put up to. I told her it was no use. That all I knew of you was that you were a woman who honestly earned your own living. I gave her three dollars because she said she hadn't eaten and hadn't a cent. I asked her why she didn't go to you. She said her daughter and her husband would send her to Blackwell's Island, that wretched dumping ground for hopeless debtors and the insane, if she did. I write this to you to put you on your guard and return proof that the parties behind your mother mean you harm.'"

I quickly read over the paper that had accompanied the letter. It was in Polly's handwriting and most certainly a blackmail attempt. I pinned my mother with a merciless stare. "Is this what you meant when you said you got in touch with some old friends on your last journey home? You and Polly are back to blackmailing people? Why? Tennie and I provide for all your needs and even your selfish whims. How could you do this? Is this your idea of fun? Polly, get down here," I commanded, raising my voice so it would carry through the floors above to a sister who could not mistake its gravity.

Before Annie could form a response, Tennie collapsed into a chair, tears falling thickly. "What have you done? Never, never will I ever go back to that life." She scrubbed at her cheeks, halting suddenly and staring at her mother. "You've written to Cornelius too, haven't you? When I went to his house yesterday, the butler told me he wasn't at home even though we have a standing date. Then later I received word that he no longer wished to keep our appointments." Her tears began anew. "I believed the note was another trick of William's, an attempt to drive us apart, but now I know. Oh, God." She dropped her head into her hands.

"There's more," I said, fingering a second envelope. "This message informs us that Mr. Vanderbilt will no longer be a contributing patron of the brokerage or the paper." I flung the second letter at my mother and sister. "You've done it, Mother. You've ruined us. The commodore values trust above all, and now that you've broken that, he will never forgive us."

Annie made a dismissive noise. "Don't neither of you need the old coot. You got your own money and your own jobs. Well, you do." She waved at me. "Like I said, this one is useless." She dipped her head, indicating Tennie. "Now, if you'd come back to your father's business, then you could contribute to this family somethin' proper."

"I will never—" Tennie began.

"Get out, all of you," I bellowed, shaking with rage. "I will not have such vile thieves in my house. I don't care if you are my family." My vision blurred with anger. "You have thirty minutes to pack your things. You too," I added to Polly and her husband, who had arrived unnoticed during the exchange. "And you'd better believe I will have maids stationed with the silver and our jewels. If even one seafood fork or a single earring is found missing, I will bring suit before you can say spit. Do you hear me?"

"They have nowhere to go," Tennie said in a small voice, sounding much as she did when we were children.

"So?"

"At least put them up in a boardinghouse."

"I will do no such thing. I have spent my entire life in the shadow of their schemes. I'll be damned before I let them ruin what we have worked so hard to build. Mark my words, not another dime of my money will be spent on the lot of you."

I turned, intent on storming out, but Canning blocked my path. I shoved past him, which wasn't difficult since he was already imbalanced from drink.

"Do I have to go too?" he asked quietly. "I didn't blackmail anyone."

I closed my eyes and took in a long, ragged breath, fighting for control. "No. Go to your room for now. I'll deal with you later."

He wasn't supposed to be drinking, the doctor said so, but that was such a trifling matter in comparison to all we'd lost I hardly cared. As the door was closing behind me, a snippet of conversation rose above Annie's wails of how she'd been wronged.

"Don't worry, Ma," Tennie said. "I'll put you and Pa up in a boardinghouse. I have money of my own."

I balled my hands into fists at my sides. Tennie would never learn. She was the wounded puppy who always returned to her abuser.

Rubbing my temples, I made a decision. I may not have been able to save my family, but I might be able to save our relationship with Mr. Vanderbilt if I could show him that Tennie and I had nothing to do with our family's scheming. Pocketing the letter from Ohio, my one precious bit of proof, I summoned the coachman.

❀

THREE DAYS LATER, AFTER brokering a tacit truce with Mr. Vanderbilt, I sat on the stage of Apollo Hall before a sold-out crowd of suffragists and laborers as part of the National Women's Rights Convention, only minutes away from giving the keynote address.

Over the last few days, dozens of women had given speeches, and as a body, we had ratified my idea that women had already been given the right to vote by the Fourteenth and Fifteenth Amendments. Even though Elizabeth Cady Stanton and Lucretia Mott were running the business of the meeting, the press had begun calling it "the Woodhull Convention" and the attendees "Woodhull's Women."

Could it be true? Was it possible that a mere two years after attending my first convention, I was the unofficial leader of this one? The suffragists in their bloomers, breeches, and gowns chatting happily with plainly dressed Spiritualists seemed to think so, as did the businessmen, politicians, and members of the International Workingmen's Association Section 12, who sat elbow to elbow, exchanging ideas with a contingent of madams from the local brothels. They were all here to see me, to hear what I had to say.

Normally I would have tried to dissuade myself from such hubris, but I would need all the confidence I could get to make it through this speech. Though the crowd was made up mostly of supporters, a fair contingent of journalists were also pressed in among the crowd, ready to deliver my words to a much less forgiving public.

While I was introduced, I fanned myself and prayed I would not faint. One would have expected Apollo Hall to be hot with so many people present on an unusually warm May night, but tonight it was suffocating. We'd discovered earlier in the day that the windows had to stay shut in order to hear the speakers over the clops and creaks of the horses and carriages outside. I sipped my water and took my place before the crowd.

"Why do I war upon marriage?" I asked by way of introduction. "Because it is, I verily believe, the most terrible curse from which humanity now suffers, creating more misery, sickness, and premature death than all other causes combined. Sanctioned and defended by marriage, night after night, thousands of rapes are committed under the cover of this accursed license. I know whereof I speak."

A spool of stories of neglect and abuse told to me by clients over the years unwound in my mind. I could still hear their voices as clearly as the day they'd confessed their shames to me.

"Millions of poor, heartbroken, suffering wives are compelled to minister to the lechery of insatiable husbands when every instinct of body and sentiment of soul revolt in loathing and disgust."

Memories of all the nights I had to submit to Canning's drunken advances against my will assailed me—his calloused hands upon my thighs, his whiskey-soured breath in my mouth, his clammy skin rubbing against mine. Shame flooded me, bringing with it heat so strong my cheeks and neck tingled. This was why I spoke so freely—or bravely, as some said. I had to use the humiliation of my past to help free other women from similar bondage. It was the only way I, or they, would ever be free.

I let my repressed fear, anger, and betrayal color my voice. "Prate of the abolition of slavery, there was never servitude in the world like this one of marriage."

A rumble flowed through the crowd as listeners commented to their neighbors. From the expressions of those in the front row, the opinions ranged from nods of agreement to scowls of indignation.

I held up a palm to quiet the crowd. "I have asked for equality, nothing more. Sexual freedom means the abolition of prostitution both in and out of marriage, means the emancipation of woman from sexual slavery and her coming into ownership and control of her own body. Rise and declare yourself free." I motioned, encouraging the women to stand and cheer.

"Women are entirely unaware of their power. If the very next Congress refuses women all the legitimate results of citizenship, we shall proceed to call another convention expressly to frame a new Constitution and erect a new government."

Cheers, applause, whistles of approval, and the chant "Woodhull! Woodhull!" filled the hall. The audience was replaced by a sea of white with occasional splotches of bright color as women waved their handkerchiefs.

When I turned to take my seat, I found Lucretia Mott crying. She hugged me before I could take my seat, whispering, "You truly are an evangel."

It took nearly a quarter of an hour for the crowd to settle down enough that Elizabeth could speak. She gave a brief statement about my new political party before inviting me to once again take center stage.

This time I spoke plainly, although not without conviction. "I have had ample occasion to learn the true worth of present political parties, and I unhesitatingly pronounce it is my firm conviction that if they rule this country twenty years to come as badly as they have for twenty years past, our liberties will be lost or the parties will be washed out by such rivers of blood as the late war never produced. Therefore, it is my conviction, arrived at after the most serious and careful consideration, that it will be equally suicidal for the woman suffragists to attach themselves to either of these parties. We will have our rights. We will say no longer 'by your leave.' We have besought, argued, and convinced, but we have failed; and we will not fail.

"Though the right to vote be now denied, it must eventually be accorded. Women can be neither Democratic nor Republicans. They must be humanitarian. They must become a positive element in governmental affairs. They have thought little; they must be brought to think more. To suggest food for thought, a new party and a new platform is proposed for the consideration of women and men; the party, the Cosmopolitical—the platform, a series of reforms."

I proceeded to read the platform document, which had mostly been written by Stephen. Reactions were about as expected. Reform of the government, including a one-term presidency, brought some vocal agreement. The room was silent when I spoke of governmental and prison reform, while they greeted labor reform—especially the idea of an eight-hour workday—with raucous foot stomping and whoops of adulation. More cheers arose at tax reform but died to silent apathy as I explained my proposed system of national education and foreign policy.

Finally, the moment I had been anticipating for months had arrived—my final proposal, the one that required government to stay out of personal affairs and paved the way for Free Love, which would bring an end to marriage being an iron trap for women. My words were couched in carefully arranged language so as not to arouse too much ire or undue excitement—I never called it Free Love—but several of the patrons were wise enough to connect my earlier speech about marriage reform to my call to limit the government's involvement in personal issues.

As I finished the closing remarks of my speech, the phrase "Free Love" began a slow ripple across the hall. I could actually follow its progress as one head turned to the next and the general level of chatter grew. By the time my speech ended, the level of applause scarcely drowned out the catcalls. I walked off the stage a woman both revered and reviled.

By the morning, the press was crying "Free Love" as though the phrase had never before been uttered. For all my trepidation over what people were going to say, I now reveled in the coverage. The more scandalized the papers were, the more of them people bought and the more my name was on everyone's lips. I could live with my name being temporarily associated with loose morals and marital infidelity if it meant my platform was spreading farther across the country. I still had eighteen months to help the American public understand what

I truly meant by the term. If I had learned anything from Stephen in the last year, it was that the exposure could do me no lasting harm as long as I followed it up with something positive.

Besides, I was vindicated by the unlikeliest of sources—the *Tribune*, Horace Greeley's traditionally conservative paper. The *Tribune* was not quick to dole out praise, but they lauded me for standing up to defend my beliefs, writing, "*For ourselves, we toss our hats into the air for Woodhull. She has the courage of her opinions. She means business. She intends to head a new rebellion, form a new Constitution, and begin a revolution beside which the late war will seem but a bagatelle, if within exactly one year from this day and hour of grace, her demands be not granted out of hand. This is a spirit to respect, perhaps to fear, certainly not to be laughed at. Would that the rest of those who burden themselves with the enfranchisement of one-half our whole population, now lying in chains and slavery, had but her sagacious courage.*"

I cut the clipping as soon as I read it and sent copies to my loudest detractors. I smiled, imagining their scowls as they read such high praise for my courage. Let them call me a misguided fool now.

CHAPTER TWENTY-FOUR

"James, Tennie, where is the paper?" I called.

I'd spent the better part of an hour searching for the *Times*, eager to see if there had been any additional coverage of my speech or the nasty letter-writing battle that followed. I couldn't find it in any of the usual places; it wasn't on the table in our bedroom, the sideboard in the dining room, not even in James's favorite chair in the parlor. Stranger still was that even the servants had claimed not to have seen it.

Giving up, I donned my cloak and walked to the nearest newsstand. I paid my ten cents and scanned the headlines as I returned home. I was about to climb the front stairs when a notice in the legal section—which had increasingly been carrying threats against my firm by companies exposed in the *Weekly*—gave me pause. This couldn't be right. It couldn't. Leaning against the stone wall for support, I read the article again, shaking my head in disbelief.

"Roxanna 'Annie' Claflin, mother of the self-appointed presidential candidate Victoria Woodhull, appeared before one Justice Ledwith a week ago Monday and swore out a warrant for the arrest of James H. Blood, alias Dr. J. Harvey, on charges that he 'has succeeded in corrupting her daughters Victoria and Tennessee' and had 'entirely weaned them from their affectionate and never to be consoled mother.' In addition, she had 'often heard Blood insist that Tennessee should make efforts to secure the attentions of different married gentlemen of wealth in order that they might make money out of them.' Such men as were secured, she charged, were blackmailed by Blood. A trial date has been set for May 15."

I covered my mouth with my hand and sank onto the cold stone steps, letting the paper fall at my side. There had to be some mistake. My mother might have been a vengeful old bat, but even she wouldn't take her family to court, would she? I laughed, a bitter, mirthless sound. Of course she would. This was the same woman who had blackmailed every person she could. She likely had my thieving father's full support, not to mention that of the equally indignant Polly and her husband, Dr. Sparr.

I took a deep breath, momentarily calmed until I recalled the date mentioned at the end of the article. May 15. That was tomorrow. Why had no one told me? What was I to do? Did James know? He had to. Realization dawned like a punch to the gut. This was why I could not find the paper this morning. James didn't want me to know and had been trying to hide it. Frantic in mind but overcome in body and spirit, I drew my knees to my chest and laid my head on them, trying to think, all the while torn between anger at my mother, betrayal that James had kept this from me, and utter despair.

I was still in this position when a pair of brightly polished black boots crunched into my field of vision. James's coat and hat came into view as he bent to retrieve the paper.

"You know." It was a statement, not a question.

I said nothing, remaining still as a statue.

James placed his walking stick and hat on the banister before sitting next to me. "I was hoping this whole situation would be over before you even heard of it." When I didn't reply, he continued with a deep sigh. "I suppose this is my fault. I was there when the affidavits were read. The judge said he would dismiss the complaint unless I insisted on a trial."

I raised my head. Had I heard him correctly? He'd had the chance to stop this and chosen not to?

James passed a hand across his face. "Damn my pride. I couldn't let that woman ruin my good name. I told the judge I wished for a trial so I could disprove the charges against me."

I struggled to speak, opening and closing my mouth several times before finding my voice. "Why would you do such a thing?" I took hold of James's shoulders and shook him. "Have you any idea what this could do to us? To the firm? I can see the headlines now—'Future Presidentess Attacked by Own Mother.' Oh, you are a fool." I rose, ignoring the protestations of my stiff joints, and stomped up the stairs.

James was after me like a shot. "Victoria, please, I'm sorry."

Ignoring him, I flung open the door and made for our bedroom. On the landing outside our room, I whirled on him, one hand already on the doorknob. "Apologies will do us no good now. We have to find a way to undo this. I will speak with the firm's lawyer and see if it can be hushed up."

"I have already secured a lawyer. There is nothing to be done but see it through."

I regarded my husband coldly. That his contrition was sincere was plain enough in the pleading of his eyes and his wrinkled brow, but that did not change the facts. This man, whom I loved more than anything, had chosen to indulge his pride rather than save all of us the embarrassment of a public trial. What was worse, he had given Ma a bit of vindication simply in acknowledging her suit, a concession she would twist as far and as long as she could. I shuddered, dreading the following day. Annie Claflin may have been evicted from her daughter's home, but she was not about to go down without a fight.

***

THE LARGE, OPEN ROOM of the Essex Market Police Court was a hive of anticipation the following morning while its patrons waited for Judge Ledwith to appear. I sat next to my husband, still refusing to speak to him, straining to pick out snippets of the conversations buzzing around me. I hadn't been the only one to note the legal notice, which had been inflated from a fine-print article yesterday to full-page speculation today, calling Ma's suit "The Great Scandal" and painting her claims as slanderous "revelations," giving them a ring of truth that the more honest term "allegations" lacked. I'd feared walking into a hornet's nest when we entered the courtroom today, but thus far, no one was paying us any mind.

James stood and shook the hand of a tall, barrel-chested man with hair so white it had to have been originally blond. He introduced the man as John DeNoon Reymert, our lawyer.

His name was so similar to that of my lover's in Washington, Judah DeWitt Reymart, my heart skipped a beat and my blood turned to ice. This couldn't be a coincidence. But what did it mean? Did James know? Was this man his way of getting revenge on me? No, I was being foolish. None of this meant anything. Many people had similar names. I had to stop this nonsense and focus on today's trial.

Soon the judge entered and proceedings began. As the one bringing the suit, Ma was called to the stand first. My jaw tightened as Polly helped Ma, hobbling for effect, into the testimonial seat as though she were an invalid; the whole family knew she could walk fine. It was her mind that was defective, not her body.

Ma's lawyer, a man called Mr. Townsend, asked her to tell the court why she had brought this claim against Colonel Blood.

Ma gave the judge her most piteous look. "Judge, my daughters were good daughters and affectionate children afore they got in with this man, Blood. He's threatened my life several times, and one night last November, he came into tha house on East Thirty-Eighth Street and said he would not go ta bed 'til he'd washed his hands in my blood." Her chin trembled, and her voice shook as though she would burst into tears.

"I'll tell you what that man Blood is. He is one of those who have no bottom to their pockets; you can keep stuffin' in all the money in New York, but they never get full up. If my daughters would just send this man away, as I always told them to do, they might be millionairesses and go riding around in their own carriages. I came here because I want to get my daughters out of this man's clutches. He has taken away Vickie's affection and Tennie's affection from their poor old mother." Sniffling loudly, she took hold of the Bible used to swear her in and grasped it to her chest. "S'help me God, Judge, I say here and I call Heaven to witness that there was tha worst gang of Free Lovers in that house on East Thirty-Eighth Street that ever lived—Stephen Pearl Andrews and Dr. Woodhull and lots more of such trash."

Eyebrows raised at how wildly his client had veered off course, Mr. Townsend snapped, "Keep quiet, old lady."

Ma wagged an arthritic finger at him. "Yes, yes, I'll keep quiet. But I want to tell the judge what these people are. I was afeared for my life all tha time I was in the house. It was nothin' but talkin' 'bout lunatic asylums. If not for my son-in-law, Dr. Sparr, they would have put me on Blackwell's Island." She harrumphed and nodded for emphasis.

Shaking his head, Mr. Townsend ended his questioning there. Mr. Reymert wisely chose not to question Annie lest he give her a venue to vent her spleen in additional detail that might harm his client.

Polly was called next, and as expected, she affirmed her mother's testimony. Though she tried to appear prim and the picture of a good daughter, it didn't take long for her real feelings to show.

When asked about Ma's relationship with Tennie and me, she answered, "Of course she's upset over the colonel taking them away. She always did like them two best. My whole life, all I heard was how wonderful Vickie and Tennie were. Never once did she praise me." She crossed her arms defiantly. "But now look who's here to take care of her in her old age. Me. Not them two. They turned us out into the street."

"Did you ever witness Mr. Blood acting in a violent manner toward your mother?" Mr. Reymert wanted to know.

Polly thought before answering. "No. But she was right about Blackwell's Island. Once I seen Tennie and Vickie invoke the spirit of Demosthenes, Vickie's spirit guide, who, speaking through Vickie, threatened my mother that she would be taken to an insane asylum."

My grip on the banister in front of me tightened, forcing the blood from my knuckles as I fought the urge to rise and pummel my sister or, at the very least, raise my voice in self-defense. How dare the little traitor use my religion against me? Polly had never witnessed any of my séances, especially not the private ones where I consulted Demosthenes. Those were for James and me alone. What Polly said made no sense. Why would a spirit threaten our family? But then again, Polly had never been concerned with the finer points of Spiritualism, preferring, like Ma, the flash and showmanship that could easily part unwitting people from their coins.

The lawyers looked at one another, seeming not to know how to follow that bit of information. When neither made a move to question her further, the judge dismissed Polly and called James to the stand.

Mr. Townsend wasted no time getting straight to the point. "Did you never make any threat to Mrs. Claflin?"

James shook his head. "Nothing except one night last fall when she was very troublesome. I said if she was not my mother-in-law, I would turn her over my knee and spank her."

Mr. Townsend did a poor job of covering a snicker with a cough. When he recovered his composure, he asked, "Would you do that?"

James chose not to reply, letting logic speak for itself.

Changing tack, Mr. Townsend asked, "When were you married to Mrs. Woodhull?"

"In 1866 in Chicago."

"Were you married to anyone before that?"

I cringed, not liking where this was headed. We had never actively concealed our previous marriages, but neither of us wanted the uncomfortable subject resurrected, especially when there were bound to be reporters present. Still, James was under oath, so he had to answer.

"Yes. I was married in Framingham, Massachusetts."

I waited for our lawyer to object. I didn't know the finer points of law, but my past work with Mr. Butler and Judah had taught me they had to stick to the topic at hand, which this clearly was not. But Mr. Reymert didn't make a move. He rather sat passively, as though observing a pleasant conversation.

"Were you divorced from your first wife?" Mr. Townsend asked.

"Yes."

"Was Mrs. Woodhull divorced when you married her?"

James thought hard on this question, his brow furrowing, silence stretching into an uncomfortable tension before he finally admitted, "I don't know."

My mouth dropped open, and the courtroom erupted in scandalized murmurs. How could he have said that? He knew that Canning and I were divorced in 1863. Was he daft or had nerves simply wiped his mind of all memory?

Seeking to restore peace, the lawyer quickly moved on. "Were you afterward divorced from Mrs. Woodhull?"

I stiffened. We never spoke about the brief period we were separated, and now it was going to come out in open court. I rubbed my temples, which were pounding with the rush of my blood. His memory better not fail him now, or we would both appear to be illegitimately calling ourselves husband and wife. Could this day get any worse?

On the witness stand, James cleared his throat. "Yes. In Chicago in 1868, for a short time. My wife's sister Polly"—he indicated the woman who had just testified—"and her first husband said they had evidence my first marriage was still legal. They threatened to have me arrested for bigamy, with the plan that they would get ten or fifteen thousand dollars out of me for not pressing charges. I had already gone through the legal process in St. Louis, but I was worried something hadn't gone through correctly. Since Victoria and I were traveling during that time, it would have been hard for a lawyer to reach me, so I thought it wisest to divorce her before I went to St. Louis to ensure the first divorce was finalized. When I confirmed I was no longer tied to my first wife, Victoria and I were remarried."

I closed my eyes, unable to face the people around me, but I couldn't shut out their gasps of shock. I wasn't sure which was more scandalous to the good people of New York: that my sister had tried blackmailing us once before—it had actually been more than once, but I prayed her routine attempts would not come to light—or that James and I had briefly been divorced. Judging from the excited conversations, both were an equal delight to those who lapped up scandal like milk.

When the crowd finally quieted, the proceedings continued.

"I'd like to turn now to the Dr. Woodhull who was mentioned earlier. When have you seen Dr. Woodhull?" Mr. Townsend asked.

My heart sank into my stomach. Canning? Why was Mr. Townsend interested in Canning? This couldn't possibly lead to anything good. Cold sweat broke out on the back of my neck, and I searched the room for a source of egress as panic threatened to overtake me.

"I see him every day. We are living in the same house."

I rested my head on the rail in front of me as silver spots of light danced in my vision and breath was sucked from my lungs. I should have smacked my husband for answering so stupidly. I could almost hear the thoughts of those in the courtroom. The candidate for president who had held herself up as a representative woman was living with two men to whom she had been married. Our situation was innocent, but the public did not know that, nor would they listen even if I shouted it from the spires of St. Patrick's cathedral. I swayed in my chair, praying the darkness would take me soon.

A cool breeze brought me back from the brink of unconsciousness as the judge called for order. The sharp raps of his gavel echoed through my nerves, calling me back into my body. I raised my head to find Tennie furiously fanning me. Mr. Reymert thrust a glass of water into my hand.

Seemingly unfazed by the commotion, Mr. Townsend continued. "Do you and Mrs. Woodhull and Dr. Woodhull occupy the same bedroom?"

James didn't answer. He was staring at me with a stricken expression, giving no indication he had even heard the question.

Mr. Townsend raised his voice and tried again to attract James's attention. "Now, Mr. Blood, please tell the court why Dr. Woodhull lives in the same house and who supports him."

James's face went from shock to quiet rage in an instant. "The firm of Woodhull, Claflin, and Company has supported the whole of them. Mrs. Woodhull's first child is idiotic, and Dr. Woodhull takes care of him." He bit out his words through clenched teeth.

I left the courtroom then, unable to hear any more. My humiliation was complete. Now, not only did everyone know my family's squabbles and my troubled past, but they also were aware I had a simpleton for a son. I had arrived today to stand by my husband as he cleared his name—misguided though his intentions might have been—but left with more than a scarlet letter on my breast. I'd borne the full ignominy of the day's testimony all thanks to a vengeful mother who had achieved more with this suit than she could have ever dreamed. Plus, I had to pray my marriage could withstand the mess James had created. And the whole ordeal was far from over. I still had to testify tomorrow.

❖

TUESDAY WAS EVERYTHING I'D feared the first day of the trial would be. As newspapers gleefully reported the previous day's shocking revelations, people crowded into the courthouse, hoping to witness something shameful or at least catch a glimpse of the famous sisters who were set to testify. They had ample opportunity as Tennie, James, a police officer, and I slowly snaked through the clogged passageways lined with gawkers.

The courtroom itself was little better as reporters, brokerage clients, and all manner of public figures jockeyed for position. Once at the defense table, I could at least breathe, having the open expanse of the courtroom proper before me. I glanced at the empty chair beside me. Where was Mr. Reymert? He should have been there by now. Worried, I searched the room. Instead of the elderly gentleman, James was happily greeting Judah DeWitt Reymart, my auburn-haired former lover.

For a moment, the world tilted, and I feared I would faint before I was even called to the stand. But I pulled myself together, without, from what I could tell through surreptitious glances, my husband or sister being any the wiser.

"I hope you will forgive the last-minute change of counsel," the younger Mr. Reymart said in his honeyed voice. "Mr. Reymert fell ill during the night and asked me to take his place. I'm one of the partners in his firm and a distant relative, as you may have guessed by the similarity in name." He flashed us both a charming smile but gave no outward sign of recognizing me.

For that, at least, I was grateful. I sat back down, suddenly overcome with nerves. Now I not only had to undo the damage done by yesterday's testimony, I had to do it in front of my secret former lover, and chances were good I would have to speak about the same extremely personal matters that had been broached yesterday. Casting a quick glance heavenward, I silently asked, *What did I do to deserve this?*

Mr. Reymart took his seat next to me while James placed a reassuring hand on me from behind. At least, I thought that was what it was meant to mean. His palm pressed into my shoulder like a vise in which I was imprisoned by guilt—a feeling that was not supposed to accompany Free Love.

"Are you all right?" Mr. Reymart asked.

"What?" Had he somehow divined my thoughts? No, he was simply inquiring about my readiness to testify. "Oh, yes. I'm quite fine. Thank you."

"We are in the lead today, so I will walk you slowly through your testimony. Answer only what I ask of you and avoid superfluous details."

"I understand."

Once I was sworn in, Mr. Reymart began. "Please state your name and explain to the court your relationship with those involved in this case."

"My name is Victoria C. Woodhull. Colonel Blood is my husband. Dr. Woodhull was my husband. I was near fifteen years of age when I married Dr. Woodhull. I have lived seven years with Colonel Blood. My mother has lived with me at East Thirty-Eighth Street. My father lived there also, along with this man Sparr and his family of four children; Mrs. Miles and her four children; Mr. Woodhull; myself and my husband, Colonel Blood; and my sister Tennie."

Mr. Reymart smiled at me encouragingly. "How would you characterize the relationship between your husband and your mother?"

"Colonel Blood has never treated my mother otherwise than kind. Sometimes when she would become violent, he would utterly ignore her presence. I thought at times that she was insane and not responsible for what she said. I never thought my mother in danger of any violence from Colonel Blood. The most I ever heard him say was when she would come up to the door and abuse him frightfully, as if she were possessed by some fiend, he said, 'If you do not leave that door, I will go out and push you from it.' I never knew him to put his hands on her."

"You speak of your mother living with you in the past tense. What is your relationship now?"

"She left my house in April and went to the Washington Hotel to board." I glanced at Tennie, still sore she was paying our parents' room and board. "All bills for her maintenance there are paid by the firm of Woodhull, Claflin, and Company. I have always pitied my mother," I added as an afterthought, though why, I could not say. I was beginning to understand why my relatives babbled in this chair with so many curious and accusatory eyes on them.

Mr. Reymart shot me a warning glance, and I looked away, chastised. He asked his next question. "What evidence of insanity have you noticed in your mother's conduct?"

I thought for a moment, trying to decide which of the many incidents would best support our case. "Sometimes she would come down to the table and sit on Mr. Blood's lap and say he was the best son-in-law she had. Then again, she would abuse him like a thief, calling him all the names she could lay her tongue to and otherwise venting her spleen—all without any cause whatsoever. The whole trouble was that Mother wanted to get Tennie going back around the country, telling fortunes. That is the cause of this action."

Mr. Reymart thanked me and gestured that Mr. Townsend was free to question me.

"Did you ever hear your mother complain that Blood claimed the money that came in through your sister Tennie?" Mr. Townsend asked.

Mr. Reymart stood. "Objection."

Thank God. Where was the younger lawyer yesterday when we'd needed someone to object?

"Overruled."

"I will answer him. She was determined to ruin my husband. She said she would have him in the penitentiary before she died and he would end his life there."

Mr. Townsend frowned. "What was the violent language or abuse that your mother used toward Colonel Blood?"

I smiled wryly. "It was the same that most mothers-in-law give their sons-in-law."

"Did you ever say that you would put your mother in a lunatic asylum?"

"No. Her other daughter, Mrs. Utica Booker"—I indicated my curly-haired, half-inebriated sister in the crowd, who waved back like a child—"told her that if she did not keep quiet, it would be her duty to put Mother in some such place."

As Tennie and I exchanged places, Mr. Reymart stopped me with a small pat on the hand. "You did well. If Tennie can keep this up, we have a strong hope of overshadowing what took place yesterday."

My sigh of relief upon being seated was short-lived. My sister was in rare form. Upon arranging herself artfully in the witness stand, she smiled at the reporters in the front row, nodded to her attorney, and after she was sworn in, she kissed the Bible with an audible smack that made me groan.

Mr. Reymart asked the same opening question to Tennie as he had to me.

Tennie leaned forward as she spoke, ostensibly to be sure everyone could hear her but also to display her cleavage to the crowd. "I am Tennie C. Claflin. I am one of the firm. Mr. Blood is my sister's husband. I have lived with them since the firm was first started. Before

that, my mother and father lived with me. I am the martyred one."
Tennie pursed her lips in a small pout.

I rolled my eyes, feeling the tide begin to turn against us.

Tennie turned to the opposing counsel with a smile and said,
"Now go on. You may cross-examine me as much as you like. I never
knew the colonel to use any violence toward Mother. He treated her
too kind. In fact, I don't know how he stood all of her abuse. My
mother and I always got along together until Mr. Sparr came into my
house. Benjamin Sparr has been trying to blackmail people through
my mother."

It was Judge Ledwith's turn to look exasperated. "This is altogether
irrelevant. If it is objected to, I will rule it out."

Mr. Townsend nodded. "I object, but I can't stop her from talking."

Tennie reached into her reticule and produced the letter from the
man in Ohio. "I demand that it be publicly acknowledged that I am
not a blackmailer as the papers have said." She shoved the letter at the
judge. "Here, this is proof of my innocence and that my mother and
sister are guilty of the crime of blackmail."

"Miss Claflin"—the judge's tone was soft as though talking a
child—"those letters are not relevant to the case at hand. I cannot
admit them into evidence."

Mr. Reymart dabbed his forehead with a handkerchief and
attempted to steer his witness back on track. "What was the reason
your mother quarreled with Colonel Blood?"

Tennie wrinkled her brow, confused. "Hadn't I better begin and
tell the whole trouble from the commencement? My mother is insane
on Spiritualism. But she is my mother, and I love her. She has not
slept away from me five minutes until lately."

Emotion crept into Tennie's voice on her last statement, but I couldn't tell if she was acting for effect, simply overcome by nerves, or if her resolve against our mother was beginning to crack. I peered closely at her. Her cheeks were flushed, pupils enlarged. She resembled Canning when he'd indulged in morphine. Something wasn't right.

"You and your mother have been on most intimate terms?"

"Yes, since I was eleven years old, I used to tell fortunes with her..." Tennie paused as though caught in memory. When I thought she would not go on, she added unhelpfully, "She wants me to go back with her to that business. But Vickie and Colonel Blood got me away from that life, and they are the best friends I ever had." Again, her eyes were far away as she rambled. "Since I was fourteen, I have kept thirty or thirty-five deadheads—members of my family. I was their bread and butter. I am a clairvoyant. I am a Spiritualist. I have power, and I know my power. Many of the best men in Wall Street know my power. Commodore Vanderbilt knows my power."

Tennie had lost her grip on her testimony. I moved to stop her from speaking.

James restrained me. "Only the lawyers or judge can reprimand her. You have to let her speak what she wills."

"Madam," Mr. Reymart said, his voice growing strained with irritation, "just try to answer the questions."

But Tennie was lost on her own train of thought, running her fingers through her short hair with growing agitation. "I have humbugged people, I know. But if I did, it was to make money to keep these deadheads. I believe in Spiritualism myself. It has set my mother crazy because she commenced to believe when she was too old." She turned to the judge. "But, Judge, I want my mother. I am willing to take my mother home with me now or pay two hundred a month for her in any safe place. I am afraid she will die under this excitement. I am single myself, and I don't want anybody with me but my mother."

The red-faced judge scowled at Mr. Reymart. "Can't you keep her from irrelevant testimony? Approach the bench, both of you."

The two lawyers exchanged sharp words with the judge that I could not hear, but their hand gestures and expressions indicated none of them knew how to get the trial back on track.

While this was happening, Tennie started to cry. To my horror and the crowd's delight, she suddenly left her seat, ran to her mother's side, and embraced her. Ma returned her embrace, and they hugged and kissed as though they were the perfect family.

Seeking to stop the spectacle from getting worse, James went to Tennie, patted her on the cheek, and whispered, "Retire, Tennie. Do retire, my dear. You are only making yourself conspicuous."

She nodded and left the courtroom without another word.

I chased Tennie. I couldn't let her get away with that display of treachery.

I darted in front of Tennie, forcing her to halt. "How could you turn on me like that? I thought we were in this together."

Tennie's eyes were wide, uncomprehending. "Whatever do you mean?"

"I mean, how could you defend Ma when she said such horrible lies about my husband, about all of us?"

"She is our mother. I couldn't let her be slandered before God and everyone. I only told what I know to be true."

I searched her eyes. "Are you in the altitudes? That is the only way to explain the mess you've just made. You are talking like someone else entirely."

Tennie blushed. "Utica may have given me something to calm my nerves before I testified, but I swear to you I don't feel a thing."

I grasped Tennie by the shoulders. "But don't you see? You've ruined everything! Your testimony has thrown the whole case into question. Ma may well taste victory yet. We may see my husband punished before this is through."

Tennie's lower lip quivered, and her eyes brimmed with tears. "I didn't mean to—I didn't want to hurt anyone…"

We burst through the courthouse doors, greeted by the cries of paperboys hawking the afternoon edition. "Read the latest in the Woodhull War. It's mother against daughter. Who will win in this tawdry tale?"

I did my best to block their singsong mockery from my ears as we hurried into the waiting carriage. James arrived home not long after us, bringing with him a report that the judge had elected to not issue a verdict.

Not that it mattered. The whole family was already the subject of sport in the papers. Virginia Minor sent me clippings from the *St. Louis Times,* which dug into our past with cruel enthusiasm, revealing many of my father's sins, including accusations of insurance fraud and theft. It called me a madam, accusing me of running a house of prostitution in Chicago, another sin best laid at the feet of my father. But it soon became part of popular lore, with the *Cleveland Leader* calling me "a brazen snaky adventuress" and accusing me of tawdry doings in Cincinnati years before. For those not inclined or unable to read, cartoons in so-called sporting papers gave visual representation to the "disorderly family" and its most famous daughters in particular, who were portrayed as seductive, wild, and dangerous.

Following Stephen's advice, I stayed silent for as long as I could, remaining in self-imposed exile until I could take it no longer. I had to shift the public attention from my family to something else. If I didn't neutralize the effect of the trial, my candidacy, my position in the suffrage movement, and likely the brokerage firm would suffer irreparable damage. I couldn't let that happen.

Horace Greeley's *New York Tribune*, which had previously praised me for standing up for my beliefs, was now using the issue of Free Love—so much more sensationalized by the revelation that I lived with my former and current husband at the same time—to distract from my constitutional arguments, which it opposed. Two could play at that game. I could just as easily use my views on Free Love—my real belief that marriage should not be bound by a legal document, rather than an espousal of wanton behavior as the press claimed—to distract from my family's foibles. I could even tie it back into my campaign by showing how, for me, marriage and democracy were both issues of individual rights, the core of what I believed in as a presidential candidate. It was a risky move, but I could defend my views more easily than my crazy family.

I began my offensive with a letter to the editor in the *New York Times*, which I had no doubt they would print, if only to pick it apart line by line. In the darkness of my confinement, I penned my thoughts, discarding draft after draft, rebuffing Stephen and James's attempts to help. This was deeply personal, and so my response would be as well, free of all outside influence.

Only when I was ready to submit the final draft did I gather everyone together in the drawing room and read it to them.

"Think what you will of me, but I am sharing this with you as courtesy so you may have time to prepare for what may come next. I do not seek your input or your edits." I made certain both men understood before reading what would appear in the next day's paper.

"Because I am a woman and because I consciously hold opinions somewhat different from the self-elected orthodoxy, the press endeavors to cover my life with ridicule and dishonor. This has been particularly the case in reference to certain law

proceedings into which I was recently drawn by the weakness of one very near relative.

"One of the charges made against me is that I live in the same house with my former husband, Dr. Woodhull, and my present husband, Colonel Blood. The fact is a fact. Dr. Woodhull is sick, ailing, and incapable of self-support, and I felt it my duty to myself and to human nature that he should be cared for although this incapacity was in no way attributable to me. My present husband, Colonel Blood, not only approves of this charity but cooperates in it. I esteem it one of the most virtuous acts of my life.

"I advocate Free Love in the highest and purest sense as the only cure for immorality, the deep damnation by which men corrupt and disfigure God's most holy institution of sexual relations. My judges preach against Free Love openly but practice it secretly. I know of one man, a public teacher of eminence, who lives in concubinage with the wife of another public teacher of almost equal eminence. All three concur in denouncing offenses against morality. 'Hypocrisy is the tribute paid by vice to virtue.' So be it. But I decline to stand up as 'the frightful example.' I shall make it my business to analyze some of these lives and will take my chances in the matter of libel suits. I have small faith in critics, but I believe in public justice."

Silence greeted me as I set down the letter. Three pairs of eyes stared at me along with two open mouths—only Tennie remained composed.

As usual, Stephen was the first to recover. "Do you know what will happen if you run the last part? Everyone will know of whom you speak. Henry Ward Beecher's reputation is well known, and his sisters have made no secret of how much they loathe you."

"If Harriet is allowed to portray me wrongly in her plays and call it art, am I not allowed to portray her brother truly and call it justice? And before you ask about my exposure of hypocritical lives, know that I mean what I say—I will bring them to light. Let us begin with Mr. Greeley, who has been so vehement in his attacks. Dedicate space in the next several issues of the *Weekly* to investigate him and his employees. The press got one thing right—this *is* war."

CHAPTER TWENTY-FIVE

My letter was printed on the morning of May 22. Within hours, the suffragists were rallying around me. I received telegrams from Elizabeth and Susan well before noon, pledging their support and promising to defend me every chance they had.

Visitors came and went, along with our regular clients, so I was only mildly surprised when a tall, handsome man in the soft collared shirt and loose jacket of a poet or scholar strode in brandishing a copy of the morning's paper. He threw it on my desk, where it smacked against the scarred wood, and pointed at five words circled in heavy ink—"a public teacher of eminence."

"Whom do you mean by this?" he demanded.

I smiled sweetly, waiting out the infuriated man. His dark eyes were wide with emotion, cheeks red, his breath coming in short, quick puffs that made his tie bobble like a toy boat caught in a ripple at the shore. He clearly expected that I knew him, and indeed, I recognized Mr. Theodore Tilton from the suffrage convention earlier in the month.

"Why? Do you fear I am writing about you?" My voice dripped with feigned innocence.

He glowered at me, fairly shaking in his efforts to control his emotions. "Madame, you well know what I fear."

"Ah, yes, the same as so many men." I leaned back in my chair, enjoying toying with him. "Public exposure of private indiscretions is most troubling, especially when they demean you though they are not your own fault." Deciding I had tortured the man enough, I answered his question. "I mean you and Mr. Beecher. I consider it my mission to make sure his hypocrisy is brought to the knowledge of the world."

Mr. Tilton sank into one of the plush chairs situated before the desk. "But in doing so, you will expose me as cuckold. I beg you to have mercy." He leaned toward me, arms flat on the desk, hands clasped together in supplication. "Mrs. Woodhull, you are the first person I have ever met who has dared to say such things to me openly. But do not take any steps now. I have carried my heart as a stone in my breast for months for the sake of Elizabeth, my wife, who is as brokenhearted as I am. I have had courage to endure rather than to add more to her weight of sorrow. For her sake, I have allowed this rascal to go unscathed. I have curbed my feelings when every impulse urged me to throttle and strangle him. Let me take you to my wife, and you will find her in no condition to be dragged before the public; I know you will have compassion on her."

The last thing I wanted was to become embroiled in their infidelity scandal, but the man before me was so piteous that I could not refuse him. "Fine. I will meet this gentle she-devil of yours, but I have no desire to form a lasting attachment. If she moves me as you say, I will forestall further action. But be warned, sir, I will not stay my hand forever."

Much to my surprise, we were invited to dinner that very evening. As soon as James and Mr. Tilton repaired to the study to smoke cigars and continue their discussion of Mr. Tilton's history in the reform movement, Lib—as Mr. Tilton's wife insisted on being addressed— attached herself to me like a june bug. The delicate, beautiful woman kept her dark eyes downcast, hiding as much as she could behind her long brown tresses, but though she was physically meek, she was surprisingly open with her confidences.

"Please forgive me for being so forward." She ran her fingers back and forth over the cloth of her skirt. "I am so often alone here and lack female companionship. My husband tells me you are used to hearing the complaints of others from your previous profession, so I hope you will indulge mine." Her eyes flicked briefly to mine before returning to her lap. "It is only that if you seek to shame me, you should first know the full story."

Over the next hour, as I sat next to her in stunned silence, Lib confided that her husband was routinely cold to her and they were rarely intimate. The picture she painted—one of a man who spent extravagantly yet berated her falsely for her largess with their children, made her feel a failure because she was not trained in how to run a grand household, and shunned her company in public—was completely at odds with the chivalrous man Mr. Tilton appeared to be. If Lib's words were true, Theodore had treated her very badly. But that was between them and none of my affair.

"To be honest, he makes me feel so worthless I scarcely wish to live." She looked up suddenly, scooting forward in her chair and taking my hands in her tiny ones. "You can see why I strayed, can you not? Reverend Beecher gives me such confidence and makes me feel at ease, whereas with my husband, I am constantly conscious of our inequality. I knew of the rumors about Henry—Reverend Beecher—

and I resisted for as long as I could, determined to demonstrate the honor and dignity of womanhood, but in the end, his warmth and kindness won out. You cannot blame a woman for seeking comfort where she may, can you?"

I longed to tell to Lib that her relationship with the preacher need not be a source of shame if they both openly embraced Free Love, but she was too entrenched in the Plymouth Church's mindset of "thou shall not commit adultery" to listen to my explanations.

Angry as I was at the Beechers and their sanctimonious duplicity, I also was moved to pity the small woman before me. Were it in my power, I would have rescued Lib as I had Minnie, but I had no agency in this woman's life. The most I could do was honor Mr. Tilton's wishes and delay my promised exposure of Reverend Beecher, which would also spare Lib public humiliation.

"How can I thank you?" Mr. Tilton asked when I told him of my decision as we readied to depart.

"I have done nothing for *you*," I clarified, thinking of how he treated his wife. "I have simply shown mercy to a pitiable woman who is much more deserving of your attention than you credit. Besides, as I told you, I am not of a mind to forget the matter, simply delay it."

Mr. Tilton bowed his head to me. "More than I deserve, as you say. But surely there is something you wish for, some way I may aid in your cause?"

I studied the tall, trim man. He was a poet, a former journalist, and a much sought-after lecturer; that much I had divined from my connections. Yes, surely there was some way to make use of Mr. Tilton's talents.

"I'm sure you have heard Miss Anna Dickinson, the famous lecturer?" I asked.

"I have. She is the most sought-after female speaker in the country."

"I aim to use the rise in controversy surrounding my name to supplant her in that role. I would see her crushed under the heel of my boot. What say you to that?"

Mr. Tilton went down on one knee, arms raised in supplication, his fountain pen lying horizontally across his cupped palms. "Were I a knight, I would offer you my sword, dear Queen Victoria. But as I am but a humble poet, I offer my pen to your service."

I smiled at the romantic flourish of his gesture so at odds with how Lib painted him. "Then I accept."

CHAPTER TWENTY-SIX

JUNE 1871

I paced the length of the drawing room, gathering my thoughts while Theodore—Mr. Tilton would not allow me to call him anything more formal—sat waiting with pen and paper, poised to record my every word. We were there to begin writing my biography, a task that was vital if the American public was to trust me enough to vote for me.

"I don't want a repeat of the court case. There must be no more secrets left to spill. Plus, I want people to understand my family and how they could have turned on me the way they did." After a pause, I began my tale. "I was raised in a small white cottage with a flower garden in front."

"But Tennie has made it sound more like a shack."

I put my hands on my hips. "Whose biography is this? If I want a nice childhood home, I shall have one. Tennie can write about the shack she remembers in her memoirs. As I was saying... that idyllic setting hid a dark secret."

Over the course of several weeks, I continued my tale of child-hood drudgery and poverty, including cruelty at the hands of abusive and insane parents and my escape through marriage to Canning, who had turned out to be just as bad. I tried to gloss over the day I realized my son had been born an imbecile and how I'd nearly lost Zula to blood loss, but Theodore pressed me for details, forcing me to relive those days in painful detail.

It took a full day for me to recover from the emotional strain before I could continue. Wishing to move on to happier subjects, I talked about my visions, which I'd had since childhood. Reliving those happy memories boosted my spirits, so I continued with how I met James, my advent to New York, the opening of our business on Wall Street, and the events that had led me to proclaiming myself a candidate for president.

When I wasn't living in the past for Theodore, I was working on the next issue of the *Weekly*, which more often than not included a point-by-point rebuke of the latest attack on me or my views, and an expansion of some point of my party platform. Through it all, Theodore sat by my side. He proved to be a helpful workmate, making occasional suggestions for broadening the appeal of what I was writing or pressing for more details on some aspect of my life.

All of this went on while I made daily visits to the brokerage, though to be fair, Tennie managed the lion's share of the work there. I also answered the bell rung by an increasingly ailing Canning. In addition to once again shaking and sweating from withdrawal, the deep, wet cough that had him in its grip showed no inclination of abating.

The nights were my refuge, literally and figuratively, from the chaos of the day. With James heavily occupied with the firm, I took to inviting Theodore to take my husband's place with me on the roof to watch darkness fall and commune with the higher powers. Sitting stories above the other houses was like being on top of a mountain. In one direction, the East River faded into inky darkness as the flickering glow of countless gas lights brought the city to life. If I turned my head, the imposing void of the park allowed the trees to retreat into the shadow of night, and beyond, Mr. Vanderbilt's train tracks crisscrossed interspersed patches of houses and open land.

I took a deep breath. Here, I was free. I was more than human. As the stars bloomed in the ether and the chirp of crickets lulled me along with the rhythmic *clop, clop, clop* from the teams transporting people below, I closed my eyes and slowly became one with the spirit world.

For a long time, I simply sat quietly, listening to those who found me, only offering words of my own when questioned. That was one aspect most people didn't understand about Spiritualism. For the true believer, Spiritualism was about so much more than being a medium through which higher powers could communicate. That was a gift but one rarely used without a direct request from a client. In daily life, Spiritualism was about listening to the guiding forces of the spirit world and learning to heed their wisdom to fulfill one's purpose. It wasn't dramatic, but it was reassuring in an ever-changing world.

One night, I was so deep in trance I forgot Theodore was with me. When I opened my eyes, he was watching me, a slight smile playing upon his lips. I yawned and stretched, and he brushed a stray curl, loosened by the soft breeze, out of my eyes.

"She never goes to any church—save to the solemn temple whose starry arch spans her housetop at night, where she sits, a worshipper in the sky," he intoned quietly, reverently, like one reciting a sacred prayer.

"That is beautiful. Is it Emerson? I know it's not Whitman."

"It's Tilton. Watching you commune with the spirits inspires the poet in me." He ducked his head, reminding me of a little boy embarrassed by his own affection.

But not all nights were so ethereal. The roof was often the only escape when the brick house jealously guarded its heat like an oven. Plenty of nights saw Theodore fanning me while I pretended to chant an Indian invocation for cooling breezes and rain.

One such humid night near the end of June, Theodore presented me with the first draft of my biography. I took it, my eyes eagerly consuming the words as he paced. Pride swelled my heart in places where he'd elegantly described my abilities, and tears pricked my eyes when he vividly painted my most painful memories. But in the end, disappointment outweighed all other emotions.

"You dislike it?"

"No, it is a beautiful piece, but you've left out the most important part—the spirits."

Theodore fumbled with his shirt sleeves, unrolling and re-rolling them. "I know it is an important part of your life, but I thought the book would have a broader appeal if we minimized that aspect. Not everyone is as knowledgeable or approving of such things. You wouldn't want someone in the South thinking you a witch, would you?"

"No. But you must include them. To do otherwise would be as if you were writing *Hamlet* and decided to leave out his father's ghost. The spirits guide me in all I do. That must be made clear." I held out the papers.

He took them and bent them lengthwise to fit in the pocket of his discarded jacket. "I will have another draft to you in a few days."

I nodded and pulled my legs beneath me, leaning against one of the many stone chimneys. The roof was faintly cooler in its shadow. Theodore sat next to me, his shoulder inches from mine.

I couldn't get the manuscript off my mind. "I must say, you make me sound like a saint." I gave a small tinkling laugh. "You do realize I am running for president, not pope?"

His laugh was much heartier, shaking him from shoulders to hips. "Perhaps I overdramatize, but I want the whole country to see you as I do."

I angled my body toward him. "How is that exactly?"

He unconsciously shifted so that his posture mirrored mine. "A woman made strong by her faith, who finds courage in doing what is right, and who will not rest until injustices are vindicated. Are there any finer qualities we can ask of our presidentess?"

I laughed. He couldn't be serious. "Now you make me out to be a hero of myth, a female Hercules."

"And so you are, but you are very much real. Think on it. You rose from nothing to become an extremely wealthy woman in your own right. You and Tennie were the first women to sell stocks on Wall Street. You were the first female to speak before Congress on woman's suffrage. Soon, you will be our nation's first female ruler. If that's not heroic, I don't know what is."

I turned away, not wanting him to see me blush. My stomach twisted, my gut telling me what my mind refused to admit—there was more behind his words than professional admiration. "You regard me too highly."

Suddenly, my hand was in his, and he was kneeling before me.

"No," he said firmly. "It is others who do not regard you highly enough. My dear Victoria, you are queen of my heart."

His lips brushed the top of my hand, and I inhaled sharply. I should have pulled away, discouraged him, but his touch was so gentle that I found I could not. What was worse, I suddenly realized that the reason I had been so aloof with him—from our very first meeting until now—was that I was attracted to him. Try as I might to deny it, it was true.

Theodore raised his head, the slight upturn of his lips telling me he read the emotion in my eyes. His thumb caressed my palm in lazy circles, asking questions his lips dared not form. I didn't move but gave myself over to the sensation of his touch, eyes riveted on his as though by some preternatural force. His hand slipped from mine and gently traced the veins up my arm, over the soft curve of my shoulder. I shivered as he ran the flat of his fingernails along my collarbone and up my neck. With an artist's grace, he slipped a finger under my chin, tilting it up toward him.

A connection was forming between us unlike any other I'd ever experienced, even with James. If I hadn't known better, I'd have sworn an oath that Theodore was a mesmerist who now held me under his spell. Anticipating his kiss, I felt like a girl again, pure in the innocence I'd never had the chance to experience due to my foolish youthful betrothal.

Slowly, he leaned in, and I did the same, closing my eyes only when I trusted he would not pull away. Our lips collided with a soft sigh, the meeting of two souls in bodies pledged to others but unable to deny their connection any more than iron could resist a lodestone.

That kiss was the physical expression of all of my Free Love ideals. The guilt that had marred my encounter with Judah was absent, as was the sense of betrayal. I was not cheating on my husband but expressing the bond of love that had formed with Theodore. As long as that was present, I was free to do what I chose.

As I reached up to run my fingers through his thick, wavy brown hair, Theodore pulled away.

"I wish you to know," he said, holding my head, "that I have separated from my wife. You need have no fear where she is concerned."

"And neither should you. You have heard me speak of Free Love, yes?"

He inclined his head.

"A popular objection against Free Love is that it breaks up families. My answer is that a family which falls to pieces when Free Love strikes is already broken up and waiting for a loophole through which to escape."

Theodore's smile matched mine. "And so we are free."

I pressed my forehead to his, placing a palm along each side of his jaw. "And so we are."

Our lips met again, this time with cautious curiosity that soon turned to wild abandon as we followed the instincts of body and soul, which for the first time in my life, were in perfect unison.

That night before bed, I removed my petticoats, wincing as something stiff and sharp scraped my thigh. I felt around for a loose pin or perhaps a thorn, but I found only that I had failed to empty the pocket of the innermost layer. I couldn't remember storing anything away there, but the day had been so busy that I could have simply forgotten.

I removed a small square of paper and held it to the light, surprised to see it covered in an elegant hand. It read simply, "My dear Victoria, put this under your pillow, dream of the writer, gather the spirits about you, and so good night. Theodore Tilton."

❧

THE SUMMER PASSED IN a halcyon haze of happiness. When Tennie and James complained that the brokerage was faltering, I closed my ears, trusting they would handle things. There was no place in my life for negativity or bad news. My priorities were the *Weekly* and my campaign, which was stronger than ever thanks in no small measure to Theodore. Having him by my side not only made me happy, it gave me credibility as a politician by association with his past reform successes with abolition and his key role in getting President Johnson impeached.

Because of this, I was not shy about appearing with Theodore in public. He was, after all, now on staff at the paper, a campaign advisor, and a legitimate part of my inner circle. One day he took me rowing in Central Park, and the next we found ourselves on the beach at Coney Island.

"It was very thoughtful of you to bring me here today," I said, running my fingers through the sand as the waves crashed against the shore. "Can you believe I've only seen the sea once since we moved to New York? When we first came here, we took Byron and Zula to see it, but James is not fond of the ocean. I, on the other hand, find its majesty inspiring."

"It seemed a suitable place to take a woman of means who enjoys watching others," Theodore said distractedly as he unpacked the wicker hamper containing our meal.

I leaned forward, peering inside the container, but I could only make out small round crockery bowls with matching lids and two sets of silverware. I tried to take one, but Theodore playfully slapped away my hand.

"I eat at your table often enough; it is my turn to serve you." He pulled at one of the lids, which was not inclined to budge.

I shifted my attention to the visitors around us. Families gathered in clumps near the water, children the only ones brave enough to remove their shoes and toddle into the surf, giggling and shrieking as the cold foam enveloped their feet. Nearby, a group of young women clustered under parasols, tittering to one another and making eyes at Theodore, who was oblivious to their attentions. I took the jar Theodore offered, gave the girls a smug smile and a finger wave, then turned my back on them.

"I appreciate your glowing words about me in the *Weekly*," I said before digging a fork into the spread and lifting it to my lips. The creamy mayonnaise mixed with the wild tang of rare beef to set my taste buds alight. I groaned in appreciation as I chewed. "Cook has truly outdone herself." After swallowing, I picked up my original train of thought. "I was hoping you'd be willing to be a little more open about your stance on Free Love."

He chewed, considering. "Am I the best person to endorse you there? I would think you would do better with a preacher or someone whose opinion would lend validity to your argument."

I glared at him, champagne flute frozen halfway to my mouth. "Why do I have a feeling you have someone particular in mind?"

He chuckled, swallowing a mouthful of his own wine. "Because you know me far too well."

"No. Not him. I will not do it. I distrusted Reverend Beecher from the moment I first heard those rumors about him in Washington, and save Isabella, his family has done nothing to endear themselves to me since."

"Is that how you found out about his affair with Lib?"

What an odd question. Why did he care? "No. In Washington I was acquainted with the rumors of his lasciviousness. I heard about the affair from Paulina some time later. Lib had confided in her, and Paulina couldn't keep her confidence with something that monumental, so she told me. Knowing she is a gossip, I didn't put much store in it until Elizabeth confirmed it was true."

Theodore hung his head. "So the entire women's movement knew before I did. What a fool I am."

I continued eating forkfuls of the spread. "When did you find out?" If he could ask, so could I.

Theodore steeled himself, clearly not wanting to answer. He took several gulps of wine, finishing his glass and refilling it before he answered. "I heard rumors upon returning from a lecture tour in the West. I didn't want to confront Lib until I knew for certain what was true and what wasn't. Luckily, one of my daughters is incapable of lying to me, so when I pressed her, she told me the whole sordid tale." He shifted onto his side, wrinkling his nose in distaste as though the conversation had spoiled his appetite. "It didn't take me long to realize the child Lib then carried wasn't mine but Beecher's. I confronted her, but she neither confirmed nor denied it."

Shame dulled his expression, and he flicked his gaze toward the ocean before returning it to me. "Then she miscarried. I'm not proud of what I did next, and I swear I will never treat you thus. I was simply blind with rage. I tore the wedding ring from her finger and held it up before her, shouting about her infidelity. Honestly, I wanted to shove it down her throat and make her choke on it. But I will not raise my hand to a woman. Instead I tore the photo of Beecher from the wall, shredded it, and condemned it to the fire. Finally, I dragged Lib outside and stamped the ring into the ground at the child's grave as though I could bury her sins with it."

Theodore's expression darkened when I chuckled.

"Such dramatics. Need I remind you that you are no vestal virgin? Rumors abound about your prowess outside the marriage bed."

He scowled at me. "So I've heard. But it gets worse. When Beecher found out what I knew, he tried to get Lib to sign a statement saying that nothing untoward ever took place between them."

"What is it with that family? They think they can do whatever they wish with no recrimination. Harriet gets a pass when she says

I'm a 'snake who should be given a good clop with a shovel,' but if I say anything in response, I am vilified. Henry demands one of his mistresses perjure herself and yet is held in higher esteem by his congregation than the president." I shook my head, adjusting the strings of my bonnet to better shade my face.

Theodore sighed. "I tell you this not to upset you but to show you that Henry lives the life you speak of even if he cannot yet admit to it. He might be more open to endorsing Free Love than you think if you try to get to know him."

"But why would he do that if he tried to get Lib to deny their affair?"

"Because he is a man who struggles to reconcile what he lives with what he preaches. He's deathly afraid that people will find out." He held up a hand to silence my comment. "Please, let me finish. He knows of the rumors, but no one can prove them. He's scared someone will. You see, this isn't his first public brush with Free Love. Two years ago, he was involved in a scandal in which he officiated a wedding between a divorced woman and her dying lover, who was shot by the woman's abusive ex-husband. The legitimacy of the divorce was called into question as it took place in Indiana where the laws were less strict than here in New York. Her ex-husband claimed he was merely defending the sanctity of his marriage. The aftermath nearly cost Beecher his church. So you can see why he is hesitant to attach himself to the phrase 'Free Love' or even the more respectable euphemism, 'social responsibility.'"

"Yet he continues to practice it," I whispered, lost in my own thoughts. The more I thought about it, the more I became convinced Reverend Beecher was a man who would care a great deal for the truth. "I wonder if having lived the life that he has and entertaining the private convictions he does, I could perhaps persuade him to come out and openly avow his principles and be a thorough, consistent radical and thus justify his life in some measure, if not wholly, to the public."

Theodore smiled as I came around to his way of thinking. "You should at least try."

My lips twitched as I formulated a plan. I already had the perfect leverage. Stephen had set the stage last October when he threw down the gauntlet against Reverend Beecher in the *Weekly*. Now I could add a little additional weight to the threat of exposure, and I was certain he would do as I wished. It was blackmail, but after all, I was my mother's daughter.

Reverend Beecher was quick to accept Theodore's proposed meeting with me, so on a hot Sunday morning, Theodore and I attended services at Plymouth Church. The plan was to speak privately with the reverend after the congregation returned to their homes.

I was never one for organized religion. The revival meetings of my youth still gave me nightmares—all those people trembling uncontrollably and babbling gibberish they swore was a divine language. Then, as now, the only part that truly captured my interest was the fire with which the preachers delivered their sermons.

Reverend Beecher was certainly an impassioned man, intoning his words with a force most actors would have envied. His deep voice resonated throughout the church, likely clear even to those who stood outside on the street.

"God values men according to what they have had to walk through. Some men are so made that they are obliged to hold perpetual warfare with themselves. They must have a hand always on the engine, or something will blow up in them every minute."

Interesting. He could well be speaking of himself—or perhaps his words were aimed at me. He did know I would be in his congregation today, so it was possible.

"There are doubts and troubles that never can be settled. The only thing to be done with them is to lay them down and leave them. *This*"—he slammed his hand onto the pulpit to punctuate the word, making me and half the congregation jump—"the Christian must do if he wants peace; and if the impenitent won't do it, they will torment him to death."

So he was saying there were troubles that we would never settle. We should leave them to God. I agreed with that, but there were others who were greatly alleviated when their public and private lives were one. I was willing to wager I could convince him of the same.

That goal was at the top of my mind when the three of us stepped into the preacher's small office tucked away behind the altar of his massive church. Theodore remained only long enough to make the introductions, preferring to withdraw to the sanctuary to give us the space to speak in confidence. At Reverend Beecher's invitation, I took a seat in front of his heavy wooden desk.

He cleared away a pile of papers—likely drafts of more sermons—and rested his arms on the empty space, fingers entwined. "Now, Mrs. Woodhull, my friend Mr. Tilton said you wished to speak with me. How may I be of service to you?"

Candor was likely the best approach. "I was hoping you would be willing to stand up with me on the subjects of social responsibility and marriage reform. The endorsement of a man of your standing in the community would do much to convince others that I truly have their best interests, rather than the degradation of society, at heart."

"You speak of Free Love."

"Among other things, yes. Surely you have heard my views." *Your sisters certainly have.*

He leaned forward on his desk. "Mrs. Woodhull, I know that our whole social system is corrupt. I know that marriage, as it exists today, is the curse of society. Marriage is the grave of love." His tone hinted that he knew its sting from personal experience. "I never married a couple that I did not feel were already condemned."

As had been the case with the president, I could not hold my tongue. "If you hold such strong feelings in your heart, why do you not preach them every Sunday?"

He laughed ruefully. "Because I should preach to empty seats. It would be the ruin of my church. Most people cannot handle such thoughts, lost as they are in tradition. I am twenty years ahead of my church. I preach the truth only as my people can bear it. Milk for babies, meat for strong men, as they say."

"Considerate as that may be, do you not feel it is time to introduce soft food?"

He smiled. "Perhaps. How do you propose I do such a thing?"

I sat forward, removing a sheaf of papers from the Bible I carried. "I will be speaking at Steinway Hall in August on the subject of social responsibility. I was hoping you would be willing to introduce me there." I held out the papers. "This is an early draft of my speech. I would be honored if you would read it and offer your learned opinion."

I nearly choked on the last phrase. I also failed to mention that the papers were a toned-down version of the speech, heavily edited by Theodore to make the preacher more amenable.

As I waited, he read it, pursing his lips. He grunted in agreement with a few points and twice picked up his pen, making notations in the margin.

When he finished, he handed back the papers. "I agree with much of what you say, but would not introducing you be tantamount to endorsing your views?"

"In some ways, yes. But you need not say anything so explicit. Your presence would speak for itself." I struggled to maintain the humility I'd practiced with Theodore. "I simply thought your reputation would be safer if you owned up publicly to living a Free Love lifestyle rather than being found out later."

"And you would be the one to reveal my secrets?" There was menace in his voice.

"Perhaps. You know I have it in my power, but I am by far not the only one."

The reverend was quiet for a moment, drumming his fingertips on his desk as he turned my proposal over in his mind. Finally, he sighed, shaking his head. "I am not fit to stand by you, who goes there to speak what you know to be the truth. I should stand there a living lie. I promise to think on it, but I am in doubt I would be able to endure the public disgrace."

He stood then, extending his hand. Our meeting had come to an end.

As I took his hand, he added, "Until such time as I give you my answer, I trust you will keep what you know to yourself."

CHAPTER TWENTY-SEVEN

JULY 1871

Music filled the halls of 15 East Thirty-Eighth Street as twilight fell, competing with the laughter and chatter bandied about by Tennie and a few close friends gathered with us for an evening of socializing and revelry.

"To our hostess, Mrs. Victoria Woodhull, and her indomitable sister, Tennessee. Our sincere felicitations on your appointment as leaders of Section Twelve of the International Workingmen's Association and best wishes for your continued success. May your concern for laborers and women take you to the highest office of this great nation," Stephen said, kicking off the evening's celebrations.

James raised his glass, seconding the sentiment. "Hear, hear."

"And there are many more victories to come," concurred Jesse Grant, the current president's father. "I'm so happy you started hosting parties again. I so missed speaking with you and your intelligent group of radicals." He gave me a warm smile.

"Mr. Grant, you flatter me," I said coyly, batting my eyelashes.

"Should you not be out stumping for your son's reelection rather than consorting with his rival?"

"I love my son and wish him all the best." Mr. Grant took a sip of his gin. "But he has had his time in office and, in my opinion, has squandered it trying to curry favor from all sides rather than taking action. It's time for someone else, someone who is not afraid to fight, to take up the mantle of power."

I dipped my head in acknowledgement of the compliment. "Thank you. Your support, even if only in private, means more than you can know."

Slowly, the party moved to the drawing room, where bankers, lawyers, editors, clergymen, politicians, and their wives dropped the formalities of high society and relaxed, knowing they were among friends. The atmosphere became like that of a private club as gin, brandy, whiskey, and port were consumed, softening the edges of personalities and turning thoughts to brotherhood and camaraderie.

I raised my voice so all could hear. "I wish to thank you for being here tonight not in your social roles but as friends. This year has been one of both tumult and joy, and I wish to express my gratitude that you have stood by me. As they say, it is only in your darkest hours that you learn who your true friends are."

"To friendship," someone in the crowed toasted.

After we had all sipped from our drinks, I continued. "Looking around at your joyful faces, it strikes me that there is great power in this room. We are, in a way, a Congress of the People, representing all walks of life from the common laborer"—I nodded at tinsmith and reformer William West, who was highly active in the IWA—"to the very wealthy." I singled out a few well-known couples with a brief nod. "We are the future of this country, the reformers who will set it on its due course to true equality. That power does not lie in the hands of politicians—no offense to those present—but in the hands of the people who will use their voices and their votes to shape the path ahead."

"As we are a group of like-minded individuals," Tennie mused, fiddling with the enormous jet buttons on her black jacket, "wouldn't it be wonderful if we were a political party and could endorse you publicly?" She sat up straighter. "I mean, I know I am your sister, but the whole country needs to hear what you have just said."

"You may be on to something," Benjamin Butler said, puffing away on his cigar. "Victoria is, in essence, relaunching her campaign to prepare for the final year of stumping for votes. This would be the perfect time to resurrect her Cosmopolitical party." He turned to me. "You will need to be nominated by a national party to get your name officially on the ballot."

I pursed my lips, considering. "You're right. But I want it to better represent the union of women's and laborers' rights. It must hold in no doubt my position on equality, for no matter what subject we consider—be it suffrage, marriage, or work—that is the basis."

Stephen disappeared and quickly returned with pen and paper. "We have an issue of the *Weekly* set to go to press in the morning, but I will discard my column in favor of a letter marking this monumental development. I ask all of you, do we dare call our party the Equal Rights Party?"

That got everyone's attention. The muffled din of conversation rose as individuals consulted with their neighbors.

I turned the idea over in my mind. The Equal Rights Party was a name steeped in history and controversy, having first been used by a Democratic splinter group before the Civil War to protest anti-labor practices. In that way, it would immediately envelope half of my platform. Coupled with my obvious association with the suffrage movement, it might well be the perfect name.

We spent the next several hours debating the finer points of our new party and what it stood for and composing the letter that would appear on behalf of our group—a new movement in politics we hoped the letter would encourage others to join—in the *Weekly* to mark the upcoming Independence Day holiday.

On July 4, 1871, *Woodhull and Claflin's Weekly* ran the following letter.

> *"A number of your fellow citizens, both men and women, have formed themselves into a working committee, borrowing its title from your name and calling itself the Victoria League. Our object is to form a new national political organization, composed of the progressive elements in the existent Republican and Democratic parties together with the Women of the Republic, to be called the Equal Rights Party.*
>
> *"We ask you to become the standard bearer of this idea before the people, and for this purpose nominate you as our candidate for President of the United States, to be voted for in 1872 by the combined suffrages of both sexes. Offering the assurance of our great esteem, and harboring in our minds the cheerful prescience of victory which your name inspires, we remain, cordially yours, the Victoria League."*

Tennie added fuel to the fire by implying to a reporter that she had it on good authority that the Victoria League was backed by Cornelius Vanderbilt. As everyone knew she was still occasionally seeing the elderly tycoon—thanks in no small part to my efforts after our mother's blackmail debacle—the rumor was assumed to be true. When questioned, the commodore would say nothing, which would set tongues wagging even more.

For my part, I pretended to be shocked and honored by such a spontaneous outpouring of support. I responded to the invitation in the next issue of the *Weekly*.

> *"Your timing could not be more fortuitous, as I have returned to my humanitarian objectives of uniting suffrage with labor reform under the platform of human rights. The freedom of women and the freedom of the laborer are conjointly the cause of humanity. The fusion of the women and the workingmen and the Internationalists will render the Democrats and Republicans as parties unnecessary. The National Labor Union, just now convening in St. Louis, has, for the first time, invited women upon equal terms to that convention. It is, of course, noticed that neither Republicans nor Democrats have invited us yet to their political assemblages.*
>
> *"I will admit, in the spirit of openness, that my announcement as a candidate a year ago was for the mere purpose of lifting a banner, of provoking agitation, and creating a rallying point for suffrage. But now, seeing as how people support me and have taken to my cause, I have little doubt of the possibility of success. Little as the public think it, a woman who is now nominated may be elected next year."*

PART THREE
"Mrs. Satan"

CHAPTER TWENTY-EIGHT

NOVEMBER 1871

One year remained until the presidential election. The event I had carefully planned for today tested exactly how a woman attempting to vote would be treated. At best, our band of reformers would gain notoriety for succeeding; at worst, we would be arrested like so many suffragists before us. Either way, I was sure to make the papers. I even invited Johnny to accompany us as we made our way to the polling place to ensure every moment would be documented in the *Herald* for posterity.

Approximately a dozen women, including Tennie and me, were gathered in the drawing room of our Murray Hill mansion when the clock struck half past two. We had registered to vote two days before without anyone trying to stop us, so the atmosphere was one of hopeful excitement. Pray God we would be able to cast our votes as easily.

"Ladies, please, if I may have your attention," I called above the chatter. "Today, buoyed by the rights granted us in the Constitution of the United States, we set out to become the first female voters in the great state of New York. We will be meeting John DeNoon Reymert, a seasoned lawyer of some repute, at our polling place in case there are any questions as to the legality of our actions. But to quiet any last-minute fears you may have, Tennie will now read the Fourteenth and Fifteenth Amendments of the Constitution for us."

After Tennie concluded, we opened our parasols as we emerged onto the sunny street and marched to the little furniture store at 682 Sixth Avenue, which doubled as the polling place for our district and ward. We sang hymns of freedom as we walked, attracting a small following of ordinary citizens and a reporter from the *World*.

Inside the store's large waiting area, we met my elderly lawyer, who greeted us warmly. This plus our very presence at a polling place—traditionally a male haven—attracted quite a bit of attention from those standing around.

"What's the likes of you fair pusses doing here? You lost?" one man asked with a guffaw at his own wit.

I stared him down. "I am here to exercise my privilege as a citizen of the United States to vote."

Before the man could harass me further, I, followed by the other women, strode into the smaller inner room where voting took place. Up ahead, at the end of the long, disorderly line, a glass voting window separated the election officials from the voters. The man casting his vote had to step up onto a platform, in full view of everyone else in the room, and hand his ballot to the official, who put it in the corresponding box out of reach of the voter but within sight of all present. There was absolutely no question for whom he had voted when he left the platform.

Ahead, two men were elbowing one another, arguing over who was first. A strolling police officer admonished everyone to "form an orderly line," but some still cut in or assumed a front place because of their surname or occupation, much to the grumbling of the common men.

However, once word trickled up the line that there were women present, the men remembered their gallantry and insisted the ladies go first. I was quickly ushered to the head of the line, curious spectators of both sexes behind me.

I had been hoping for a little less attention, but I would play the hand dealt to me. Squaring my shoulders, I stepped onto the stage and presented my ballot to the inspector.

He recoiled as though I was handing him his death warrant. "I can't take it. I can't even look at it."

"You refuse to take my vote?" My eyebrows rose even though this was the reaction I'd expected.

"We can't receive it," the small man with the badge of an election official repeated.

"By what right do you refuse to accept the vote of a citizen of the United States?"

"By this." He thumped a copy of the Constitution, clearly annoyed.

Mr. Reymert mounted the platform. "But refer to the second article. You will see that 'all citizens,' not 'all males,' are entitled to vote."

"We haven't a copy of the Amendments here, and even if we had, I could not take the vote."

I produced the copy of the Amendments we had read from earlier. "Here. Read the Fourteenth and Fifteenth articles and tell me if you still have legal grounds for denying my vote."

"I cannot."

"Cannot or will not?"

"I have been instructed to accept no votes from women."

"Is it a crime to be a woman?"

While the lawyer and election officials tried to sort out the scene I had created, I stepped aside. There was no better opportunity than this to deliver my Constitutional Equality speech, to educate people during a moment when their minds were already attuned to politics. At least this way, they would know what the scene playing out before them was about.

I recited it from memory. A few people looked genuinely interested, but most of the men were gathered around to gawk and laugh. Above them carried Tennie's high-pitched, "You will regret this when my sister is president," when she too was turned away. Amidst the chaos, I tracked quiet Mrs. Miller, who slipped behind the arguing men to silently drop her ballot into the box. It was a small victory, one likely to go unnoticed by the history books but a victory nonetheless.

Over the next week, I learned just how much attention my revolutionaries and I had garnered with our little stunt. Brokerage clients relayed that we were the focus of every social gathering from Harlem to Five Points and even out to Brooklyn, as well as the subject of more than one Sunday sermon. Every step of the event was chronicled in the *Tribune* and *World*.

Later in the month, *Harper's Weekly* printed a half-hearted report of our doings along with a sketch that depicted me forcefully exerting my right. I didn't care much for the article, but the sketch was perfect. With my arm raised, fingers clutching my ballot as the baffled election officials looked on, they'd captured my spirit and strength better than any words ever would.

❧

MY SPEECH ON SOCIAL freedom at Steinway Hall was in less than twenty-four hours, and I still hadn't received any assurance from Reverend Beecher that he would introduce me. I had no choice but to reach out to him, to remind him of what he had to lose if he didn't stand up for me.

> *"Two of your sisters have gone out of their way to assail my character and purpose. You doubtless know that it is in my power to strike back and in ways more disastrous than anything that can come to me. I do not desire to do this. I simply desire justice, and a reasonable course on your part will assist me to it. I must have an interview tomorrow. What I shall or shall not say will depend largely on the result of the interview."*

Within two hours of sending the letter, I had his agreement to meet me at his church. Once again, Theodore accompanied me, but this time, he stayed to witness the exchange. Reverend Beecher remained sequestered behind his desk while I sat on a settee near the door, at which Theodore stood guard.

When the reverend made no effort to begin the conversation, I said, "You know my position. The only safety you have is in coming out as soon as possible as an advocate of social freedom. You don't have to proclaim yourself from the pulpit, but introducing me would go a long way to bridge the gap between what you do and what you say."

Reverend Beecher stood, wailing, "I cannot! I should sink through the floor. I am a moral coward on this subject, and you know it." He rounded the desk and came to kneel on the cushion beside me. To my horror, he wept, pulling at my arm like a child and begging, "Let me off."

I pulled away, wiping my hands on my dress to rid them of his cowardice. "I shall do no such thing. Powerful men with secrets to hide may rise, but they also fall. Someday you have got to fall." I stood, wishing to be away from this pathetic craven. "If I am compelled to go upon that platform alone, I shall begin by telling the audience why I am alone and why you are not with me."

Reverend Beecher was sobbing, his breathing far too shallow and too rapid. "I cannot face this thing." He moaned. "If you are to do as you say, let me have proper notice so that I might take my own life."

"Oh, come off it," Theodore snapped, crossing to his former mentor in three long strides. He took Reverend Beecher by the shoulders and shook him. "She is only asking you to introduce her, not stand before the world and give a full confessing of your sins. If you can preach for two hours every Sunday, surely you can speak two paragraphs about this woman."

The preacher regarded him with red-rimmed eyes. "This thing you ask of me is a great cross." He sniffed. "But it will be as you say if I can bring my courage up to the terrible ordeal."

That night, as our carriage sloshed through the sodden city streets, rain beating incessantly against the windows, I wondered aloud if Reverend Beecher would be good to his word.

"I cannot imagine who would come out in all this rain," Tennie said. "Perhaps God is telling you not to give the speech." She made a disgusted face as she peered into the night. Tennie's intake of breath drew my attention outside.

The steps of Steinway Hall were lined with ten-foot-high red banners with gold letters proclaiming, "Freedom! Freedom! Freedom!" At the door, seven-foot-high posters left visitors in no doubt of the night's subject: "Victoria C. Woodhull: The Principles of Sexual Freedom – Free Love, Marriage, Divorce, and Prostitution." They were drenched with rain, and a few were twisted from the wind, but their message still blared to all within sight. On the stairs, people from all walks of life were crammed cheek by jowl, waiting to get in and huddled under umbrellas. My biography may have been poorly received by everyone save the Spiritualists, but no one would have been able to tell judging from the crowd waiting in the rain. I would have to give Stephen a raise; he and his band of promoters had outdone themselves.

The carriage dropped us off at a back entrance, where we were escorted to a large dressing area to await the eight o'clock hour. I paced, practicing my speech quietly to distract myself from the unease taking root in my belly.

I stopped in the wings and peered out at the crowd, which was quickly filling the hall to its three-thousand-person capacity. With still an hour before the lecture, every seat on the ground floor, two balconies, and every bit of standing room in the aisles was filled. Some of the men close to the stage leaned on it, and others bowed over the balconies. They were talking loudly, some fanning themselves with the memorandum I had placed on each seat explaining the purposes of my speech so there could be no doubt.

> "Victoria C. Woodhull speaks tonight for the express purpose of silencing the voices and stopping the pens of those who, either ignorantly or willfully, persistently misrepresent, slander, abuse, and vilify her because of her outspoken advocacy of and supreme faith in God's last and best law. She wishes it to be distinctly understood that freedom does not mean anarchy in the social relations any more than it does in religion and politics; also that the advocacy of its principles requires neither action nor immodest speech."

By ten minutes after eight, the audience was growing restless, pounding their feet and clapping and chanting, "Woodhull! Woodhull!"

Where in tarnation was Beecher? Not wanting to make them wait any longer, I made for the stage, but the building manager rushed in front of me.

"Mrs. Woodhull, do not go out there. Certain members of the crowd both outside and within are trying to break up the meeting with violence, and some are threatening your life if you speak on what you say you will."

I threw up my hands. "Oh, this is preposterous. No man will silence me with threats. Have they not learned that by now?" I turned on my heel, headed in the direction of the stage.

Theodore stepped in front of me.

"Are you going to introduce her?" someone asked.

"Yes, by Heaven, since no one else has the pluck to do it," Theodore said.

When we emerged onto the stage, the crowd surged forward, some perilously close to the gas footlights. I was suddenly acutely aware of every pair of eyes on me, examining me, scrutinizing my black silk dress with the white rose at my throat, silently comparing the woman in the flesh before them to the one they had dreamed up based on gossip and lies.

Theodore took center stage and opened his arms wide. "Ladies and gentlemen, happening to have an unoccupied night, which is an unusual thing for me in the lecture season, I came to this meeting actuated by curiosity to know what my friend would have to say in regard to the great question that has occupied her for so many years of life. I was told she was coming upon this stand unattended and alone. Now, as to her character, I know it and believe in it and vouch for it."

Applause rose, cut through by a few lewd whistles. I fought to keep my expression neutral, raising my chin against the implications that our relationship was more widely known than I had suspected.

Theodore motioned for the audience to be silent. "As to her views, she will give them to you herself in a few moments, and you may judge for yourself. It may be that she is a fanatic; it may be that I am a fool, but before high heaven, I would rather be both fanatic and fool in one than to be such a coward as would deny to a woman the sacred right of free speech."

This assertion was greeted with boisterous applause.

"Allow me the privilege of introducing you to Victoria C. Woodhull, who will address you upon the subject of social freedom."

More applause filled the air as Theodore stepped back, ceding the stage to me. I took in the crowd, my eyes flicking first to one box, in which Tennie sat, then another, which was filled with my friends and—oh God—my family. Doing my best to ignore them, I began to speak.

"Our government is based upon the proposition that all men and women are born free and equal and entitled to certain inalienable rights, among which are life, liberty, and the pursuit of happiness. Now what we, who demand social freedom, ask is simply that the government of this country shall be administered in accordance with the spirit of this proposition. *Nothing more, nothing less.*"

As I spoke, the spirits gathered around me, encircling me with their arms joined, as if channeling their higher powers into me. Slowly, I deviated from Stephen's carefully prepared script, inserting my own thoughts.

"Two persons, a male and a female, meet and are drawn together by a mutual attraction—a natural feeling unconsciously arising within their natures of which neither has any control—which is denominated love. Suppose after this marriage has continued an indefinite time, the unity between them departs. Could they any more prevent it than they can prevent the love? It came without their bidding; may it not also go without their bidding? It is therefore a strictly legitimate conclusion that where there is no love as a basis of marriage, there should be no marriage, and if that which was the basis of a marriage is taken away, that the marriage also ceases from that time, statute laws to the contrary notwithstanding."

At this, half of the crowed leapt to their feet, cheering, while the other portion hissed.

Theodore stepped from the wings and did his best to get them to sit down and be quiet by shouting "Ladies and gentlemen!" several times, but he was drowned out by the commotion, which lasted a full ten minutes.

Oh, this was ridiculous. They were a crowd of adults, not rowdy schoolchildren. But if they wished to behave as such, I would treat them as such. I stamped my heeled boot on the polished stage. The echo reverberated like thunder, making the hall fall suddenly silent.

"Let the gentleman or lady who is capable of hissing or inter-rupting me come forward on this platform and define their principles fairly." If they were going to challenge me, they could state their opin-ions publicly, just as I did.

A woman in a pink dress stood unsteadily in one of the boxes directly to my right. I took a few steps in her direction, relatively cer-tain that that was the box in which I had seen my family seated. I bit my cheek, dreading what might follow.

Just before she spoke, I recognized my sister Utica. "How would you like to come into this world not knowing who your father and mother was?"

I stared at my sister, not quite certain as to how her question pertained to the subject at hand. But that was irrelevant. It had been asked before the whole forum, so I had to address it as best I could.

"I assert that there are as good and noble men and women on this earth suffering from the stain of illegitimacy as any man or woman before me. God knows I do not know how many illegitimate men or women are in this hall tonight."

A scandalized murmur swept the crowd only to be replaced by Utica's shouts of "I am her sister. Unhand me," when a police officer tried to drag Utica from her box. This angered the crowd even more, and the officer was forced to exit the box to a chorus of "Shame!"

Theodore once again came to my rescue, calling to Utica, "You shall all be heard if you give us time. I must say, however, that this lady"—he gestured to me—"has hired the hall and is entitled to be heard first."

I mouthed my thanks to Theodore before turning once again to the audience. I was sweating profusely, pulse pounding, hands shaking. *Please, God, let there not be any further interruptions.* "Now, let me ask, would it not rather be the Christian way, in such cases, to say to the disaffected party: 'Since you no longer love me, go your way and be happy and make those to whom you go happy also.' I know of no higher, holier love than that."

"Are you a Free Lover?" shouted someone.

I screamed inwardly. Was that all these people cared about—what I did and with whom? Did no one wish to hear the reasoning behind my beliefs? No, they were more concerned with branding me an adventuress.

I hurled my script pages to the floor, shouting as they scattered at my feet. "Yes, I am a Free Lover! I have an inalienable constitutional and natural right to love whom I may, to love as long or as short a period as I can, to change that love every day as I please." A growing wave of hisses threatened to drown me out, but I raised my voice even further. "And with that right, neither you nor any law you can frame have any right to interfere, and I have the further right to demand a free and unrestricted exercise of that right."

I was shouting to be heard, but be heard I would be, even if I tore my vocal chords in the process. These were words the crowd needed to hear.

"I believe promiscuity to be anarchy and the very antithesis of that for which I aspire. But I protest, and I believe every woman who has purity in her soul protests, against all laws that would compel her to maintain relations with a man for whom she has no regard and for which is often added the delirium of intoxication. I protest against this form of slavery."

Utica stepped to the front of her box again. The crowed stilled to hear what she would say.

She pointed at me. "I would ask her, how can we reform the women she speaks of and at the same time teach them to live promiscuously with men?"

I shot back, "Were the relations of the sexes thus regulated, misery, crime, and vice would be banished and the pale, wan face of female humanity replaced by one glowing with radiant delight and healthful bloom and the heart of humanity would beat with a heightened vigor and renewed strength and its intellect be cleared of all shadows, sorrows, and blights. Contemplate this and then denounce me for advocating freedom if you can, and I will bear your curse with a better resignation."

Theodore suddenly appeared at my side and whispered into my ear, "The police are threatening to shut the event down. It is time for us to go."

With that, he ushered me off the stage and signaled to the workers to douse the footlights.

I refused to come out of my room for two days after the speech, preferring to remain curled up in my blankets with the windows shuttered. My head ached, my heart ached, and the tears would not stop falling. My ungrateful family had done it again—wrecked what would have otherwise been a glorious night for me. If they truly were seeking to ruin me, they were doing excellent work.

I sat up as a memory danced through my mind—Stephen's beautiful wife in a trance, warning me to "beware the Judas kiss." I should have listened, been prepared. Of the countless messages I had heeded, why had I chosen to ignore that one? It was foretold all along that they would ruin me in my hour of greatest triumph. I was a fool.

A knock sounded at the door, and Tennie pushed in, balancing a breakfast tray and a pile of newspapers, both of which she set at the foot of the bed. I nibbled on a crust of toast, thumbing through the papers. Some had stayed quiet, but many others were ruthless in their denouncement of my views and me. The *New York Herald* declared, "Victoria and Theodore: Mrs. Woodhull claims the right to change her husband every day in the presence of three thousand people," while the *Gazette's* front page pronounced, "Died of Free Love, November 25th in Steinway Hall, the Woman Suffrage Movement."

I groaned and tossed the papers to the floor, curled my arms about my ribs as if for warmth, and stared at one of the green-and-gold walls. "Free Love is not what I asked for nor what I pleaded for. What I asked for was educated love; that one's daughter be taught to love rightly so that she could, under no circumstances, love unworthily."

Tennie asked, breaking her silence, "Do you remember when Stephen advised us that it is not what we say but what people hear that's what matters?"

I forced myself to look up. "Yes. Why?"

"Well, thanks to this press coverage, plenty of people heard you have radical, even scandalous, views and are anxious to hear them firsthand."

I squinted at her, shaking my head in confusion. "What are you saying?"

Tennie stood and opened first one then a second set of shutters, allowing a golden stream of light to wash in. I blinked. Tennie was smiling, glowing even, with suppressed joy.

"You are the most in-demand ticket in town. While you've been up here wallowing in self-pity, I've been arranging your next lecture tour. You've received thirteen invitations in less than forty-eight hours. Three of those conflicted, so I could only book you in eleven."

I threw off the covers and jumped to my feet. "Why did you not tell me?"

"Because you needed your rest. You'll be visiting eleven cities in thirteen days. It's all arranged. You leave first thing in the morning."

❦

THE LECTURE TOUR WAS well-timed and beneficial in many ways. It gave me much needed publicity in other cities—the *Pittsburgh Dispatch* called me "the most prominent woman of our time"—but more importantly, it brought in coin that would keep the landlord at bay a little longer. If Wall Street had taught me nothing else, it was that money was more persuasive than the false concern for virtue that fed my neighbors' complaints against me. I would enjoy watching their efforts to have me evicted backfire; my newfound cash would outweigh even this latest scandal.

However, I hadn't been expecting such a chilly homecoming. While the rest of the Northeast was singing my praises, the doors of many of my closest companions were suddenly closed, allies turned to enemies. Even the firm suffered; James reported we had lost several of our biggest clients.

What was worse, I was not alone in this sudden shunning. Theodore, as the man who had introduced me, fared far worse than I. He appeared on my doorstep, a sobbing mess, the night I returned. He reeked of brandy. I quickly shuffled him into the parlor where we could be alone. I guided him onto the royal-blue lounge where we had planned so many issues of the *Weekly* and laid his head on my chest while he wept like a babe.

"I am undone," he said between sobs. "My reputation is ruined."

I rocked him, patting his head and cooing affectionately, "There, there. It cannot be so bad."

Once Theodore regained some measure of control, the story came pouring out of him. "I have nothing. While you were off on your whirlwind tour, all my lecture dates were canceled, invitations to events and parties rescinded." He gave me a wry look. "Everyone may want to see the female Free Lover, but no one dares associate with the one who introduced her. I bet Beecher is thanking God and all the saints he was too much a coward to do it himself."

And that I didn't have the heart to denounce a man who wasn't there to defend himself. I pulled Theodore to me again, this time laying my head on his shoulder. "You know how fickle these society people are. They may have their backs to you at the moment, but give them time and they will come around. Someone always has to be on the outside looking in. It is simply your turn."

Theodore grunted dubiously. "I do not think so. I'm ashamed to admit this, but I even tried making excuses to get them to change their minds. I…I blamed you—your interjections and deviation from the prepared speech—for what happened so they wouldn't cast blame on me. Can you ever forgive me?"

I sat up so I could look at him, cupping his cheek. "There is nothing to forgive. What you say is true. If I had stayed to the script, things likely would not have ended so badly, but I did as my heart moved me. That is an end to it."

Theodore nodded and kissed me softly on the cheek. "Thank you."

I sighed. "So where do we stand?"

Theodore blew out a breath, less addled now that he had confessed all. "As far as I can tell, you still have the suffragists, Spiritualists, and Section Twelve. If you can keep them, you still stand a fair shot as a candidate next year."

"I have no fear from any of those, so that pleases me. But the negative media attention has to stop."

"Speaking of fear, has Tennie told you of the curious letter the *Weekly* received from a Miss Mary Bowles?"

"No. Why?"

"I think it may be just the thing we need to strike fear into the heart of Wall Street." He stood, searching through the oak partner's desk Tennie and I shared as he spoke. "All those tycoons and their haughty wives have secrets they wish to keep hidden. Well, thanks to Miss Bowles, we now hold the key."

"Oh, I am intrigued."

"If I could find the blasted thing." He opened drawers and stuck his hand in cubbyholes, examining and discarding scraps of paper. "In short, she says your words at Steinway Hall touched the hearts of many on Broadway and the Bowery. She's offering you unprecedented access to her client rolls—and what's more, Miss Wood and Madame de Ford have agreed to do the same. Ah, here it is!"

I took the letter, skipping over the woman's life story and her plans to close her brothel to the important bit. I read aloud. "'If you, in the prosecution of your blessed mission as a social reformer, have any need to see more behind the scenes and to understand the real state of New York society better, I will give you access to my two big books. You will find in them the names of all classes—from doctors of divinity to counter jumpers and runners for mercantile houses. Make what use of them you please.'" I looked up, a broad smile blossoming across my face. "This is a goldmine."

Theodore yawned from the couch, eyes growing heavy. "It is. Tennie wants to publish both it and a reply thanking her for her kind offer and implying you may well make use of them." He leaned his head back on the cushions, seemingly content.

"She is brilliant. This will go a long way toward scaring our detractors into silence. You may even get your invitations back."

Silence.

"Theodore?"

He was fast asleep.

CHAPTER TWENTY-NINE

DECEMBER 1871

My election as co-president of the International Workingmen's Association, Section Twelve, back in July had been a major coup in my plan to make my presidential dreams a reality. But at the time, it was largely ceremonial. Now, as Tennie and I took the reins of power in earnest, I vowed to show the country its workers were a force to be reckoned with, a populace not to be ignored.

But first the public had to understand what the workers were fighting for. Stephen had read Karl Marx's *Communist Manifesto* to me, translating it from the original German, but most people hadn't had such an opportunity because no one had yet printed it in English. With Stephen's help, I would see that changed. The lengthy document was set to run in the December 30th issue of the *Weekly* while people still railed against the killing of the three Communards in Paris, a full six months after the revolution had ended. Even those who didn't sympathize with the movement saw the killings for what they were— murder—so now was the time to shed light on their cause.

News of Section Twelve's protest against the killings reached me in Washington. While Tennie and I were happily making nuisances of ourselves at the American Woman Suffrage Association convention—paying young boys to hand out copies of our paper and ensuring they were left on every seat so that my name would constantly be before the eyes of Catharine Beecher and Lucy Stone—Section Twelve planned a funeral march without us. I read with horror Stephen's note detailing the illegal march of nearly one hundred souls and the subsequent arrest of six IWA leaders.

I rushed home to find Stephen, acting as president in our absence, was actively organizing a joint parade of Sections Nine and Twelve for the following Sunday.

"Stephen, I don't think this is wise. Let tempers cool before you act," I cautioned.

"We can't expect the men to sit around and do nothing. These are people used to working with their hands and getting into fights. They needed to expend their pent-up energy and anger at the deaths of their Parisian counterparts and the unjust arrest of their leaders. To ask them to do otherwise would be a grave insult."

"And that justifies a possible riot? Ha."

"There will be no riot. The police will be there, as they were last week."

"So are you willing to be arrested as leader of this illegal rabble? I am not." I crossed my arms. "I will not go along with this without police approval."

Stephen smiled at me wickedly. "Actually, you have to and so does Tennie. Part of your duty as president of the IWA is to lead any organized events held by our section. The only reason you weren't called into service the first time is because you were out of town."

I wanted to wring his neck. The bastard had trapped me. If I said no, I risked the fury of the members, who would take it as a personal betrayal. I couldn't afford to lose their support. I would have to attend and pray nothing went wrong.

When the carriage bearing Tennie, James, Stephen, Theodore, and me arrived at the Cooper Institute that Sunday, I remained in my seat. Stephen took me by the arm and tried to drag me onto the street, but I held fast to the door frame.

"The police are doing nothing to quell the growing crowds. I will not put myself in danger," I said.

I wasn't being melodramatic. People donning red sashes, ribbons, and banners were everywhere, lining the parade route, peering down from windows and balconies, even sitting on overhanging tree branches.

"Madame, I must insist you join us," the mustachioed grand marshal said, offering his hand to help me down.

Once again, I was cornered. But that didn't mean I had to go along quietly. "Ridiculous! An outrage to public safety. Isn't that part of what we are fighting for?"

I carried on my protest but took my place at the head of the throng, behind the black-draped wagon containing an empty bier that would lead the mourners. Tennie stood by my side, carrying the flag of the Paris Commune. James, Stephen, and Theodore flanked us on three sides like knights of old.

Behind us stretched row upon row of people lined up five abreast. These included Negro Civil War veterans who were playing a funeral march on their drums along with various male and female members of Sections Twelve and Nine carrying a banner that read, "Honor to the martyrs of the Universal Republic." Cuban revolutionists carried banners of blue and white while the French carried red. Sprinkled in between were Irish, German, and Italian groups along with the Printer's Society and various other revolutionaries.

Some blocks away, a church bell tolled twice, and the parade set out, the pace slow, the atmosphere somber. From both sides of the street, the mocking, jeering crowd called us all manner of derogatory names. Several times, I was nearly hit by rotten produce, and once, a rock grazed my elbow. Still, the police made no move to control the situation.

"They are hoping for a riot," I whispered to James, who held my arm firmly, body angled in to shield me from anything else thrown by the crowd. Despite our ups and downs, he rose to my defense when it mattered.

At the corner of Bowery and Great Jones Street, an overturned wagon and team blocked the route, so we veered from Bowery onto Great Jones Street, passing the house where Tennie and I had first lived after coming to New York. Katherine stood on the stoop, grinning and bouncing a baby in her arms. She waved and called to us. I waved back. It was wonderful to see my old friend again, and looking so well.

As Union Square grew visible in the distance, the crowd swelled with even more people pouring out of every side street to join the marching throng. Tennie and I were forced shoulder to shoulder as James, Theodore, and Stephen formed an even tighter barrier to protect us from the crush. From somewhere in the crowd, a band began a dirge to accompany us the final blocks.

At Union Square, the press of people was so great I could hardly breathe. "James, please, let me out."

"I can't. They will rush toward you, knock you to the ground. I will not let them harm you."

He was right. From every side came shouts of "Speech! Speech!" and demands for us to lead the rallying cry for justice. When the men around me declined, the crowd turned on us.

"Can our lady presidentesses not speak for themselves?" some-one asked.

"Aye, they are not fit to lead. Presidentesses my arse," came another.

Stephen detached himself from our retinue. "Get them out of here," he said softly before raising his arms to the crowd. "My fellow IWA members, we come here today to protest a grave injustice."

I didn't hear the rest of his impromptu speech. My world became a mass of sweaty wool and greasy hair as I pushed and elbowed through the crowd amid shrieks and curses from those I disturbed. Keeping one hand in James's, I tried not to trip on my skirts or the uneven paving stones while keeping the waiting carriage in sight.

We were nearly there when half a dozen men detached from the crowd and stepped between us and our method of escape.

"Look what we have here, Bennie," a sharp-featured, dark-haired man in a pipe hat and moth-eaten workman's clothes called. A wicked grin split his face. "I do believe these are the Bewitching Brokers."

I froze, panic seizing my limbs and rendering me immobile. My eyes darted from the men to the carriage to James and Theodore then to Tennie. A thought passed between us, a shared sense of desperation. There were too many of them. We'd never be able to flee without some sort of altercation.

"You are worth a pretty penny, are you not?" The heckler fondled the gold watch chain hanging from my suit. "Let's have a look."

I willed myself not to flinch. If all he wanted to do was rob me, I would not stop him. I could buy another watch. Other far darker dangers threatened in a crowd such as this. As long as I could escape unharmed, nothing else mattered.

James made a move toward me but was quickly restrained by one of the other men. Out of the corner of my eye, I caught another move-ment, a blur of brown that heaved itself upon my would-be attacker.

The whole group staggered, caught unawares, providing the opportunity we needed. Tennie and I raced for the carriage, followed closely by James and Theodore.

"Go, go!" James yelled to the driver as he shut the door behind us all.

As we sped away from the square, I glanced back just as a mob, much larger than the six original men, descended upon our anonymous savior, raining down blow after blow upon him under the watchful gaze of the police, who did nothing to stop the violence.

My would-be assailant limped on behind the carriage for a few blocks, brandishing a knife at us. "Take care, Madame Presidentess. I am not the only one who would see you silenced."

CHAPTER THIRTY

The backlash from the parade was swift and harsh. All I could do was watch as, one by one, my remaining allies turned against me.

Shaken by the alarm raised by the *New York Times*—which compared me to Karl Marx, insinuating I shared his belief that a violent overthrow of the capitalist class was inevitable, if not imminent—many of the firm's most lucrative clients quietly closed their accounts, leaving the brokerage with barely enough business to keep the collectors from our door.

How we would keep even that small clientele was questionable now that Josie, still our main source of tips after all these years, had abandoned us for Paris. When her lover, Mr. Vanderbilt's loose-lipped stock market rival, Jim Fisk, was brutally murdered, she didn't wait around for suspicion to fall on her innocent shoulders.

But that was, in many ways, the least of my troubles. The Unionists and Marxists were accusing me of using the funeral march as a publicity stunt, which was not sitting well with the Section Twelve workers. I couldn't lose them at such a critical juncture in my campaign. To maintain their loyalty, I would have to make a bold move, one that placed me firmly on the side of the working class, a gesture no one could ignore.

Starting in January, I began calling out the rich and powerful in the columns of the *Weekly*, especially those who depended on the labor of the poor, and revealing the inside deals that had made them rich, of which we had knowledge thanks to Josie. I hadn't wanted to go this far, but the aftermath of the parade had forced my hand, and I was tired of the duplicity of the rich.

No one was sacred—not even Cornelius Vanderbilt. That made Tennie nervous, but I no longer cared. If he wished to withdraw his support, that was his decision. But I could not in good conscience shine the light on others while allowing our patron to remain in the dark. I was against hypocrisy in all its forms, and to do so would have made me a practitioner of the worst sort.

I followed up the columns with the most explosive speech of my career, titled "The Impending Revolution." It was a scathing indictment of the wealthy and the crimes their fortunes allowed them to perpetrate without even a second glance, whereas the average man was jailed for far less.

After I debuted the speech in Boston, James and Tennie begged me to not speak such words again, especially not in New York, where my name was increasingly linked with violence.

"You're taking a terrible, unnecessary risk," James said. "Please, as you once asked Stephen, let tempers calm before you set the town on fire again."

"Why should I cede the tide of popular opinion because of a minority who wish me ill?"

Tennie growled. "Sometimes you can be so bullish, Vickie. Have you forgotten the break-in at the firm or the threats made against your person? Or do you desire to end up a female Abraham Lincoln?"

"No one will shoot me."

"Can you be so certain?" James asked. "Are a few votes really worth your life?"

"No. But I spent my childhood in fear of my father and my maidenhood in fear of my husband. I will *not* succumb to fear of what may or may not occur in my adult life. I will speak the truth, and the spirits will guard me."

Three days before I was due to give the speech in New York, *Harper's Weekly* got wind of it and published a cartoon depicting me with the caption "Get thee behind me (Mrs.) Satan." It showed me in the foreground as a winged creature with horns coming out of my short hair, gesturing to a page that read, "Be saved by Free Love." Behind me was a woman in rags, saddled with dirty, crying babies and carrying on her back a drunkard of a husband.

I stared at the image, unsure whether to laugh or cry. In truth, I wanted to do both. On one hand, the drawing was absurd, but on the other, its message was clear: I was equal to Satan for suggesting Free Love could save woman from her circumstances. Any God-fearing female was better off enduring her circumstances than following me to perdition.

I dropped the paper in the rubbish bin. Either way, worrying over it wouldn't do any good. What was done was done; now I needed to show the public that the press was wrong.

On February 20, I waited backstage at the Academy of Music on Fourteenth Street, watching the crowd grow larger and larger until they were squashed together like bound firewood. One of the janitors mentioned I was so in demand that the sold-out venue was still admitting patrons who held scalped tickets. According to him, the fifty-cent tickets were being sold for as much as ten dollars. Well, if nothing else, the damned cartoon had drawn people to see for themselves if I had horns. Smiling, I patted my hair and hoped they wouldn't be disappointed.

Thirty minutes remained until I was scheduled to take the stage, but the audience was growing unruly as profit trumped safety. I had asked the building manager not to admit anyone else, but he clearly wasn't listening. As patrons pushed in from the back, the women in front were crushed up against the stage. Three women had to be carried out after they fainted in the muggy, sweat-laced air of the ground floor.

The manager may have had no problem treating his patrons like cattle, but I did not wish to see my audience penned in like animals. It was time to put a stop to this nonsense before it set off a chain reaction of hysteria. I straightened my black jacket and tie and stepped onto the stage.

My notoriety negated the need for an introduction, so I began straightway, my voice strong and powerful. "A Vanderbilt may sit in his office and manipulate stocks or make dividends, by which in a few years, he amasses fifty million dollars from the industries of the country, and he is one of the remarkable men of the age. But if a poor, half-starved child were to take a loaf of bread from his cupboard to prevent starvation, she would be sent first to the Tombs and thence to Blackwell's Island.

"An Astor may sit in sumptuous apartments and watch the property bequeathed him by his father rise in value from one million to fifty million, and everybody bows before his immense power and worships his business capacity. But if a tenant whose employer discharged him because he did not vote the Republican ticket fails to pay his month's rent to Mr. Astor, the law sets him and his family into the street in midwinter.

"Is there any common justice in such a state of things? Is it right that the millions should toil all their lives long, scarcely having comfortable food and clothes, while the few manage to control all the benefits? A system of society which permits such arbitrary distributions of wealth is a disgrace to Christian civilization.

"But it is asked, how is this to be remedied? I answer, very easily. Since those who possess the accumulated wealth of the country have filched it by legal means from those to whom it justly belongs—the people—it must be returned to them. When a person worth millions dies, instead of leaving it to his children, who have no more title to it than anybody else's children have, it must revert to the people who produced it."

I continued on in a similar vein for two hours. When my speech ended, instead of the usual laudation, I was greeted with stunned silence followed by polite applause. Unlike in Boston, where I'd been treated to both cheers and jeers, this audience was oddly subdued upon leaving the theatre, mumbling to one another but otherwise unmoved.

I mentioned this to James afterward.

"My love," he replied, "you have just declared war on not only their heroes but their neighbors and colleagues. It is far easier to scoff at the tycoons of Wall Street and Fifth Avenue from the safe remove of several states away. It is far different to do so when you will see them at church on Sunday."

For the next two days, the same silence I experienced from the audience extended to the press. But then the *New York Times* found the courage to speak out against my speech, accusing me of inflaming the poor against the rich and being a hypocrite.

"*Why should not Mrs. Woodhull prove her faith in the theory that property is crime?*" they wrote after asking, incorrectly, why I didn't include Vanderbilt in my speech. *"Let her kindle a bonfire in Union Square and head a procession of women like-minded with herself, who will cast their wicked wealth into the flame. When her best black silk and her jaunty sealskin jacket, her diamond rings, and her golden necklaces have cracked and burned in the fire, the intelligent working men of the city will, at least, credit her with a desire not to enjoy luxuries which she has not earned by manual labor."*

Furious, I immediately sent a reply, pointing out their errors and defending myself. *"I never objected to the accumulation of wealth. I want everybody to have all the wealth of which he can make good use, and if equal conditions are secured, everybody may have that amount. But I did, and always shall until it is remedied, object to a certain few holding all the wealth. One class of people has no right first to monopolize the wealth and afterward to put labor in bondage by its power.*

"I do not monopolize either dresses or jewels, since of the first I only possess sufficient to render myself comfortable while with the last I have nothing to do. I believe money should be simply the means to better ends and not the end itself."

When my reply was returned with a terse message that the paper "cannot possibly afford space for your letter," I crumpled the note and set to work printing it in the pages of the *Weekly*.

Once the *Times* set the standard, other papers followed suit, happily condemning my speech.

Weary of the constant journalistic backbiting, I sequestered myself at the brokerage, only to be surprised by a visit from Mr. Vanderbilt. He had never once visited us there, preferring to remain in the shadows. His connection to Tennie and me had stayed as ephemeral as smoke, especially since our mother's failed blackmail attempt. His presence spoke volumes, so much so that he needed not speak for the purpose of his visit to be clear. He was gravely upset over my speech.

He declined the seat I offered and instead stood erect as a naval captain, hands clasped behind his back. "I have just been to see Tennie. It should come as no surprise that I am withdrawing my commitment to fund the *Weekly*. How you finance it, and any of your other ventures, is no longer any of my concern. We shall put it about that my wife caught me embracing Tennie, but we both know the true reason I wish to end our association." He stared at me pointedly.

I nodded mutely, a lump forming in my throat. This was my doing, was inevitable even, but the loss of our friendship was still a terrible blow. Then there was the financial consideration. It cost three hundred dollars a week to run the paper, more than it made, so we would have to find a new source of backing to keep the presses running.

But more than that, I was affected by the hard tone of finality that colored his words, like a disappointed father disinheriting a persistently unruly child. That was what he had become to me—a surrogate father who had taken in my sister and me when we were but orphans in a strange new city, taught us a trade, and saw to it that we prospered. I began to weep.

"Why did you do it, Victoria?" The commodore's voice cracked, and his icy blue eyes softened a touch. "Why, after all these years, did you turn on me? You could have given the same speech without using my name, and we would not be where we are today."

I regarded him, tears streaming down my cheeks, but was unable to find words. How could I explain to this man that I thought what I had done was just, that I was afraid of being called his pet, of being accused of sheltering him while I gleefully snitched on everyone else? How could I justify the hubris that had made me think I no longer needed him?

In the end, I said nothing, shaking my head and praying he would see my sorrow and regret in my wrinkled brow and hear my pleas to forgive me within my sobs.

Mr. Vanderbilt sighed. "Do you remember the first day you came to work for me? You channeled the spirit of my mother. She warned me away from you, said I would rue to the day I took you in." He shook his head. "God, that I would have listened."

After Mr. Vanderbilt departed, I left feeling as though I had been run over by a carriage. When I opened the front door to my home, I nearly screamed, not expecting to meet Mr. Langley, my landlord, in the foyer. He was dressed formally, a briefcase resting at his side as though keeping him company while he waited for me. He rose when I entered.

"Mr. Langley, to what do I owe pleasure of your company?" I asked, forcing warmth into my voice that I did not feel, upset as I was by the afternoon's events.

I made to shake his hand, but he backed away. So this was not a social call. My smile faltered as I offered him a brandy.

"No, thank you. This will not take long." He opened his briefcase and removed a long sheet of paper. "I am here to serve notice that you and your family are to vacate the premises at the beginning of next month."

My jaw dropped. "But why? We have not been late on our payments." To illustrate my point, I reached into my purse and withdrew a fistful of cash, which I thrust at him. "Here, here. We are not paupers. What is wrong with our money?"

"Nothing. It's not your money." He cleared his throat. "There are those who do not wish to have your name associated with this neighborhood."

"And why not? We have caused no disruption." But I was a radical, and those with money had no desire to associate with my kind. With more bravado than my frayed nerves would allow me to feel, I added, "You have no legal grounds on which to evict us."

Mr. Langley dug the toe of his highly polished shoe into the pile of my blue-and-white carpet. "Perhaps. Perhaps not. That is a matter for our attorneys to decide."

I wasted no time in escorting my landlord to the door. "So it is. Mine will be in touch," I assured him as I slammed the door.

CHAPTER THIRTY-ONE

I sat at my desk, head in my hands. It was all getting to be too much. Despite old Mr. Reymert's best efforts, we'd had to vacate my beloved mansion and sell off all of my lovely possessions. Gone were the crystal chandeliers, the mirrors twice the height of a man, the fine furnishings. Now we were interlopers in my sister Maggie's modest brownstone—just as when the mill had burned so many years before—stretching it to its limits with the addition of my brood of seven.

Then Canning died. He had been ill for quite some time with a lung ailment, and when the doctor tried to cut back on his dosage of morphine in an effort to end his addiction, his body gave out. No dramatic scene ensued—no deathbed apologies or pithy final words. Canning was too ill and too inebriated for any of that. He simply closed his eyes and, shortly thereafter, stopped breathing.

Grieving for him—little as he deserved it—would have been a strain on its own, but then Utica, Canning's consort in all substances legal and illegal, had to go and cry to the coroner that he'd died under suspicious circumstances, blaming the doctor. The press jumped on the story, making it sound as though I or, more popularly, Colonel Blood was implicated in Canning's untimely death.

Of course, as soon as the coroner did his job, it was proven that Canning died of congestion in the lungs and had been ill for many years. But by then, Maggie had taken it upon herself to host a reporter for tea and give him all the sordid details, including recounting the night Canning came to live with us and revealing that Utica took morphine daily. So now not only was *I* a pariah, but the entire newspaper-reading world knew my sister was addicted to drugs—yet another spot on my family's already tarnished reputation. Many people were beginning to ask if I came from the kind of stock they wanted in their president.

I had hoped my run of bad luck would be buried with Canning, but it continued unabated. Earlier that morning, Stephen had informed me that Karl Marx himself had suspended Section Twelve. Stephen tried to make light of it by telling me it was a matter of ideological differences, that Marx and those in London were more concerned with wages, rights, and communal living than the individual rights Section Twelve and I espoused. But no matter how much sugar he poured on it, the stark truth was the same—by failing as the leader of Section Twelve, I had lost the loyalty of its members and, with that, the workingman's vote. All the risk I had taken on, all the friends I had alienated—it was all for nothing.

"The fact is you're too much trouble, Victoria." Stephen was the one to give voice to the unspoken thought we both shared.

Now all I had left were the Spiritualists and the suffragists. But if I faced the truth, the loyalty of the suffragists was questionable. The gossip about me in the papers was relentless, most of it coming from women who were supposed to be my allies. I could understand when it came from the American Woman Suffrage Association and their Boston bluebloods, but lately my sisters in suffrage—Elizabeth Phelps, Laura Curtis Bullard, and Lillie Devereux Blake—were found to be the source of some of the rumors swirling about me.

Susan B. Anthony was by far the worst offender, spewing bile whenever she could. The sudden change of heart she had displayed at the conference in January had taken permanent hold. I couldn't know for certain, but I suspected my former friend was jealous I was eclipsing the power it had taken Susan twenty years to gain. Be that as it may, it was no excuse for intimating Tennie was an adulteress and I a practitioner of humbuggery.

I raised my head, peering out the rain-streaked windows at the gray New York streets. An idea was forming, one that might put an end to the worst of the slander. From a young age, Ma had taught me that secrets were the most valuable currency, so for some time, I had quietly been collecting tidbits about the indiscretions of these very women in case I ever needed to use them.

God knew I didn't want to use the information, but there were only six months left before the election and I was losing supporters faster than the clouds could loose the rain. I certainly didn't need help from the suffragists in that regard. I had spent nearly two years of my life and the balance of my fortune in my bid to become president. It was my birthright, preordained from the moment I was named; I wouldn't let it slip away because of a few spiteful tongues.

Setting pen to paper, I combined my information into a single damning article that would expose all of their secret sexual relations—some outside of marriage, others with members of their own sex—if they didn't end their abuse. If they ceased their hateful speech, no one ever need know. The beauty of it was that with all of my own skeletons already exposed, they would have nothing to use against me. Even if one of them was brave enough to reveal my threats, she couldn't do so without taking herself down at the same time.

A weight slowly lifted off my chest. Tomorrow, five of the most powerful women in the suffrage movement would receive unsolicited envelopes, and within a matter of minutes, their tongues would be silenced.

CHAPTER THIRTY-TWO

The arrival of summer brought with it sunshine and a sense of optimism to my life. Why shouldn't I have been happy? I was the unofficial leader of the Suffragist Convention taking place at Steinway Hall—site of some of my most momentous speeches—later that day. Not only that, I'd succeeded in getting permission to have the audience expanded again to include Spiritualists and laborers. Plus, though Elizabeth was irritated I had signed her name to a call to join the Equal Rights Party without her permission, she'd privately endorsed the party. Susan was spitting mad about all three things, not to mention the threatening article that no one spoke of publicly, but there was little she could do. All signs pointed toward a successful event, both for women's rights and my campaign.

I was scheduled to speak early, and for that I was glad. I could get my message out before Susan had a chance to co-opt the meeting for her own ends, which were always solely focused on suffrage. I, however, was more interested in getting the crowd to support the broader range of reforms that working-class women sought.

"The eyes of the world are upon this convention," I declared proudly from the podium, beaming at the crowd of enraptured faces. "Its enemies have sneered and laughed at the idea of combining reformers for any organized action. They say that women don't know enough to organize and, therefore, are not to be feared as political opponents. I have even heard some confessed reformers say they don't want anything to do with those who belong to 'our clique,' but I trust this policy may not succeed. I hope all friends of humanitarian reform will clasp hands with each other."

With a final glance at Susan—who was studiously studying her lap—I steeled myself and played my trump card. "Now, I move that the convention adjourn and meet jointly with the Equal Rights Party at Apollo Hall."

Susan's head shot up. "You cannot move for such a thing without a vote of the members, and as president, I refuse to call one. You, madame, are out of order." Susan shuffled toward me, no doubt intent on forcing me off the stage.

I clung to the podium and called out my own motion. "All in favor of the parties meeting jointly at Apollo Hall, say aye."

Hundreds of cheers of "aye" rose from the assembly.

Scowling like a startled hen, Susan yelled over them, "Most of you are not members of our organization. You have no right. You can't vote. The meeting is adjourned. We will meet in the same space tomorrow." Susan doggedly pried my fingers one by one from the podium.

"We shall do what the spirit of freedom moves us to," I shot back, fighting to keep my hold. "In this case, that is to come together, despite our varied interests, as one party focused on equal rights—suffrage, labor reform, and women's rights. For until such time as true equality is granted, women will still be seen as slaves in this great land."

Clapping and waving their arms in agreement, the crowd chanted, "Woodhull! Woodhull! Woodhull!"

Susan finally gave up trying to forcibly remove me and disappeared backstage. I grinned. *She finally realizes I am younger, stronger, and possibly even more stubborn.* But my triumph quickly faded when Susan returned with a smug smile. Moments later, all the gas lights in the hall went out with a soft whoosh, leaving the crowd to grope in darkness for the exit.

Susan may have put a dramatic end to the meeting, but many of the attendees of the National Women's Rights Convention—including Ada Ballou, Laura Cuppy Smith, and a shining new star of the women's movement, an attorney named Belva Lockwood—defected to Apollo Hall to see how I would follow up my stunning performance.

The hall carried a festive atmosphere, with joyous voices shouting to one another and laughter ringing out. Nearly seven hundred delegates from over half of the states in the Union rubbed elbows with another six hundred fifty suffragists, Spiritualists, and other reformers. This crowd was little like the staid, conservative audience gathering across town at Steinway Hall. While a fair number of suits and fashionable gowns were spotted among the participants, there were also women in the pantaloons and short hair of sex radicals, men with the long hair and loose coats of free lovers, and quite a number of women who made their living in the streets of the Bowery.

I took the stage to deafening cheers. "Go where we may in the land," I said, raising my arms toward the delegates, "we see inequity and injustice, but we will tolerate this no longer."

For the next hour, I repeated my call for revolution in business, education, politics, and private life. Before I could end my speech, the crowd charged forward, chanting my name.

I held up my hand for quiet, ending with the rallying cry, "Let us have justice though the heavens fall!"

The crowd went wild, women waving their handkerchiefs and crying openly and men tossing their hats in the air while shouting until they were hoarse.

Judge Carter from Kentucky leapt onstage. "I believe that in what I am about to say, I shall receive the hearty concurrence of every member of this convention. I therefore nominate, as the choice for the Equal Rights Party for the President of the United States, Victoria C. Woodhull."

Suddenly, the crowd around me disappeared, and time stood still. I had done it. Despite the ups and downs, the nasty rumors, the lost friendships, and both the odds and the powers that be against me, I had lived to see another step in Demosthenes's prophecy come true—this was the first time any party had endorsed a woman for president. For the space of three heartbeats, Demosthenes was at my side. Then the whir of the crowd came rushing back, and I was ushered once again to the podium.

Looking out upon the smiling faces turned up toward me like flowers to the sun, I couldn't help but shed a few tears of joy. "I feel this honor more deeply and sensibly since I have stood before the world so long, sometimes receiving its approval but oftener encountering its rebuffs. It is with great joy that I accept your nomination. I promise to carry the principles of the Equal Rights Party into governmental practice. I thank you from the bottom of my soul for the honor you have conferred on me tonight."

Later in the night, Frederick Douglass was nominated as my running mate, uniting an abolitionist and a suffragist, a white woman and a black man, one who had started out poor and the other a slave, on one ticket under the banner of Equal Rights.

CHAPTER THIRTY-THREE

JUNE 1872

Ma had always said that for every blazing sun in the noonday sky, there was a waning moon waiting; it was the way of the world. I'd dismissed the aphorism as rot until my joy came to a crashing halt in the sweltering heat of summer.

Things had been going so well. My family moved out of Maggie's brownstone and into the Gilsey House hotel, and my electoral chances were better than ever. But then as I was packing for a much-anticipated speaking tour out West, I began to shake uncontrollably. I slid to the floor in a heap, and the world went black.

It was a faint from which I could not seem to wake. I could open my eyes for short periods of time, but when I did, my arms, legs, and head were like lead. I was constantly hot and sweating and could barely choke down the water James poured down my throat as soon as my eyelids fluttered.

In those brief periods of consciousness, I conceded I was powerless to continue on with my plans.

"Tennie," I said, "please take my place out West. You know my positions as well as I do. We can't afford to pass up the speaking fees. Show Ma she was wrong. Prove to her you are not worthless, as I always knew."

As the days dragged on, my periods of consciousness lengthened, though I wished they would not. The news being brought to my bedside was anything but good. While I was ill, James had pulled Zula from school then enrolled her at new one under an assumed name because parents didn't want their children around her. Elizabeth, who had apparently found out about my springtime scheme to keep the gossips at bay, turned against me. Belva Lockwood, whom I was beginning to see as a spiritual and political daughter, announced her intention to back Horace Greeley for president, while Frederick Douglass—who had never officially accepted his nomination as my vice president but did not ask to have his name removed from the ticket either—came out campaigning for Grant. If that wasn't bad enough, Ma was suddenly feeling maternal and insisted on staying by my side until I recovered.

The crushing blow came when Theodore came to visit me one humid afternoon. I was sitting up in bed in only my chemise. He took my hand so warmly that I dared to hope I may be back in his favor.

"I'm glad to see you are recovering."

I gave him a wary smile, sensing reservation in his tone. "Slowly."

"But you are, and praise be to God for that." He kissed the top of my hand as he sank onto the bed next to me. "I came to tell you I'm going to the liberal Republican convention with Whitelaw Reid. He's asked me to report it for the *Tribune*. I wanted to tell you myself before you read about it in the papers."

My smile evaporated along with my feeling of euphoria. The *Tribune* was run by Horace Greeley, an open antagonist of mine. But if Greeley got elected, his job as editor would be available, a position Theodore had coveted for as long as I'd known him. He'd finally found a way to get it—by betraying me.

"You are a liar." I wrenched my hand from his and moved as far away from him as I could. "Why not be truthful and admit you are going to the convention to nominate Mr. Greeley for president?"

"Victoria… I—"

I didn't hear any more of his protestations. I was suddenly swept into a trance. Before me was Theodore walking behind a wagon that bore a coffin. When I strained to see inside, I almost screamed. It was carrying the body of Horace Greeley.

Grasping at his lapels as I came back to myself, I told Theodore of the vision in a babbling rush, ending with, "You will be responsible for putting him in that coffin, responsible for his death. Don't go, Theodore, I beg of you."

But he was already standing, shaking his head. His expression said he thought me either mad or falsifying my vision in a bid to get him to stay. Without another word, my former lover walked out of my life.

❧

A few weeks later, I was feeling up to getting out of bed, so I paid a visit to the brokerage. After a few hours of work, I returned home for a nap to find Minnie, Zula, and Byron on the sidewalk in front of the hotel, surrounded by our luggage. Before I could ask what was going on, Zula ran to me and burst into tears.

"Oh, baby girl, what is it? What's happened?" I wrapped my arms around my daughter and held her close.

"They said—they said we were no longer welcome here," Zula hiccupped between sobs.

"Who did?"

"The landlords, ma'am," Minnie answered. "They were all fired up about Tennie's association with the Spencer Grays, said they 'don't want no nigger lovers in their hotel.'"

My shoulders sagged. I had told Tennie not to get involved with the black military regiment, but still smarting from Ma calling her worthless, Tennie couldn't resist their request to become their colonel.

"I want to show that women can go to the front of any group," she had said. "You aren't the only one who can make a political statement."

And now my sister's stunt had gotten us thrown out of yet another home.

"They stood there while we packed, but—" Zula dissolved into tears again.

"We weren't fast enough, so they threw the rest of our things into the street along with us," Minnie finished for her. "I gathered everything up once the children were calm."

I smiled softly at Minnie. "You did very well." The best thing I had ever done was take that girl in. I thought for a moment. "Well, we'd better get you back to the firm. At least you'll have a proper place to sit down while I figure out what to do."

Once there, Tennie, James, and I traded ideas. Many of our remaining friends were gone on holiday for the summer and so couldn't be prevailed upon for a room. There was no way any of us were going to stay with Buck and Annie or any of my half-crazy brothers and sisters. That left Madame de Ford and Miss Wood, but a brothel was not an ideal place to shelter two young children.

Then Tennie, bless her, remembered Katherine at 17 Great Jones Street. "We can at least ask. She may have two rooms to rent."

Katherine rented us two of her rooms but only for a week, as she had additional guests scheduled to arrive. I thanked her profusely, paid in advance, and soon we were back in the same rooms we'd occupied in 1869.

We were fast running out of options, so I swallowed my pride and appealed to the most powerful man I knew. Reverend Henry Ward Beecher owed me a favor for failing to appear at Steinway Hall. The least he could do was put in a good word with one of the many hotels in New York so my family could have a place to live.

"*Dear Sir,*" I wrote. "*The social fight against me being now waged in this city is becoming rather hotter than I can well endure longer, standing unsupported and alone as I have until now. Within the past weeks I have been shut out of hotel after hotel and am now, after having obtained a place in one, hunted down by a set of males and females who are determined that I shall not be permitted to live even, if they can prevent it.*

"*Now I want your assistance. I want to be sustained in my position, from which I am ordered out and from which I do not wish to go—and all this simply because I am Victoria C. Woodhull, the advocate of social freedom. I have submitted to this persecution just so long as I can endure. My business, my projects, in fact everything for which I live, suffer from it, and it must cease. Will you lend me your aid in this?*"

His reply was swift, brief, and obviously written by someone else. He regretted being unable to help me in this matter.

"Ungrateful bastard." I crumpled up the note. We had to be out of Great Jones Street by five o'clock that evening, and I had no idea where we would go.

The family roamed the streets for a full night without being able to find a place to sleep—hotel after hotel either had no vacancies or refused to serve us. Finally, we went back to the brokerage, where we slept on desks, on couches, in chairs, and on the floor.

Exhausted and dispirited, I relapsed into my illness. I was not conscious when the presses went silent on my beloved *Weekly* at the end of June due to lack of funds, but I was crushed all the same.

"It's because of my candidacy," I said one day not long after. "No one wishes me to succeed. I know newsmen are being bribed to exclude it from the stands. I've seen them tossing bundles into the garbage. It's the same reason the newspapers won't cover my plight. All those we've called out are banding together against us because we want to change the system."

"Don't be silly," Tennie said. To our mother, she added, "It must be the fever talking."

"That ain't no fever talking," Annie said. "It's her pride. Even an animal knows not to bite the hand that feeds it. But you gone and done it anyway with those articles and speeches. Now you're surprised at what happens." She shook her head. "You've always been that way, thinking you're better than the rest of us, what with your airs and all."

How dare she? I sat up, overwhelmed by dual waves of dizziness and nausea, and sank back down into the pillows. "My 'airs,' as you call them, were fine when they were putting bread in your belly and rum in your cup."

Then it hit me. My mother was not the only one with that attitude.

"Everyone else was the same, friendly only when I had money. Sure, then I was entertaining and useful. Now I'm a pathetic shell of a woman." I moaned.

My depression only deepened when the brokerage's landlord realized we were living there. Seeing an opportunity for profit, he raised the rent by one thousand dollars and demanded we pay immediately. We couldn't, and so were back out on the streets, the once glorious firm of Woodhull, Claflin, and Company remaining only in name.

Tired, depressed, and sick to my bones, I gave up. No one in New York City would rent to Tennie or me. Our names and faces were too well known. Maggie took us back and was eventually able to find us a small apartment, rented under an assumed name and paid for with campaign funds since it also served as the headquarters of the Equal Rights Party and the brokerage office.

How the mighty had fallen. The future presidentess who had once cowed all of Wall Street and lived in the tallest mansion on the block was now running a faltering campaign from a single room on borrowed funds. Where had it all gone so terribly wrong? My conscience and the spirits gave me the same answer loud and clear—my pride had brought us there. It was all my fault, and only I could undo the damage.

CHAPTER THIRTY-FOUR

The summer had worn me down to my bones, sucking out the marrow of my iron will and ambition until I resembled the woman who had announced her candidacy two years before as much as winnowed grain resembles the tender shoots of spring.

Though finally recovered from my mysterious illness, I had no desire to attend the National Convention of American Spiritualists in Boston. But as their president, it was my duty.

On the second night of the convention, I mounted the stairs to the stage with growing resignation. No one knew this was to be my final speech to my beloved supporters, as I intended to step down as the group's president. It would be a simple speech expressing my gratitude for their unwavering dedication and pledging my support to the group for years to come, albeit in a lesser role.

While Laura Cuppy Smith introduced me, I recited my habitual pre-speech prayer to the spirits for guidance. I was suddenly taken out of myself into a great blinding light.

"Paradise was lost in Genesis through woman and regained in Revelation through woman," a female voice said with the force of a gale. "Through woman and not through man will the world be saved. The time has come to at last unburden yourself of all you know of Henry Ward Beecher and his affair. By doing so, you will save the world from the hell of a sexual double standard and sexual hypocrisy and usher in a new era—paradise found."

Blinking rapidly, I returned to myself in time to hear Laura say my name and turn toward me, inviting me forth. I was barely conscious of the walk to the podium, still suffused with that heavenly light.

When I parted my lips, my voice rang out as though from a distance, repeating the words spoken by the spirits. "Paradise was lost in Genesis through woman and regained in Revelation through woman. Through woman and not through man will the world be saved. For this paradise to be found, we must no longer allow a standard of sexual hypocrisy to exist. As you know, I have myself been a victim of this falsity, privately and publicly charged with vulgar sins I did not commit, oftentimes by those I know for certain were guilty of the same crimes with which they charged me and worse.

"That is why today, I have come before you to reveal the most heinous of these crimes. Many of you have no doubt heard the rumors about the so-called 'clerical weakness' of Plymouth Church leader Reverend Henry Ward Beecher. I am here to verify that they are all true. I know from the mouths of all parties involved that he did in fact seduce the young, vulnerable parishioner Elizabeth Tilton, who was, at the time, married to Mr. Theodore Tilton. This beloved preacher used his power and charisma to form an unholy union with her, convincing her that their sexual affair was an expression of God's love, a right and holy thing. Not only that, but a child resulted from this union, one which was untimely cast from its mother's womb by the forces of nature which saw it for what it was—the forbidden fruit of criminal passion.

"I call this sin only because of the hypocrisy with which the act was treated. Were the affair undertaken under the auspices of Free Love, then no harm would have been done. But no, even though Reverend Beecher holds these views in his heart—he has told me so—he continued to deny that such an act ever took place even when confronted by Elizabeth's cuckolded husband.

"I have held this information in confidence for years because I did not wish to expose those involved to undue scrutiny. However, the time has come for all to be revealed; at the urging of the spirits, I have told you what I reliably know from all involved. May we who hear these words take into our hearts and minds the lesson contained herein—that if sex and love are to be held up in private or public as the vital forces that they are, this must be done equally between the sexes with no expectation that what is right for man is shameful for woman. The responsibility for the behavior of two must be equally borne if our nation is to move toward becoming a just society."

Word quickly spread about my speech, raising more than a few hackles among local Spiritualists. A Boston newspaper, no doubt influenced by the relentless Beecher sisters, accused me of slander, a charge I vehemently denied.

"I may have spoken against a public figure, but all that I said was true," I said to the assembled *Weekly* staff. "In this situation, I must either endure unjustly the imputation of being a slanderer, or I must resume my previously formed purpose of relating in formal terms, for the whole public, the simple facts of the case as they have come to my knowledge. I have decided to do so in the *Weekly*, as it has always been the vehicle through which I speak."

"But that would mean resurrecting it," James pointed out. "Can we afford that?"

"For a limited time, yes. The funds from my delayed lecture tour out West should be more than enough to cover the expenses. I want the story to be released to coincide with the reverend's silver anniversary so that it comes out when the most attention is already focused on him."

"Don't you think that's a little cruel?" James asked.

"Not after what he's done to me. I have only ever asked two things of the man: to stand with me before I made a speech and to put in a good word when I could not find shelter for my family. But he could not be bothered with either, and so now I will give his needs equal consideration."

"You will be doing your campaign no favors coming out so near Election Day," Stephen observed.

I whirled on him. "You think not? I think the opposite. This will be the grandest example of everything I've been speaking about for the last three years—a coup de grâce, if you will. This is no mere act of revenge; it is an illustration of the principles of equality, Free Love, and free speech in action."

Stephen gave me a dismissive gesture as if to say, "I give up. Do what you will."

Tennie, who had been silent up to this point, finally burst out, "I think you are absolutely right. But if you are going to raise a ruckus, I'm banging on the pots with you. I want to tell everyone what Luther Challis and Charles Maxwell did at the French Ball all those years ago. It's an injustice that's been chafing my heart for years and another example of men getting away with lurid behavior while women pay the consequences."

I had nearly forgotten about that obscene night four years earlier, when Josie had dragged us all to the American Academy of Music for the annual hedonistic tradition that dated back to before the Civil War. For that one night, daring members of high society mingled with brothel owners and workers along with anyone given to carousing, drink, or open sexuality.

Challis and Maxwell had been no different from thousands of other men who took their pleasure openly—only one of their conquests had been less than willing, and the other had been Minnie, for whom I'd always felt a motherly protection. When Tennie and I protested, the men carried the girls off to Madame de Ford's, where no one cared to stop their debauchery. Tennie had vowed that night that one day the girls would be revenged. She'd finally found her opportunity.

I took Tennie's hand. "We'll be like the female Frank and Jesse James."

Tennie grinned at me. "Making waves and breaking laws to the last."

James sighed. "Let's all pray you meet a better end."

I worked nearly around the clock in the weeks leading up to the reemergence of the paper from its financial slumber. While Stephen and I tried to find the best way to present my story to the public, Tennie worked on her exposé with Minnie, who agreed to help her piece together that night and its aftermath on the condition her identity not be revealed.

I also spearheaded the layout of this most important issue. I didn't want to scream what could be considered libel from the front page. No, this was a subtle, but deadly, attack. Sitting on the shelf next to other newspapers, the *Weekly* would appear like any other publication. Readers would have to buy it and wade through pages of Spiritualist articles and advertisements to get to the hidden powder kegs within.

Blue copying pencil in hand, I poured over the final proof of the issue. My article was set to appear on page nine under the headline

"The Beecher-Tilton Scandal Case: The Detailed Statement of the Whole Matter." It was written in the form of a mock interview in which I, after a brief introduction, answered questions from a made-up reporter about the affair.

"I propose aggressive moral warfare on the social question, to begin in this article with ventilating one of the most stupendous scandals which has ever occurred in any community. I refer to the conduct of Reverend Henry Ward Beecher in his relations with the family of Theodore Tilton. I intend that this article shall burst like a bombshell into the ranks of the moralistic social camp.

"I have no doubt that he has done the very best which he could do under the circumstances. The fault I find with Mr. Beecher is of a wholly different character, as I have told him repeatedly and frankly, and as he knows very well. I condemn him because I know that he entertains one conviction, sub-stantially the same views I entertain on the social question; that under the influence of these convictions, he has lived for many years, perhaps his whole adult life, in a manner which the religious and moralistic public ostensibly condemns; that he has permitted himself, nevertheless, to be overawed by public opinion, to profess to believe otherwise than he does believe, to persistently maintain, for these many years, that very social slavery under which he was chafing and against which he was secretly revolting both in thought and practice; and that he has, in a word, consented and still consents to be a hypocrite. The fault with which I therefore charge him is not infidelity to the old ideas but unfaithfulness to the new."

I marked a few errant spelling and grammar mistakes, moving into the section where I detailed what I knew of his affair with Lib Tilton. Flipping more quickly through the pages of advertisements and articles of trivial consequence, I stopped on page fourteen, where Tennie's damning story appeared under the somewhat-veiled headline "Beginning of the Battle."

> "A governor of a state and a pastor of the most popular church, president of the most reliable bank or the grandest railroad corporation may constantly practice all the debaucheries known to sensualism, and he, by virtue of his sex, stands protected and respected, so much so that even though the other sex cry shame on the exposer, the newspapers pretend not to know anything detrimental to public morality has transpired. But let a woman even so much as protect herself from starvation by her sexuality, and everybody in unison cries out, 'Down with the vile thing,' while newspapers make it their special business to herald her shame, utterly forgetting there was a man in the scrape.
>
> "We propose to take leading personages from each of the several pursuits of life and lay before the world a record of their private careers so that it may no longer appear that their victims are the only frightful examples of immorality. To that end, I give you the story of Mr. L. C. Challis."

I made a few marks as Tennie laid out what had transpired at the French Ball in 1869. I considered striking the final line, *"And this scoundrel, Challis, to prove that he seduced a virgin, carried for days on his finger, exhibiting in triumph, the red trophy of her virginity."* It was overly dramatic, but we tried not to edit one another's work too heavily. I could live with it. It added shock value of Biblical proportions, which would be good for sales.

James oversaw the secret printing and ensured subscriber issues were mailed before the paper hit newsstands on October 28. Finally, there was nothing to do but wait.

The paper made exactly the impact I was hoping for. Within a few hours, people were referring to it as "The Scandal Issue" and with good reason. As word spread, papers flew off the shelves, quickly depleting the first run of ten thousand copies and forcing the printers to work overtime to meet demand. By evening, issues that normally went for a dime were selling for over two dollars each.

By the time we opened our home/office the second morning, clients were telling us all sorts of outlandish rumors. Supposedly, one copy sold for forty dollars. Buck, ever enterprising, proudly bragged that he was renting his issues to others to read for a dollar a day. Returning from the printer, Stephen reported seeing copies being burned in Union Square by Reverend Beecher's supporters.

When the first one hundred thousand copies were depleted, our distributor, American News Company, refused to replace it on the stands. So Tennie and I used our network of contacts to get word to the newsboys that they could pick the papers up from our offices in person.

For the next two days, young boys in suits with rolled up cuffs and jaunty caps paraded in and out of our tiny office as though it were a schoolhouse, exchanging their coins for packs of papers tied with string. Some didn't even wait until they hit the corner before shouting about their newly obtained wares.

One of them, upon obtaining his latest pack, thanked me, adding, "I don't know how to read or who Mr. Beecher is, so I don't know what's got these papers so hot, but I'm glad they are. My family will be able to eat this week thanks to what I've earned."

My heart warmed to hear the issue had some positive unforeseen consequences. But that did little to loosen the knot of anxiety growing in my belly with each passing hour. We were opening ourselves up to possible libel suits, so I kept waiting for some response from Beecher or Challis. But so far they were silent, which unnerved me more than if they had barged in demanding Tennie and I be arrested.

By the time the gaslights were lit, despite the brisk sales and satisfaction of finally exposing the two, my skin was itching with anticipation. Were Beecher and Challis plotting against us? It was the only possibility that would explain why neither of them had yet issued a statement or even hinted that they were aware of what had been written about them. They were probably holed up in some secluded club or hotel room, colluding to ruin the two women who dared speak against them.

Late that night, I voiced these fears to James.

"My dear, you are being ridiculous," he said.

But I knew better. The sprits were whispering for me to prepare. But for what?

CHAPTER THIRTY-FIVE

NOVEMBER 1872

The paper sold more than two hundred fifty thousand copies in three days, and now, halfway into our fourth day of sales, Tennie and I were on our way back to the office with three thousand more copies tied in freshly printed bundles on the seat and floor and lashed to the back of our carriage. The woody scent of paper pulp was bravely trying to hold its own against the astringent bite of the ink, both of which were stinking up the cabin.

We were only a few blocks from our office when the driver stopped the carriage. At first, I paid no attention to the male voices outside, thinking it a routine stop for traffic or so that the driver could help someone in need. But then the door was wrenched open to reveal a mustachioed police officer in his navy uniform. He politely tipped his cap before looking between Tennie and me.

"Mrs. Victoria Woodhull and Miss Tennessee Claflin?" he asked.

I shaded my eyes to see the officer in the glare of the noontime sun. "I am Victoria. May we help you?"

The officer frowned. "I regret to inform you that I must arrest you on charges of sending obscene material through the United States Postal Service. You are hereby under police custody and will be delivered to the local police station to undergo the routine procedures." He flashed a document at us.

I assumed it was a warrant but was too shocked at the moment to read it.

"I will be driving your carriage, and Officer O'Malley here will be seated with you."

"What?" Tennie spluttered. "Whatever does this mean?"

Officer O'Malley, a handsome boy of about eighteen, stuck his head into the carriage. After seeing the piles of papers crowding the seats, he carefully settled on Tennie's lap. She responded with a flirtatious smile.

At the police station, heavy iron manacles were secured to my wrists, and I was sent through a series of procedures to make my arrest official, Tennie only a step behind. Then we were hauled in front of the police captain, who was grinning as though he'd inherited a fortune. I glared at him, imagining how much he must be relishing my humiliation. I was well aware that he had disliked me from the moment I started speaking in public.

"What do you have to say for yourselves?" the police captain asked.

"They are refusing to speak until they obtain counsel," the first officer, whose name was Miller, said. "They request contact with Mr. J.D. Reymart."

The captain grunted. "Well, see if Mr. Reymart is available. Until then, the two of you will have to get comfortable in a cell." He shooed us out with a gesture usually reserved for animals.

❧

THE FOLLOWING MORNING, WE were dragged before a judge with Mr. Reymart at our side. From what Mr. Reymart had told us during our brief session before being taken into chambers, the charge stemmed from a man named Anthony Comstock, who took objection to Tennie's use of the phrase "red trophy of her virginity" even though she'd taken it from the book of Deuteronomy.

"Who is this man?" Tennie asked. "I've never heard of him."

"He is the United States Postal Inspector, a rather zealous fellow who sees himself as a crusader against vice. He claims you violated the law by mailing the issue to him."

"Did we mail a copy of the paper to him?" I asked.

"You did, upon his request. He furnished the paper along with an envelope bearing a local postal mark and a note in your hand thanking him for his request."

"So the rat set us up," Tennie sneered.

"It appears that way, yes. Mr. Comstock is a powerful man, so getting these charges dropped will not be easy. The police are even now searching your offices, probably seizing and destroying the presses." He turned to me, his expression full of concern. "I'm sorry to tell you that the colonel and Mr. Andrews have been arrested and sent to Jefferson Market Prison."

I closed my eyes as if doing so could unmake his words. Jefferson Market Prison was one of the worst in the country, notorious for its prison fights and filth, and hence, normally reserved for hardened criminals. I drew in a shaky breath. How would James fare in a place like that? He would be fine. He was the same man who had been shot six times during the Civil War and once even removed the bullets himself. I exhaled loudly, willing myself to be calm.

"Why would they send them there instead of bringing them here?" I demanded.

Mr. Reymart shrugged. "Probably to make a statement about how seriously they are taking this case. My point is that they will likely find or manufacture evidence that leads to additional charges, so it is my recommendation that after bail is set, you do not pay it but remain here."

"Why would we do such a thing?" Tennie asked, obviously appalled.

"Do you want to suffer the humiliation of being arrested again? Because that is exactly what they'll do as soon as you set foot outside these doors."

Tennie pouted but said nothing more.

Our appearance in the courtroom was brief, with Mr. Reymart speaking on our behalves. Bail was set at eight thousand dollars each—but not before a court official editorialized that "an example is needed and we propose to make one of these women."

We were then escorted to cell eleven, a sparsely furnished eight-by-four-foot room meant to house common criminals. No matter how many times Officer Miller apologized that the nicer guest quarters for notable inmates were full with the warden's family and the citizen bedroom was occupied by a merchant, I still found it fitting that we ended up with the common population, sleeping in a spare room right next to criminals. It wasn't too different from the way we had grown up.

To help make up for our living conditions, Officer Miller smuggled in copies of the paper to us the following morning. The *New York Times* declared, "The female name never has been more disgraced and degraded than by these women."

The *Herald* tut-tutted, "These women cannot even be classified with the unfortunates. It is a greater depth of infamy to which they belong."

"That's a pleasant way to start trial day," I muttered as we waited to be transported to the courthouse.

Though my heart was pounding, I told myself not to worry. We had a strong defense thanks to Mr. Reymart and two additional lawyers we had hired. They were going to argue that the language Comstock found so offensive was also repeated in the plays of Shakespeare, the poetry of Lord Byron, and the Bible. Therefore, if he insisted on pursuing these charges, he would have to also arrest anyone who had ever shipped one of those materials in the mail.

When we arrived at Jefferson Market Court, surrounded by half a dozen officers, we were greeted by a clerk barring the door to the courtroom.

"I'm sorry you were not informed, gentlemen," the agent of the court said to the trio of lawyers, "but the federal grand jury has already met."

"Now see here, it is a violation of the law—"

The clerk held up a hand to stave off further argument from Mr. Reymart or any of the lawyers. "Sir, I am only the messenger. I was told to relay to you that Mrs. Woodhull and Miss Claflin were each indicted on individual counts and one joint count of sending obscene material through the mail. These charges carry a maximum of one year in prison and a five-hundred-dollar fine. They will be held until you can enter a plea tomorrow."

Back in our cell, Mr. Reymart apologized for the confusion and promised to investigate whether any of our rights had been violated by the grand jury meeting without representation from the defense. "I should probably also tell you something I overheard at the courthouse, but you aren't going to like it."

"Tell us," I said.

"Stephen Pearl Andrews was arraigned this morning. He told the court he had disassociated himself from the paper over a year ago and had never heard of Luther Challis until he read the issue as a subscriber."

"That weasel!" I made an exasperated noise. "He helped me edit the article. And he certainly had heard plenty about Mr. Challis from Tennie. What did the court say?"

"I suppose they believed him. He was released when he made bail."

I shook my head. "He's a man. Why should we expect differently? Any word on James?"

"He was released as well."

I blew out a breath. "Thank God for that."

Mr. Reymart patted my hand. "I'm sorry I couldn't get you out in time for Election Day. We tried. Honestly, we did."

"I know. There's one thing you can do to make it up to me."

"What's that?"

I gave him a wry smile. "Vote for me."

❦

A SOMBER PALL LAY over cell eleven on Tuesday, November 5. Even the inmates in the surrounding cells maintained a respectful silence. They must all have known that a presidential candidate was in their midst, unable to even attempt to cast a vote in her own name. The pitying glances of the guards told me that they—well, most of them at least— were sorry I was detained for this momentous occasion.

While Mr. Reymart was in court entering pleas of not guilty for both of us, Tennie and I were stuck in our cells with little to do and nothing to distract us from the election taking place without us.

Trying to focus on the big picture, I leaned my head against the wall and closed my eyes. All was not lost. I might not have been able to cast my own vote, but many others would be voting for me. At that very moment, men and women across the country were clipping Equal Rights Party ballots from their local papers, accepting them from election volunteers, or writing in my name on other parties' tickets. Somewhere, not too far away, Paulina Wright Davis was fulfilling her promise and doing her best to cast her ballot in my name.

Tears slipped unbidden from beneath my lashes. I was no fool. I had little chance of winning, especially given the events of the past six months, but I should have at least been able to try, to scrape together what little support remained—to end my campaign with the same vigor with which it had begun.

Sitting in a damp cell was definitely not how I'd envisioned Election Day when I'd announced my candidacy or when I'd been formally nominated. On both occasions, drunk on heady optimism, I'd pictured myself striding confidently to my polling place with James on my arm, a train of hundreds of suffragists—both male and female—in our wake. James would cast his vote for me first. Then, with my ballot clutched firmly between my fingers, I would ascend the platform, hold it up for all to see, and hand it to the official. In some of my fantasies, he would take it almost reverently, sensing that to be part of a historic moment like that was a great honor. In others, I was verbally or physically denied, but I fought my way to the ballot bowl and dropped my ticket in right before I was dragged off to jail. The other women present, of course, would follow suit, beginning a riot that would make national headlines.

Later in the day, another inmate confirmed that my vision had been eerily accurate but for one small detail. Not far away, in Rochester, New York, Susan B. Anthony had completed the historic act of which I could only dream. She had successfully cast her vote and had subsequently been arrested, along with fifty friends, family, and supporters, in an act of defiance that would surely be remembered for generations.

I bowed my head, accepting defeat. I had lost the war.

❦

WHILE PRESIDENT GRANT WAS celebrating his reelection, Tennie and I were being slapped with more charges, and James was rearrested.

"It seems that Luther Challis finally found his balls," Tennie said when Mr. Reymart told us that libel charges were being added to the mounting list against us. "I bet that boat-licker Maxwell follows suit."

Fortunately, she was wrong. When the preliminary hearing rolled round on Friday, the only charges being discussed were those from Challis.

Jefferson Market Court was jammed with people, including many heavily veiled women who wanted to witness the proceedings but not be recognized. Tennie, James, and I sat at the defense table next to Mr. Reymart; Mr. William Howe, our main lawyer; and his partner, the rail-thin Mr. Abraham Hummel. Mr. Howe was a large, muscled man with a lion's mane of wavy gray hair and a mustache that made him resemble a walrus. Eccentric but effective, he was attired in plaid pantaloons, a purple vest, and a blue satin scarf held in place with a diamond pin, with more diamonds on his fingers, watch chain, shirt studs, and cuff links. He was well-known for his courtroom theatrics but also as one of the best defense attorneys in the state.

The first to testify was Luther Challis, who still had the same loosely trimmed black hair, mustache, and goatee. He had aged into a ruddy-faced drunk rather than the gentleman of means he claimed to be.

"Did you attend the French Ball in 1869?" Mr. Howe asked.

"Yes, I met a friend there," Challis replied.

"And is that friend present here now?"

"Yes. Just there." He pointed at Mr. Maxwell.

"Were you accompanied while at the ball?"

"If you mean were we with any women, yes, we met two young ladies there."

"And did you, as Miss Claflin claims, get them drunk and seduce them?"

"Absolutely not. We drank only a small bottle of wine with them before tiring of the scene and leaving."

"Small bottle?" I whispered to Tennie. "They were practically pouring wine down the girls' throats. Perhaps his memory is failing in his old age."

Mr. Reymart shushed me and advised me to remain silent for the rest of the proceedings.

"Did you leave alone?"

"Yes. The girls stayed behind. If anything untoward happened to them after that, I cannot say, but I would be truly sorry if it did."

When the next witness was called, I had my first glimpse of our accuser in the other upcoming trial, Anthony Comstock. He was a tall, portly man with no hair save a bristly mustache and even larger ginger mutton chops. He didn't look the sort to be obsessed with morality, but they never did.

"Mr. Comstock, will you please tell the court how you came to be in possession of the offending issue of *Woodhull and Claflin's Weekly?*" Mr. Reymart asked.

"At first I obtained it by visiting the offices of the paper on Broad Street and purchasing a copy. It was so popular that was the only way one could get ahold of it. Mrs. Woodhull, Miss Claflin, and Colonel

Blood all were in the office at the time I purchased it. Later I lost that copy and so sent a request asking them to deliver a copy by mail."

"That's a lie," Tennie hissed. "I've never seen that man in my life."

Mr. Reymart sent her a warning glare, which she acknowledged by crossing her eyes at him.

Mr. Reymart stood. "Mr. Comstock, can you please identify Colonel Blood for the court?"

Mr. Comstock shifted in his seat, eyes sweeping the crowd once from left to right then from right to left. "I am afraid I cannot. I must not have gotten a good look at him."

"Hmm... that is most interesting because he is sitting right in front of you." Mr. Reymart interlaced his fingers behind him, leaning toward the witness. "Related to the second copy, the one that you obtained by mail, is it true that you receive half of the fines paid by people who are charged with violating the law that bears your name?"

Mr. Comstock glowered at the lawyer. "It is."

"And so you would have motivation to entrap innocent people with such claims?"

"Objection!" the prosecution's lawyer yelled.

"Sustained. Counsel, you've been warned," the judge growled.

But Mr. Reymart had gotten his point across.

I cringed as the next witness was called. Buck Claflin shambled to the stand, leaning forward and cupping a hand to one ear and holding an ear trumpet to the other. He had been going deaf for years. I had no idea why he had been called because he was not at all involved in the paper. I could only guess it had to do with confusion over his involvement with the firm.

"Mr. Claflin, I will make this brief since I know you are hard of hearing. Did you have any knowledge of your daughter Tennie's plans to write her libelous article against Mr. Challis?"

Buck nodded into the ensuing silence as though he were just catching up with what was asked of him. "Oh, yes. I warned my daughters both against printing the article. I told them it would end up badly. But that man"—he pointed at James—"insisted they go ahead with it. I always said he was a bad influence, and this proves it."

I put a warning hand on Tennie's thigh, silently begging her not to make a scene. I was pressing my lips together, fighting the urge to blurt out something about Pa constantly reviving the same old grudges. Neither of us relaxed until the judge told Buck he could sit down.

The final witness of the day was Mr. Maxwell, who had been with Mr. Challis at the French Ball. I gritted my teeth, waiting for him to side with his pal, Challis.

After being sworn in, he looked straight at Tennie and me, and without waiting for the lawyer to question him, he said, "I will make this easy on everyone. I was there. I saw what happened, both at the ball and after. Every word Miss Claflin wrote was true."

I grinned at Mr. Maxwell as the courtroom burst into an excited buzz of conversation. Finally, someone had done right by us.

Vindicating though it was, Mr. Maxwell's testimony did us little good. Weeks passed without a decision by the judge or any indication we would ever be released. Mr. Reymart did his best to fight on legal grounds, but nothing moved the court or the police.

Frustrated, I reached out the only way left to me—by mail. I poured my heart out to the American people through the *Herald*, the only publication that had ever treated us fairly. My request was simple—that my sister and I be tried for our words and actions, not the claims of others regarding us.

Johnny wrote back, saying my letter would run on Sunday. Plus, he was confident it would be picked up by papers across the country as the public was growing impatient with the increasingly unfair treatment Tennie and I were receiving.

On November 20, I sat in my cell, reading my own appeal.

"To the Editors of the Herald—

"No one can be more conscious than I am that prudent forethought should precede any appeal made to the public by one circumstanced as I am, and I think I have not ignored that consciousness in asking the attention of the public through your columns.

"I have been symmetrically written down as the most immoral of women, but no act of mine has been advanced in support of this charge. My theories have been first misstated or misrepresented and then denounced as 'revolting.'

"But what is the great danger which the public pretends to fear from me? The plain statement of what I desire to accomplish, and it is this at which the public howls, is this—I desire that woman shall be emancipated from sexual slavery maintained over her by man.

"The great public danger then is not my exposure of the immoralities that are constantly being committed but in the feat that their enactors will be shown up to the public they have so long deceived. The public is in no danger from me. To the public, I would say in conclusion that they may succeed in crushing me out, even to the loss of my life, but let me warn you that from the ashes of my body, a thousand Victorias will spring to avenge my death by seizing the work laid down by me and carrying it forward to victory."

CHAPTER THIRTY-SIX

We were released from jail days before Christmas. James and Tennie urged me to take some time to rest before returning to the public eye, but I could not. Demosthenes had foretold I would be queen of this land. I may have lost the presidential election, but that was no reason for me to go into hiding. On the contrary, it gave me all the more reason to speak even louder. He never said 1872 was the year; that had been my assumption. There would be other elections.

By the beginning of the year, I was itching to speak out about my experiences at the hands of the United States justice system. I wrote my speech "The Naked Truth, or Moral Cowardice and Modern Hypocrisy" partially from my jail cell and wholly with the purpose of debuting it in Boston, right under the noses of the Beecher family. But I hadn't counted on how red-hot their hatred of me still was or how powerful they really were. Catharine had me banned from the city.

More resolute than ever, I booked the Cooper Institute auditorium in New York, determined that my fellow citizens learn exactly how the government treated its people.

I was rehearsing my speech only hours before I was due to give it when Laura Cuppy Smith knocked on my door. Her face was pale, and she was panting.

"Victoria, you have to get out of here," she cried as soon as she crossed the threshold. "Mr. Comstock has laid eight new charges on you and your sister. You will be arrested for certain."

"Oh, God. Tennie has gone out. How will we warn her?"

"I'll find her, ma'am," Minnie said, already grabbing her cloak, one foot out the door.

"I know a place where you will be safe." Laura urged me toward the door.

"But what about my speech tonight?"

"We'll come up with something on the way there."

"There" was a hotel in Jersey City, where I remained until it was time for my lecture. Laura and I had crafted the perfect plan. It wouldn't hold the police off forever—but long enough for me to get my say.

A carriage dropped me off at the Cooper Institute as if I were any other patron. Dressed in the gray dress and black coal scuttle bonnet of an old Quaker woman, I made my way into the auditorium. Thanking the spirits yet again for my time on the stage in San Francisco, I hunched my shoulders, pulled my shawl up over my head, and slowly shuffled toward the stage, feigning deafness so I could push ahead of those already claiming a place. Sweat was trickling down my back. I passed several police officers, one of whom even helped me through the crowd of nearly a thousand, never once showing any sign of recognition.

As we had agreed, Laura Cuppy Smith was onstage, announcing that she would read my speech in my stead just as I reached her.

"No need," I called, jumping up onstage, tearing off my disguise, and facing the astonished crowd with a look of triumph. "You have come to hear me, and I shall speak. I was compelled to pass through doors surrounded by five deputy marshals with warrants in their pockets for my arrest, but I eluded them thanks to this disguise. And now, as I am here, I may go on with the lecture, but when it is delivered, I must go to jail.

"I come into your presence from a cell in the American Bastille, to which I was consigned by the cowardly servility of the age. I am still held under heavy bonds to return to that cell or to meet my trial in a United States court upon a scandalous charge trumped up by the ignorant or the corrupt officers of the law, conspiring with others to deprive me, under the falsest and shallowest pretenses, of my inherited privileges as an American citizen."

I painted a picture for the audience of my rise to fame and fall from grace, describing how in a little over two years, Tennie and I had gone from being lauded as the "The Fascinating Financiers" and the "Queens of the Quill" to being satirized as "Political Harlequins."

"The change began after I spoke before the House Judiciary Committee in January 1871. That was when I—and with me, all women—became a real threat to men. Soon after, the press began to call Tennie and me humbugs, frauds, prostitutes, and most recently, blackmailers. Now, by these we have been brought into public dishonor and dispute while not a single fact of crime to justify a single one of the various charges has ever been advanced by any journal. Imagine, for a moment, how easy a thing it is to ruin the usefulness of any person by this system of insinuation and innuendo."

I paused to allow the audience to envision how their own lives could be ruined by a single false remark. Then I thundered back with more energy than I'd possessed in months. "The old, worn-out, rotten social system will be torn down, plank by plank, timber after timber, until place is given to a new, true, and beautiful structure based upon freedom, equality, and justice to all—women as well as men.

"Stop our presses they may, but our tongues? Never!"

AFTERWORD

At the end of her speech that night, Victoria walked to the edge of the stage and extended her hands to the waiting officers so that she could be arrested. She and Tennie were jailed and rearrested several times over the next several months. In all, more than a dozen charges were brought against them, but Reverend Beecher never sued them for libel. Between court appearances, they managed to survive on lecture fees earned as both women toured the country, taking advantage of the public's desire to see the "female jailbirds."

The trial over the obscenity charges finally took place June 26-27, 1873. The Challis libel case didn't reach court until March 1874. Victoria and Tennie were found not guilty of all charges in both cases.

Theodore Tilton went on to sue Henry Ward Beecher for willful alienation of his wife's affections on January 11, 1875. That trial, which was the O.J. Simpson case of its time, lasted six months, riveting the nation with its tale of sex and scandal. Victoria was originally scheduled to testify, but in the end, she was only called to present evidence in form of letters from Tilton. The trial ended in a hung jury, and Beecher was never convicted. He came out of the matter richer and more popular than ever, with his church members paying for the trial.

On January 4, 1877, Cornelius Vanderbilt died, and William Vanderbilt finally succeeded in getting Victoria and Tennie to Europe. Afraid they would be called to testify to his father's belief in Spiritualism—and thus give credence to the idea that his father was not of sound mind and the will should be invalidated—William was rumored to have paid the sisters a large sum to relocate to England.

Tennie found her confidence there, crusading for women's suffrage in both England and America. In September 1884, she married Viscount Francis Cook and became a viscountess. She died in 1923.

Victoria divorced Colonel Blood before leaving for England, the first step in a long quest to reinvent herself. That included distancing herself from and outright denying her earlier radical statements and adopting new philosophies, such as a belief in eugenics. In 1883, Victoria married John Biddulph Martin, a wealthy banker. Though living as an expatriate in England, she ran for President of the United States twice more, in 1884 and 1892, though with far less fanfare and even less success than the first time.

Both sisters lived to see women get the vote in America on August 18, 1920. Though it would be poetic to be able to say one or both returned to America to cast the votes they had so long fought to achieve, no record of this exists, and failing health made it unlikely for either one.

Victoria lived to the age of ninety, finally passing away in her sleep on June 10, 1927. At her direction, she was cremated and her ashes scattered over the Atlantic Ocean between the two countries she loved.

In 1928, the first biography of Victoria, *The Terrible Siren* by Emanie Nahm Sachs, was published. This highly suspect portrayal was vindictive and brutal, and Victoria received barely a footnote of mention in Susan B. Anthony and Elizabeth Cady Stanton's three volume, 900+ page work on the history of the suffrage movement.

These are largely believed to be the reasons why Victoria has all but been written out of the history books, even nearly one hundred years after her death.

GLOSSARY

Adventuress – A loose woman, sometimes slang for a prostitute

Altitudes, in the – The state of being drunk or high

Big bugs – Important people, aristocrats or leaders

Bosom friend – An especially intimate friend

Boat-licker – An ass-kisser

Bully for you! – Good for you!

Burglared – To have one's house or other establishment broken into at night. If committed during the day, it was called "housebreaking."

By the horn spoons – An expression of surprise or shock

Cherry – Vulgar term for a young woman

Coumarin – A fragrant substance obtained from the tonka bean, sweet clover, and certain other plants used in soaps and perfumes

Confound it – A mild oath

Coot – A fool or simpleton

Cussed – A somewhat acceptable swear word meaning cursed, contemptible, mean, etc.

Cut a shine, to – To pull a prank or practical joke

Deadhead – A person who does not pay for services or things but takes a free ride

Devil – A powerful expletive

Flâneur – A lazy person, a loafer

Hornswoggler – A cheat or hoaxer

Humbug, Humbuggery – A trick or hoax, a person who employs such fakery

Idiot – Someone who was brain-damaged or mentally retarded

Lightskirt – A prostitute

Periauger – A type of sailing vessel

Pompkin – A colonial term used to refer to a man or woman from the area near Boston or that part of the country. (Victoria purposefully misuses the term to mean any rich woman from a big city; Anna is from Philadelphia.)

Puss – An endearing term for a woman

Rotgut – A blend of moonshine, burnt sugar, and tobacco juice

Seven by nine – Something or someone of inferior or common quality

Six of one, half a dozen of the other – The same thing

Tarnation – Euphemism for damnation, an oath

SOURCES:

Cassell's Dictionary of Slang by Jonathon Green
A Nineteenth Century Slang Dictionary, compiled and edited by Craig Hadley

BEFORE YOU GO...

Thank you for reading this book. If you enjoyed it, please leave a review on Amazon and/or Goodreads. Word of mouth is crucial for authors to succeed, so even if your review is only a line or two, it would be a huge help.

To be the first to find out about future books and insider information, please sign up for my newsletter. You will only be contacted when there is news, and your address will never be shared.

Also by Nicole Evelina:

Daughter of Destiny (Guinevere's Tale Book 1) (Arthurian historical fantasy)
Camelot's Queen (Guinevere's Tale Book 2) (Arthurian historical fantasy)
Been Searching for You (a contemporary romantic comedy)

Future releases include:

Mistress of Legend (Guinevere's Tale Book 3)—2017

Please visit me at **nicoleevelina.com** to learn more.

❧

I love interacting with my readers! Feel free to contact me on Twitter, Facebook, Goodreads, Pinterest, or by email. You can also send snail mail to: PO Box 2021, Maryland Heights, MO 63043.

Author's Notes

This story started with a pin on Pinterest. Seriously. I was just fooling around when a black-and-white photo of a woman from what looked like the 1800s caught my eye. The caption said: "Known by her detractors as "Mrs. Satan," Victoria Claflin Woodhull, born in 1838, married at age fifteen to an alcoholic and womanizer. She became the first woman to establish a brokerage firm on Wall Street and played an active role in the woman's suffrage movement. She became the first woman to run for President of the United States in 1872. Her name is largely lost in history. Few recognize her name and accomplishments."

I knew then and there I had my next book subject.

As I researched, I became more and more fascinated with Victoria and determined to help restore her name to the history books where it belongs. I also came to learn that history really is stranger than fiction. So much of her family's antics and Victoria's own actions are more grandiose than I could ever invent. That's why this book is extremely historical, with less emphasis on the fiction than one may expect.

Where possible, Victoria's words are her own as recorded in letters, speeches, articles, and interviews. When evidence exists, I've also used real quotes for other characters, especially Theodore Tilton, Henry Ward Beecher, Catharine Beecher, Susan B. Anthony, Elizabeth Cady Stanton, and other suffragists. Most of Victoria's speeches, articles, and the testimony of their many trials have been shortened for the sake of the story but are otherwise accurate. If you are interested in the full text, I recommend *The Victoria Woodhull Reader* (which carries her speeches in their entirety), *Notorious Victoria* (which offers the most ample quotes of any biography), and actual issues of *Woodhull and Claflin Weekly*, which can be accessed through certain universities or in a condensed form through the book *The Lives and Writings of Notorious Victoria Woodhull and Her Sister Tennessee Claflin* by Arlene Kisner.

Some dates differ by as little as a day or as much as a year in various sources (for example, the May 1872 National Womans Suffrage Association Convention can be dated as either May 9 or 10). I've chosen to use the dates that are most common among my sources. Other times I have compressed the timeline slightly to make for a better story.

Pinning down the real Victoria Woodhull is about as easy as harnessing the wind due to contradictory depictions of her in the press during her life, varying remembrances of her after her death, and most importantly, her constant need to reinvent herself during her life. Victoria often gave conflicting statements about her early years, changed her story to suit different audiences, and flat out denied things she was on record as endorsing. In order to decide how to portray her, I read all of the available sources, and most of the time I went with the prevailing opinion, but sometimes I chose what I believed most likely to be the truth or what suited my story best. After all, as highly historical as this book is, it's still fiction.

One quick note on word usage in this book: I've chosen to use "Madame" when referring to Victoria, rather than "madam," to help distinguish her from the madams (a.k.a. brothel owners) who play a role in this book. (However, Madame de Ford is French, so that is the normal mode of address for her.) Technically, the word "Madame" should only be used to refer to a French woman, but I think Victoria, being named after a queen and believing she was destined for greatness, would appreciate being referred to by a more lofty, exotic title.

PART ONE: THE LITTLE QUEEN

ONE SUBJECT I WANT to get out of the way right away is that of abuse. It's commonly believed that Buck Claflin physically abused his children. The vast majority of biographies agree on that, and really, it was common practice at the time, so it shouldn't be too surprising. Some also intimate that he sexually abused his daughters. That's a subject I'm honestly not sure about, so I chose not to include it, though other authors have chosen differently. There is a pretty strong argument that he introduced at least some of them into prostitution, though I don't believe Victoria was one of them. She appears to have escaped that fate through her marriage to Canning. Tennie, however, does not appear to have been as lucky.

The personalities and professions of Victoria's parents are also points of contention. Most portray Buck as the untrustworthy con artist you see in these pages. He may or may not have had a successful, perhaps even lucrative, career in law or real estate before Victoria was born, but most agree that the family was in financial trouble by the time she was four or five. Buck is variously credited with being a school teacher, a farmer, a storekeeper, a tavern owner, a gun dealer, a lumber merchant, a raftsman, a racehorse breeder, a hotel keeper, a gristmill and sawmill operator, a lawyer, a speculator, and a doctor. He is often said to only have had one eye, though I never found an explanation for what happened, whether it was gone completely or blinded.

His wife, Roxanna, or Annie as she was often called, is commonly credited with being a religious zealot at best, "drunk on Spiritualism" as Tennie would later say, and insane at worst. She is said to have praised her children one moment while cheering on their beating the next. But she was very smart and had an excellent memory. It is said she could recite the Bible backwards.

The mill fire, the event that opens my story, is recorded in many biographies, though its cause is questionable. Some say it was insurance fraud on the part of the Claflins, while Annie always claimed it was a terrible accident. The citizens of Homer appear to have leaned toward the former because they really did take up a collection to have the family run out of town.

The spiritualist encounters Victoria has while working at her father's shop are based on rumored experiences attributed to her, which I dramatized for sake of the story. The methods Buck teaches Victoria and Tennie to get information from clients are detailed in Barbara Goldsmith's amazing book *Other Powers* as common among Spiritualist charlatans. The long hours Victoria worked after moving into the shop are actually taken from Tennie's later time working at her father's many healing clinics. But I assumed that if he worked her that hard then, it would make sense that he'd done it before and it would be a plausible reason why Victoria fell ill.

Victoria's illness is the historical basis for her meeting Canning. (A few sources name him as Channing, but Canning is much more prevalent, so I have used that spelling of his name.) Their rapid courtship is also historically accurate, though we know few details outside of his asking to accompany her to the Fourth of July picnic and his proposal that very night. His nicknames for Victoria of "my little chick" and "my little puss" are also recounted numerous times.

The stories of Canning's lover/mistress who bore his child and of his frequenting brothels are commonly recounted in biographies of Victoria, and she even talked about them in the biography she directed Theodore Tilton to write. However, I did invent his marital rape of Victoria in the carriage. It is meant to symbolize his brutish treatment of her and also serve as a possible explanation (at least to the 19th-century mind) as to why Byron was born mentally retarded. Some sources say Byron became so as the result of a childhood fall, but I went with the idea that he was born that way.

I could find no reason given as to why the Woodhulls moved from Cincinnati to San Francisco, so I used the imaginary threat of Canning's lover. I have condensed the period of time they spent there for the sake of the story. Victoria did work as a seamstress for actress Anna Cogswell and may have been a prostitute (or "cigar girl" as they were called) for a time, but I don't believe so. The plays Victoria appeared in are real, and her vision of Tennie appears in Tilton's biography, but her meeting at that time with Josie Mansfield is entirely my own invention.

Buck ran "cancer clinics" in Columbus, Chicago, and a multitude of other cities while Victoria was suffering through her marriage to Canning. Many of these came with rumors or charges of prostitution, which is how I have portrayed Tennie's life once Victoria returns to her family. The violent incident with Byron is fictional, intended to give Victoria and Canning a reason to leave her family and go to New York, a motivation whose truth is lost to history. Victoria's daughter is called both Zulu and Zula in biographies. I have chosen the name Zula because it is the one I prefer. The story of her birth and near death due to blood loss is true according to what Victoria instructed Tilton to write in his biography.

This same biography gives us the details of Victoria and Colonel Blood's meeting in St. Louis, including the "betrothal by the powers of the air." It is thought likely that he introduced Victoria to Virginia Minor, who was to be so influential to her position on women's right to vote being part of the Constitution.

Part Two: Future Presidentess

VICTORIA HERSELF WAS THE source for the story of how she came to New York at the urging of her spirit guide, Demosthenes. The work of Victoria and Tennie with prostitutes appears in several biographies, and it appears Madame de Ford and Miss Wood might both have been historical people, though I have taken liberty in fictionalizing their interactions with the sisters.

Minnie is completely fictional, as are all of her interactions with Victoria and her family. I invented her to embody and symbolize all of the women Victoria worked with during her time in the brothels, the women who inspired her to run for president.

How exactly Victoria and Tennie met Cornelius Vanderbilt is up for debate. Some say Buck had something to do with it, while others say the sisters made the acquaintance on their own or even that James was involved. But both of them worked for him, and he did back them in their desire to become stock brokers. His training and contributions to their knowledge of the financial world are fictional, but they had to have gotten it somehow. Given their poor upbringing and meager education, I thought it logical for him to have been involved. Also, it is commonly believed that Josie Mansfield, through her real-life relationship with Jim Fisk, was the source behind Victoria's stock tips, not the spirit world as Victoria and Mr. Vanderbilt claimed.

James was a supporter of the suffrage movement and was likely the reason Victoria became involved. The January 1869 convention in Washington goes by different names in different sources: National Woman's Rights Convention, the National Female Suffrage Convention, the American Equal Rights Association Convention, and National Convention of Woman Suffrage. The quotes from Elizabeth

Cady Stanton are mostly her own words. As noted in *The Woman Who Ran for President*, Douglass' speech from that day didn't survive, so I pulled from a letter he wrote about the convention after it was over reflecting on the contents of the speech he gave. The debate between Tennie and Victoria is my own invention, but Victoria is recorded as siding with Douglass over Stanton. The newspaper accounts from after the event are all historical.

Victoria and Tennie briefly operated their stock company out of another location in January 1870 before moving and having their official grand opening on February 5. I omitted the January location for the sake of clarity and have combined the description of the two offices, as my sources disagree to which office the descriptions belong. Walt Whitman did indeed visit their office, and the poem attributed to him in the story is made of his own words, though he did not deliver them in poetic form. The many strange visits of Edward Van Schalck and Hugh Hastings on opening day are factual, as are their actions and comments. However, the vandalism of the brokerage firm is fictional. I chose to add it because I wanted something to show the resistance to and danger of women entering the male sphere.

The incident at Delmonicos about Victoria and Tennie nearly being removed for not having a man with them is the stuff of legend surrounding Victoria, as is her "tomato soup for three" comment, but it may have actually happened. However, we don't know for sure how she and Stephen met, so my use of that location for their first meeting is fictional.

Victoria's biographers disagree on exactly when Canning Woodhull reentered Victoria's life after they divorced. Some say he never left it. Others tell a story that about a year and a half after James and Victoria's marriage, Canning was delirious with illness and called for her.

She and James brought him back and took care of him for six weeks. He paid them, and they said he was welcome any time. From that day on, when he needed her, he came. She knew others were scandalized by it but considered it her Christian duty to take care of him. I have chosen to use a variation of this story, having him track her down after the national press coverage of the opening of their stock company and her announcement as a candidate for the presidency.

In some cases, I have moved the timing of content in *the Weekly* to suit my story. All that is mentioned in the book really did appear in the paper, though perhaps not exactly in the order it is in my novel.

James and Stephen Pearl Andrews were the prime sources of Victoria's political writings. Some biographers believe her political career was entirely their doing and she was just along for the ride, but I agree with those that give her a more active role. A woman as shrewd as Victoria would not have allowed herself to be totally manipulated. She would have allowed it when it suited her, but she would also have had her say.

There is no evidence of an affair between Victoria and J.D. Reymart. In fact, my sources disagree on his actual name and its spelling (Reymert vs. Reymart). I have taken advantage of this to create two characters, one with each surname, and to create a fictional familial relationship between them.

Only *Other Powers* gives J.D. Reymert a full name, James "John" DeNoon Reymert, which is the name of a historical lawyer practicing in New York since 1861, and which I have used for the elder of the two lawyers in this novel. In *Other Powers*, he is only mentioned as James Blood's aging lawyer at the trial instigated by Annie Claflin, with no reference to Washington at all.

In my other sources, beyond a few brief references to a J.D. Reymart as the lawyer who helped Victoria with her memorial, there is no relationship at all, nor have I been able to find any biographical details about him. While the man likely existed and interacted with Victoria on a business level, the name Judah DeWitt Reymart is a fabrication, as are his age, appearance, all the details of his relationship with Victoria, and his familial relationship to the historical James "John" DeNoon Reymert. However, there were rumors that Victoria had an affair with Congressman Benjamin Butler while she was in Washington. While I doubt that was more than idle gossip, I used it as the basis of her affair with the younger Reymart.

Victoria's memorial is reproduced in this book minus one paragraph because of its importance to the history of the women's movement. Victoria did meet with President Grant while she was in Washington D.C., but she never divulged the details of their meeting, so I had to make that up. But it is commonly rumored that he said she would one day occupy the presidential chair.

After the rejection by the House Judiciary Committee, Victoria amended the memorial to take it to the New York legislature, where Representative Bingham, the same man who wrote the majority opinion on the memorial, blocked her efforts. I have omitted this step from the book for brevity and let Representative Bingham's threat stand in its place.

Victoria's carriage ride with Catharine Beecher is also included in many biographies. While I have fictionalized the particulars, everything Catharine says to Victoria is historically accurate, culled from letters and other interactions between the two women.

The letter Victoria intercepts from Ohio is included as written in at least one source, as are Annie's many blackmail attempts. Annie's charges against Colonel Blood and the resulting trial are also real. I have used actual trial testimony, although Victoria wasn't actually present at the first day of the May 1871 trial that pitted Col.

Blood and her mother against one another. I took license to have her there so that the reader could see the events as they happened rather than having them recounted to her after. Several variations of the trial testimony exist. Many believe that which was recorded in the *New York Herald* to be the most accurate – and it is claimed to be the most widely distributed – so I have used that as my main source with bits from other accounts thrown in as I saw fit. Nearly all of the proceedings, save a few questions by the lawyer to break up Victoria's monologist testimony, are the actual quotes as recorded in works by Underhill, Goldsmith, and Macpherson. Blood's comments about Polly's extortion are not part of the trial testimony but come from an interview he and Tennie gave to the *Brooklyn Herald* before the trial. I used them to connect the dots for the reader that were left out of the testimony.

Tennie's odd testimony at the trail is real. Tennie and her mother had a strange sort of codependent relationship that made them hate one another one moment and be the most loving of relatives the next. I made up Tennie's possible drug use on the day of her testimony as I needed a reason why she would say such strange things that aren't otherwise in keeping with her attitudes toward her family.

Victoria's first meeting with Tilton is based on recorded recollections of that day, and his poem and note to her are historically accurate. I fictionalized Victoria's interaction with Lib from accounts given in Goldsmith's book.

PART THREE: "MRS. SATAN"

VICTORIA AND A GROUP of women did attempt to vote in November 1871, an event which was memorialized in a drawing in *Harper's*

Weekly, which Victoria said was her favorite depiction of her of all that had appeared during her lifetime.

The words of Rev. Beecher during his two meetings with Victoria are based on her recollections.

It is believed by some that a madam (possibly named Mary Bowles) did indeed offer the sisters use of her client books. In some sources, she is substituted for Annie Wood or Madame de Ford, so I have combined this information to make all of them supportive in helping the sisters unmask hypocrisy among the rich and powerful. However, a few biographers are beginning to question the reality of this occurrence, speculating that Tennie may have invented the incident to help the sisters' cause.

The strange exchange between Utica and Victoria during her Free Love speech is well documented in the historical record. The threat of violence before her speech is also real, as is Theodore's introduction.

The IWA funeral parade was a historical event, though whether or not Victoria and Tennie participated willingly is unknown. The details were well-recorded in the papers, so I only had to fill in some blanks. The attempted robbery and threats against Victoria and Tennie after the IWA funeral parade are my own invention, but the threat to their safety in Union Square was very real, as was the mob's beating of an innocent man trying to keep the peace while the police looked on, doing nothing.

For a brief period of time in 1872, Victoria's political party (which had started out as the Cosmopolitical Party, then was rebranded the Equal Rights party in July 1871) was called the People's Party. I have chosen to refer to it consistently as the Equal Rights Party after July 1871 so as not to confuse the reader.

Victoria suffered a series of misfortunes in early 1872, including being evicted from her home, losing the brokerage building, and being unable to find a place to live. She appealed to Henry Ward Beecher for help. This letter and his reply were as shown in the book. The details of Victoria's illness in the summer of 1872 are fictional, but she was known to be ill and depressed that summer, refusing to speak publicly until September.

While the validity of Victoria's vision of Tilton being responsible for Greeley's death (as told in *Other Powers*) is anyone's guess, it is true that Horace Greeley died only a week after the presidential election of 1872, before the electoral votes were cast.

I have included only a brief introduction to Victoria and Tennie's "scandal" articles against Beecher and Challis to save space. Anyone who wishes to read them in full may find them online or printed in Underhill's book, p. 221-226.

I have combined the two days of testimony at the Luther Challis trial into one for ease of reading. The account of the French Ball which Challis attended comes from *Other Powers*. It is also cited in *Documents of the Senate of the State of New York, Volume 12* and *City of Eros: New York City, Prostitution, and the Commercialization of Sex, 1790-1920*. I have also streamlined Victoria and Tennie's time in jail. They were moved around quite a bit, and according to at least one source, may have spent time in the Tombs, the most feared prison in New York City.

If you would like to know more about the sources I consulted in writing this book, please see the selected bibliography on the next page or visit my website, **http://nicoleevelina.com**, and click on the "Research" tab under the section for *Madame Presidentess*. You may also wish to search my blog, located on the same site, for additional information on many of these topics.

Selected Bibliography

Bensel, Richard Franklin. *The American Ballot Box in the Mid-19ᵗʰ Century.*

Brody, Miriam. *Victoria Woodhull, Free Spirit for Women's Rights.*

Frisken, Amanda. *Victoria Woodhull's Sexual Revolution.*

Gabriel, Mary. *Notorious Victoria.*

Gilfoyle, Timothy J. *City of Eros: New York City, Prostitution, and the Commercialization of Sex, 1790-1920.*

Goldsmith, Barbara. *Other Powers: The Age of Suffrage, Spiritualism and the Scandalous Victoria Woodhull.*

Havelin, Kate. *Victoria Woodhull.*

Kisner, Arlene. *The Lives and Writings of Notorious Victoria Woodhull and Her Sister Tennessee Claflin.*

Krull, Kathleen. *A Woman for President – The Story of Victoria Woodhull.*

MacPherson, Myra. *The Scarlet Sisters.*

Sachs, Emanie Nahm. *The Terrible Siren.*

Stern, Madeleine B. *The Pantarch: A Biography of Stephen Pearl Andrews.*

-----, ed. *The Victoria Woodhull Reader.*

Stiles, T.J. *The First Tycoon: the Epic Life of Cornelius Vanderbilt*

Tilton, Theodore. The Golden Age Tract No. 3 "Victoria C. Woodhull, a Biographical Sketch."

Underhill, Lois Beachey. *The Woman Who Ran for President.*

ACKNOWLEDGEMENTS

THANK YOU SO MUCH to Liv Raincourt for pinning the Pinterest pin that started it all. I bet you had no idea you were launching a book, did you? Thanks also to the unknown person who pinned the original photo and wrote such an alluring caption. You drew me in and made me want to learn more, which I have in turn shared in this story.

Thanks to my editor Cassie Cox for asking the tough questions and helping this story shine, and to Devon for catching all my last-minute errors and saving my butt on a few historical missteps. I owe you both so much! Also, thank you to Terri Valentine for editing an early draft of this manuscript. Your patience and attention to detail helped shape Victoria's story and make it all the richer. Thanks as well to Kiffer Brown and Chanticleer Reviews for their belief in this tale and championing of it. My gratitude also goes to Jenny Quinlan for the beautiful cover and The Editorial Department for their layout and attention to detail.

Hugs and kisses to my beta readers, Courtney, Kerry, and Lauren. Your feedback was invaluable. Eternal gratitude to my mom for listening to every single detail of this story as it flowed from my mind to the page and for being one of my first readers.

I'd also like to thank the Missouri History Museum, especially reference librarian Jason Stratman, for providing their information on Victoria and James' time in St. Louis. Thanks as well to Myra Macpherson, author of *The Scarlet Sisters*, for answering my questions about Victoria's later life.

I can't leave out my fur babies, Connor and Caitlyn, who are the best editorial assistants in the world. You have my heart and all my love. Thank for you your patience and support. (Yes, I am the crazy cat lady.)

As always, thanks to everyone who reads this book. Your willingness to read about someone you've likely never heard of is commendable, and I appreciate it. By that simple act, you are helping Victoria's story be known, helping her to be restored to the historical record. In a year when we may well see the first female president of the United States, it is time for the woman who made that journey possible to take her place among the annals of history.

ABOUT THE AUTHOR

NICOLE EVELINA is an award-winning historical fiction and romantic comedy writer. *Madame Presidentess* was the first place winner in the Women's US History category of the 2015 Chaucer Awards for Historical Fiction, earning the distinction months before it was released to the public.

Nicole's debut novel, *Daughter of Destiny*, the first book of an Arthurian legend trilogy that tells Guinevere's life story from her point of view, was named Book of the Year by Chanticleer Reviews, took the Grand Prize in the 2015 Chatelaine Awards for Women's Fiction/Romance, won a Gold Medal in the fantasy category in the Next Generation Indie Book Awards and was short-listed for the Chaucer Award for Historical Fiction. Her contemporary romantic comedy, *Been Searching for You*, won the 2015 Romance Writers of America (RWA) Great Expectations and Golden Rose contests.

Her mission as a historical fiction writer is to rescue little-known women from being lost in the pages of history. While other writers may choose to write about the famous, she tells the stories of those who are in danger of being forgotten so that their memories may live on for at least another generation. She also writes from the female point of view since the male perspective has historically been given more attention.

Nicole is one of only six authors who completed the first week-long writing intensive taught by #1 *New York Times* bestselling author Deborah Harkness in 2014. She is a member of and book reviewer for the Historical Novel Society and Sirens, a group supporting female fantasy authors, as well as a member of the Romance Writers of America, Broad Universe, Women Fiction Writers Association, the St. Louis Writer's Guild, and Women Writing the West.

When she's not writing, she can be found reading, playing with her spoiled twin Burmese cats, cooking, researching, and dreaming of living in Chicago or the English countryside.

Made in the USA
Middletown, DE
24 June 2019